PUFFIN BOOKS

DUTY CALLS
BATTLE OF BRITAIN

Historian and bestselling author James Holland was born in Salisbury, Wiltshire, and studied history at Durham University. He is the author of numerous historical non-fiction titles and the Jack Tanner fiction series, and presented *Battle of Britain: The Real Story* and *Dam Busters: The Race to Smash the German Dams* for the BBC.

A member of the British Commission for Military History, his many interviews with veterans of the Second World War are available at the Imperial War Museum and are also archived at *www.secondworldwarforum.com*.

Find out more about the Duty Calls series and the Second World War at www.dutycallsbooks.com

JAMES HOLLAND

DUTY CALLS
BATTLE OF BRITAIN

PUFFIN

PUFFIN BOOKS

Published by the Penguin Group
Penguin Books Ltd, 80 Strand, London WC2R 0RL, England
Penguin Group (USA) Inc., 375 Hudson Street, New York, New York 10014, USA
Penguin Group (Canada), 90 Eglinton Avenue East, Suite 700, Toronto, Ontario, Canada M4P 2Y3
(a division of Pearson Penguin Canada Inc.)
Penguin Ireland, 25 St Stephen's Green, Dublin 2, Ireland (a division of Penguin Books Ltd)
Penguin Group (Australia), 250 Camberwell Road, Camberwell, Victoria 3124, Australia
(a division of Pearson Australia Group Pty Ltd)
Penguin Books India Pvt Ltd, 11 Community Centre, Panchsheel Park, New Delhi – 110 017, India
Penguin Group (NZ), 67 Apollo Drive, Rosedale, Auckland 0632, New Zealand
(a division of Pearson New Zealand Ltd)
Penguin Books (South Africa) (Pty) Ltd, Block D, Rosebank Office Park, 181 Jan Smuts Avenue,
Parktown North, Gauteng 2193, South Africa

Penguin Books Ltd, Registered Offices: 80 Strand, London WC2R 0RL, England

puffinbooks.com

First published 2012
004

Set in Sabon Mt 10.5/15.5 pt
Typeset by Palimpsest Book Production Limited, Falkirk, Stirlingshire
Made and printed in Great Britain by Clays Ltd, St Ives plc

British Library Cataloguing in Publication Data
A CIP catalogue record for this book is available from the British Library

ISBN: 978–0–141–33220–8

For Jude Petrie

CONTENTS

GLOSSARY

Ack-ack	Anti-aircraft fire, also known as flak
Adj	Adjutant
Angels	Code for height in thousands of feet, e.g. angels ten is ten thousand feet
AOC	Air Officer Commanding
ATA	Air Transport Auxiliary
AVM	Air Vice-Marshal
Bandits	Enemy aircraft
Beat up	Fly over very fast and very low
Big jobs	Bombers
Bind/binding	Grousing, giving someone a hard time, a nuisance
CAS	Chief of the Air Staff
CO	Commanding Officer
CRU	Civilian Repair Unit
DCT	Director Control Tower
DFC	Distinguished Flying Cross
Drink	Slang for sea
EFTS	Elementary Flying Training School
Erk	Slang for ground crew

Fitter	Ground crew responsible for engines and related controls
FTS	Flying Training School
Glycol	Radiator coolant, effectively antifreeze
Huff-Duff	HF/DF – high frequency direction finding
IFF	Identification Friend or Foe
IO	Intelligence Officer
Irvin	Sheepskin leather jacket issued to pilots
Kite	Slang for aircraft
Little jobs	Fighters
Mae West	Life jacket
MO	Medical Officer
OTU	Operational Training Unit
RASC	Royal Army Service Corps
RDF	Radio Direction Finding (radar)
Rigger	Ground crew responsible for airframe
R/T	Radio Telegraphy – i.e. radio
Shoot a line	Show off, exaggerate
Sigint	Signal Intelligence
Skipper	Captain, slang for the CO
Snappers	Enemy fighters
Sortie	A single flight, so twelve aircraft flying together would be twelve sorties
Stick	Slang for control column
Stooge	Fly around without any action
Tit	Slang for gun button
U/s	Useless, broken
Vic	Inverted 'V' formation of three aircraft
X raid	A false alarm

Visit www.dutycallsbooks.com for more information.

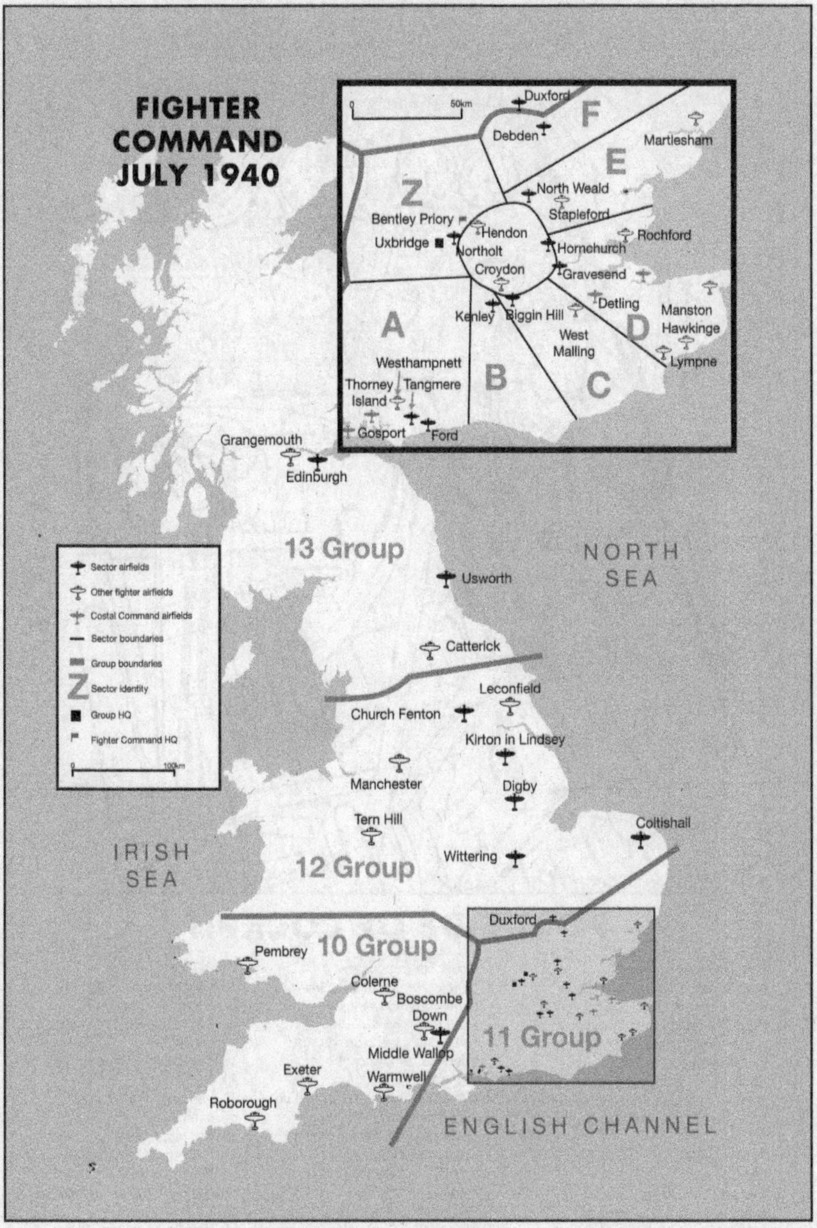
FIGHTER COMMAND JULY 1940
0
50km
Duxford
Debden
F
E
Martlesham
Z
North Weald
Stapleford
Bentley Priory
Hendon
Uxbridge
Northolt
Hornchurch
Rochford
Croydon
Gravesend
Detling
Manston
Hawkinge
Kenley
Biggin Hill
A
West Malling
D
Lympne
Westhampnett
Thorney Island
Tangmere
B
C
Gosport
Ford
Grangemouth
Edinburgh
13 Group
NORTH SEA
Usworth
Sector airfields
Other fighter airfields
Costal Command airfields
Sector boundaries
Group boundaries
Z Sector identity
Group HQ
Fighter Command HQ
0
100km
Catterick
Leconfield
Church Fenton
Kirton in Lindsey
Manchester
Digby
Tern Hill
Coltishall
IRISH SEA
Wittering
12 Group
Duxford
10 Group
Pembrey
Colerne
Boscombe Down
11 Group
Middle Wallop
Exeter
Warmwell
Roborough
ENGLISH CHANNEL

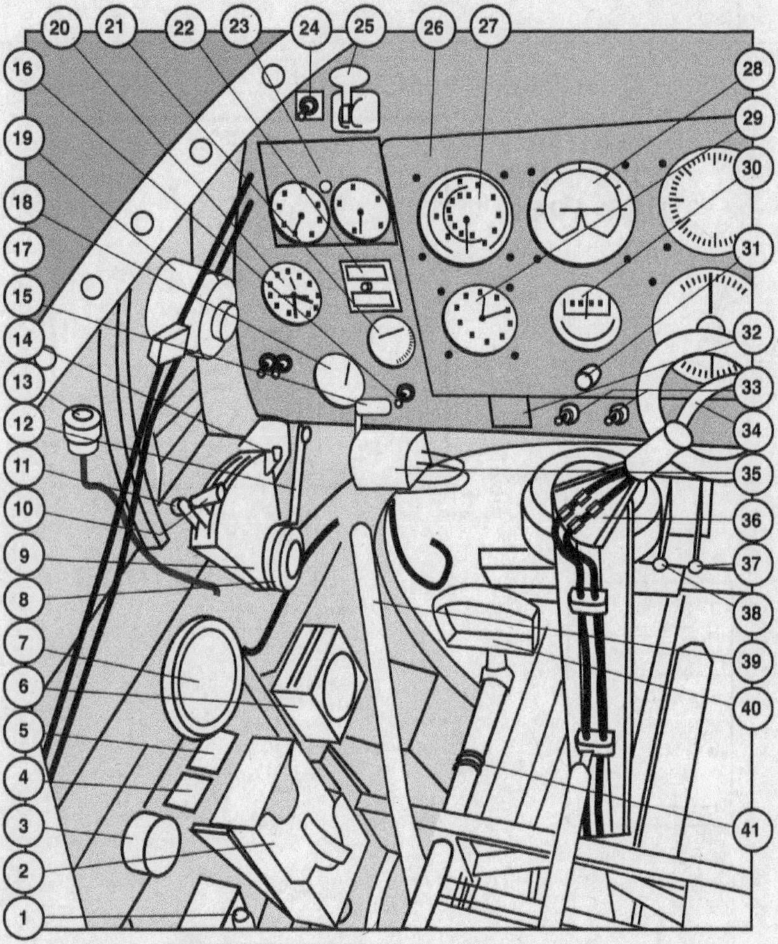

PORT SIDE OF COCKPIT

1. Flare release control
2. Map stowage box
3. Rudder trimming tab control
4. Pressure head heating switch
5. Camera-gun master switch
6. Writing pad container
7. Elevator trimming tab control
8. Throttle and mixture friction adjusters
9. Push switch for silencing warning horn
10. Throttle lever
11. Mixture lever
12. Airscrew control lever
13. Connection for cine-camera footage indicator
14. Boost cut-out control
15. Landing-lamps dipping lever
16. Landing-lamps switch
17. Main magneto switches
18. Brake triple pressure gauge
19 Wireless remote controller
20. Clock
21. Elevator trimming tabs position indicator
22. Undercarriage position indicator
23. Oxygen regulator
24. Navigation lamps switch
25. Flaps control
26. Instrument flying panel
27. Air-speed indicator
28. Artificial horizon
29. Altimeter
30. Direction indicator
31. Setting knob for (30)
32. Compass deviation card holder
33. Cockpit lamp dimmer switches
34. Brake lever
35. Landing-lamps lowering control
36. Control column
37. Fuel cock lever (top tank)
38. Fuel cock lever (bottom tank)
39. Radiator flap control lever
40. Rudder pedals
41. Rudder pedals leg reach adjusters

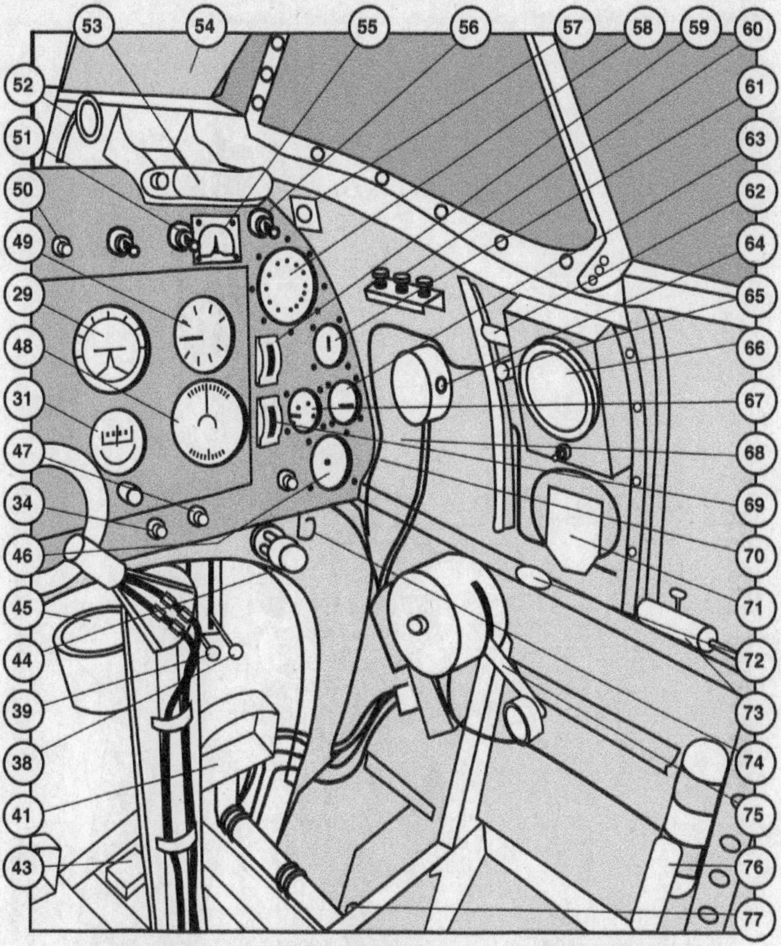

STARBOARD SIDE OF COCKPIT

29. Artificial horizon
31. Direction indicator
34. Cockpit-lamp dimmer switch
38. Fuel cock lever (top tank)
39. Fuel cock lever (lower tank)
41. Rudder pedal
43. Brake-relay valve
44. Priming pump
45. Compass
46. Fuel contents gauge
47. Engine starting pushbutton
48. Turning indicator
49. Rate-of-climb indicator
50. Reflector sight main switch
51. Reflector sight lamp dimmer switch
52. Lifting ring for dimming switch
53. Reflector gun-sight mounting
54. Dimming screen
55. Ammeter
56. Generator switch
57. Ventilator control
58. Engine-speed indicator
59. Fuel-pressure gauge
60. Spare fillments for reflector sight
61. Boost guage
62. Cockpit lamp
63. Radiator temperature guage
64. Signalling switch box
65. Oxygen socket
66. Wireless remote contactor mounting and switch
67. Oil-temperature gauge
68. Engine data plate
69. Oil-pressure gauge
70. Cartridge starter reloading control
71. Height and air-speed computer stowage
72. Control locking lug
73. Harness release
74. Slow-running cut-out control
75. Undercarriage control lever
76. Undercarriage emergency lowering lever
77. Control locking lug

SPITFIRE MARK I

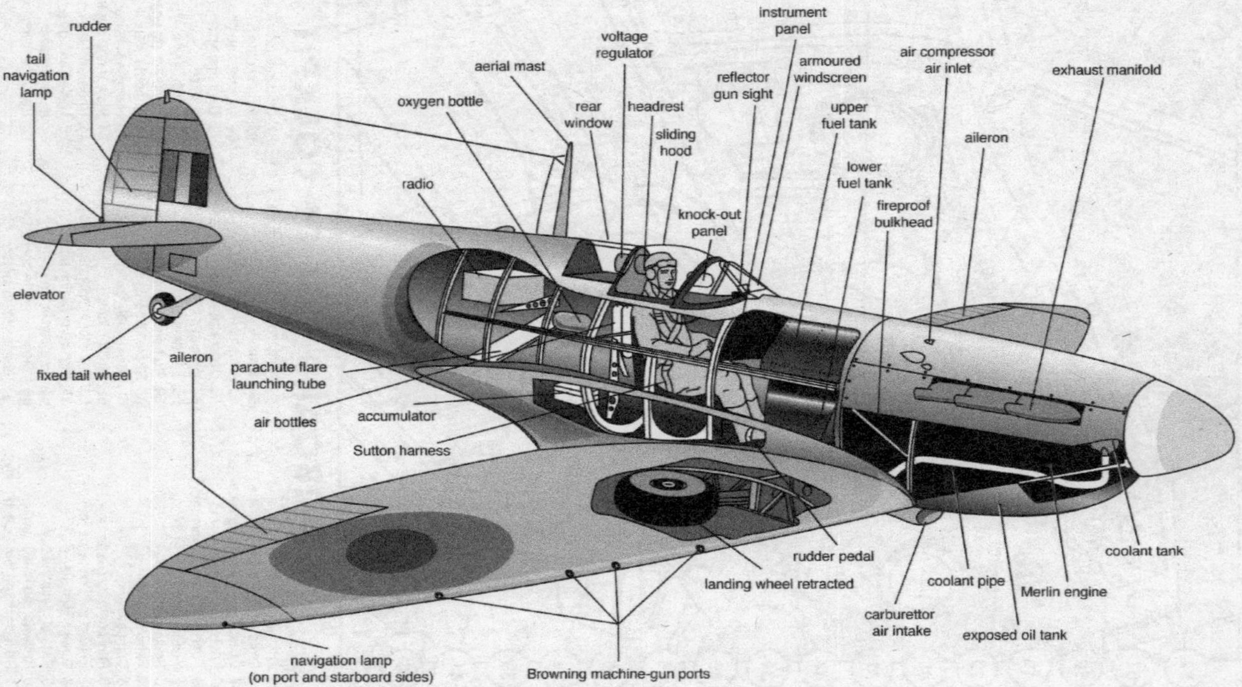

rudder
tail navigation lamp
elevator
fixed tail wheel
aileron
radio
oxygen bottle
aerial mast
rear window
voltage regulator
headrest
sliding hood
knock-out panel
reflector gun sight
instrument panel
armoured windscreen
upper fuel tank
lower fuel tank
fireproof bulkhead
air compressor air inlet
aileron
exhaust manifold
parachute flare launching tube
air bottles
accumulator
Sutton harness
rudder pedal
landing wheel retracted
carburettor air intake
coolant pipe
exposed oil tank
Merlin engine
coolant tank
navigation lamp (on port and starboard sides)
Browning machine-gun ports

1

SCRAMBLE

Around 10 a.m., Friday 24 May 1940. The sun was already high, and warm too. The early morning mist that had shrouded London when the squadron had flown down to Rochford at first light had long gone. So, too, had the morning dew. When Archie Jackson had clambered down from his Spitfire and walked with Ted Tyler and the others over to the dispersal hut, his black leather flying boots had been sodden, but now, some four hours later, they were as dry as the surrounding grass.

It already felt as though half the day had gone by: up at four, shaken awake by their batman, a quick shower, a lukewarm mug of sugary tea, and then they were on the bus being driven to their dispersal. Ten minutes later, having collected Mae Wests, parachutes and flying helmets, they had been tramping towards their aircraft. Irving and Green, Archie's fitter and rigger, had already been there – Green giving the canopy one last polish, Irving battening down a bolt on the cowling. A cheery greeting from Green, a weary nod from Irving.

Just five minutes later, he'd been airborne, along with five others from A Flight and six from B, led by their CO, Squadron Leader Dix. Archie had wondered then whether he would ever see Northolt again. *If I do,* he had thought, *it will be after my first combat sortie. I will have survived.*

Rochford was their temporary forward base, a place to refuel and wait for the order to take off and patrol the French coast. New, unfamiliar ground crew – erks as they were universally known by the pilots – had descended on their aircraft, and Archie had followed the others to the dispersal hut on the western edge of the airfield. After a short while, a van had drawn up bringing Thermos flasks of tea and bacon sandwiches. The tea had been lukewarm, the bacon limp, but he had not struggled through his sandwich because of the taste.

'Make sure you eat, Archie,' the CO had told him in an avuncular tone. 'You don't know when you might get the chance again, and there's no point in flying to France on an empty stomach.'

Archie had nodded silently as a new wave of nausea had coursed through his stomach. Gingerly, he had taken another bite.

That had been around 6 a.m. – four hours ago. Four hours! Four hours of sitting, waiting, doing little, the knot in his stomach tightening, first in the crew room of the wooden dispersal hut, and then, as the sun warmed the air, outside. Some managed to read, others played cards. Archie couldn't face either. All he could think of was the mission that lay ahead of him, like a giant chasm waiting to swallow him up. He wasn't sure what gnawed at him the most: the thought of being killed, or the prospect of somehow messing up. He could not imagine what it would be like, or how he would react, when he saw a German aircraft for the first time. *A real German.* In a real plane.

An hour ago, the Spits of 74 Squadron had returned from

an earlier patrol. Archie had watched them come in, one after the other, then rumble around the perimeter. The red canvas patches that covered the gun ports had all been shredded, smoke from the guns streaked the underside of the wings, and some had visible battle damage – jagged silvery metal sticking out where a bullet had torn into it. The pilots then clambered out and staggered over to the crew room. Archie saw the expression of one: it was a look of shock, his eyes wide and disbelieving, his hair clammy with sweat.

'Well, you can hardly miss Dunkirk,' said one, as the pilots dropped off their kit and reported to their Intelligence Officer. 'The oil depot's on fire and there's smoke rising ten thousand feet into the air.'

'Or more,' said another. 'Honestly, you've never seen anything like it. Thick black smoke. Damn hard to see anything much below.'

Two aircraft had not returned. There had been some speculation over what had happened to them. Several of the pilots had seen Sergeant Mould bail out of his, and were convinced he had done so on the right side of the lines, but no one could be sure what had happened to Flying Officer Hoare.

'He was trailing white smoke,' said one.

'Glycol,' said another.

'But he had his kite under control,' said the first. 'I'm sure he's just landed it somewhere.'

Three others were gesticulating wildly at the IO, making steep diving motions with their arms.

'So that's a third of a kill each, then,' said the IO eventually. The three men had looked deflated.

Archie had listened to all this with a mixture of excitement and dread. His stomach felt heavy, while the salty taste of bacon lingered sourly in his mouth. He'd watched them take off shortly after he had landed, and now two were still in France, possibly wounded, possibly dead. He struggled to take it in. Soon after, the pilots had disappeared, tramping back to the messes. Quiet had descended once more.

Archie closed his eyes a moment and felt the warmth of the sun beating down on his face, and the comforting orange glow through his lids that reminded him that summer was on its way once more. For a moment, he thought about summery things: lunches outside, cricket, golf at Strathtay, the tiny nine-hole course near his home, the sound of a bee on the air, cut grass and skylarks. There was one twittering away nearby, chirruping madly, and he now looked up, his hand shielding his eyes, and tried to spot it. Where was it? *No, can't see him.*

Giving up, he glanced around. Ahead lay the open expanse of the airfield, while away to the south a couple of large hangars loomed over a cluster of buildings. Aircraft lined the perimeter: twin-engine Bristol Blenheims of Coastal Command, Spitfires of 54 Squadron and their own machines from A Flight. Some hammering began from somewhere near the two hangars and then, a moment later, a fuel bowser began rumbling around the far side of the field. To his left, sitting in a battered old leather armchair, Will Merton-Moore, the A Flight commander, was reading a copy of the *Daily Express*, and tutting occasionally. Archie glanced across. Merton-Moore was holding the paper so that the upper half of his body was almost entirely hidden, revealing the headlines in the process. The news from France was not good – not good at all – but sitting here on this fine May morning in south Essex, Archie found it hard to imagine such terrible things going on just the other side of the Channel.

The Channel. His stomach lurched. For a few blissful minutes, he'd managed to put the task ahead out of his mind, but now it came crashing back, sweeping over him like a heavy weight. For so long he had been chomping at the bit, itching to have a crack at the enemy, but now that that moment was almost upon him, he felt consumed by an urge to fly straight back to Northolt. Archie swallowed hard, then turned to look at Ted Tyler sitting beside him in another deckchair. His friend's leg was jiggling, and he was rapidly tapping his hands together, only pausing occasionally to sweep back his overly long dark hair.

He heard Ted sigh, then saw him reach into his trouser pocket and pull out his cigarette case. Plucking a cigarette out, he tapped it swiftly on the case, put it between his lips and then, noticing Archie watching him, turned and offered him one too.

'Jesus,' he muttered.

'Thanks,' said Archie, taking one.

'Jesus,' said Ted again. 'How much blinking longer?'

'Calm down, Ted,' said Will Merton-Moore. The flight commander was older than most in the squadron – twenty-eight – and tall, with a slow, dry voice. 'I can feel your impatience assaulting me. I'm trying to read the paper. It's really very off-putting, you know.'

'Sorry,' muttered Ted, 'but I just wish we could get on with it. Four hours we've been sat around here.' He lit his cigarette then tossed the matches to Archie.

Archie caught the box and was about to light his cigarette when he realized his hands were shaking. Anxiously, he glanced around, saw that no one seemed to be looking at him, hastily struck a match and then held it with one hand gripping the other to steady himself. He wished he could feel as calm as Merton-Moore. He ran a hand round his neck, the collar of his shirt blissfully unbuttoned, his tie replaced by his new silk scarf.

He had bought it only the day before, in London. It was bright orange and at first he had thought it rather dashing. Now he was not so sure. The other pilots had ribbed him mercilessly.

'How's the scarf, Baby?' said Will, without looking up from his paper.

Archie immediately brought his hand back down again. Will had given him the nickname almost as soon as he'd joined 629 Squadron. It was not just that he was still nineteen; he had a thick mop of strawberry blond hair, and a wide, open face with barely a bristle on it, which made him look younger than he really was. 'Extremely comfortable, thank you,' he replied.

'That's the main thing, Archie,' said Mike Drummond from his deckchair behind Merton-Moore. He grinned. 'Even if you look like you're wearing a carrot.' There were sniggers from the others.

Archie thought about a riposte, but then decided against it. He was glad of the scarf – after all, it was far better to be able to move one's neck freely – but privately, he determined that when he next had a chance he would buy another, more sombre-coloured one: navy blue, perhaps, or maroon.

Next to him, Ted suddenly stood up. Like Archie, he was only nineteen, although a few months older; both were about the same height too – just under six foot – but there the similarities ended. No one would be calling Ted 'Baby' in a hurry:

he had dark hair, shaved every day, and had a leaner, more muscular face. Archie had been brought up in the country – well, halfway up a Scottish mountain – the son of a local doctor, while Ted's father was Group Captain Guy Tyler DSO and Bar, MC, DFC, a flying ace of the last war with more than thirty kills to his name. Ted had lived all over England and all over the world. He'd been born in India, had learned to walk in Iraq and to fly in Palestine; at least, that's how Ted liked to tell it.

'Come on,' said Ted.

'Where?' said Archie, glad of the distraction and the chance to get away from the others.

Ted shrugged. 'Dunno. Over to our kites? I can't sit here any longer.'

Archie stood up and followed him.

'I just want it over and done with,' said Ted, taking a jerky puff on his cigarette.

'You're not the only –'

Archie stopped mid-sentence as the telephone in the dispersal hut rang. Both men turned and froze. Will had lowered his paper a fraction. Others looked up too.

'For you, sir!' the orderly called out to the CO through the open window.

Dix hurried over, the others watching him disappear inside. Archie felt rooted to the spot.

A moment later, the CO reappeared. 'We're heading over the Channel, boys,' he said in a loud but calm voice. 'Patrolling Dunkirk to Calais, angels fifteen.' He glanced at his watch. 'Let's aim to be airborne in ten minutes – so, 10.15, all right?'

Archie swallowed again, glanced at Ted, then waited for the others as they flung down newspapers and cards and hurriedly began walking towards their aircraft. Will cuffed him lightly on the back of his head as he passed.

'What are you waiting for, Baby?' he said. 'I thought you and Ted were desperate to get going.'

'I was – I am,' stuttered Archie, now hurrying after him.

Moments later, they reached the first of the planes. He saw Mike Drummond, one of the longest-serving members of the squadron, already up on the wing and clambering into his cockpit. Then he reached Ted's plane and watched his friend jump up on to the wing root. Ted shot him a glance, smiled uncertainly, and hoisted himself over the half-lowered door.

Now Archie reached his own Spitfire. Snatching the parachute from where he had left it at the end of the wing, he lobbed it into the cockpit, then jumped up himself. A fitter and rigger were waiting; the rigger, standing at the edge of the wing root, hastily placed the parachute on his bucket seat.

'Thank you,' said Archie, his tone mechanical. With one hand on the top of the windscreen, he hoisted one leg over the door, then the other, standing briefly on his parachute, then slid down on top of it, his feet slotting into and resting on the two rudder pedals. Parachute straps on, then the Sutton harness.

'Nice and tight, sir,' said his rigger. Archie nodded as he slipped the ends into the fastener with a click and then tightened the straps. His helmet was still on the control column, but he took it now and pushed it over his mop of gingery blond hair. Radio leads in, oxygen lead too. He felt for his goggles, perched on the top of his head, left his oxygen mask dangling free – he hated its claustrophobic smell of rubber – then went through his basic cockpit drill, murmuring the now ritual mnemonic:

BTFCPPUR. Brakes, trim, flats, contacts, pressure, petrol, undercarriage, radiator. All in order. Everything set. He nodded to the rigger, who closed the door, gave a wink then slid off the wing.

Archie glanced across at the Spitfires either side of him, both now bursting into life, then shouted, 'All clear? Contact!'

The fitter pulled the chocks clear and signalled to Archie, who began manipulating the hand-pumps and the starter buttons. Ahead of him, pointing imperiously upwards, was the huge engine cowling and beyond it the three-bladed airscrew, black with yellow tips. Slowly, it began to turn, the engine whined and then suddenly, with a flick of flames and smoke from the exhaust stubs and a muffled roar, the machine burst into thunderous life, shuddering as it did so.

Opening the radiator wide, Archie watched the engine temperature quickly begin to rise, then released the brakes, opened the throttle a fraction and began rumbling forward, following Dennis Cotton – like Drummond, one of the long-serving originals, and his section leader – as they began taxiing round the edge of the field. He glanced behind him: there was Ted, weaving from side to side so that he could see beyond the cowling. Twelve Spitfires, airscrews nothing more than a blur, all rolling forward. The CO led the first vic of three on to the grass, then, through his headset, Archie heard the ground controller at Rochford say, 'Nimbus Leader, you may scramble now, you may scramble now.'

'Roger, Moonstone,' Dix replied. Suddenly they were thundering across the grass, and then the next three, Green Section, were moving up to take their place. Moments later, they too began hurtling across the field, and then it was Blue Section's turn and Archie was turning to the left of Drummond, just a little behind him, with Ted on the right.

'Blue One,' said the ground controller, 'you may scramble now.'

With his heart hammering in his chest, Archie felt a trickle of sweat run down his neck. He touched his scarf, looked anxiously at Cotton, then, seeing him nod, glanced at his engine temperature – 105 degrees – and opened his throttle. The noise was immense, and the airframe seemed to shake violently as the plane bumped and surged across the field. Archie pushed forward with the control column – just a bit – and felt the tail lift and the cowling lower. *Good.* He could see now. Faster and faster. Eighty miles per hour, ninety, and then suddenly, as he pulled gently back on the stick, the rattling bumping stopped as the beast glided into the air. Archie looked out to his right, saw the huge elliptical wing scything through the air and, behind him, his shadow retreating, and managed to smile to himself. Swapping hands so that his left was on the stick, he began pumping the undercarriage as the Spitfire continued to climb. A click, a green light – wheels up. Keeping his left hand on the stick, he slid the canopy forward, and felt himself enclosed in the machine, his shoulders almost touching the sides of the cockpit. He and the plane had become one.

Ahead, Dennis Cotton was curving his Spit gently to starboard. Archie followed, looked across at Ted, then swivelled his head and looked around. It had only been eight weeks since he had first flown this wonderful machine, and he never ceased to be amazed at how quick it was. It was as though they had barely taken off, and yet already they were climbing high, Rochford far from view. Below lay the wide expanse of the

Medway estuary, dark and twinkling, while away to the right he could see London, shrouded in haze, and all around the chequered expanse of southern England.

But it was slipping ever further away. As they continued to climb, Archie watched the altimeter turn – five thousand, six thousand, seven thousand, until some twelve minutes after take-off they were at fifteen thousand feet – angels fifteen. And now the long tongue of Kent slid beneath them so that moments later they were out over the English Channel. Away to his left, he saw a convoy moving down the East Anglia coast, a series of white streaks following the ships, and below him were several heading back from France.

France. Archie swallowed again and felt his chest begin to hammer once more. Ahead, the vast flat continent stretched endlessly beyond. The continent where the war was being fought, where enemy aircraft and anti-aircraft guns lurked. An enemy who would try to kill him. His life had gone by in a flash. When he was a boy, being an adult had seemed an eternity away, but now it felt as though he'd barely lived. He didn't want to die. He wanted to live. *Oh, help,* Archie thought to himself.

2

FIRST COMBAT

They were flying in four tight vics of three in line astern, one vic behind the other, their formation flying impressively steady and tight. Up ahead, near the French and Belgian coast, lay a bank of fluffy cumulus, rising high and white. In a trice, they had flown into it, the bright morning light changed into a strange milky glow and all sense of speed stopped. Beside him, Dennis's Spitfire wisped through the cloud. It looked rather ghostly, Archie thought, then wondered whether it was an omen. 'Don't be ridiculous,' he said to himself out loud. Then the cloud thinned, the huge power of the Spitfire obvious again as the knife-like wings sped on over the Channel.

Ahead, Archie could now see Dunkirk, a giant column of thick, oily smoke rising high into the sky, obscuring much of the town and beaches below. In fact, the smoke was so high it had dispersed into a kind of dark shroud that seemed to lie just beneath them. It was worse than the thickest pea-souper he'd ever seen in London and a renewed sense of dread washed over him; he couldn't help it. The dark cloud of smoke seemed so sinister.

'My God,' muttered Archie to himself, and he felt his heart lurch. His mouth, he realized, was horribly dry – as dry as chalk.

The only war he'd seen so far was what they showed on the newsreels at the cinema; and now here was the evidence of it, stark and real. *But what were you expecting?* he asked himself.

The 74 Squadron pilots had warned them of the smoke at Dunkirk, but he felt shocked by what he saw. It was a stark reminder that he was now, at long last, after months of training and then sitting on his backside waiting for things to happen, on a combat sortie. Not for the first time that day, he felt overwhelmed by an urge to flip his Spit on its side, bank hard and head for home.

'Keep your eyes peeled, chaps,' the CO's voice crackled in his ear. Archie craned his neck, glad to feel the soft silk of his new scarf against his neck.

He was still looking around keenly when suddenly he saw them, a dark formation of, he guessed, around thirty Stukas, and above them the same number of fighters, twin-engine Messerschmitt 110s. He recognized both types immediately – the Stuka with its distinct gull-wings and static undercarriage, the 110s with their twin engines and twin tail fins. A bolt, like an electrical charge, coursed through him. Fear? No, something more – *excitement* too.

'There!' he shouted out. 'Below us!' Then, remembering he was supposed to use the correct code, he added, 'Bandits, angels twelve!' Already he could see the Stukas beginning their dives, peeling off one after the other.

'Roger, I see them,' crackled Dix. 'Red and Yellow Sections head straight for the Stukas, Blue and Green go for the fighters. Number One Attack, go!'

Archie dropped into line astern behind Dennis Cotton, then saw the CO peel off and dive down, leading Red and Yellow

Sections. Following Dennis, Archie pushed the stick forward and to the right and felt himself thrust back into his bucket seat as the engine whined louder and the Spitfire hurtled down. Fifteen thousand feet to just twelve in a matter of seconds, the Messerschmitts suddenly looming larger so he could now clearly see their grey mottled camouflage and the stark black crosses on the wings. It seemed unreal, and for a moment Archie felt as though he were somehow not himself at all, but a spectator watching the scene unfold. He glanced at his speedometer – almost four hundred miles per hour! – and eased the stick back towards him. The enemy fighters appeared not to have seen them yet and Archie now felt another surge of adrenalin.

Without thinking, he flicked off the gun safety catch at the top of the oval handle of the control column, and held his thumb poised. A quick glance at Dennis, then Archie picked out the 110 in the middle and carefully lined himself up. He was gaining on the Messerschmitt. *Wait,* he told himself. *Let him fill the gunsight.*

He was now just seven hundred yards away and still rapidly closing, but that was not yet close enough. Four hundred yards was the prescribed distance, but he had never forgotten what his instructor had told him at flying school – that a fighter pilot should always get as close as he possibly could before firing. Archie had listened to that advice – Mick Channon had been an ace in the last war. He'd listened to the advice of Ted's father too. 'The closer you are, the more your bullets are going to hurt,' Group Captain Tyler had told them both. 'And the more you hurt them, the less time you spend firing. The less time you spend firing, the less chance you have of being surprised by some sneaky Hun coming up behind you.'

Since rejoining 629 Squadron, Archie had listened to Dix's oft-repeated line about firing at the prescribed four hundred yards, and had read the various discourses on fighter tactics issued by Fighter Command, but it had always seemed to him that four hundred yards was quite some distance. Secretly, he'd told himself he would try and get closer if he ever had the chance.

He had that chance now, as his Spitfire screamed towards the formation of 110s at nearly four hundred miles per hour. Another quick glance behind – fleeting – but the skies seemed clear, and now he fixed his eyes on his target. Still the 110s had not seen them. Six hundred yards, five hundred, and then Dennis began to fire, beads of tracer flicking from his gun ports.

'Too soon,' muttered Archie to himself. Where was Ted? He couldn't see. Another quick glance behind. Nothing, and now, ahead of him, the enemy fighters had spotted that they were under attack. The Messerschmitt in front of him began to weave, then banked to port and at the same time the rear gunner opened fire. Archie saw orange sparks of tracer arcing towards him, slowly it seemed, but then suddenly they seemed to flash wide past him.

'He's firing at me!' Archie said out loud. He opened the boost, felt the Spitfire surge forward as he swept across the sky, still just managing to keep the Messerschmitt in his gunsight. And he was gaining on him, the height advantage giving him the extra speed he needed to catch the 110. Four hundred yards, three hundred, two hundred and fifty. A bit more . . . *Now!* Archie pressed his thumb down on the tiny red button. A long burst of his eight Browning machine guns and the Spitfire shuddered from the recoil, jolting Archie in his seat. The

Messerschmitt ahead seemed to wobble and now, within just two hundred yards, the 110 huge and close, Archie opened fire again, his mouth set in a determined grimace as he did so. The return fire stopped immediately and he saw from his own lines of tracer that he had raked the fuselage. *Have I killed a man?* he thought, but then a puff of dark smoke came from the Messerschmitt. It banked to the right and stalled, and for a split, heart-stopping second, Archie thought they were going to collide. Instinctively, he ducked his head – not that it would do him any good – as his Spitfire flashed past a huge grey wing, missing it by what seemed like only inches.

Boy, that was close, thought Archie, gasping heavily, his chest hammering. But he'd shot down an enemy plane – his first combat sortie and he'd scored already! A wave of exhilaration consumed him. He glanced around and saw a Stuka diving down away to his right, a long stream of smoke following behind. Archie banked and began to climb once more, thinking he should try to rejoin the fray, but he was amazed by how far away they already seemed – distant specks towards the coast. Could it really be? He watched another plane dropping from the sky – another Stuka he thought – and so pulled back on the stick and began to climb towards them.

Orange flashes whipped past his cockpit and he heard machine-gun fire crackling in his ears. Momentary panic gripped him as he frantically looked behind him – there was nothing, but a moment later he saw two Messerschmitts diving at him from the north, and more tracer curling towards him. And these were not twin-engine 110s, but single-engine fighters, Me 109s. Archie cursed, the words of the station commander at Northolt ringing in his ears: 'Watch your back!' he'd said.

Archie had been – repeatedly – but in the excitement he'd briefly forgotten and now he had two 109s diving down on him. The hunter had become the hunted.

Momentary panic. His mind went completely blank. *What the hell do I do?* He could hear his breath, laboured and heavy, in his oxygen mask, but then another piece of advice suddenly forced its way into his addled mind. 'Always turn in towards your attacker,' Channon had told him. His breathing heavy, his heart hammering, Archie now did so, and felt his harness cut into his shoulders and his goggles slip down from his helmet and partially cover his eyes. Frantically, he pushed them back, and saw he was now heading straight for one of his attackers. He pressed down on the gun button, the Spitfire jerked, and to his utter amazement the Messerschmitt belched a gush of black smoke and dropped out of the sky. Another flush of elation, only to be instantly replaced by raw fear as he saw a third 109, this time attacking from the right.

'Oh my God!' he said out loud as more tracer hurtled past him. *Where is everyone?* There was a sudden clatter, the Spitfire jolted, and he saw a line of bullet holes across the wing, but his machine still seemed to be flying all right. A Messerschmitt thundered over him, its pale underside streaked with oil, the black crosses vividly clear, the wash of its passage jerking his Spitfire with sudden turbulence. But no sooner had it gone than more tracer whipped past him. Archie banked again, as tightly as he dared, and felt himself pressed hard into his seat, his vision blurring and greying. As he emerged from the turn, sweat now pouring down his face, he glanced in his mirror and saw the 109 still doggedly on his tail.

'Damn it! Damn it!' exclaimed Archie. More tracer curled

towards him, and he flung his Spitfire one way then another, radio static and chatter still crackling in his ears, the horizon sliding back and forth, his stomach whirling and churning. Frantically, he kept glancing back, the Messerschmitt just visible in his peripheral vision, but no matter what he did the 109 was still on his tail. Archie felt helpless, unsure what he should do, but then there was an ear-splitting crack, and the Spitfire jolted.

'Christ!' whispered Archie. Where had he been hit? Another punch as a cannon shell tore into his plane, so hard it was like a giant fist ramming into him. Smoke now burst from the engine and flooded into the cockpit. His Spitfire was knocked upside down and he was spinning, the control column limp in his hands. He was falling out of the sky, his plane out of control and smoke billowing behind him, the sky and the ground spiralling, his altimeter spinning backwards too fast to read. *I'm going to die,* he thought to himself.

A moment later, the control column hit his leg and, clutching it once more, he felt the stick respond after all. Pushing it forward and applying the left rudder hard, he was amazed to feel the Spitfire miraculously recover from the spin. He gasped, opened the canopy so that the smoke whipped out, then wiped his brow, pulled off his oxygen mask, pushed his flying helmet back off his forehead and glanced upwards. Two 109s were still circling but they were several thousand feet above him.

He sighed and briefly closed his eyes, but then, with a splutter and a cough, his engine died and he was left gliding. After the constant deafening roar of the engine, there was now a startling silence, save for the wind whistling through the cockpit.

'Damn it!' he exclaimed again. Where on earth was he? Away

to his left he could still faintly see the coast, but was that Allied or enemy land below? He glanced at his altimeter – eight hundred feet. Could he bail from that height, or was it too low? While he wondered, his mind addled once more, he lost another three hundred feet. Well, that was that. Five hundred feet was definitely too low.

For several moments he sat there, unable to think clearly, but then realized there was only one option. He would have to crash-land somewhere. Sweat ran down his neck and his back. His free hand was shaking. Four hundred feet, the ground getting ever closer. To the north, he saw a town, on a high promontory that stood out from the largely flat surrounding countryside, but before it the ground looked flat enough. If he could just find a big enough field, but his sense of scale and proportion was warped by the height he was at. Below there were a couple of villages and then further to the south puffs of smoke – guns? – and suddenly a renewed sense of dread swept over him as he realized that even if he did survive he would probably find himself in the middle of a battle.

Archie sighed – a helpless, resigned sigh. He could not imagine dying – that was impossible to think of – but he could not see how he would ever get out of this mess. Or perhaps he *would* die. Perhaps this was it. One sortie, and he would be gone.

A strange sense of calm now glided serenely over him. It had been a good life, after all. Too short, but pretty decent as far as it had gone. And he wasn't dead yet. Would it hurt? *Don't think about it.*

'Oh, well,' he said out loud, 'hope for the best. Here goes.' Banking the Spitfire, he lowered the flaps, praying he'd judged it correctly. Just three hundred feet now, the village away beneath his port wing, but there was a field, a lush grass field, and about as flat as he could hope for. At one end was a wood, and to the left a thick hedge and a barn, but the field looked to be long enough. He hoped it was long enough.

He pressed down the undercarriage lever, but nothing happened. The hydraulics must have been damaged. He cursed, but there was nothing for it: a belly-landing it would have to be. Checking the buckle on his Sutton harness and tightening the straps, he watched the ground loom towards him. Moments earlier, he had thought he would die, then he'd thought he'd been spared. Now he wondered whether he would die after all, or be horribly maimed for life, or shot at the moment he clambered out of his stricken aircraft. Over some trees, a hedge, grass rushing towards him, and then crack . . .

3

CROSS-COUNTRY ON A BSA

The motorcycle sped on, its engine throbbing as it roared down the long, straight road that led north, away from Cassel. Archie clutched the waist of the despatch driver, a blur of poplars rushing past him on either side of the road. A glimpse of a large concrete blockhouse away to the left, and a vague impression of some Tommies nearby, then an old brick farmhouse, and over to the right a windmill – no, two – sails out, turning slowly. A pothole, nearly avoided, which made the motorcycle jolt, knocking Archie upwards and then hard back down again on to the small second seat. Archie gasped, felt his head throb again with renewed intensity. He had his flying goggles over his eyes, but it had been too painful to get his leather helmet back over his scalp as well, and he was now glad he had not: the wind through his hair was soothing.

It was just a couple of hours since he'd brought his Spitfire down, and had survived the crash with nothing more than a nasty gash to his head. Unfortunately, it had been in no-man's-land, right smack between the outposts to the south of Cassel and the advancing Germans. Fortunately for him, however, Tommies from the King's Own Yorkshire Rangers had got to him before the Germans, had pulled him out of his plane and set it on fire. Despite coming under heavy machine-gun fire from the woods beyond, under the cover of the smoke from the burning Spit, they had managed to get him back to their farmhouse outpost.

And then there had been further good fortune: instead of pressing forward, the Germans had miraculously pulled back. The lieutenant at the farm had been as perplexed as the rest of them, but it had allowed Archie to have his head bandaged and be escorted up the hill to the town, and to Battalion Headquarters. There, in an ancient building on the town square, he had been told by the colonel that the enemy troops to the south had most likely been reconnaissance, probing forward. They had pulled back while waiting for the rest of the division to catch up, at which point they would attack. The colonel had been certain about that. 'It's just a matter of time,' he had told Archie, 'so we're going to get you out right away. Once the fighting starts, you won't be able to go anywhere, I'm afraid.' The quickest way was by catching a lift with a despatch rider. 'Happy with that?'

'Of course, sir,' Archie had replied. He'd wanted to get back home as quickly as he possibly could. One of the men who had led him up to Battalion HQ in Cassel had made it clear that he would far rather be a soldier than an airman. What was it he'd said? 'You wouldn't get me up in one of those things. I prefer being on my own two feet.' Archie smiled ruefully to himself. *You wouldn't get me being a soldier,* he thought. Not after what he'd seen so far that day. They had been good sorts, those Yorkshiremen, and in any case they had saved his life; he'd given the men his orange scarf as a memento. It wasn't much as he had wanted to get rid of it anyway, but they'd seemed pleased. He hoped they would survive the onslaught.

Now, directly in front of him, Chalmers, the despatch rider, looked strangely robotic. The noise of the wind and the single-cylinder, air-cooled 496 cc engine was too great for there to be any conversation, and so instead Archie studied the silent back of the man's head, in its hard helmet, rounded like a football sliced in half, and the leather strapping covering his neck.

A memory suddenly came back to him: taking his younger sister, Maggie, on his first motorcycle, a 120 cc Norton. She had laughed at first, and he could remember, as though it were yesterday, her long hair blowing across his cheek. Down the track and out along the road to Strathtay, he had accelerated and her laughter had turned to screams. Her hands had tightened around his waist, so hard that her nails had dug into him. When he eventually stopped, he had turned to her, grinning, and only then saw the tears running down her face. Had he deliberately been trying to scare her? He couldn't remember, but he did recall the roasting his father had given him.

'She's only thirteen!' he had scolded him. 'It's always far more nerve-wracking being the passenger when you're not in control. Do that again, and I swear it'll be the last time you ride that motorcycle of yours!'

That Norton had been his pride and joy, a machine bought in bits from McAllister's garage in Pitlochry, saved and saved for, and painstakingly, during several school holidays, put back together, until finally the day had come, just a week or so after he had turned sixteen, when he fired up the engine and took his first ride. He still had that Norton; it had served him well over the years. He thought about all the hours he had spent on it, outside the garage, his mother repeatedly scolding him for bringing oil into the house. *Home.* Home seemed a million miles away.

Up ahead, a mass of British troops, some on foot, walking along the road, but beyond them, a convoy of trucks. Chalmers swerved out into the road to overtake, nearly went straight into a French cart, pulled back in, then, once it was clear, gunned the throttle and sped past. Archie gasped, even more aware of what it must have been like for his little sister those three summers ago. His father was right: it was infinitely more nerve-wracking riding pillion.

Ahead, a town, houses and a church spire were outlined against the blue, early summer sky, and immediately the traffic began to thicken. At the side of the road, Archie saw several trucks and cars, some spattered with bullet holes, others nothing more than burnt wrecks. An upturned cart, and, spread out across a young cornfield, the contents of what appeared to be several suitcases, the clothes strewn for thirty yards and more. Now there were not just army vehicles, but lines of trudging civilians, some tramping, heads bent, others with mules and carts piled high with belongings.

The despatch rider slowed at last, until he was weaving at little more than walking pace. Archie glanced at a family of two small boys and a girl – perhaps ten years old – who eyed him with a mixture of stunned disbelief and fatigue. The mother held one of the boys, the father led the mule. Archie looked away.

Chalmers stopped, unable to get through the dense mass of refugees and soldiers, trucks, cars and hand carts – there was even a pram piled high.

'We're coming into Wormhout,' he said, turning to Archie.

'This is terrible,' said Archie.

'I know, sir. If only the French would stay at home.'

'Where are they trying to get to?'

Chalmers shrugged. 'Away. I'm not sure they've thought about where to. But wherever it is, they're getting in our way.'

'Frustrating.'

'You can say that again, sir,' muttered Chalmers. 'It's been like this the past few days. The French have gone mad, if you ask me.' He leaned forward, his booted feet on the ground, and looked about him, then said, 'Look, sir, do you mind if we do something a bit cheeky?'

'What's that?'

'We could get snared up here for hours if we're not careful – that is, if we're not shot up by Jerry aircraft first. I've learned it's sometimes a whole load quicker to go cross-country. Over the fields, like. It's a bit bumpy, but the ground's dry enough.'

'Of course,' said Archie. 'She seems as though she's up to it.'

'Oh, aye,' said Chalmers, 'she's up to it all right. I was thinking more about your head.'

'It's fine. Honestly.'

Chalmers grinned. 'Hold tight, then, sir.'

He throttled gently, dodged behind an army truck, the men in the back jeering at them enviously. 'You should be in the bleedin' air, mate!' someone shouted.

'I wish I was!' Archie yelled back, as the BSA lurched up on to the bank and rolled bumpily into the field.

They rode over one, then another, then sped along the edge of a small winding brook before finding an old wooden farm bridge, which they gingerly crossed, before reaching another road, which was busy but not gridlocked like the one from the south. Chalmers raised his thumb, wove his way forward past yet more refugees, then cut left up a track, on to another road leading towards the town. They took another track before finally rejoining the road north towards Bergues and Dunkirk.

Archie breathed in deeply, but swallowed a mouthful of choking dust as Chalmers gunned the throttle and the BSA lurched forward. *Christ,* he thought, clutching on for dear life.

Suddenly there was a roar overhead, so loud that it could be heard over the throb of the bike's engine. Instinctively, Archie looked up, and saw half a dozen Stuka dive-bombers peeling over one after another and diving down towards the town. Chalmers glanced up, then, leaning forward, gunned the throttle again, the bike accelerating as he did so. Behind them, Stukas were now screaming down over the town, their awful sirens wailing as they dived. A moment later, Archie felt the pulse of the first bomb exploding and looked back to see a cloud of smoke billowing up from the western edge of the town, precisely where they had been just a minute or two earlier. More bombs were falling, one to the north of the town, exploding not three hundred yards behind them. Another quick glance behind from Chalmers, but the despatch rider clearly had no intention of stopping. Instead, he leaned even lower over the handlebars, straining to make the machine go faster.

Behind, Wormhout disappeared behind a cloud of smoke and grit. *My God, that was close,* thought Archie. Yet another brush with death: someone was looking after him, it seemed.

They sped on, the roads always busy with troops and refugees alike, but the traffic not so heavy as to completely hinder their progress. The flat Flanders landscape stretched around them as they flashed past villages and farms, and down long poplar-lined roads. The journey from Cassel to Dunkirk was little more than twenty miles, Chalmers told him, and an hour after leaving

Cassel, they were nearing the port. Archie now saw the huge cloud of oily smoke that shrouded Dunkirk up ahead and felt that same sense of menace he had experienced as he had flown over it. Through the town of Bergues, teeming with troops and vehicles, but passable, and then on to Dunkirk itself.

The city had already been badly bombed. There were smashed and burnt-out vehicles at every turn. Tram wires lay twisted and curling on the roads. Craters pocked the streets. A number of houses were burning, and many more had suffered some degree of damage. Walls had tumbled into the streets. Half-destroyed roofs shorn of their tiles hung above exposed bedrooms or attics. Archie was astonished by the debris: masonry, rubbish, even the dead body of a Frenchwoman. The stench was cloying – of dust and smouldering rubber and oil.

They reached the port. Much of it was already wrecked, particularly the inner harbour. Several ships lay half-sunk, blocking any further approach to the docks where they had been moored, but further out, towards the eastern mole that stretched beyond the port, they saw two Royal Navy destroyers tied up alongside a still-functioning part of the quayside. Chalmers carefully and slowly inched towards them, finally coming to a halt alongside the second. Men were boarding, shuffling up a gangway on to the main deck.

'What's going on?' asked Archie. 'Why are they leaving?'

Chalmers shrugged. 'Getting them away while they can, I s'pose,' he said. Across the far side of the port, a mile or two to the west, Archie watched the oil depot still burning, thick, black smoke billowing upwards. He could smell it on the air, heavy and cloying. Away to the south and west, he could hear the faint boom of distant guns, could feel the trace of a shudder in the ground. The battle was getting closer. Swallowing, his mouth felt dry as sand. Chalmers wheeled the BSA and rolled the motorcycle over to a tin-helmeted naval officer standing beside the gangway watching the men boarding the ship.

'Excuse me, sir,' he said, feeling inside his jacket for the note from the colonel of the Yorks Rangers. 'This here is Pilot Officer Jackson, who needs a ride back to Blighty.'

The officer snatched the note, read it, then said, 'All right. Better get on board.'

Chalmers turned to Archie, lifting his goggles as he did so. 'Well, sir,' he said, a rueful grin on his face. 'Your carriage awaits.'

Archie clambered off stiffly, rubbed his bruised backside, then shook Chalmers' hand. 'Thank you,' he said. 'And good luck.'

Chalmers nodded. 'And you. Give those Stukas hell next time you're in the air, sir.'

Archie stood beside the officer; a naval lieutenant.

'Just a moment,' said the lieutenant. 'We'll get this lot on first, if it's all the same to you.'

'Of course. Why are they leaving? Won't they be needed?'

'They're what's known as Useless Mouths,' said the lieutenant. 'Base troops, mostly RASC. Soldiers, but not front-line troops. If they're not absolutely essential, they're going home while there's still a chance.'

'Are things that bad? What about the rest of the army?'

'Hear those guns?'

Archie nodded.

'They're Jerry guns. Calais's fallen, you know.'

'Do you mean there's no chance for us, then? What about the French? Won't there be a counter-attack?'

The lieutenant did not answer.

Good God, thought Archie. Even after all he had seen that day, it had not occurred to him that all hope had gone. He looked at the men now boarding the ship, and noticed they were scowling at him. *Why?* he wondered.

'Where the hell have you been?' snarled one suddenly as he stepped up to the gangway.

'What do you mean?' said Archie, startled.

'We've been bombed to hell,' said the next in the line, 'and where have the RAF been while Jerry's been bombing us to his heart's content?'

'We-we've been up there,' stammered Archie. 'I was up there earlier.' He felt his cheeks flush.

'Bloomin' useless,' muttered the second man.

'I'll have you know –' began Archie, then stopped. It was not right to brag.

'That's enough,' snapped the naval officer at the men. 'Stop grumbling and get on board.'

'Honestly,' said Archie to the lieutenant, 'we've been flying. But we operate above the cloud base.'

'Ignore it,' said the lieutenant. 'We can't see you from here, that's all. What we do see are Jerry bombers and Jerry bombs. And with things as they are – well, let's just say the men are not in the best of moods. There are some other airmen on board already, as it happens.'

'Really?' said Archie, brightening.

'All wounded, though,' said the lieutenant. 'We've been evacuating the hospitals.'

Archie felt his spirits drop once more. The thought of being surrounded by hostile Tommies for the trip across the Channel was hardly something to relish.

'You'll be all right,' said the lieutenant, reading his thoughts. 'You're an officer and most of them are not. And after all, it's not as though you haven't been doing your bit. What do you fly?'

'Spitfires.'

'A fighter pilot, then. Get any Huns?'

Archie nodded and grinned. 'Two, actually. One after the other this morning.'

'Tell them that, then.'

'I wouldn't want to shoot a line, though.'

The lieutenant patted him on the back. 'Look, just be thankful you're going to be back in England in a few hours' time. You're getting another chance. There are plenty out there not so lucky.'

A little after 4 p.m., that same Friday, 24 May. Could it really be the same day, Archie wondered? He'd been awake for twelve hours, had flown from Northolt to Essex, Essex to France, been shot down, walked to Cassel, then gone by motorcycle to Dunkirk, and was now on a British destroyer inching out of Dunkirk and heading back across the Channel.

The deck was crowded with men, some standing, others sitting wherever they could. Archie had been told he could go below to the Ward Room, but for the moment he decided he would remain on deck and watch the ship leaving port. Standing near the stern of the ship, beneath the X gun, he leaned on the metal railing. The gun crews were at their stations, dressed in navy denim overalls and wearing white cotton balaclavas beneath their helmets. Behind them were the damage-control parties, waiting expectantly.

The destroyer slid slowly out of port. Archie looked back along the vast stretch of beach that he had seen earlier from fifteen thousand feet. It had looked like a narrow golden line then, but now he could see what must have been, the previous summer, a lovely seaside resort, with a wide, open beach and dunes behind. In contrast, the town, shrouded as it was by the great pall of smoke, looked dark and menacing and broken.

He noticed the men around him were all looking skywards and glancing at one another anxiously. Archie followed their gaze, but he could see nothing – only the smoke cloud.

'I wish they'd get a bleedin' move on,' said one man nearby. 'We're sitting ducks going this speed.'

They won't attack through this, thought Archie. Bombers needed to see what they were bombing.

They crept past the rickety-looking outer moles that extended like spider's legs from the harbour and then, once clear, they suddenly accelerated and turned north, rather than directly across the Dover Strait. Archie was impressed by the sudden surge of speed.

'Now where the bleedin' hell are we going?' muttered the same man. 'Ain't Dover straight across?'

'There are minefields, you dolt,' said another beside him. 'Or do you want to become fish bait?'

In what seemed like no time at all, they were out in the open sea, clear of the smoke cloud and once more bathed in warm sunshine. Archie looked out at the deep blue water and the startlingly white wake that was being furrowed by the ship's passage and felt his whole body lighten. He could not help smiling. *This is more like it,* he thought. Soon he would be back in England. Back with the squadron, and with Ted. *Thank God.*

He closed his eyes and felt the sun on his face and a light spatter of seawater on the air, but then immediately opened them again. *What was that?* Engines. Aero engines. Faint, but distinct, and now suddenly getting louder.

Around him, the men were murmuring and pointing, and then the klaxon rang out. Shouts now. Next to him, on the X gun, he heard the gun layer relay the orders he had received from the gunnery officer in the Director Control Tower: 'Dive-bombers, bearing green 375.' The twin 4.7-inch guns were quickly elevated, clicking as the barrels rose. Archie watched, open-mouthed, and then saw that the second stern gun, Y gun, was following suit. Desperately, he scanned the skies, shielding his eyes with his hand.

'There!' he said out loud, spotting them.

'Where?' said the man next to him. 'I can't see them.'

'Nine of them,' said Archie.

'Jesus,' said the man, 'have you got field glasses for eyes or something?'

Archie could not think what he meant. The noise of the aircraft grew rapidly louder.

'Now I see them,' said the man. 'Holy Mother of God.'

They were almost above them now, and Archie saw the already familiar outline of the wings, black against the sky. *Stukas.*

A moment later, he lost them in the sun. *Where are they?* He couldn't see them. But then he could hear them – that terrible wail of the siren as the first began its dive, and then the second and third, screaming down towards them.

4

CHANNEL DASH

As one, the four guns, two at the bow and two at the stern, opened fire, the 4.7-inch shells hurtling into the sky with a deafening boom, while the pom-pom, in the centre of the iron deck and the only weapon able to fire independently at will, pumped away. The terrible wail of the Stukas was getting ever louder, but then the ship suddenly lurched as she changed course, so that Archie nearly lost his footing. A moment later, the first whistle of a falling bomb – men cowered and clutched their heads. The whistling of the missiles could be heard over the ear-shattering din of guns, then huge fountains of spume and spray erupted like sea monsters into the sky. One bomb hit the sea no more than seventy yards away on the starboard side, spray lashing across the deck. Archie ducked as water drenched him. His wound stung painfully, and he cursed.

He could see three of the Stukas now, just a thousand feet or so above them, pulling out of their dives. *Christ,* he thought, *they're almost standing still.*

He glanced back at the gunners, traversing and elevating their 120 mm tube in response to orders from the DCT. One man was gathering the shell, the loader placing it in the breech, and the layer giving the signal that the gun was ready to fire.

When all four guns were ready, the gunnery officer in the DCT triggered each of them as one. Another deafening boom as the guns fired, the breech recoiling, and the empty casing clattering out on to the metal deck behind.

The ship swerved violently again as the bombs continued to fall. *How many was that? Seven? Eight?* Behind him, the pom-pom continued to pound, black smudges of flak peppering the sky, but none of the Stukas appeared to have been hit. But then the dive-bombers hadn't hit their ship either. A further bomb whistled down, this time landing even closer, just fifty yards from the stern of the destroyer. A fountain of water erupted a hundred feet into the air, lashing the men once more. A few seconds later, a third salvo was blasted by the ship's guns, but the Stukas were now on their way.

A lot of noise, a lot of water, but neither dive-bombers nor ship had hit their target.

'Christ!' muttered the man beside Archie. 'Christ Almighty! Oh my God!' He was crouched down, clutching his helmet.

'All right, Sid,' said the man next to him. 'They've gone now. You're all right.'

Archie felt inside his Irvin and fumbled for his tunic pocket, then pulled out a battered packet of cigarettes. Despite the soaking, the thick sheepskin Irvin had done its job: the cigarettes were quite dry.

'Here,' he said, offering the packet.

The man slowly looked up. With a shaking hand, he took one, as Archie felt in his pocket again for his matches. His fingers touched the cool metal of the small silver matchbox his parents had given him on his eighteenth birthday.

'Thank you,' said the man as Archie struck a match and

cupped his hand, lighting the fellow's cigarette and then his own. 'I never thought I'd be this twitchy,' he added. 'But we've had a bit of a pasting these past few days . . . It's got to me, rather.'

'Well, with a bit of luck, that's the last of them,' said Archie. He stood up, smiled weakly at the man, then made his way to the railings. The attack had lasted less than a minute – so quick, he had barely had time to feel frightened. In fact, he had been pleasantly surprised to discover how calm he had felt. His ears were ringing, and his head throbbed with renewed vigour, but he could not help feeling a sense of exhilaration. He had watched those Stukas carefully. When they'd come out of their dives, they had been so slow they were almost hovering in the air for a moment, and then had slowly – very slowly – climbed back into the sky again. That, he reckoned, was the time to try to hit them. It would be like shooting rats in a barrel. When he got back, he would tell the others.

His trousers and hair were damp, but he moved himself into the sun, joining several other men leaning against a locker near the stern of the ship. One of them looked at him suspiciously, but the man next to him had his eyes closed, seemingly asleep. *Good,* thought Archie. He did not feel like talking very much. A group of others had begun playing cards. The destroyer was steaming full speed ahead, the wake furrowing behind blindingly white.

Not long after, a glint of light twinkled high overhead and the distant but unmistakable thrum of Merlin engines could be heard. British fighters heading over to France. Archie closed his eyes again. He had always loved planes, ever since he was a boy. He had been captivated by the thought of being able to take to the air, to be part of an entirely new and different world. The sense of freedom it promised. It was why he had also loved spending so much time as a boy tramping the hills above the Tay Valley, making dens in the woods and dams across the little brooks that ran off the mountains; it was that same freedom, and sense of space.

But aeroplanes also offered excitement and speed. His parents always used to tell him the story of how he had been sitting out in the garden one day as a very small boy – he'd been only three or four at the time – and had seen an aeroplane fly over, only a few hundred feet above their house. He had pointed and laughed and jumped up and down. He could not remember it, but apparently from then on, aeroplanes had been his first love. Certainly, he could not recall a time when he had not been interested in them. As he had grown older, he had devoured the Biggles books, and anything else he could read about the Royal Flying Corps and the RAF. He knew all about the aces: Mannock, McCudden, Ball, Richthofen, and had wooden models, painstakingly made, hanging from the ceiling of his bedroom.

He developed a fascination with machinery – motorcycles, cars, even ships. Speed. The thrill of going fast. His father had had a car for as long as Archie could remember, much needed for his numerous house calls in their remote part of Scotland. But although his father had shared his son's fascination with engines and machinery, and had taught him to drive from the day he had been tall enough to reach the pedals, Archie had longed for a machine of his own.

It was his father who had told him about the Norton in McAllister's garage. McAllister was one of his father's patients, and had kept the motorcycle and its boxed-up bits of engine aside for young Archie until he had saved enough to buy it. That had taken more than a year of window cleaning, clearing out of sheds and yards and other tasks, but now, thinking back, Archie guessed his father must have accepted the Norton as a form of part-payment for some visit or cure. Certainly, it had been worth more than the few pounds Archie had managed to scrape together.

He smiled to himself. Those had been happy days – tinkering in the shed, slowly putting the engine and the Norton back together. When the bike was ready to ride, it had given him even greater freedom, going further afield to the mountains around Loch Tummel and Loch Rannoch, sometimes with friends from school, sometimes on his own.

Speeding along the winding valley roads, the wind in his hair, had been great fun, but he had never lost his desire to fly. Throughout his early teens, he had been determined to join the RAF and become a pilot. On leaving school, he had fully intended to apply for a commission and hoped he would go to Cranwell, but his parents had dissuaded him. 'Get a degree first,' his father had urged. 'You're a bright lad, Archie, and you're good with your hands. Why not get an engineering degree, then, if you still want to join the RAF, we'll not stop you.' Archie had resisted at first, but his father had pointed out that flying was a young man's game. 'When you're older, you'll be grateful for that degree. It'll give you more choice.' Archie had taken off on his motorcycle, played a round of nine holes at Strathtay, and, by the time he returned home, had decided his father was right.

*

High above, and a little way off, he suddenly heard the distant sound of an aircraft. He looked up but could not see it at first. *Ah, yes,* he thought, when at last he spotted it, although he couldn't see quite what it was. Not an enemy plane at any rate – or at least not one intent on attacking them. He thought about the others. He hoped Ted had got back all right, and then felt a sudden flutter of anxiety. He'd hardly given Ted a moment's thought until then, but it was, he now realized, quite possible that others had been hit too. *No,* he thought, *not Ted*. His friend was one of the best pilots he had ever come across, which, admittedly, was not saying much, but it was widely accepted that Ted was among the very best fliers in the squadron. A natural, who had received an 'Exceptional' mark in his wings examination.

Archie looked back across the Channel. The French coast – or was it Belgian? – was now just a faint strip on the horizon. Earlier, he had been relieved just to be alive, then grateful to get away from Cassel. Now he felt nothing but impatience. He wanted to be back at Northolt, in the Mess with the boys.

The man next to him had begun snoring. Archie gave him a gentle nudge, the man snuffled, opened his eyes briefly, then went straight back to sleep.

'Can sleep anywhere, can Norm,' said another of the men to Archie. He snapped his fingers. 'Out just like that.'

'I wish I could,' said Archie, although, in truth, he'd been quite enjoying thinking about the past. He closed his eyes again. His eyes stung with fatigue, his head ached, but sleep eluded him because he began thinking about when he and Ted had joined the squadron.

He had met Ted Tyler in his first week at Durham University, more than a year and a half ago now. Ted was in a different college, but next door to Archie on the Bailey, and studying engineering too. It had been during their first tutorial, when Ted had made some reference to the differences between an air-cooled and liquid-cooled engine, that Archie had suddenly taken notice of this dark-haired young man sitting near him. 'Like the new Rolls-Royce Merlin, for example,' Ted had said.

'As opposed to the Bristol Pegasus air-cooled radial engine,' Archie had replied. They had looked at each other and grinned.

Afterwards they had discussed their mutual love of machinery and flying. Archie could remember that conversation as though it were yesterday.

'Why didn't you join the RAF straight away?' Archie had asked him.

'My father said I should get a degree first,' Ted had replied.

'So did mine,' Archie had laughed.

It seemed Ted had been every bit as obsessed with flying since he was a boy, although, unlike Archie, he had already flown a number of times and even had his civilian licence. His father was still serving in the RAF – a group captain at the Air Ministry.

And then it had suddenly dawned on Archie. 'Your father,' he had said, 'he's not by any chance Group Captain Guy Tyler DSO and Bar, MC, DFC?'

Ted had laughed. 'Yes! Yes, he is.'

'My God, but I know all about him. I read about him in my *Air Aces of the Great War.* That's incredible! He's one of my heroes. He's only got something like thirty-one victories to his name!'

'Thirty-one exactly. You'll have to meet him,' Ted had

grinned. 'He's a good sort is Pops.' He had raised his glass. 'You know what, Archie? I think you and I are going to be pals. Great pals.'

Ted had been right: they had become the best of pals, and almost from the moment they had first met. Archie smiled, remembering. The very next morning his new friend had come and found him in his digs in college, bursting into his room in great excitement.

'I've got a plan, Archie,' he said. 'It suddenly occurred to me last night in the pub, but I didn't want to say anything until I'd spoken to Pops.'

'What?' Archie had said, bemused. 'What are you talking about?'

'Well,' said Ted, pausing to stand still. 'Have you ever heard of the Auxiliary Air Squadrons?'

'Of course, they were founded by Trenchard just after the war. A kind of yeomanry of the air.'

'Exactly. The "Weekend Fliers" as they're known. Well, there's sadly no University Air Squadron here, but there are two Auxiliary Squadrons – 607 County of Durham and 629 City of Durham. And my old man knows the CO of 629.' He sat down on the edge of Archie's bed.

'You mean we can join them?'

'I'm hoping so. At least, I think so.' He stood up again and paced the room. 'Or rather, I'm praying so, Archie!' He now turned and faced Archie once more. 'Do you have any wheels?'

'I have a motorcycle.'

'Good, that'll do. Will it take me too?'

'At a push, yes.'

'Excellent. Apparently, the CO has strict criteria for who

joins. You've got to be the right sort – have your own transport, outgoing, like sport. Do you play anything?'

'Golf. Rugger, football. Cricket. Played it all at school.'

'Even better. We're the right age too – he won't take on anyone older than thirty-four, even though he's thirty-eight himself. He doesn't want anyone to come from too far either. Wants local types.'

'Where are they based?'

'Spennymoor. It's only six or so miles south of Durham. Christ, we could almost walk it! A grass 'drome, used in the last war and then turned back to farmland, but it's on Fitzwilliam's land.'

'Fitzwilliam?'

'The CO. He served under my father in the last show. Anyway, he's turned it back into an airfield and that's where 629 City of Durham Auxiliary Squadron is based.'

Archie ran his hands through his hair, then breathed out heavily. He could scarcely believe what Ted was telling him. 'And they really can fit us in? Aren't they massively oversubscribed with local landowners' sons?'

Ted shrugged. 'I don't know. Pops thinks there will be room for us. Squadron Leader Fitzwilliam is going to see us next weekend.'

For the rest of that week, Archie had thought of little else, and when Saturday finally arrived the two of them had ridden down on his Norton with mounting nervousness. What if the squadron had changed its mind? Or if Fitzwilliam did not like them? Archie was particularly worried that Ted might get in but not him. No, Ted had assured him: they would both be accepted or not at all.

Neither of them need have worried. They had gone to Fitzwilliam's home, a large Queen Anne farmhouse on the edge of the airfield, and, having been given stiff drinks, had been sat down in two armchairs in his library. Squadron Leader Fitzwilliam admitted they had been inundated when they had formed the squadron a year earlier. 'Enough applicants for three or four squadrons,' he told them, but his strict criteria had brought that number down, and since then two of their members had dropped out due to illness and injury, another had gone to Cranwell to gain a permanent commission, while a fourth had joined the Guards. 'You chaps are just what we need,' he told them. 'Young bloods with a bit of gumption.' He had nothing but praise for Ted's father and had been impressed by Archie's mechanical skills. 'Useful that – damned useful.'

Fitzwilliam promised to apply on their behalf for Auxiliary Air Force commissions for both of them; they were to become the fifteenth and sixteenth pilots in the squadron, along with some sixty auxiliary ground crew, all of whom were now receiving instruction in various aspects of aircraft service work. The squadron had two Avro Tutors for what Fitzwilliam termed '*ab initio*' training, a Tiger Moth donated by himself, and two Hawker Hind biplanes handed over by the Air Ministry for service training.

'I'm afraid you won't get much flying,' Fitzwilliam told them. 'About five to twelve hours a month, but at least you *will* be flying. Next summer you'll come with us on summer camp – a couple of weeks in tents where we all get up bright and early and fly as much as we possibly can, then have a bit of a laugh in the evening. Oh, and there's an annual dinner too. Everyone present. You know, we all take the flying pretty seriously, but we're here to have fun too. We're all friends here.' He had paused at this point, stretched, then grinned at them affably. 'I've always loved flying. Not so keen on fighting. Tell the truth, it was pretty bloody in the last show, but this squadron now is what it's all about. Flying over this beautiful country of ours, pirouetting about the sky, feeling a bit like a god or something, then having a good time with one's mates when back on the ground. I'm proud of our squadron. It's full of first-class fellows, all of whom I know will do more than their bit should it ever come to war, and all of whom share a great bond. In fact,' he added, 'you couldn't have come to a better squadron. The best in all the AAF.'

Archie smiled again to himself, remembering. It had been such fun – fun and exciting. He recalled his first flight – with Fitz in the Tiger Moth, sitting up front with the CO behind. A beautiful aircraft, Archie had thought, even though it was made of little more than wood and doped canvas. There had been no wheel at the rear, just a little strip of metal, and as they had begun their take-off, they had rattled and bumped and Archie had wondered how such a flimsy thing could ever possibly get airborne. But then suddenly the shaking and bumping stopped, the hedge at the end of the field had disappeared, the ground had stretched away from them and they were effortlessly rising into the air. Archie had laughed out loud with the thrill of it all. He was flying! He was actually flying!

Fitz had turned north, climbing to around two thousand feet. They had circled over Durham. The great cathedral and castle dominated the countryside for miles around, so huge, so solid compared to the town that had built up around them, yet from the air they were dwarfed. Fitz had turned and Archie had marvelled at the silvery snake of the River Wear, the patchwork of fields, the small clusters of villages and towns. Away to the east, he had seen Newcastle and Sunderland and, beyond, the North Sea, stretched out so that Britain, which had always seemed so large on the ground, had, like the cathedral, shrunk into a much, much smaller place. It had been a cold day, that early November Saturday in 1938, but bright: tall banks of fluffy cumulus had towered above them, casting vast shadows on the countryside below. But then there would be gaps and the sunlight would pour down shafts of gold, bathing the fields and villages beneath them in glittering light. Fitz had said they were like gods up there, and he had been not far off the truth. Archie had felt empowered, intoxicated, as though he had been touched by God.

'Well?' Fitz had said as they landed and rumbled across the field.

'It's – it's quite the most overwhelming . . .' Archie had been unable to finish. He had felt quite giddy as he had stumbled back towards the wooden dispersal hut, his feet light, his legs shaky. But he knew that he had just experienced something he would never, ever forget.

'I think our man is hooked!' Fitz had grinned as they'd rejoined the others. 'Isn't that so, Archie?'

Archie had nodded mutely. Yes, he was most definitely hooked. In fact, he and Ted had lived for flying and for the weekends at Spennymoor. During the week, they had attended lectures and tutorials, and Archie, at any rate, had dutifully completed all the written and practical work expected of him. He had made a few other friends, but, as Fitz had suggested, all the companionship he had ever needed he found at the squadron. Most were a bit older – in their early and mid-twenties, and with embryonic careers. There were a couple of solicitors, a sculptor, a number of farmers. One or two had family estates, another a motor-car business: men like Harry Dix, Mike Drummond, Will Merton-Moore and Pip Winters.

Fitz's house had been an unofficial Mess, and it was either to there or to a pub down the road that the pilots would retire as soon as the flying was over. It was all that Archie could have ever hoped for: flying, flying machines, camaraderie. Those had been wonderful days.

Archie opened his eyes, his reverie interrupted by movement from the men around him. Most were now getting to their feet, pointing and talking with one another. Archie remained where he was a moment, his head throbbing painfully once more, then wearily stood up too and made his way to the rail on the port side of the ship. Ahead, quite clear now, were the white cliffs of Dover, and above them a string of six metal lattice masts, dark against the early evening sunshine. The men around him were animated now; the low spirits of earlier had evaporated at the sight of home.

It was strange, Archie thought, how *English* the cliffs appeared; there were no doubt chalk cliffs in France too, and it was most likely that many of the men had never set foot in Dover before – he knew he certainly had not. And yet they now seemed as familiar to him as any part of Britain he had ever seen. He, too, felt his spirits rise. Soon he would be on home soil again. Soon he would be back with the squadron – no longer the best Auxiliary Air Squadron in the RAF, but, to his mind, the best squadron in all the Air Force. How lucky he had been, he thought to himself, to have met Ted, and to have been given the chance to join 629 City of Durham Squadron. To be flying the best, fastest, most modern aircraft in the world. He thought about those soldiers from Yorkshire who had rescued him earlier, and wondered what they were doing now. Were they fighting? Or were they still dug in at their farmhouse? Already, that place seemed like a thousand miles away – another world.

Suddenly his spirits sagged again. If the Yorks Rangers' colonel had been right, and if Chalmers and the naval lieutenant had been right, things looked very bleak indeed in France. He thought of all the refugees he had seen on the roads, the endless troops and vehicles, all heading one way: towards the coast. Was it really possible? Could Britain lose in France? Could France, one of the most powerful nations in the world, really have been knocked over with such apparent ease?

A sense of shame swept over him. He supposed he was a bright enough fellow, and yet he knew so little. His life had been so sheltered. He had barely ever read a newspaper, hardly ever listened to the news, and although he had seen newsreels of the fall of Poland at the cinema, it had never really occurred to him that he would soon be taking on the Luftwaffe's best himself. How callow he had been; he could strip and rebuild an engine, could hole a putt from fifteen yards, and could fly an aeroplane, but he knew little else. He had had little interest in anything else.

Even last August, at his and Ted's first summer camp, he had barely given the war a thought. Of course, they had heard the talk of imminent war, but when he had arrived at RAF Yeadon, he had not been thinking that soon he would be part of Britain's first line of defence, tussling with Messerschmitts. He had been thinking about flying, about twirling around the sky, and, hopefully, seeing some modern fighters for the first time. War talk had been banished from the Mess. He thought about it now – what could he remember? Fitz's opening speech, that song they had sung every night, a long discussion about golf with Mike Drummond, nearly choking on his first cigar and he and Ted having their trousers stolen one night after a particularly heavy session in the Mess. But war talk? Nothing.

And even up till now it had never really occurred to him that Britain would ever be in grave peril – that they might *lose,* and that he would be in the vanguard of those who were supposed to stop the German juggernaut. *Christ,* he thought, *this is getting serious.* He was only nineteen – barely a man at all – but it was, he realized, time he grew up a bit.

The ship inched into Dover harbour, seagulls swirling and calling around them. Archie breathed in deeply – a familiar smell to any port of seaweed and coal smoke. The port was heaving with ships. There were other naval vessels: destroyers, two much bigger cruisers and a number of others, including pre-war Channel cruisers, fishing boats and merchantmen. On the quayside, stevedores and sailors scurried about, then the destroyer gently berthed, ropes were lashed and, minutes later, the Useless Mouths were filing down the gangway.

Archie hovered at the rear, waiting his turn, then he was on the gangway himself, and, a few steps later, his feet landed on the quayside.

He was back on English soil once more.

5

FIRST FLIGHT

Archie had intended to ring through to Northolt, but, having been directed to a naval office at the harbour, he had seen that the telephone at the front desk was busy and so had decided against it. The thought of arriving unannounced appealed to him, in any case. More dramatic. The previous summer he and Ted had seen the latest Errol Flynn film, *The Dawn Patrol,* all about a flying squadron in the last war. There had been a bit in it when Flynn's character, Captain Courtney, thought he had lost his best friend, Scotty, played by David Niven. But later that night, Scotty had burst into the Mess, clutching several bottles of champagne, miraculously back from the dead and grinning like a Cheshire cat.

Archie had loved that film, and wondered whether he might turn up out of the blue, too, rather like Scotty.

The harbour was busy, not least with the sudden influx of four hundred troops and servicemen from Dunkirk. No one was very interested in Archie. His head still hurt like mad, and he was conscious that the medic at the farm who had bandaged the wound had told him he needed stitches, but Archie was impatient to get back; he had put up with it all right so far that day, so he reckoned a few more hours would not make much difference.

On the quayside he spotted a row of trestle tables where ladies were handing out sandwiches and hot tea to the arriving troops. Only then did Archie realize how hungry and thirsty he was. Having devoured a bully-beef sandwich and drunk a mug of the sweetest tea he had ever tasted, he felt remarkably revived. The troops were being directed towards special trains that were waiting at the station, but Archie did not want to go to Pirbright – he wanted to get to Northolt, or London, at any rate.

He took another sandwich, then made his way to the railway station. The first of the troop trains was slowly huffing away, but another train had arrived and this one, he was told, was the usual South Eastern fast train to London. It was due to depart at 19.45, which was in ten minutes' time.

'I say, sir, are you all right?' the porter asked him.

'Oh – er, yes, thank you,' said Archie, lightly touching the bandage on his head. 'It's nothing.'

'Looks like a nasty wound, that's all,' said the man, a small, round fellow with a bristling moustache.

'I banged my head,' said Archie, then realized what a foolish comment it was, so hastily added, 'could have been worse.' He smiled and hurried on towards the train, still clutching his flying helmet and with his bulky Irvin under his arm.

Finding an empty compartment, he sat down next to the window and stared out, then breathed on the glass just as he had done in the back seat of his father's car when a boy. With his finger, he slowly drew the numbers '629', then sighed. The door opened, and a middle-aged couple stepped inside, so he hastily wiped the glass clear.

'Not disturbing you, are we?' asked the man, who had a thin, kindly face and greying hair.

'No, no, not at all.'

The couple talked to each other in low tones, the man placing their bags and coats on the netted luggage rack above them, before settling down next to each other.

The lady cleared her throat, then said in a very clear, precise voice, 'You look like you've been through the mill, rather, young man.'

'Yes, I'm sorry,' said Archie. 'I must look a bit of a sight.' He touched his head again and winced, which prompted a wince of sympathy in return. 'It's a bit of a cut. Nothing too awful.'

'You were flying today?' said the man, adjusting his tie.

'Yes, yes, I was – this morning.' He wanted to tell them about it, but did not want to admit to having been shot down – at least, not without having told them he had brought down two enemy planes first. But to tell them that would be to show off, and that, he reminded himself, was not really the done thing.

'Over there?' asked the man, nodding towards the Channel.

Archie nodded.

'Do you fly fighters or bombers?'

'Fighters.'

The man nodded thoughtfully, his brow creased. 'And, er, did you get any? Huns, I mean?'

Archie felt a wave of relief. 'I did, actually, yes. A couple, but then unfortunately I got hit myself and had to bring her down in a field. That's how I cut my head. I'm afraid I was knocked out cold for a bit, but some soldiers hauled me out, and I managed to get a ride back to Dunkirk, and then across the Channel, and so here I am.'

'My goodness, what a day!' said the woman.

'Well, good for you, young fellow,' said the man. They were

all silent for a moment and then he said, 'And just how bad is it over there?'

'Um,' said Archie, unsure how to answer. He did not want to seem defeatist, yet was there anything to be gained from misleading him? 'It's pretty bad. A lot of refugees on the roads.'

'They're starting to bring the troops back, Harold,' said the lady, turning to the man.

'Only the Useless Mouths,' said Archie, 'the Royal Army Service Corps types. The fighting men are still there. I was in Cassel and the men there certainly meant to keep fighting.'

'So that's from the horse's mouth, my dear,' the man said to his wife; at least, Archie assumed they were man and wife. The lady certainly wore a wedding ring.

'It's hard to know what to think.' She sighed and shook her head. 'These are certainly worrying times we live in. To think we might have the swastika fluttering just across the Channel.' She gave an exaggerated shudder. 'It turns one quite cold.'

They were silent for a moment, then heard a whistle blast from the platform, the hiss of steam, which rolled down the platform in great gusts, and then the carriage lurched and they were off, moving slowly at first, the chuffing of the engine gathering speed until it became one rhythmical beat.

'So what is it you fly, if you don't mind me asking?' said the man at length.

'A Spitfire,' Archie answered, and felt a touch of pride as he said the word.

'A Spitfire,' repeated the man with relish. 'And is it as marvellous as they say it is?'

'More so.' Archie grinned. 'It's quite the most incredible machine. A thoroughbred, all right.' He smiled, leaned against the high-backed seat and looked out of the window, the Kent countryside already rushing by.

A thoroughbred. That was what Will Merton-Moore had called it before Archie had made his first flight in that glorious machine. That had been a magical day, and one that had felt like a very long time coming – a time when his future as a pilot and his future with the squadron had been far from certain.

Everything had changed for Archie the previous August, a couple of weeks before war had been declared. Before that first summer camp had ended, the news had reached them that the squadron was to be put on a war footing and fully mobilized. Initially, no one was quite sure what that meant – not even Fitz – but a few days later, orders were received. The squadron was to move to Drem, near Edinburgh, where it would become 629 Fighter Squadron, but Archie and Ted Tyler were among six of the squadron's pilots who were to be sent for immediate pilot training. As 'weekend fliers', they had learned the basics of how to fly, but little more. Even Ted had much yet to learn. They were to report to No. 7 Initial Training Wing at Cambridge in four days' time. Whether they would ever return, however, was another matter. 'I very much hope we will get you back,' Fitz had told them, 'but I'm afraid I cannot guarantee it.'

So had begun seven long months of uncertainty. Parade-ground drill at Cambridge for a month, then to No. 16 Elementary Flying Training School at Burnaston near Derby. Archie had already made his first solo in one of 629 Squadron's Tutors, and he and Ted had arrived at Burnaston confident they were several steps ahead of the others. Archie's confidence, however, had been misplaced. 'Your aerobatics are terrible,' his instructor had told him. 'Your slow roll was disgraceful, and you're heavy-handed too.' It had been a shock, and with it had come the awful realization that he might be transferred to bombers rather than remain as a fighter pilot. Even worse, that he might get thrown off the course altogether.

He had worked hard from then on; when the others went to the pub, he stayed behind, studying his textbooks in his room. He listened carefully to everything his instructor told him, made notes afterwards, and concentrated so hard his head hurt. It had all paid off, however, because suddenly he discovered he knew what he was doing; he no longer had to think about everything. The plane began to go where he wanted it to, and do what he wanted it to do; the heavy-handedness evaporated. He had mastered other potential stumbling blocks too – navigation, night flying, recovering from a vertical spin – so that in March, at Flying Training School, when he had taken his wings examination, he had passed with an 'Above Average' mark. Ted had passed too; he had been top of the entire course. Then had come a terrible wait for their postings, until at last they had been pinned up on the notice board at Burnaston. He remembered now the sense of panic he had felt as the twenty-six who had gained their wings had gathered round. He'd not been able to see the board at first. Some had groaned as they learned they would be joining Army Co-operation or bomber squadrons, and then, as the jostling crowd thinned, Ted and Archie had finally learned their fate: they were to go back to 629 Squadron.

'Thank God,' Archie had said, closing his eyes and leaning against the wall.

'We're sticking together,' Ted had added. 'We've done it, Archie. We've gone and damn well done it!'

*

That had been at the very end of March. Spring had been well on its way by then, the longer days, the green tinge in the hedgerows, the sunshine a welcome change after a bitterly cold winter. That was one of the reasons why their training had taken so long: there had been many days when flying had simply not been possible. Too wet, too much snow. Too damned cold.

It had been good, though, to rejoin 629. Most of the fellows were still there: Will, Pip, Mike, Dennis Cotton – the pre-war stalwarts, although Archie had been saddened to learn that Fitz had been forced to stand down. At thirty-eight, Fitz had been too old to fly and so he had been promoted to wing commander and made station commander of a bomber airfield somewhere in Lincolnshire; Henry Dix had become CO. They were now together all the time, rather than just at weekends, and at a different airfield too – Drem was especially convenient for Archie, whose home was less than three hours' ride on his Norton – but the pre-war atmosphere seemed much the same: the jokes, the banter, the passion for flying. Seven months of war – long winter months in which they had not once seen a single enemy aircraft – had done little to change the City of Durham boys.

The only real change, as far as Archie could tell, was with the aircraft. Before the war, the squadron had made do with a handful of old biplanes. Now it was fully equipped with Spitfires: 1,000 British horsepower, an astonishing top speed of three hundred and fifty miles per hour, and eight .303-calibre Browning machine guns. As Will Merton-Moore had pointed out, it was like driving an old Morris capable of thirty miles per hour and then being told to take a Grand Prix-winning Bugatti for a spin.

From the moment they had arrived at Drem, both Archie and Ted had thought about little else other than flying these wonderful machines for the first time. Walking down the flight line that first evening back, fifteen Spitfires all lined up, their noses pointing imperiously towards the sky, they had marvelled at the promise of power, at the curves, at the feline beauty. Like a beautiful, angry beast, Archie had thought. Just looking at them made his heart race. He was desperate to fly one, but apprehensive too, worried that he would struggle to control that power. During training, he had progressed from Tutors and Tiger Moths to the new American Harvard, a modern, single-engine, all-metal aircraft with a retractable undercarriage like the Spitfire, but although it had felt like a great leap forward after the biplanes, the new trainer had still been only 400 horsepower. The Spitfire had one and a half times more power – more, if the others were to be believed.

Archie looked out of the window, the Kent countryside rushing past, but he barely noticed. He was thinking of that first flight. What a moment that had been! Thursday 11 April, three days after their arrival at Drem. A bright enough morning, but cold and crisp, with a touch of frost still twinkling and crunching underfoot at nine o'clock. As Archie reached his Spitfire, he had thought, *My first flight is just minutes away.* A light breeze drifted across the airfield, the air cool and sharp as he breathed in deeply. In the distance a mechanic working, a spanner tapping on metal, resounded across the quiet morning air.

For a moment, Archie had stood just looking at the aircraft. The wide curve of the wings, the slope of the nose – barely a straight line anywhere. He ran a hand over the cold stressed metal of the wing, wet with condensation as the frost melted.

'She's a thoroughbred,' Will had said as they had walked out together, 'an absolute thoroughbred.' The sun was well over the hedgerows at the far end of the field and as Archie walked around the engine cowling he was suddenly blinded by the brilliant light.

'All right, sir?' said his fitter, who was standing on the wing root and polishing the canopy with a cloth.

'Yes, fine, thank you. Perfect flying weather,' said Archie, hoping he sounded calmer and more nonchalant than he felt.

'Perfect,' agreed the rigger, who was busy fixing the cable from the starter trolley into the nose of the Spitfire. Archie looked back up at the fitter and noticed he was smiling. Was he laughing at Archie's inexperience or just being friendly?

'When you're ready, sir,' said the fitter, in a thick Scottish accent.

Archie muttered, 'Yes, absolutely,' then stepped up beside him. The paintwork by the footplate was chipped, revealing flecks of bare steel. The tiny half-door hung open, allowing him to lower himself into the narrow cockpit. His fitter helped strap him in.

'OK, sir?' asked the fitter. 'Lean forward a little for me.'

Archie did so, then looked behind him. Only if he really strained could he see the rudder, but the harness felt binding and secure. He nodded to the fitter, who then shut the door. Archie took a few deep breaths, the air around him suddenly close, then began going through his cockpit checks and trying to remember everything he'd been told. Throttle, undercarriage pump, magnetos, canopy release, temperature gauges, oil pressure. Look at it any longer and he'd never get off the ground.

He waved a gloved hand at the two ground crew, then pressed the starter button. A chug from the engine, then another, the propeller creaking, then suddenly flames spurted from the blackened exhaust stubs, the propeller whirred and the Merlin burst into life, a deep, guttural roar, noisier than any engine he'd heard before. Its pounding pistons vibrated his seat and shook the airframe.

Blimey, he thought, *this is the moment*. The moment he'd looked forward to – yearned for – ever since he'd first seen pictures of a Spitfire in one of his magazines four years earlier. Ever since he'd been sent for training. Wasn't it the dream of every boy in Britain to be doing what he was doing now? And yet he knew he had just one chance to get it right. There was no instructor sitting behind him talking him through what he had to do. Will's casual briefing had not given him much confidence.

'Oh, you'll be fine,' he'd told Archie, as they had walked around the machine. 'Yours for an hour. Go and have some fun.' Then he'd turned back and said, 'Just watch you don't push the nose too far forward when you take off or else you'll flip over. And another thing: bear in mind that this machine is much, much more powerful than anything you've ever flown before. Oh, and I almost forgot: wreck this aircraft and there'll be hell to pay. Serious hell to pay.' Then he'd winked and wandered off.

Some briefing, thought Archie. He loved the laid-back attitude of the squadron's pilots – the devil-may-care approach to everything – but sometimes, just *sometimes,* he wished Will and Pip Winters and the other seniors would take life a little more seriously.

Above his feet lay a tank full of high-octane fuel; beyond

that, the giant Merlin engine; ahead of that, the whirr of the variable-pitch propeller, very different from the single-speed Harvard. The Spit was unlike anything he'd ever flown before. Nausea rose from his stomach. His mouth tasted sour. The airframe shook; he could feel his entire body shaking with it, like an electrical charge pulsing through him.

He closed his eyes a moment, breathed in deeply, opened them again and then released the brakes and gently rolled forward. He couldn't see anything, then he remembered Will had warned him that forward vision was terrible and that during taxiing he should weave from side to side until ready to start his take-off. He'd also been warned that the controls were more sensitive than those of any other plane he'd flown – well, he could tell that just from the way the rudder responded.

He swung the plane round at the far end of the airfield. A glance at the temperature gauges – already above a hundred degrees. Now facing into the wind, he counted to three. *Here goes.* Brakes released, throttle open, and then the Spitfire was hurtling across the grass, the surge of power intense. Archie glanced at the vast elliptical wings, visibly straining as the Merlin growled deeper and the speed increased. Stick forward a shade, and the nose dropped, so that he could now see the perimeter rushing towards him. Fifty miles per hour, sixty, seventy, ease back on the stick and suddenly the two of them had left the ground and were surging through the air.

Hedgerows, houses, trees flashed beneath him. In what seemed like a few moments, the airfield was nothing but a tiny patch of grass behind him. Beads of sweat ran down his forehead as the Spitfire continued its rapid climb. Turning his head from side to side, he tried to work out where he was.

Shocked by the unaccustomed power, Archie felt completely out of control, as though the Spitfire were running away with him. *Think,* he told himself. Throttle back, coarsen the pitch – *much better.* Then he remembered the undercarriage. A manual pump. He looked down and realized he needed to swap hands, but as soon as he started pumping with his right hand, he found his left began aping it and the Spitfire started bobbing through the air.

As soon as both wheels clicked into place within the wings, he levelled off. *Six thousand feet already! And so light on the controls!* Perhaps this machine wasn't quite so formidable after all, and, for the moment, his fears evaporated. As Archie took the plane through a gentle turn, the horizon tilted. Arcing through the sky, he left behind the expanse of clear blue and flew into a mass of rolling white cumulus. He shouted out loud with joy – how many hundreds of thousands of people would wish to do what he was doing, cavorting and dancing around the sky in this wondrous machine? Effortlessly, he climbed over a towering column of cloud, then, laughing, rolled and dived and climbed once more.

This is perfect, he thought. For this moment in time, he had become the master of all he surveyed: the sky, the clouds were his. Time had stopped. The war no longer existed. A glorious solitude, in which he had discovered harmony with both machine and nature. The morning sun gleamed across the top of the clouds, capping them with shining gold, and Archie understood why many believed heaven lay somewhere high in the sky. At just the slightest command, the lightest pressure, the Spitfire twisted and pirouetted as it was bidden, a mighty beast indeed, but one already tamed.

'Trim her properly,' Will had told him, 'and you'll find her controls are as light as a feather.' Archie laughed again, climbed and rolled the plane, watched the great wings slice through the sky and felt his stomach churn as the Spitfire effortlessly cork-screwed. Never before had he experienced such pure, unbridled joy.

What a thrilling moment that had been. He remembered finally landing again, clambering out of the cockpit and jumping down on to legs that suddenly seemed so weak they could barely support him. The mighty Merlin engine had ticked impatiently as it cooled. But the moment of pure joy had passed. Today he had used his Spitfire for the purpose it had been designed for: destroying other aircraft. Killing pilots. He'd killed three men that morning, something he had hardly dared think about until now. He'd barely killed a living thing in his life before – perhaps the odd fly, but that was all. Now three young men were dead because of him. It was incredible, impossible to comprehend. A lump rose in his throat. Outside the rushing train, the Kent countryside looked a picture of peacefulness. A patchwork of fields, woods, villages and farms. He looked at one farmhouse with its high conical-roofed oast house, bathed in late evening sunlight. The trees and hedgerows all seemed to be bursting with life. England looked so beautiful.

If they lost in France, Britain would be next, and the scene outside his window might be lost for ever. Lost for ever unless he and his comrades in the squadron and in the RAF managed to stop the enemy.

The enormity of this responsibility now overwhelmed him. *I just wanted to fly,* he thought to himself. *Not kill anyone. Not be shot at*. That lump in his throat refused to go away and he now felt tears begin to prick at the corner of his eyes. He glanced at the couple opposite him. The lady looked at him with such pity, such compassion, that he could do nothing but quickly look away and close his eyes.

It had been such a long and difficult day, and yet Archie knew that this was just the very beginning . . .

6

GROUNDED

It was after half-past eleven by the time Archie finally reached Northolt. The train had pulled into Charing Cross by ten, and he was wondering how he might get to north-west London when it occurred to him that someone at the RAF Club might be able to fix up a lift. At any rate, he had thought it worth a try. Walking up through Trafalgar Square, and then down Piccadilly, he had reached the club twenty minutes later.

No sooner had he walked into the main hallway than an air commodore had looked at him and said, 'My God, are you all right?' Archie had explained that he had just arrived back from France and that really, he ought to get back to Northolt.

'I was going to get a bus or something,' he'd said.

'Nonsense,' said the air commodore. 'I've got a driver outside. He'll take you.'

And so he had, right up to the main entrance of the Mess.

'Here we are, sir,' said the driver, as he brought the car to a halt. He jumped out and hurried around the front of the car to hold the passenger door open.

'Thanks so much,' said Archie.

'You'll be all right now, sir? Get that head looked at, won't you, sir?'

'Yes, of course.' Archie smiled, then shook hands. The driver bade him farewell and drove off. For a moment, Archie stood there, looking up at the sky. It was clear, the stars twinkling brightly. He could see his breath on the night air as he peered towards the bar. The windows had been blacked out, but he suddenly heard laughter. *Good*, he thought. *There're some still there.*

The intense fatigue he had felt earlier had now gone and so had the sombre thoughts that had plagued him. His head still throbbed, but a sudden wave of excitement allowed him to force the pain into the background. *I've made it*, he thought, and, grinning, he pushed open the door and headed to the bar.

Pip and Will were playing billiards, but a number of other pilots were still gathered around the bar. Archie glanced at them all, unable to stop grinning, then spotted Ted, slumped against the counter, head in his arm.

'Well, look what the cat brought in!' said Will, looking up, then slamming the end of his cue on the floor. 'Honestly, Baby, we thought you'd bought it!'

Still grinning from ear to ear, Archie now saw Ted suddenly look up, a startled expression on his face. He looked as though he had seen a ghost. And then his expression changed to one of relief and then joy. Pushing back his stool, he jumped down and hurried over to Archie.

'Archie, thank God, I can't believe it –' He stopped, looked him up and down, then held out his hand, clasping Archie's firmly. He was laughing now. 'It's good to see you, Archie. Damn good to see you. I thought I'd lost you. Everyone thought . . .'

'What the hell happened?' asked Will, slapping an arm round his shoulder.

'One minute you were shooting down a 110,' said 'Pinky'

Parmeter, another of the A Flight pilots, 'and then I lost sight of you.'

'Dennis here thinks you might have got a 109 too,' said Will.

'I definitely saw you on the tail of one,' said Ted, 'then the next minute I was being nobbled myself. I rather had other things to look at then – like my own backside.'

'But I saw you in a spin,' said Pip, 'or at least, I guessed it was you. It was certainly a Spitfire, had smoke trailing and looked as though it was plunging straight into Flanders.'

Archie glanced around, unable to shake off the inane grin he was wearing. 'I think it probably was me,' he said. 'I hit a 109 but then there were two more and one of them got me. It was like being punched sideways, and the next thing I know, the Spit's on its back and the world is going round.'

'Ah, told like a true raconteur!'

Archie looked up to see the CO. Dix was a tall man, with a long, square chin and aquiline nose, and wavy, straw-blond hair. He had always seemed an age older to Archie. 'Welcome back, Archie,' he said. 'And congratulations. Your 110 has been confirmed.'

'Thank you,' said Archie.

'And what about his 109?' said Will, an expression of mock outrage on his face.

Dix smiled. 'You'll need to talk to Calder about that. He's the IO. You definitely saw it go in, did you?'

'Oh, yes,' said Archie. 'It must have done.'

Dix raised an eyebrow. 'Well, you can sort that out with Calder in the morning.'

'What I want to know,' said Pip, 'is how on earth you got out of that spin.' Archie had always liked Pip. He was a small-framed man in his mid-twenties, who always spoke slowly with a tone of perpetual amusement, as though life were all a bit of a joke. Nothing seemed to faze him; Archie envied him that.

'I honestly don't know,' said Archie. 'I felt the stick respond, pushed it forward and kicked on the rudder. Next thing I know I'm crash-landing in a field. I was rescued by some Tommies, given a lift to Dunkirk, put on a ship and here I am.'

'Quite an adventure, Archie,' said Pip. 'Quite an adventure.'

'I've been lucky,' said Archie.

'Well, good for you, Baby!' said Will. 'Now, what you need is a drink, young man.' He led him to the bar and ordered him a double Scotch.

'Did we get any others?' Archie asked.

'One or two,' said Will.

'He reckons he bagged a 109,' said the CO, 'but we all know what a line-shooter Will is.'

Will laughed. 'I'm not even going to begin to respond to such blatant jealousy. The skipper thinks it's his right to claim the squadron's first kill.'

'Touché,' said Dix. He turned to Archie. 'We've put in claims for six – seven if you include your 109. Ted got two as well, so it looks like you're both keeping pace.'

'Well done,' said Archie, turning to his friend.

'I can't believe you're back,' said Ted. 'I really thought you'd had it.' He looked up at the bloody bandage. 'What have you done to your head?'

'Cut it a bit – on the reflector sight, I think.'

'Down that,' said Ted, 'then let's go and find the MO.'

'MO?' said Will. 'MO? Who needs an MO when there's whisky? Come on, Archie, drink up!'

Archie glanced at Ted then knocked back the Scotch. The spirit burned his throat and he spluttered slightly as it closed his windpipe, then gasped.

'Another!' called out Will. Several of the others cheered.

'Where's Dennis?' said Archie, looking round. He hadn't noticed Dennis was not there until now.

'Dennis bought it,' said Will, his voice flat, the exuberance suddenly vanished.

'Bought it? How?' Archie felt the blood draining from his face.

Will made a plunging movement with his hand.

'Got hit by 109s,' said Ted. 'No doubt about it. I saw him hit the ground.'

'He didn't get out?'

Ted shook his head.

'Everyone else got back, though?'

'Yes. It was just you and Dennis,' said Ted.

'Now,' said Will, clearing his throat, 'what about another drink?'

'No, no more,' said Archie, putting his hand over the top of the glass. 'Sorry, Will, but I suddenly feel all done in.'

'Ah, Baby needs his sleep, does he?' Will patted Archie on the shoulder. 'All right, Archie. You get your kip.' He smiled. 'I'm glad you made it back. One down in the squadron is bad luck, but two was looking downright careless.' The others laughed, but Archie turned away.

'See you in the morning,' he muttered, and stumbled with Ted towards the door.

They found the medical officer, who grumbled a little at being called upon so late, but who none the less cleaned Archie's wound. The bandage had stuck to the congealed blood, but carefully, using warm water, Flight Lieutenant Dr Grady prised the bloodied bandage free, gave Archie four stitches and then put on a fresh bandage.

'I'm grounding you for twenty-four hours,' he said. 'You'll be fine, but if you've suffered concussion, you should stay off flying for a day.'

Archie agreed, then, with Ted, they walked in silence up to their digs, a simple square room at the Mess with two iron beds, cupboard, writing desk and chair. Archie thought he was exhausted – his body ached, his eyes stung with fatigue – and yet once he was finally in bed sleep eluded him. For a while, he just lay there, staring at the ceiling, marvelling that he was still alive, that he had somehow made it back all the way from that field in no-man's-land somewhere in France. He'd been so lucky, and yet Dennis was now no more. Dennis, who had been laughing and joking that morning, who had led Archie and Ted in their section, was now no longer a living, breathing, thinking, functioning person, but snuffed out. Dead. It was incomprehensible. And what about those Germans? Three he'd killed earlier that day.

'Archie?' whispered Ted suddenly.

'Yes?'

'Oh. So you are awake,' he said, no longer whispering. 'I thought you were, but wasn't sure.'

'I can't sleep. It's ridiculous. I can't stop thinking about Dennis. I can't believe he's gone.'

'I know.' They were silent for a moment, then Ted said, 'I know this sounds stupid, but I never really gave much thought to people actually dying. I mean, I was nervous this morning – actually, I was terrified – but I hadn't really considered that anything would happen to anyone else – that you'd get shot down. I can't believe how naïve I've been. Too busy thinking about flying to really consider what we were getting into.'

'I was much the same,' admitted Archie. 'It all feels very real now, though, doesn't it?'

'Yes – yes, it does. At least we've shot down some of theirs. Avenged Dennis.'

'Yes, but don't you feel – I don't know . . . We've killed people now, Ted.'

'But they were trying to kill us. It's war.'

'I know. I don't *feel* any different. I'm the same person, but . . . Oh, I don't know what I'm saying, really. My brain's gone to pot. I love flying, that's all I ever wanted to do – fly. Not kill people.'

'Or get killed.'

'I'd really rather not.'

Another pause, then Ted said, 'What did those Tommies who rescued you think was going on?'

'I don't know. They said it had been chaos. They blamed the French – they said it was the Frogs withdrawing either side of them that meant they then had to pull back too. The despatch rider who gave me a ride to Dunkirk reckoned we were done for.'

'Do you think he was right?'

'I don't know. It did seem pretty chaotic. Refugees everywhere, Jerry dive-bombers attacking at will. We missed a Stuka attack by a whisker. One bomb fell only a few hundred yards behind us. It was pretty hairy, I must admit.'

'Blimey.'

'There were Jerries right where I came down. I was so lucky, Ted, really I was. These Tommies pulled me out. I was out cold at the time and when I came to, there were Jerry machine guns firing at us, bullets whizzing over our heads. I thought we'd never get away. But we did. Our chaps had set fire to my Spit and the smoke gave us cover.'

'Must have been terrifying.'

'I was still a bit too dazed to feel really scared.' He sighed. 'What a day! Honestly, I can't believe I'm here.'

'So do you think France will throw in the towel?'

'I don't know. I always thought France was supposed to be pretty strong, but when you have Jerries firing at you and bombing you, it does make you think it's all going rather badly.'

'We'll be next.'

'Yes, I suppose so. And it'll be up to us to try and stop them. I think that's why I can't sleep. I'm scared, Ted. To tell the truth, I feel out of my depth. I've been lucky today, but even if I was a cat, I reckon I've used up at least three lives today.'

'Look on the bright side – at least you know how to get out of a vertical spin with your engine on the blink.'

Archie laughed. 'That's true. Every cloud has its silver lining. And actually, talking of Stukas, I must talk to the skipper tomorrow. They're not all they're cracked up to be, you know.'

'Really? They looked pretty damn ferocious to me.'

'Well, yes, maybe if you're underneath one when they're dropping bombs, but they're sitting ducks when they come out of a dive. They go so slow they're almost at a standstill. I reckon you watch them attack, then pounce. We could slaughter 'em.'

He yawned, then heard Ted follow suit. A moment later, he finally drifted off to sleep.

Archie slept in, not waking until nearly nine o'clock. There was no sign of Ted – his bed was made and only a damp, scrunched up towel showed that he had been in the room that morning. A quick shower, and then Archie dressed and went downstairs, checking his pigeonhole before heading off in search of some breakfast. There was one letter for him, from his mother, in her familiar, slanting handwriting.

He was ravenous, and, having persuaded the cooks to make him some tea and toast, he sat down to read the letter.

Dear Archie,

I hope this finds you well. All is fine here, I think. The May dawn chorus is louder than ever and the hill is full of spring flowers. How is your flying? I do hope you are being careful. Your father has joined the Local Defence Volunteers, and has brushed down his uniform from the last war and managed to dig out an old service revolver and his shotgun. He says the uniform still fits him like a glove, but Maggie and I have been teasing him and telling him it's far too tight and that he needs to lose weight. As you can imagine, he's getting very cross with us and says that in a time of war there are more things to worry about than an old service tunic being a little bit tight around the girth. God only knows what good he'll be if he and the others ever come up against a German paratrooper, because they are mostly men over fifty and, to be fair to your father, he's about the fittest. Maggie says they ought to be called the Old Age Defence Volunteers. Your poor father – he's feeling very outnumbered at the moment. He needs you back to balance things out. Do you think you might get any leave? I suppose it is unlikely at the moment, what with everything that's happening in France. We've been listening to the news and reading your father's Times, *and praying things improve over there.*

Archie smiled. *Poor Dad,* he thought. Still, he guessed his father and his friends would be enjoying strutting around in their uniforms, feeling as though they were doing something important for the war effort.

He read on.

Your sister has got it into her head to become a pilot too, and join what is called the Air Transport Auxiliary. Will you write to her, Archie, and make her see sense? I've never heard of anything more ridiculous, but she's absolutely determined to apply. She needs our approval at the moment, but she's eighteen next week and can then do as she pleases. Don't forget her birthday, will you? I know you have a lot to think about, but it would mean a great deal to her if you remembered.

Mrs McDuff and I were cleaning your room the other day and found that little toy dog you loved so much as a boy. Do you remember the tears when you lost it? My, we turned that room upside down looking for it, but there it was, wedged behind the chest of drawers, there all along!

Anyway, I've washed him and he looks much better. I've put him on top of the chest of drawers, where he sits watching over your room.

Do take care, Archie.

Your ever loving,

Mum

P.S. I saw Mr McAllister the other day. He asked after you and wants to know if that motorcycle of yours is still going strong.

Archie finished reading and put the letter into the top pocket of his tunic. Leave – fat chance! He wished he could go home – May was his favourite month. When he had last been back, before rejoining the squadron, there had still been snow on the hills and it had been cold. Spring always arrived late in Perthshire and then summer arrived with a gallop. He shook his head. A year ago, he'd been back for the Easter holiday, without a care in the world.

Wandering over to dispersal, he found the rest of the pilots. It was a warm day and some were already sitting outside on the grass in deckchairs.

'Ah, here's our wounded hero at last,' said Pip, looking up. 'How's the head, Archie?'

'Almost right as rain,' he replied. 'Where's the skipper?' Then he saw Ted standing in the doorway looking restless.

'In the hut,' said Pip. 'Doesn't look like we're needed today.'

Archie found Dix sitting in one of the battered leather armchairs, talking to Will and Calder, the Intelligence Officer.

'Just the man,' said the CO, looking up. 'You can tell Cally about your 109.'

'I'd forgotten about that,' said Archie.

'Such modesty,' said Will. 'No line-shooting from Archie.'

'So,' said Calder. 'You reckon you got an Me 109, do you?'

'I'm certain,' said Archie. 'I saw bits of it flying off and smoke poured out and then it began diving towards the ground.'

'But did you actually see it hit the ground?'

'Well, no, because by that time I was in a vertical spin myself, but –'

'Can't give it, I'm afraid,' Calder cut in.

'Hang on,' said Archie. 'What I was going to say was I heard from at least four different men of the King's Own Yorkshire Rangers that it had gone down and exploded.'

'I'm convinced,' said Dix.

'How did they know it was your one?' asked Calder.

'They all said so. They saw me shoot it down then saw me get hit myself. I was practically over Cassel at the time. I'd say ask them, but they're probably a bit busy fighting the Germans at present.'

Calder rubbed his chin thoughtfully. 'Oh, all right,' he said at length. 'You know we're supposed to have proper corroboration, not second-hand confirmation, but you've such an innocent face, Jackson, I'm willing to believe you this time.'

'Thank you,' said Archie. He turned towards Dix. 'Actually, Skip, I had something to tell you. From yesterday, that is.'

'Oh, yes?'

'Yes, it was on the trip back across the Channel. We were attacked by Stukas.'

Will raised an eyebrow. 'Anything else happen to you yesterday, Baby?'

Archie explained. 'It's just a thought,' he said when he'd finished.

'You obviously have to make sure there aren't swarms of Messerschmitts about, but, yes, it's a thought,' Dix said. 'I've already seen more than I care to of them on the newsreels. Jerry obviously thinks they're the bee's knees.'

'So it would be even more satisfying to start knocking them out of the sky,' said Will.

'Wouldn't it?' Dix smiled. 'Could you write me a little report, Archie? Then I can forward it to Fighter Command HQ. Actually, we could give it to Ted's old man as well. He's in Air Intelligence, isn't he?'

'Yes, Skip,' said Archie.

'Good,' said Dix, clapping his hands together. 'And I hear you're grounded?'

Archie nodded. 'But I'm fine. Honestly.'

'I'm sure, but we're not on ops today and it's B Flight's turn tomorrow, so I'm going to give you and Ted twenty-four hours. You've both got a couple of Jerries to your name, so I think you've probably earned it. Anyway, I'm not sure I can cope with seeing Ted hanging about here fidgeting all day long.'

'Are you sure, Skip?' said Archie.

Dix waved him away. 'Go and have some fun, and come back tomorrow lunchtime ready for action.'

Archie grinned. 'Thanks, Skip!'

An hour later, they were on their way, speeding out of Northolt on Archie's Norton, and heading east along Western Avenue towards London.

'You're to come and stay at my place,' Ted had told him, 'and then tonight we'll go out. We could see a show, or go to a club. We'll decide nearer the time. The point is, we're going to have some fun. God knows, if things are really that bad, we might as well while we've got the chance.'

'All right,' Archie had agreed. 'For twenty-four hours, let's forget about the war.'

7

INTELLIGENCE BRIEF

Saturday 25 May, around 11 a.m. Group Captain Guy Tyler sat at his desk in the main Air Ministry building in King Charles II Street reading through the minutes of the morning's Joint Intelligence Committee meeting. As Deputy Director of Air Intelligence, he had a seat on the JIC. Every morning at eight, he and other members of Air Intelligence would meet with their counterparts in the Navy and Army and the previous day's, and night's, intelligence would be gathered together and discussed. It was then written up and sent as a single intelligence summary to both the War Cabinet – the prime minister and his four senior ministers – and the Chiefs of Staff, the heads of the British Armed Services. It was on the basis of these intelligence summaries that many of their decisions were made.

Guy Tyler sighed wearily, rubbed his forehead, then sat back in his chair and turned to look out of the window. His office was on the fourth floor and, from where he sat, he could see Whitehall a short distance to his right, St James's Park away to his left, and in the distance, through the rapidly blossoming trees, Buckingham Palace and the golden Victoria Memorial. This was the heart of Britain – of her Empire – not much more than a stone's throw from where he sat, and yet he wondered now whether he was about to witness its end, whether soon there would be Nazi swastikas fluttering overhead, not Union Jacks, or royal banners.

He remembered how, after the last war, as a twenty-seven-year-old squadron leader, he had nearly left the RAF, but then had had a change of heart and remained. As Britain had faced one financial crisis after another, as the nation was crippled by national strikes, he had found little cause to regret his decision. He had a job, a regular monthly income, could provide his two children with decent educations, and make sure his wife lived a comfortable and largely secure existence. It was precisely the kind of life he'd gone through hell for in the last war. What's more, he'd been given the chance to see a bit of the world. He'd been posted to India, Iraq and then Palestine, before being posted home and given a job in Air Intelligence.

He'd been thrilled at the time. It had been the right moment to settle back in England, what with his children growing fast and his wanderlust satisfied, and the prospect of being able to help build a picture of what was going on in Germany, Italy and other European countries was both exciting and stimulating. It was vital work, after all.

But ever since the German invasion of Norway in April, Group Captain Tyler had found his job increasingly depressing. His task was to collate and co-ordinate all the latest knowledge they had on the German air force – its intentions, its strength, its dispositions, its reserves of both aircraft and aircrew – as well as their daily losses. Most of this came from the 'Y' Service, young men and women in Air Intelligence whose job it was to listen to as much intercepted radio traffic as they could. This might be a pilot talking in his aircraft, or a wireless station in Berlin, or some other signal.

Tyler knew there were also people busy trying to break enemy cipher codes, and some had indeed already been cracked, but he was conscious that code-breaking was only another strand in the intelligence network. There were also their own aircraft, taking photographs as they flew over France and the Low Countries and even Germany itself, just as he had done countless times himself in the last war. The film was then developed and carefully analysed. The results would then be sent to Air Intelligence HQ, here at the Air Ministry.

And he found they made for dismal reading. It had been bad enough in April, as the Germans had swept up through southern Norway, and the Luftwaffe had waltzed in and occupied the country's airfields. By the time the RAF had reached Norway, it was too late. Their planes were knocked out barely before they'd touched down.

At the Air Ministry, Tyler had then watched it all get horribly worse. He wasn't alone in thinking the French Army of the Air seemed incapable of doing anything much, while the Luftwaffe seemed to hold all the aces: they were the attackers and had concentrated their forces at the point of attack. As in Norway, by the time the Allies had responded, it was too late. On 10 May German forces had plunged forward through the Low Countries while the Luftwaffe had attacked the airfields. The Dutch air force had been knocked out on the ground, the French air force was spread all round the country, and the RAF could only respond belatedly to whatever reports came in.

If the air picture wasn't bad enough, the story on the ground was worse. Guy Tyler almost wished he didn't know, that he had been kept in the dark, but the JIC had met every morning for the past two weeks – meetings that had been held in an atmosphere of unrelieved gloom. Within five days, Holland had surrendered, as the Germans swept through the Netherlands and into Belgium. In the south, near Sedan, the Germans had breached the French defences. The day that Holland capitulated, the Germans punched a hole fifty miles deep and the French front had begun to collapse. As it did so, the Belgians and the British Expeditionary Force, the BEF, had been forced to pull back too.

Five days ago, the Germans had reached the French coast, south of Calais, and were turning north, squeezing the BEF and what French forces remained in the north into a narrow corridor. Soon the Belgians would surrender too – it was as certain as night following day – and then the BEF would be trapped in a giant pincer movement, with nowhere to go but back into the sea – that is, if the Germans didn't link up behind their backs first, and with the fall of Calais, that seemed more than likely.

As Tyler was aware, plans were hurriedly being put in place to evacuate the entire BEF through Dunkirk. The Royal Navy was massing ships, and RAF Fighter Command, established purely to defend Great Britain, was now being forced to send more and more aircraft over to France to provide air cover. As the evacuation began, so Fighter Command's precious fighters would be expected to protect the men and ships from the Luftwaffe. Tyler could see what would happen: far too many would be shot down or destroyed, leaving Britain's air defence horribly weakened when Germany turned on England. And what was so terrible was that it would be a wasted effort in any case.

Tyler had always thought of himself as an optimistic fellow, a glass-half-full sort of chap, but that morning, as he read through the latest intelligence summary, it looked odds on certain that within a few days the whole British field army – men, guns, vehicles, ammunition, tanks, everything – would cease to exist. And to make matters worse, his son – his precious, adored only son – was one of those now expected to help the retreating BEF. To help save Britain.

Tyler sighed again and rubbed his hands over his face. He supposed his own parents must have felt every bit as worried about him during the last war as he did about Ted now. He'd not thought much about that at the time. Flying had been such an adventure. He'd enjoyed the war on the whole. It had been exciting, a thrill to fly ever-improving biplanes, and, because he had been both a good pilot and an excellent shot, he had always flown with a degree of confidence that he knew many others did not share. The losses had been appalling – of course they had – but one got strangely used to it; one learned how to become detached. And during the winter, when those poor beggars on the ground had been swilling around in the mud, he and his fellows had been twenty miles behind in decent digs and getting fed and watered pretty well.

He knew that Ted was cut from the same cloth as himself. They even looked much the same, although Tyler's once-dark mane of hair was now rapidly greying; he guessed he would be quite white before this war was over. But he recognized in his son the same spirit of adventure and hunger for excitement. By all accounts, he was proving to be a first-class pilot, although being a very good pilot was not quite the same as being a very good *fighter* pilot. *He'll be all right,* he told himself. *He has a good eye, he's got plenty of flying hours under his belt.*

Impatience – that was the one trait Ted needed to rein in. Surviving in the air was about constantly keeping your wits about you – watching your back.

There was a knock at the door, and Squadron Leader Mulligan walked in.

'Sir?' he said. 'It's time.'

Tyler looked at his watch, nodded wearily, then, gathering his intelligence summaries, put them into a briefcase and headed for the door.

Mulligan was his right-hand man, his assistant deputy director, tall and thin, and some years younger than himself, but a good sort – reliable, discreet and, like him, a naturally positive person. It was hard, though, to keep cheerful when they knew what they knew.

They reached Headquarters RAF Fighter Command at Stanmore, on the north-west edge of London, a little under half an hour later. Bentley Priory, once an eighteenth-century country house, then a hotel and then a girls' school, had been bought by the RAF some fourteen years earlier, and when Fighter Command was formed just two years ago, it seemed an ideal place to house the new command's headquarters. Close to London, it was none the less away from the hubbub of Whitehall, close to Northolt and Uxbridge, and, from the hill near Harrow on which it was perched, it had commanding views south towards Britain's capital. It was light and airy too – Tyler had always liked it, and reckoned Air Chief Marshal Dowding had one of the best offices in the country.

They were ushered into Dowding's office straight away. Air Vice-Marshal Park, commander of 11 Group, was already there, and stood up as they entered, even though he outranked them. A tall man, with a trim moustache and twinkling, pale blue eyes, he said, 'Good to see you, Tyler – and you too, Mulligan.'

Dowding, spectacles perched on the end of his nose, remained seated behind his desk.

'Good morning, chaps,' he said brusquely, then leaned forward, resting his elbows on the desk, his hands brought together as though in prayer.

Tyler had known both men since the last war. In fact, he had strongly supported Dowding's efforts to try to get parachutes introduced. 'Boom' Trenchard, commander of the Royal Flying Corps and then of the RAF when it was formed in 1918, had vehemently opposed Dowding, and it had almost cost the latter his career. But Dowding was a dogged, determined old fellow and had risen through the ranks during the years of peace, and thank goodness too. Tyler rated both men highly – at least, thank God, they had the best two men in the most important jobs: Dowding co-ordinating and overseeing the whole show, Park commanding south-east England, the group in Fighter Command that would undoubtedly see the heaviest action should Britain come under attack from the Luftwaffe. It was certainly Park's squadrons that were the most busy at the moment.

'So, gentlemen,' said Dowding, 'what glad tidings do you bring us today?' Just the faintest flicker of a smile creased his lips.

'Nine Fighter Command aircraft lost yesterday and three damaged but repairable,' said Mulligan. 'A total of sixteen aircraft lost yesterday. So all in all, not too bad.'

Dowding drummed his fingers on the leather-topped desk.

'Hmm,' he said, 'but it's not going to stay that way, is it? We may have stopped sending more fighters over to French airfields, but we're going to have our work cut out over the next few days if this evacuation really does get underway.'

'It's going to, sir,' said Tyler. 'Operation Dynamo will start tomorrow night. The plan is to start lifting men in the early hours of Monday the twenty-seventh.'

'At least if we're operating from bases in the south-east,' said Park, 'then they won't be destroyed on the ground. As we know, most fighter losses in France have been at the airfields rather than in the sky.'

Dowding's brows knotted into a frown. 'It's just so damnably frustrating. Fighter Command's job is to defend Britain. We've built our air-defence system around operating over our own territory. We have radar, we have the Royal Observer Corps, there are General Pike's anti-aircraft gunners, we have the Defence Teleprinter Network, we have Huff-Duff, ground controllers and a centralized and standardized operating system that every Tom, Dick and Harry in Fighter Command knows and understands. And yet we can't use any of it over Dunkirk.'

'But lose the entire BEF and we won't be fighting an air battle over Britain or anywhere else, sir,' said Park.

'That's true,' muttered Dowding. 'There's panic among the politicians. There are some – whose names I won't mention – who are already muttering about suing for peace.'

'And it'll give some of our squadrons important experience against the Hun,' added Park. 'Don't forget that if we can shoot down some of theirs, they'll have fewer too. How's Beaverbrook getting on?'

'Very well. He might be a press baron, but Winston was absolutely right to put him in charge of aircraft production. He's got things moving already. He told me he'll have four hundred new fighters a month by the end of June and is increasing the output of repaired aircraft fourfold. The trouble is, can we wait until then? It might all be a little late.' He sighed, then sat up. 'Ah, well, we can only do what we can do. The rest we must place in the hands of God.' He turned to Tyler. 'So what are the latest figures for the Luftwaffe, Tyler?'

'The latest intelligence we have suggests the Messerschmitt factories are only producing two hundred or so new fighters per month,' he said. 'Production appears to be concentrated on bombers – the Ju 87 Stuka and the Ju 88 medium bomber. We've still got a very clear picture of all their units, and I'm afraid that it's rather sobering, sir. Our estimates are that they have around four thousand front-line aircraft.'

'And we have five hundred and seventy-four fighters in the Command,' interrupted Dowding.

'Yes, sir. But as the air vice-marshal says, the numbers are growing all the time.'

'So long as production does not exceed wastage.' Dowding stroked his moustache a moment, then said, 'Remind me, Tyler, on what are you basing this figure of four thousand?'

'Assuming their *Staffeln* are the same as our squadrons – that is, with around twenty aircraft and twenty-four pilots – then we have our figure. They have further units still in Germany, though.'

'Well,' said Dowding, 'let's hope you've overestimated rather than underestimated that figure.'

'Our intelligence suggests their units operate in similar ways to ours, sir, which is why we have assumed they are the same size. I don't think they would be bigger. In my estimation, four thousand is the most we would find ourselves up against.'

Dowding nodded. 'All right. Well, thank you, gentlemen. On that cheery note . . .' He let the sentence trail, then turned back to his papers. It was the signal for Tyler and Mulligan to leave. They stood up, saluted, then turned and left.

In the car on the way back, Tyler and Mulligan sat in silence, smoking, both deep in thought. Swirls of tobacco smoke clouded the rear of the Wolseley before being sucked out of the narrow slit of the open window.

'We need to understand their squadron make-up, Mully,' said Tyler at length. 'There must be a way. Some snippet of information, some reference – somewhere. There has to be.'

'Nothing has come up yet, sir.'

'Because we've been assuming they're the same as us.' He clicked his tongue against his teeth. 'But we operate with a very generous overlap, don't we? We never have more than twelve aircraft from one squadron airborne at any one time, but there are usually twice as many pilots as that and almost twice as many aircraft. What if the Luftwaffe don't allow for that? What if they have just fourteen or fifteen aircraft and men per squadron? That would change the equation considerably.'

'They'd still have an enormous advantage.'

'Yes, but not overwhelmingly so. We must find out, Mully. We really must. Confidence is half the battle. We've got to believe we've got a chance. Without that . . . well, let's face it, Mully. We're probably finished.'

8

BAG O' NAILS

A little after midnight on Sunday 26 May. In the cab on the way back to Pimlico, Archie felt a little drunk, but enough in command of his senses to know he felt absurdly happy. Happy because he'd had a night he felt sure he would remember always; happy because he was alive.

Beside him was Ted's sister, Tess. She had been with them all evening, which was why they had not gone to a show, but had instead headed to Shepherd's, a pub just off Piccadilly, where she had planned to meet another pilot friend she knew. 'Don't go to some boring silly old show,' she had said. 'Come with me to Shepherd's.'

'Oh, Tess, don't be so bossy,' Ted had retorted. 'We rather want to go to a show.'

'Which one?'

'I don't know. I thought maybe *Swinging the Gate* at the Ambassadors. Someone told me it's very funny.'

'I've seen it and it's awful. You'd hate it, darling, I promise you. Hermione Gingold being decidedly unfunny. Come to Shepherd's with me instead.'

Ted had looked at Archie. 'What do you want to do, Archie?'

'Honestly?' Archie had replied. 'I'd rather go to Shepherd's.'

The pub was already a well-known fighter pilots' haunt not far from the RAF Club, down a narrow side street that led to Shepherd's Market. Archie had been there once before and liked it, and, in truth, he had wanted to spend the evening with Tess as much as her brother, not that he would ever admit as much.

Her pilot friend had been at the pub with a group of other friends, and after a few drinks they had all gone on to the Bag o' Nails club in Kingly Street in Soho. Someone had said that Al Bowlly was playing; he was not, as it happened, but there had been a live band all the same. Someone had produced a bottle of champagne, and Ted had got chatting to a young girl he vaguely knew and had disappeared on to the dance floor. Tess's pilot friend had vanished, and that left Archie and Tess alone, sitting at their table, drinking the champagne and talking.

Tess was eighteen, a year younger than her brother. Archie had last seen her the previous autumn, after he and Ted had finished their square-bashing in Cambridge. She had left school that summer, and was very much the younger sister – always chirpy, always bright, friendly enough on the few occasions Archie had met her, but a girl still.

Something had happened over the intervening months. The rather plain dresses and loose teenage hair had gone, and in their place were silk stockings, mascara and crimson lips. She had joined the WAAF – the Women's Auxiliary Air Force – and was working at the Air Ministry like her father. 'It's become quite a family business, joining the RAF.' She laughed. 'Poor Mum feels a bit left out.' It was secretarial work, but she seemed to find it interesting enough. She had seen Archibald Sinclair, Secretary of State for Air, and Sir Cyril Newell, Chief of the

Air Staff, and even, fleetingly, the prime minister himself – enough important people to make her feel as though she were at the centre of things, even if most of her day was spent taking notes and typing.

Tess used to be pretty, but, Archie thought, she had now been transformed into someone quite beautiful: a young woman with the same raven hair as her brother, but with a sleeker, more finely sculpted face and a pair of pale blue eyes that Archie found quite bewitching.

Later, they had danced together, his hand on her waist, her fingers in his. It had been one of the most intoxicating moments of his life. Now, in the cab, he felt her hand reach for his once more, and as her warm, smooth fingers folded around his, a new spark of pleasure coursed through him.

She held up his hand, then that of her brother too. 'Thank you, boys,' she said. 'I've had a lovely evening.'

'So have I,' Archie grinned.

'Me too,' said Ted. 'I think I might be in love with Polly.'

'But you've only just met her,' said Tess. 'You've had too much beer and champagne.'

'No,' said Ted. 'I've met her before. Once. For about three minutes. She's what's-his-name's sister. Chap I was at school with. He was a bit dull, to be honest, but Polly's lovely. I think I might marry her one day.'

'You are ridiculous,' Tess laughed. 'She might be awful in daylight.'

'Polly? No, not possible.' Ted sighed happily. 'To think you almost made me go to that silly show, Archie.'

'I did no such thing. I never wanted to go.'

Ted laughed. 'You were quite right, sis. Thank you for saving us from the terrors of *Swinging the Gate*.' He sighed happily again, then suddenly sat up. 'Whatever happened to that pilot chum of yours?'

'I made a mistake,' she said. 'I thought he seemed quite nice last time I saw him, but I was wrong.'

'I thought he seemed awful. Poor little sis,' said Ted, resting his head on her shoulder. 'Snubbed by a first-class bore.'

'I don't mind. Archie looked after me.' She patted his leg. 'We had a lovely time together, didn't we?'

'Lovely,' said Archie, meaning it.

As they reached the house in Winchester Street, the cab driver nearly hit a car parked outside the house next door.

'Blast it!' he cursed.

'Blackout, eh?' said Ted.

'Oh, it's terrible,' answered the cabbie. 'Bloomin' terrible. The lights they allow us now are hardly enough to see three yards in front. A mate of mine hit a horse the other night. Just didn't see 'im till it was too late. I reckon more people will be killed in this war because of the blackout than by Jerry bombs.'

They paid him and then Ted struck a match, lighting up his face in an orange glow. The key was kept in a conch shell at the foot of the steps that led to the front door.

'Don't you worry that someone will find it and break in?' asked Archie.

'Trust me,' said Ted, 'there's far greater chance of my sister losing the key if she kept it with her than of any would-be burglar finding it.' He held it up. 'Anyway, in this blackout you'd never know. I find it hard enough finding it with just a match.'

Archie breathed in deeply. The cool night air smelled sooty, and he immediately thought of his burning Spitfire in that field near Cassel. He wondered about the men there; wondered whether they were still alive.

'Come on, Ted,' said Tess. 'I'm cold.' She gripped Archie's arm as they waited for Ted to fumble the key into the lock, and Archie felt another spark of pleasure.

The door opened and they stumbled in, closed it behind them, and only then switched on the lights.

'Mama's asleep,' said Ted.

'It is half past midnight, you know,' said Tess.

'Early!' said Ted, and Archie smirked, familiar with his friend's ability to make a rare night out last as long as possible.

They went into the drawing room, a comfortable, high-ceilinged room just off the hallway at the front of the house. There was a gramophone there on a table in the corner.

'I'll get the drinks,' said Ted. 'You put on some music, Archie.'

'Oh, yes, please!' said Tess. 'I want to dance again. Put on Al Bowlly, Archie. He might not have been at the Bag o' Nails but we can have him in the drawing room.'

Archie laughed. 'All right,' he said. There was a stash of records on a stool under the table and he soon found the record he was after. He liked Al Bowlly too. His parents had hardly ever played music at home – only what was broadcast on the radio, and that was always classical; there was no gramophone in the Jackson household. But since going to Durham and joining 629 Squadron, he had discovered the magical new world of dance music. Al Bowlly, Cole Porter, even comic songwriters like Noel Coward – they had been played continually. The squadron had had a battered old gramophone that Fitz used to bring down to dispersal; it had followed them to Drem, bequeathed to the squadron pilots by their former CO, and then to Northolt when they had moved down a week ago.

He pulled the record from its brown paper sleeve, placed it on the turntable, wound up the gramophone and then gently lowered the needle. A crackle, and then the opening bars of the piano rang out.

With Ted still fixing the drinks, Tess held out her hand to Archie.

'Dance with me,' she said.

Archie grinned, took her hand and they began gently turning around the room.

Tess sang along softly. Archie, who knew most of the words, and with his confidence buoyed, joined her. He was pleased not to have made a fool of himself by standing on her foot as they danced. Ted re-entered the room with two tumblers and a glass of wine, and then they were all singing, no longer softly, but more loudly.

Suddenly the door opened and standing there was Group Captain Tyler.

'What a racket you're all making,' he said.

'Pops!' said Ted, hurrying over to him. 'We didn't hear you come in.'

'No, well, unlike you lot, I've learned to come in quietly and not disturb your poor mother.' He kissed his daughter, then turned to Archie. 'Hello, Archie. How nice to see you.'

'And you, sir,' said Archie.

'Poor Pops,' said Tess. 'Always home so late.'

'Let me get you a drink, Pops,' said Ted.

Their father looked at his watch. 'It's awfully late . . . well, go on, then. Just a quick one. I need to see my son and his friend when I get the chance.' He took off his cap, smoothed his hair and sat down in one of the wing-backed armchairs. 'Ah, that's better.'

'You're working such long hours, Pops,' said Tess, sympathy etched on her face.

'There's a lot to do.' He smiled weakly and rubbed his eyes, then turned to Archie. 'So how have you been getting on? What happened to your head?'

Ted came back in with his father's Scotch at this moment. 'He pranged his Spit over in France. Not before he'd shot down a 110 and a 109, though.'

The group captain nodded. 'Well, that's good.'

'And I got a couple too, Pops,' added Ted, grinning.

'Don't get overconfident,' said his father. 'Overconfidence is deadly. But well done. Well done, the pair of you.'

Archie looked down at his glass and felt a flush of pride.

'What happened, Archie? When you were hit? Take your eye off the ball?'

'No, sir – well, I was bounced rather. Suddenly I had three 109s swarming all over me, but I managed to get one and then got a cannon shell in the radiator, I think. At any rate, there was white smoke, the oil temperature went mad and the force of the shell knocked me into a vertical spin.'

Tyler winced. 'Nasty. But did you spot the 109s diving down on you?'

'Not until too late.'

'I'm sure you've been told this a hundred times, but you've got to keep looking round all the time. I know it's hard to see right behind you, but keep scanning the skies. Even those with the very best vision can't see a fighter more than a couple of miles away. With the kind of speeds you're all flying at these days, that means you've got around five to ten seconds, depending on which direction they're coming from, in which to see them.'

'So look around every three seconds or so,' said Archie.

'Absolutely. And if you're outnumbered, don't try to take them. Get the hell out of there. Turn into them or dive away and hit the deck. Better to live to fight another day. You'll always have other chances. In the last show, it was all about manoeuvrability, and of course the speeds involved were a lot less. That's all changed, as Dowding has realized. Now it's about speed of climb, speed of dive and packing a short, sharp punch when you have the chance. Nine times out of ten, you'll be hit because of a mistake you've made, not because of the other chap's flying brilliance. Cut out those mistakes, and you'll have a much better chance of staying in one piece.'

'The trouble is,' said Ted, 'we've been taught how to fly but not really how to fly in combat. Archie and I both had Mick Channon as our instructor at FTS, and he used to pass on a few words of wisdom, but since we've been back with 629, we've mainly practised formation flying and the six standard attacks. Having been in our first scrap, I'm not sure how effective they are, to be honest.'

Tyler smiled. 'You're both good pilots. You know how to handle your kites. I'm going to give you three rules. One: keep watching all the time – every few seconds. Two: don't fly straight and level in the combat zone for more than two seconds. And three: get as close as you possibly can to the target before opening fire. This is really important. If you open fire too soon, you won't hit him and at the same time he'll know you're behind him. What's more, you'll be tempted to keep firing. You'll think, a couple more seconds, I know I can get him, and then bang! Some blighter's come up behind you and hit you instead. Trust me on this: to get the best from your guns, you need to be within one hundred and fifty yards.'

'But ours are harmonized at four hundred yards, Pops,' said Ted.

'Well, that's one point on which I disagree with Dowding. Change them.'

Archie and Ted nodded.

'Thank you, sir,' said Archie. 'We will, won't we, Ted?'

'Most certainly.'

'Gosh,' said Tess, a pained expression on her face. 'This makes it all seem so horribly real. I can't bear the thought of you boys being up there and being shot at.'

Her father smiled. 'They'll be all right. I've every faith in them. It's not so dangerous when you know what you're doing, you know.'

Tess sat there a moment, looking at them, then said, 'I suddenly feel rather tired. I'm going to bed.'

'Call in on me in the morning, sis,' said Ted. 'Before you go.'

She nodded, then kissed them all in turn. 'Come and see me again when you can, Archie. I've had a lovely evening.'

Archie felt his cheeks redden and hoped that Ted and his father had not noticed.

'I should be getting some sleep too,' said Tyler. 'We all should.'

'Before you go, Pops,' said Ted. 'Archie – tell him about the Stukas.'

His father turned to Archie, an eyebrow raised inquisitively. 'Oh, yes?'

Archie told him what he'd noticed on the trip back across the Channel.

'Interesting,' said Tyler. 'Very interesting. Yes, thank you for sharing that, Archie.' He got to his feet. 'And now, if you'll excuse me. Goodnight, both of you.' He embraced his son. 'Look after yourselves. And remember what I told you. It's important. Vitally important.'

9

RETURN TO DUNKIRK

Thursday 30 May, around noon. They had been woken at dawn, Archie opening his eyes to the distant sound of the Spitfires being run up; it was important to have the engines warm before a flight. Half an hour later, they had been on their way, this time to Manston, on the tip of the Kent coast. Another long morning of inactivity had followed, although they'd seen a number of Hurricanes and Spitfires flying back and forth across the Channel.

Then, eventually, the squadron had been ordered into the sky. Two flights of six, Dix leading A Flight and the squadron. Archie had been put into Yellow Section, with Will Merton-Moore leading and Ted on his port side. As they climbed, Archie glanced across at Ted, then behind him and watched the arrow-head shape of the east Kent coast disappear behind him. He looked back at Will up ahead, leading the vic. A check on his dials: oil temperature OK, manifold pressure OK. Fuel fine. The needle on the altimeter continued to climb. Down below, he saw the wake of several ships returning to England – ships that he knew were now crammed full of troops.

The evacuation had begun, just as everyone had told him during his own return five days earlier. God only knew how many would be taken off, but by all accounts there was no let-up in the number of ships toing and froing back and forth across the Channel.

Up ahead, he could already see the oil cloud over Dunkirk, like a black hole that seemed to be drawing them into a different world of war and mayhem. They levelled off at eighteen thousand feet and Dix now turned them northwards, leading them well to the west of the continental coast, so that they could turn and fly back down along the coast with the sun behind them. It was hard to see much now. Thick cloud covered most of the French and Belgian coastline, while the dark clouds of burning oil masked Dunkirk itself entirely.

Lightly, ever so lightly, and without really thinking about it, Archie eased the stick to his left as they turned in a wide arc. It was amazing, he thought to himself, how they could be flying at around three hundred miles per hour, and yet, at eighteen thousand feet and all flying together, there was little to suggest such colossal speeds. The engine too, which made such a deafening roar on the ground, had turned into a muffled monotone, still loud in his ears even with his flying helmet on, but muted somehow, as though he were flying silently.

This was the squadron's third combat patrol – they had carried out a second, uneventful one two days before – but it was Archie and Ted's second. Both had now harmonized their eight Browning .303 machine guns so that their combined fire met in a cone of bullets at just one hundred and fifty yards, as Ted's father had suggested. Dix, to their surprise, had been against this. The order to have them harmonized at four hundred yards had been given by the commander-in-chief of Fighter Command for a reason, he said. 'No offence to your father, Ted,' he had said, 'but Stuffy Dowding is a little higher up the pecking order.' They could do as they pleased, he told them, but he was keeping his at the prescribed distance. The rest of the squadron had taken the CO's lead.

There had also been time to practise. The squadron had been sent up in sections to simulate dogfights. The six prescribed attack methods, which mostly involved spotting a target and then following the leader in a dive or beam attack one after the other, had always broken up within moments, but both Archie and Ted had acquitted themselves well enough. No one else in the squadron had managed to get on Archie's tail, at any rate.

'Don't get overconfident,' Group Captain Tyler had told them, and yet that late-night conversation with Ted's father *had* given Archie confidence. Before they'd taken off, he'd had that familiar nausea in his stomach and he'd felt tense and on edge, but, once he was airborne, his fear had largely left him, replaced by a strange sense of exhilaration – he was almost willing them to be drawn into action. And, of course, he now knew what to expect. Fear, he had once read, was of the unknown; at least he had tasted action, had experienced shooting down and being shot down. He was surprised, as they flew north-east, parallel to the coast, what a difference that made.

They now turned, heading south-west. A slight gap in the cloud and there was the Belgian coastline – the dark of the sea, a strip of pale sand, and Flanders beyond – and then it was gone again.

A crackle over the headphones, and Archie heard Dix's voice.

'This is Red One. Keep a good watch out, everyone. I know there's plenty of cloud, but there's sure to be Jerries about. Over.'

Archie looked around him. Nothing. The cloud rose to around fourteen or fifteen thousand feet, he guessed. He glanced around again. Still nothing. Up ahead, the oil cloud darkened the sky. *So we're getting close to Dunkirk,* he thought. They droned on. Archie glanced round again, and there was a flash of something, away to his left. He looked again. *Yes, there it was*: a flash of sunlight sparkling on something. *Aircraft*. Had to be.

'Bandits, one o'clock,' said someone. Tony Simmonds in Red Section up ahead.

'And bandits at nine o'clock,' said Archie.

'I see them,' said Ted.

'One at a time, you lot!' snapped Dix. 'Remember your damned radio discipline! Yellow Two, I can't see any bandits at nine o'clock.'

Archie looked again, and this time saw several indistinct dots. 'Red One, this is Yellow Two, they're two miles plus. Six bandits, maybe more.' He now looked ahead and below and saw a formation of bombers – Ju 88s or Dorniers, he wasn't quite sure. They were close to the top of the cloud, wisping in and out of view.

'This is Red One. We're going for the bombers, but keep a close eye on those bandits away to port. Number One Attack – go!'

They dived down in line astern, peeling off one after the other, the bombers getting ever closer. *Junkers 88s,* Archie decided, as his Spitfire screamed in its dive, but then the bombers disappeared into the cloud. He glanced back up and now saw half a dozen Me 109s hurtling towards them, perhaps only half a mile away.

A moment later, they were all in cloud, scything through a mass of grey and white moisture. Archie could still see Will clearly enough but ahead, Red Three, Tony Simmonds, was nothing more than a faint outline, like a spectre.

Archie's heart began to hammer in his chest. He did not like this; he couldn't see much and the altimeter was wheeling backwards: thirteen thousand, twelve thousand, eleven, then ten, nine, eight. Eight thousand feet and nearly four hundred miles per hour on the clock. His airframe was shaking, the engine screaming. *Get me out of this cloud,* he thought. Seven thousand, six thousand.

Over the R/T, Dix was cursing, then someone else was shouting, 'I see one!'

'Watch out to port, bandits!' yelled someone else. Static screamed in Archie's ear. Flashes of light were pulsing through the cloud. *What's going on? What's going on?* He still had Will up ahead, and Ted behind him, but where were the others? Suddenly tracer was fizzing towards him, hurtling over his wing.

'Watch it, Archie!' yelled Ted.

'Jesus!' blurted Archie, pushing the stick even further forward and feeling the Spitfire dive down further, and a split second later a Messerschmitt flashed over straight above his head, making him duck involuntarily, and then was gone, disappearing into the cloud. Archie ripped off his oxygen mask and gasped. *Christ!* he thought, *Christ!* There were more voices in his ear, and Dix cursing, effing and blinding like Archie had never heard him speak before, and then the voices and static cleared and suddenly all three of them were out of the clouds. They were clear, he and Will, and, behind him, Ted, roaring over the beaches of Dunkirk. Archie gasped. Sunken ships lay half submerged off the shore. Swarms of men, nothing more than pinpricks, darkened the beaches. He could see lines of men snaking out towards several ships moored offshore. They went on and on, mile after mile. 'My God,' he muttered out loud, then realized he had stopped concentrating. Where was everyone? Where were those bombers? Ahead, the cloud base was lowering again. 'This is no good,' he mumbled to himself, but then Will's voice filled his ears.

'This is Yellow One, I'm just above you, Archie.'

Archie looked up. There, a hundred feet above and a little ahead, was the pale underside of Will's Spitfire, the wings streaked with oil.

'I see you, Will.' Radio discipline gone.

Ted now dived down alongside him, and waved. Archie waved back, then glanced around. *Keep looking,* he told himself. His heart was still hammering in his chest and he was breathing heavily. *Calm down, calm down.*

Another crackle in his ears. *Will.* 'Bandits up ahead at eleven o'clock.'

Archie spotted them immediately. In the distance, but rapidly getting closer, was the rising cloud of oily smoke over the port. *That's where they're headed*, he thought to himself. That was good – it would give them a chance to catch them.

'Roger,' said Archie, 'I see them.' He applied boost and felt the Spitfire surge forward. The bombers were now at just three thousand feet and dropped their bombs over the port. Two explosions, one after the other, both thankfully wide, but sending towers of water into the air. 'Come on, come on!' mumbled Archie. How far were they now? Half a mile perhaps, but already the bombers were turning to port and climbing away from them.

Archie leaned forward, willing his Spitfire to catch them. The gap was closing. Seven hundred yards. Archie could see them clearly now – the distinct shape of the Junkers 88, just as it was in his recognition booklet. Six hundred yards, but now wisps of cloud were curling over the bombers. Will now opened up – *too far* – his tracer arcing well short of the target.

'Come on, come on,' Archie muttered again. He could still see them – but only just. How far now? Three hundred yards. Will was still firing, pumping bullets towards them, but then stopped. *Guns jammed?* Two hundred yards, the rear bomber nothing more than a faint outline. Archie flicked the gun button to fire. 'Damn it!' he cursed, then pressed down on the firing tit. His Spitfire shook with the recoil, tracer disappeared into the cloud, and then the bomber was gone. 'Damn!' he said out loud. Where were they?

'Ted, Archie –' *Will* – 'my guns have jammed and I can't see a thing. Am heading for home.'

'All right, Will,' said Ted, 'but I'm going after that Junkers.'

'Me too,' said Archie. 'We've got to be almost touching them by now.'

And suddenly there was one of them – huge and looming, just above them, just twenty yards ahead, the dark crosses on the underside of its wings standing out through the cloud.

Archie throttled back, then pulled back gently on the stick, glanced around and opened fire. At almost the same moment, Ted began firing too. Just a couple of seconds and then they were in danger of colliding. Archie saw bits of aircraft falling off, a burst of flame, and then he had to yank hard on the stick to avoid crashing into the stricken bomber. His stomach rolled, he felt himself flung back into the seat, and then as he levelled out he realized he was quite alone. There was nothing. Just cloud and the monotonous drone of his Merlin.

Twenty minutes later, Archie was approaching Manston, Kent and southern England spread before him. There was cloud overhead, but nothing like the blanket there had been over France and Belgium; nothing like that black cloud of smoke billowing over the evacuation beaches. Ahead, shafts of sunlight poured down through gaps in the cloud, and Archie wondered whether his country was somehow blessed. It all looked so calm, so peaceful. Beneath him, a ship was pulling into Ramsgate; even that looked quite serene, belying the trauma those men had faced just twenty-odd miles across the sea.

And over England, there were ground controllers too, men sitting in station control rooms, talking in precise, clear, calm voices. Reassuring voices.

'Hello, Tartan, this is Nimbus Yellow Two,' said Archie. 'Permission to land, over.'

A hiss in his ear, and then, 'Roger, Nimbus Yellow Two, this is Tartan. Spitfire just ahead of you. Clear to land in North Field, over.'

Archie looked around, saw Ramsgate disappear beneath him and up ahead, on the open high ground west of the town, the village of Manston, and beyond that the airfield, with its cluster of buildings, barracks blocks and hangars. Opening the radiator wide, he throttled back, changed his two-speed prop to fine pitch, pulled back the hood and began his approach, the cool air buffeting his cheeks.

Directly in front of him, the engine cowling blotted out much of his view ahead, while the huge elliptical wings masked the ground either side. It could make landing difficult, especially at unfamiliar airfields, but the trick, Archie had discovered, was to keep the nose down for as long as possible and to look ahead either side of the cowling. He lowered the undercarriage and flaps, and felt the wheels click into place. Watching the air-speed indicator, he saw the needle falling. A slight wobble in the air, the ground rushing towards him – back on the stick a bit – nose up, throttle back some more, then a gentle bump and he was down on all three wheels and rolling along the grass field. A touch of left brake and the Spitfire swung round and rolled on towards dispersal and eventually came to a halt.

Switching off the engines, the rattling and shaking stopped and suddenly the great beast was still and silent, save for the furious ticking of the engine as it cooled.

Archie sat there for a moment, pulling off his helmet. His hair was damp with sweat, his legs stiff from being in the same position for ninety minutes. *So,* he thought, *I've made it again. Two combat sorties completed.*

'Are you all right, sir?'

Archie looked down to see two ground crew beside him.

'Yes – thanks,' said Archie, and heaved himself up out of the bucket seat, clicked open the half-door and clambered shakily down on to the wing.

'Fired your guns, then, sir?' said one of men. 'Get anything?'

'Yes, actually. A huge great Ju 88 at almost point-blank range. We were in cloud at the time. I say, is the CO back?'

'No, sir, haven't seen him.'

Archie slid off the wing. 'I'd better get to dispersal.'

'Well done, sir, for your Jerry.'

'Oh,' he said, 'thank you.' His legs felt weak, his eyes

suddenly stung with fatigue. He stumbled across the grass, overwhelmed with gratitude that he had made it back once more. The confidence he had felt earlier as they'd flown over the Channel had gone entirely.

Most of the squadron had already landed – a row of Spitfires, most with the canvas patches that protected the guns shredded, and smoke and oil stains streaking the pale blue undersides of the wings. Archie watched another Spitfire landing and realized it was Ted. He'd not seen him on the short flight back across the sea. He counted the aircraft. *Eleven*. Just one missing.

'Is the CO not back?' he said as he neared the dispersal hut. The men were standing around, smoking, rubbing their eyes, running their hands through their hair.

'Didn't you hear him?' said Pip. 'Swearing his head off. I thought most of France would have heard.'

'Where is he?'

'He got clobbered by that beam attack. It was damned bad luck – they were firing blind into that cloud.'

'They nearly got me,' said Archie. 'I swear that tracer was a whisker from my head. But will he be all right?'

'Pip thinks so, don't you, Pip?' said Mike Drummond.

'I followed him down – well, I thought I really ought to, since I was supposed to be his wingman. Put it this way, he waved at me as I circled around him and I'm pretty sure he fell inside the perimeter. He'll be a bit like you, Archie, and suddenly reappear in the Mess later.'

'I hope so.'

'And what about you, Baby? Did you and Ted get them?' said Will, drawing deeply on his cigarette.

'We got one. Suddenly came upon it,' Archie said, waving his hands to illustrate the point. 'It was literally right there in front of us, bursting out of the cloud, so Ted and I both let rip. Can't have been more than thirty yards.'

'Jesus, that was close!' said Pip.

'Dangerously so,' added Will.

'Well, quite,' said Archie. 'Saw bits falling off, then a burst of flame, and then I rolled hard and pulled out of the way.'

Will was shaking his head. 'Oh, dear. That's a "possible", then. You know Cally won't like it.'

Pip and Mike laughed. 'Your face,' said Pip. 'Excitement dashed.'

'I hadn't thought of that.'

'And Ted was firing too, you say?' added Will. 'You know what that means, don't you?'

Archie smiled ruefully. 'Half a possible. Oh, well. I know we nobbled him all right.'

Ted now joined them. 'Christ, did you see that Junkers, Archie?' He turned to the others, his eyes wide. 'You should have seen it! There we were, right on it! I mean, we couldn't miss, could we, Arch? Point-blank range! Rat-a-tat-tat, and thank you very much! Had to duck to avoid bits of it, I can tell you. We were so close I could almost touch it. Beast of a thing it was, wasn't it, Archie? You know, I could see that swastika on the tail just like that! There it was, right in front of me! We clobbered that one good and proper!' He whistled. 'Boy, that was quite something, I can tell you.'

He stopped, there was a moment's silence, and then everyone started sniggering.

'What?' he said. 'What's so funny? What?'

The sniggers had become guffaws, which then became uncontrollable laughter.

'Your half a possible,' said Will, barely able to get the words out.

Ted looked aghast, which made everyone laugh even more, and then his face broke into a grin, and he was laughing too. All of them were. Archie felt the tears running down his cheeks. The terror he had felt in the skies over Dunkirk, the exhaustion – both had gone in this sudden release of tension. It shouldn't have been so funny, but somehow it was. Somehow it was the funniest thing in the world.

10

MELEE

But Henry Dix did not come back that night. The squadron had flown back to Northolt that evening, only to be told that they would be flying over Dunkirk again the following day. That meant being up at four in the morning, to be on standby at Manston at six. Temporary command of the squadron was given to Will Merton-Moore.

Jenkins, their batman, had shaken Archie and Ted awake at dawn, the sound of their Merlins being run up greeting their first conscious moments. Uniforms on, flying boots and Irvin – it was cold at that time of day – a quick drink of hot, sweet tea brought by Jenkins, and then down to dispersal. The spontaneous hilarity of the previous evening had long gone as the realization hit them that Dix was now officially missing. No one said much. Will gave them their instructions – they were to fly down in flights and sections – his usual air of laconic amusement gone.

Dawn was breaking as they took off, a thin strip of pale pink and yellow light ahead of them to the east, but plenty of cloud too, which became thicker as time wore on. At Manston there was another long wait – all morning, as it turned out. Archie dozed, but in between felt bored rigid. At Northolt they had their things: writing paper, pens, paperbacks and magazines. At Manston Archie had nothing; the cockpit of the Spitfire was so small there was hardly space for much and the last thing one wanted was something falling out of a pocket during a manoeuvre and getting in the way. Mike Drummond, Pip and their American volunteer, Hank McNair, had a pack of cards between them, but Archie had never been much good at card games.

Not until 11.20 were they ordered into the air. It was still cloudy, visibility was poor and they were expected to form up with 213 Squadron and fly over together, twenty-four aircraft in all. But 213 Squadron were Hurricanes, operating from Biggin Hill, a short distance away to the south of London, and they struggled to find each other, despite help from their respective ground controllers. When they eventually joined forces, forty minutes had passed and much of their precious fuel had already been used up. Over Dunkirk, the cloud was even worse than the day before. They patrolled up and down for an hour but saw nothing. By the time they were ordered home, they were all very low on fuel and south-east England was shrouded in misty, low cloud.

Flying in Red Section with Will leading and Ted at Red Two, Archie stuck to them like glue. Mike Drummond, leading Yellow Section, also ensured they stayed close behind – Archie saw them nestling behind and to his starboard all the way back.

Will led them down through the cloud. Once again, Archie felt that strange sense of claustrophobia and weightlessness. It was disorientating; he had never enjoyed night flying either, and as he continually glanced at his dials, he hoped they were telling him the truth. According to his altimeter, they were now at only a thousand feet and still in cloud. His whole body had begun to tense. *Don't let me go into the sea, please don't let me go into the sea.* He kept glancing at his fuel gauge – the needle seemed to be flickering towards empty before his very eyes. And then it was on empty.

'Please,' he said out loud, 'please get me back. Come on, come on, come on!'

A voice in his headset. 'This is Yellow One, are we nearly there, Red One? I'm running on fumes.'

'Yellow One, this is Red One, I hope so.'

Another anxious minute, but still the Spitfires flew on. Archie listened to the thrum of his Merlin – it was not missing a beat. *But any moment now . . .* he thought. *Please, God.*

And then suddenly they were through the cloud, and only fractionally off course. There, away to their left, was the north Kent coast and the sprawl of Ramsgate and, beyond the town, Manston.

Archie breathed out heavily.

'Hello, Mongoose, this is Nimbus Leader,' he heard Will say, 'permission to land. We're all very low on fuel.'

'Hello, Nimbus Leader, this is Mongoose, permission granted.'

They circled around the airfield, and one after the other, swooped in to land. 'Thank God,' said Archie out loud as he felt the Spitfire jolt as the wheels hit the grass.

Archie watched Yellow Flight come in, but it was a couple more minutes before the first Spitfires of B Flight appeared, and then only Pip Winters and Hank McNair.

Archie clambered out and made for dispersal as the fuel bowser hurried around the perimeter, hastily refuelling their machines.

Will was standing in front of the hut, hands on his hips, staring at the sky. Then he exploded, kicking the ground. 'Where the hell are they?' He turned to Mike. 'Weren't you watching B Flight? They were supposed to stick close behind Yellow Section.'

'Don't blame me, Will,' said Mike. 'We managed to stick to you. We were following your lead.'

Pip was now walking back towards them. 'I lost them in the descent,' he called out. 'They just disappeared. Terry was behind Hank, and then Green Section.'

Will cursed under his breath and rubbed his forehead.

'They'll turn up,' said Pip.

'They'd better,' muttered Will. 'If they've ditched into the sea, I'll murder them. I'll damn well murder 'em.'

A phone call came through half an hour later. Green Section were at Eastchurch, a little further along the north Kent coast. Ian Reeves and Colin Bishop were fine, but Gordon Bowyer had damaged his undercarriage in landing. Ian and Colin were going to refuel and come back to Manston. But there was neither sight nor sound of Terry Greaves. He had just vanished.

In four combat sorties, the squadron had now lost four men, including their CO.

Soon afterwards, the sky began to clear, and within an hour the thick blanket of cloud that had shrouded them had almost gone entirely. Just a few banks of cumulus remained. The sun shone down between the clouds, summer miraculously returned. At three they were warned that they would soon be airborne again. Green Section rejoined them, all their Spitfires had been refuelled, and, at a quarter to four, they were told to take off once again and patrol Dunkirk. Apparently, the cloud bank had now shifted from there too.

Archie clambered up into his Spitfire, a sense of dread weighing on him. He could not understand how he'd felt so eager and so confident the day before. That cloud attack yesterday – it had unsettled him, and then flying back earlier encased in cloud, not knowing whether they would make it back or hit the sea or worse, had done nothing to ease his fears. His hands were shaking as he fumbled with the clip of the Sutton harness and plugged in his oxygen and radio leads. A signal to the fitter and rigger, and then he started up the Spitfire. There was the slow chug of the prop, then suddenly the engine caught, flame and smoke briefly belched from the exhaust stubs and the airframe was shaking and rattling and jolting him in his seat. A quick glance at the dials – oil pressure OK, manifold OK, fuel OK. Signal again to the ground crew to remove the chocks, and ease open the throttle. *No turning back now,* thought Archie, *and the next time I'm back down again* – well, he hoped for the best.

At least this time there was no forming up with another squadron. There were only nine of them, three sections of three, Will leading once more. They headed north-east across the Channel, climbing to seventeen thousand feet, the world shrinking the higher they flew, so that the narrow stretch between Britain and France looked more like a wide river than an expanse of sea. France and the Low Countries stretched away, bathed in pockets of afternoon sunlight where the sun shone down through the clouds, a pattern of greens and browns and yellows, before being lost to the thick blanket of cloud that was edging away to the north-east, but which seemed to cover almost the rest of the world. And then there was Dunkirk, that cloud of thick black smoke still rolling upwards, a beacon some ten thousand feet high.

Well north of Dunkirk, and still out over the Channel, they swung to the east in a wide arc, and then south-west, following the line of the coast. As they turned, the sun streaked across them, glinting over their canopies as it swivelled behind. Get the sun behind you – that was what gave an attacker the best chance of surprise. And surprise gave the attacker the best chance of shooting an enemy down.

Soon after, as they approached the evacuation beaches, they saw a flight of Dorniers, slowing heading towards the port from the south-east, at around three thousand feet below them. *Where were the fighters?* Archie craned his head, swivelling from side to side, blinking as he glanced too close to the sun, but he could not see any sign of them. Were the bombers unescorted? Perhaps. *Keep looking out for those fighters,* he told himself.

'OK, let's go,' said Will over the R/T, ignoring standard radio procedure.

Gunning the throttle, Archie followed Will as they dived towards the Dorniers, his Spitfire roaring with the strain. The aircraft loomed towards them in no time. Archie felt his ears rage with the sudden change of pressure, while his whole body was pressed into the bucket seat. His helmet slipped, so he quickly nudged it back off his forehead, flicked the gun button to fire and then strained his head, forcing himself to look around once more.

And where moments before there had been no enemy fighters, now, suddenly, there were – a dozen of them diving down from up-sun.

'109s, eight o'clock!' he shouted. *Damn it, damn it!* They must have been circling above them, watching them, hiding in the sun, just as they had been trying to do.

'All right,' Will answered, 'I see them. We get the bombers then turn into towards them.' Will pressed ahead, towards the Dorniers who had still apparently not seen them. Archie swivelled his head again. The 109s were gaining on them. *God,* he thought, *this will be close.* His heart hammered, sweat ran down his face, and he could hear his breathing in the confined rubber of his oxygen mask. He picked out a Dornier – one on the starboard edge of the formation, but once again, from too far away, Will opened fire.

Immediately, the formation of German bombers split up, planes peeling off, desperately trying to take evasive action. The rear gunners began pumping machine-gun fire towards them, but the gunner was firing high. Archie pressed on, watched the Dornier fill his reflector sight, then saw it drift out again as it banked to port. He followed, and then, at a hundred and fifty yards and with the Dornier directly in front of him, he opened fire. Bits of metal flew off and the starboard engine began to smoke, but then he glanced around, saw a 109 bearing down upon him, and a split second later orange tracer was zipping over his head and starboard wing. No time to press home the attack. Ahead of him, Will had turned in towards the attacking fire and so Archie followed him. To his relief, he saw the enemy tracer hurtle past wide. Where were the Dorniers? Disappearing out of range fast. 'Damn it, damn it!' he cursed.

And now there were more 109s among them. He followed Will as he tried to out-turn a 109 and felt his vision blur as negative-G drained the blood from his brain. Tracer continued to fizz past him and then suddenly Will rolled over and began turning in the opposite direction. Archie followed, but then saw Will fly straight into the line of fire of his second pursuer.

'No!' shouted Archie. He opened fire himself, saw the 109 peel away, but in his ears he heard Will shout, 'I'm hit, I'm hit!'

A quick look around – more tracer – a 109 attacking another Spitfire – *Hank? Pip?* – and then he saw smoke billowing from Will's Spitfire. Archie followed, fired off another burst as a 109 homed into view to try to finish off the stricken aircraft, saw his tracer hit the fuselage and the Messerschmitt bank away.

'Get out of there, Will!' Ted's voice – where was Ted? – as Archie felt a row of bullets clatter behind him. Frantically turning his head, he saw a 109 hurtle over him, the mottled grey-green paintwork and squadron markings vividly clear. He knew he needed to protect Will but there seemed to be 109s everywhere. More tracer fizzed overhead, then the aircraft jolted as bullets tore into his fuselage.

'Christ!' he said out loud, and automatically turned once more into the line of fire. Two more 109s were heading straight for him, the sun high above them, making Archie squint. Tracer curled towards him and he flung his Spitfire one way then the other, radio static and chatter – English and German – crackling in his ears, the horizon sliding back and forth. He flipped the plane over then a 109 suddenly slid across directly in front of him, so close he could see the pilot ducking, looking back at him. The wash jolted Archie's aircraft with sudden turbulence.

Where did that come from? His stomach lurched as he dived after it, then saw below and ahead of him another Messerschmitt – or was it the same one? – slowly climbing back towards the fray. A moment later, Archie was right on top of it, thumb pressed down on the gun button and pumping machine-gun bullets from his eight Brownings in a three-second burst. He saw his tracer coning, smacking into the 109, raking along the top of the fuselage, then the cowling, and then he saw the prop splinter and disintegrate. The Messerschmitt seemed to wobble a moment, then, as Archie thundered past, it flipped over and began spinning downwards, smoke trailing behind it.

Archie watched it plummet, spinning like a twirling leaf in autumn, then looked up to see another 109 hurtling towards him. The closing speed was nearly seven hundred miles an hour – a split second – and Archie broke left as the 109 did the same, the two aircraft avoiding a head-on collision by a whisker. Archie gasped, and quickly looked around. *Where on earth was everyone?* Where was Dunkirk? He was out to sea somewhere and felt completely disorientated. He craned his head, looking frantically around him, but the 109 that had missed him by inches was now heading back inland, a mile away already. Below him – well below – he saw a Spitfire turning for home, but otherwise the sky was quite empty.

He banked, circling in a wide arc, and eventually spotted the smoke cloud above Dunkirk some way to the north. How long had he been in that swirling melee? A few minutes? Nothing more. And what about Will? *Where is Will?*

He looked around once more, saw the skies were still clear, then opened the throttle and headed for home. Time to check his gauges: oil pressure still OK, fuel low, but there was enough. Manifold pressure OK too. He'd been hit in the fuselage, he was sure, so checked the rudder, yawing the Spitfire from side to side, then pushed the stick from side to side. All in working order. *Good.*

He sped on, then saw a Spitfire below him. Was it the one he had seen a little earlier? Smoke was trailing in thin puffs, so he dived down, circled around it and drew up just behind him off his port wing. BM-W were the squadron markings on the fuselage. *Ted.*

'Please let him be all right,' he said out loud, then inched forward until his Spitfire was level, and waved. To his relief, Ted waved back, and then he heard his voice.

'I got hit in the engine,' he said, 'and now it's making strange noises and losing power.'

'Don't worry, I'm with you,' said Archie. 'How's your oil pressure?'

'Rising but not critical yet.'

Archie looked ahead. There was the tip of Kent. Ten miles perhaps?

'It's not far. From this distance we can probably glide.' He looked at his altimeter. *Six and a half thousand feet.*

'I don't want to. I want to try to stay at this height.'

Archie glanced around again, then saw the engine belch another gust of thick smoke. He heard Ted cough and saw him pull back his canopy.

'Temperature's rising now,' said Ted.

'Keep going, just keep her going.'

The coast was getting closer, inching towards them. Archie could see the cliffs now and then there was Ramsgate – two boats approaching, their wakes bright across the dark sea.

'I'm losing speed, Archie,' said Ted.

'Nearly there, nearly there.' Archie pulled back on the throttle, watched the air-speed indicator approach two hundred miles per hour. Much slower, and his Spit would stall. He opened the throttle and climbed, banking in a lazy circle over Ted's stricken plane. The coast was now no more than a couple of miles away, and Manston was only three miles beyond that. So near!

He flew back alongside his friend. 'You're home and dry now,' he said.

A moment later, there was another belch of smoke and Ted cursed. 'You spoke too soon! She's gone! She's damn well gone and cut out on me! Damn it, damn it!'

'No, Ted, you'll be fine. Listen to me: you'll be fine. You're still in the air, aren't you? You can glide her in. Just glide – it's a few miles, that's all.'

He wove back and forth. His friend was losing height now, but the Spitfire was still in the air.

'Christ, if I get out of this,' said Ted, 'I never want to have to do it again.'

'Nearly there – I can see Manston. You're nearly there, Ted. You've nearly made it.'

They passed over Ramsgate at just one thousand five hundred feet. Archie prayed it was enough.

'You're doing well, Ted,' he said, as he wove over him again, and then he heard Ted say, 'Mongoose, this is Nimbus Red Two. My engine is cut, permission to land.'

A pause, a crackle of static, then Archie heard, 'Roger, Nimbus Red Two, this is Mongoose. Permission to land. Suggest keep undercarriage up.'

'Christ,' said Ted. 'All right, Mongoose. Roger, over.'

Archie flew alongside him again and now pulled back his own canopy and waved once more.

'I've never done this before,' said Ted over the R/T.

'I did in France,' Archie told him. 'Piece of cake.'

'Except you got knocked out and cut your head open.'

'But it was a field, not an airfield. Just really concentrate, Ted, and you'll be fine. Come on – you can do it. You know you can.'

They were now approaching Manston; ahead, they could see the by-now familiar buildings, and aircraft parked up around the perimeter of the North Field.

'I'm too high!' said Ted.

'Push the stick forward.'

'All right, she's dropping – Christ, Archie – ah, that's better.'

'I'm with you,' said Archie, opening the radiator and lowering his flaps and undercarriage. He glanced across, saw Ted wobble, then correct himself.

'You're nearly there, Ted, nearly there.'

'I'm going too fast!'

'No, no – you're fine. Glide in, just glide in.' But his friend was going faster than he was, and now Ted was ahead of him, rushing towards the ground. For a moment, Archie thought he was going to plough into the ground but then, at the last minute, Ted lifted the nose and the Spitfire slid on to the grass, the propeller snapping and splintering and the plane yawing as it slid across the grass.

A moment later, Archie felt himself touch down with a jolt – hardly his smoothest – then bounce lightly back into the air before touching back down again.

'Ted? Ted? Are you all right.'

He heard his friend laughing. 'Oh, my God, I'm alive! I'm alive!' he was saying. 'Oh, my God! We did it, Archie – we blinking well did it.'

Archie could say nothing. He breathed out heavily and for

a moment thought he might cry. 'Don't you dare,' he told himself. *But the relief.* They were back. They had made it. They would live to see another day. He taxied, parked and cut the engine and slowly took off his leads and helmet and unclipped his Sutton harness. A fire truck was rushing towards Ted's Spitfire, its bells clanging unnecessarily. Archie closed his eyes a moment, then gingerly clambered out, lowered himself on to the wing and slid on to the ground. His legs nearly buckled, and he grabbed the edge of the wing to steady himself, then saw a row of seven bullet holes across his fuselage. How had they not hit one of the cables that connected the controls to the rudder and elevators? By God, but he'd been lucky. *Lucky.* It was a word people kept using about him. *He* kept using about himself. But how long would it last?

11

DARKEST HOUR

Later that same evening, Friday 31 May, Group Captain Guy Tyler sat in the office of his boss, Air Chief Marshal Sir Cyril Newell, the Chief of the Air Staff, at the Air Ministry in King Charles II Street. Next to him was the Deputy Chief of the Air Staff, Air Vice-Marshal Sholto Douglas. For a moment, no one spoke as Newell perused the latest signal intelligence, or 'sigint' as it was known. Outside, it was a beautiful early summer's evening. The light was beginning to fade, casting a golden glow through the twin windows. Newell had kept one of them half open, allowing just the faintest of breezes. On the ledge outside, some pigeons were cooing rhythmically.

A scene of utter peace, thought Tyler, *but for how much longer?* Earlier that day, Newell and the other chiefs of staff had given the prime minister and his War Cabinet a report entitled 'Invasion of the United Kingdom'. The report had been put together over the past couple of days, largely on the basis of information given to the chiefs by the Joint Intelligence Committee, which in turn drew on intelligence gathered by all three services – the Army, Air Force and Navy. Some of the finest brains in the country were now working around the clock, trying to crack enemy codes, attempting to glean as true a picture of what was going on as was humanly possible. They had a good idea of German strength, and now, given the speed with which the Low Countries and half of France had been rolled over, a clear appreciation of how quickly the Germans could operate. It was the speed of this juggernaut that had caught the Allies so off guard. Pre-war planning by the French had suggested there would be another long drawn-out, largely stationary war – much the same as the Great War a generation earlier, but with more intense firepower. The Germans had obliterated that theory, as they had thundered west, troops, tanks, artillery and air force all working together in a co-ordinated strike. The world had seen nothing like it. The Germans seemed unstoppable.

Tyler had read the report earlier that morning. The Germans, it suggested, had two options. Either they could continue the battle against France in an attempt to knock her out of the war completely, or they could stabilize the front over there and launch a major assault on Britain. This struck the chiefs of staff as the more obvious option and Tyler, for one, did not disagree. The French were finished – that was obvious – and were incapable of mounting a counterattack of sufficient strength. Britain was Germany's main enemy – her most dangerous enemy; there was plenty of intelligence to support that.

The conclusion of the JIC and of the chiefs was that the Germans were very probably preparing for an all-out strike against Britain. The Navy was still strong, and the air-defence system that Dowding had established to protect Britain was a good one, but the RAF was short of aircraft compared with the Luftwaffe, and the Army was beaten. It was true that already more men had been lifted from Dunkirk than had ever been thought possible, but all their equipment – their guns, their vehicles – had been left behind. The British Army was in no position to fight anyone – not for a while. Old men with shotguns were not going to stop the Nazis.

Tyler and his team had made it clear that if the Luftwaffe struck in force – now, or within the next week or so – sheer weight of numbers meant it would be unlikely that the RAF could hold out, no matter how good Dowding's air-defence system was. He had told his colleagues in the JIC this, and he had told Newell. It was equally clear that if the Germans managed to get any troops across the Channel and secured a small toehold, it would be very difficult indeed to push them back into the sea. More and more enemy troops would follow and Britain would be overrun. Britain would lose the war.

Air Vice-Marshal Douglas rammed a pipe into the corner of his mouth, felt for his lighter, then puffed as wafts of blue-grey smoke swirled and danced into the air, only to catch the faint breeze and quickly disperse. Tyler took a sip of his whisky.

'So,' said Douglas, 'what are the evacuation figures for today?'

'It really is incredible,' said Newell at last, looking up at both men. 'By noon, one hundred and sixty-five thousand men had been brought back. Winston thought we'd be lucky to get fifty thousand in total, and he's an unashamed optimist.'

Douglas smiled. 'How much longer will it go on for?'

'Well, there's no sign of Jerry breaking through the perimeter yet, so another twenty-four hours at the very least. The big difference has been the use of the mole. No one originally thought it was strong enough to berth ships alongside – it's only a rickety wooden thing, apparently, but it's holding up nicely. The Hun simply can't hit it. Too small a target, and what's more the port's covered with the smoke cloud. That smokescreen is a godsend.'

Douglas chuckled. 'I think that's what's called being hoist by one's own petard. Jerry goes and bombs the oil depot and goes blind in the process.' He relit his pipe. 'And what's the forecast for the next couple of days?'

'Good, so from now on we're limiting the evacuation to night-time only. Our chaps need to provide cover in the evening and at dawn only from now on. Even with the smoke cloud, it's too risky by day.'

'Actually, sir,' said Tyler, 'I wanted to mention something to you about the German dive-bombers.'

'Oh, yes?'

'My son has a friend in his squadron, sir, who was shot down over France the other day but managed to get back. He noticed that the Stukas would hit a moving ship more through luck than judgement. He also noticed that they were sitting ducks as they came out of their dives. Our intelligence suggests the Stukas have suffered over Dunkirk. Not only are our chaps getting away, the Luftwaffe is taking some punishment too. If the Luftwaffe does attack Britain, sir, then I wonder whether it would be worth targeting their dive-bombers in particular. Knock those out and we would deliver an important psychological blow.'

'The Hun air force won't seem quite so invincible, you mean?' said Newell.

'Something like that, sir.'

'Hmm. Interesting. Thank you, Tyler. And how is your boy getting on?'

Tyler scratched his brow. 'He managed to nurse his Spitfire back across the Channel yesterday. His engine cut before he reached Manston, but he successfully belly-landed. They've lost their CO and their acting CO in the past two days, though.'

Newell frowned. 'I'm sorry. But he's doing invaluable work. They all are.'

'What are the latest figures, Tyler?' asked Douglas.

'Thirty-one lost today, sir, making one hundred and forty-four since the evacuation began.'

'And how many from Fighter Command?'

'Nineteen lost today and seven damaged.'

'Beaverbrook's figures look good,' said Newell. 'Here.' He passed a sheet of paper to Douglas.

Douglas puffed on his pipe as he scanned the grid. 'So at 10.00 hours this morning we had forty Hurricanes ready to leave the factories, with a further fifty-nine in the next four days, and fifty-three Spitfires ready, with twenty-eight more in the same four-day period. So at current rates, production is outstripping wastage. And his boys are repairing nearly a hundred a month too.'

'It's still not enough, Sholto. Six hundred fighters can't stop four thousand enemy planes. And certainly not if they go and attack right away.' He leaned back in his chair. 'We've got to face facts, gentlemen. We're staring down the barrel and that's all there is to it.'

Morning, around 10 a.m., on Saturday 1 June. The pilots of 629 Squadron sat at dispersal at Northolt, waiting for something to happen. It was a warm morning, so a number of them had brought deckchairs from inside the hut and set them up outside in the sun. No one said much. Some dozed, others read. In truth, most were still coming to terms with the events of the previous two days. Will was dead. Archie had lost sight of him, but Ted and two others had seen his Spitfire catch fire and plummet to the ground somewhere just south of Dunkirk; there had been no parachute. Pinky Parameter had also been killed, shot down and last seen plunging into the sea. There was no word from Henry Dix either.

It all seemed so extraordinary, so impossible to accept. Dix, Will and Pinky had been in the squadron since Fitz had first formed it, two years before. They were the squadron's lifeblood, its core. Its spirit. Archie had liked Will especially. He could be arrogant, and he had always had a waspish wit, and yet Archie had known that Will liked him, and had looked out for him. Not for nothing had Will put Archie and Ted in his section.

And now Will was gone. Archie wouldn't hear his clipped, dry voice calling him 'Baby' any more. For Pip, it was an even bigger blow; he'd known Will since they were kids. They'd even been at school together.

'I'm sorry about Will,' Archie had said to him the previous evening.

'I know,' Pip had replied. 'I honestly don't know what I'll do without him.'

Above the airfield a skylark was twittering busily, and closer by a bumble bee was hovering around the clover. The sounds of summer. The sounds of peace. Archie closed his eyes and a moment later was back in the air over Dunkirk, the tracer hissing towards him, and that Messerschmitt hurtling past, banking hard left and missing him by a thread. It was these extremes that he found so odd – one minute he was fighting for his life high in the sky over France, the next he was in the bar or sitting in a deckchair in the summer sun.

He thought of Will and Pinky and Dix and Terry and Dennis – five good chaps all gone. *Don't think about it,* he told himself. *Change the subject.* He closed his eyes and there before him was Tess, dancing with him at her house in Pimlico, her hand in his, his other on her waist. Archie smiled. *Much better,* he thought.

And there had been a letter from her too, or, rather, a package. It had arrived the day before, but last night he and Ted had been so exhausted when they reached Northolt, they had gone straight to bed; he'd not thought to check his pigeonhole.

'A parcel for you, Archie?' Ted had said, looking over his shoulder as they went down to the dining room for breakfast. Then he added, 'Hang on a minute, that's Tess's handwriting. What's she writing to you for?'

'I don't know,' Archie had replied, his heart beating suddenly much harder. He had torn the parcel open and pulled out a scarf – a silk scarf. Navy blue with tiny white polkadots.

'Crikey,' said Ted. 'I think my sis may have the hots for you, Arch old son.'

'It's a very smart scarf, though, you've got to admit.'

'A vast improvement. Pity Will's not here. What would he have made of it?'

Archie now opened his eyes again. *Will.* He cursed to himself. He didn't want to think about Will; he wanted to think about Tess. He looked around, saw that Ted was asleep and felt inside his breast pocket for the letter that had come with the scarf. He unfolded it and read it once more.

Dear Archie,

I remember you said you had lost your silk scarf, so when I saw this yesterday I thought it might make a good replacement. Thank you for such a wonderful evening the other day. When do you think you might next get away? Pops says you and Ted have been busy flying over Dunkirk. Do be careful, both of you, and come and see me just as soon as you can.

With love from,

Tess

He wondered if he was now dating Tess. Did an evening of talking and dancing mean that they were now 'stepping out'? Was this gift a further sign? He had never really had much to do with girls – apart from his sister, Maggie, but she didn't count. His school had been all boys, so had his college at Durham, and, in any case, he had spent most of his spare time with the squadron. There had been one or two dances in the holidays, and he had had dancing lessons – at his mother's insistence – but not until his evening with Tess had he ever thought about girls in anything other than a rather abstract way.

Since then, he had thought of her frequently. He wanted to ask Ted about her, but that would make an issue of it, and open himself up to a ribbing from his friend, and he didn't want that. And what if he was reading more into it than he should? What if Tess was simply being friendly? He realized just how little he knew about life. It was strange: he was expected to fly against the enemy, to take the lives of German pilots and aircrew, and yet he himself had barely lived at all.

He folded away the letter. He would say nothing to Ted, not

yet, but secretly he hoped that as soon as they were given the time, the two of them would head back to London and then he could see Tess again. In the meantime, there were letters. If he wrote back to her, then perhaps she would write back to him. Surely that was all right. She could not take a letter the wrong way. Could she?

Archie stretched and yawned, and then got up and went back inside the hut, took some writing paper from his gas-mask bag and sat down to write at one end of the table.

Dear Tess,

Thank you for the scarf. It was a lovely surprise and very clever of you to remember. It's also a much better scarf than the one I lost. I shall wear it every time I fly. Actually, you were right – we have been quite busy, but Ted and I are OK. Poor Ted had a slightly hairy time yesterday flying back with a u/s engine, which decided to cut out before we reached our 'drome. Fortunately, he glided in the last bit and landed all right. Our CO was shot down the other day, but plenty of people saw him bail out, so I'm sure he's fine. Poor Will Merton-Moore bought it yesterday, which was very sad, as he was a good friend. Oh, well, I suppose you have to accept these things. Anyway, Ted and I are fine and this morning are making the most of not flying.

I'm not sure when we'll get some time off, but I hope it will be soon and then we will come into London and hopefully we can see you. I would like that very much.

Outside, an engine suddenly started up, its deep, guttural roar tearing apart the peace and quiet that reigned over their corner of the airfield. Archie cursed to himself – the sound would wake up those who were sleeping. Sure enough, a moment later Ted appeared.

'What are you doing?'

'Catching up on some letters.'

Ted stood over him. 'Who are you writing to?' He peered down at Archie's scrawling handwriting.

'Your sister, if you must know. Thanking her for the scarf.'

Ted looked at him and grinned. 'I see.' He picked up a magazine and sat down in one of the deckchairs. 'Better let you get on with your love note, then.'

'It's not a love note,' Archie retorted, too quickly, and felt his cheeks blush.

Ted held up his hands. 'All right, all right. No need to be so touchy about it.'

Archie sighed. He signed the letter, folded it and put it in an envelope, then took out another sheet of paper. 'And now,' he said, 'I'm writing home. Long overdue.'

'Are you going to wear it, then?'

'What?'

'The scarf?'

'It's a nice scarf. Of course I am.'

Ted was quiet a moment. 'I don't mind, you know.'

'Mind what?'

'If you and Tess – you know.'

'She's just being friendly.'

'She's got the hots for you, Archie! Course she has, or else she wouldn't be sending you swanky silk scarves.'

'Look,' said Archie, putting down his pen. 'I spent a few hours with her while you were chatting up Polly, and now she's sent me a scarf. I like your sister very much but at the moment nothing's happening.'

'All right, all right,' said Ted, holding up his hands again in mock surrender. 'I'm just saying I don't mind, that's all.'

Archie turned back to his letter. He had neglected his family – he'd not written all week, and they would be worried about him. He suddenly felt a flush of irritation – cross with himself for forgetting them and with Ted for embarrassing him.

Dear Mum, Dad and Maggie,

I hope you are all well. Sorry I haven't written for a little while, but it's been very busy here. No doubt you've heard about the evacuation that's been going on. Well, we've been flying over it and it's quite a sight, I can tell you. I had a bit of an adventure the other day. I managed to bag a couple of Huns, including one of their fighters, a Messerschmitt 109, but then got hit in the engine and crash-landed in a field. Anyway, to cut a long story short, I managed to get home again OK, with nothing more than a scratch on my forehead. Since then, we've flown almost non-stop this past couple of days. Ted and I shot down a Jerry bomber and it dived down into the cloud, its engine on fire. Although Ted and I know perfectly well that that Junkers could do nothing but plough into the ground, because we can't prove it, the IO says its only a 'possible'. Since then, I've shot down another 109, which was seen, so my confirmed score is three. I got a few bullets in my kite yesterday, but it didn't really cause any damage. We've lost a few good chaps, including the CO and Will Merton-Moore. Do you remember me telling you about him? He was a good sort and will be missed.

Today is a lovely morning and we're not flying, so I've at last got a chance to catch up on my letters and write to the folks back home. How is home? I miss not being there. It's my favourite time of year. Are you getting enough petrol coupons, Dad? And I don't want you to take this the wrong way, Mum, but I think Maggie should join the ATA if she wants to. Flying is the best thing in the world and it's not as though she would have to tussle with Huns or anything like that.

No one's sure what will happen after France. Personally, I hope we're given some leave. Being a fighter pilot is tiring work!

All my love,

Archie

He put down the pen, read it through, then folded and sealed it in an envelope. The tone was about right, he thought. Not too much detail – he didn't want to worry them too much – but he did want to tell someone about his score. He couldn't talk about these things in the squadron, but it was all right to tell his own family.

He wondered whether they would be flying that day. They were still on standby, ready to be scrambled at a moment's notice, with Pip acting CO. But the squadron was now badly under strength. No replacements had come through yet, so they were down to just fourteen pilots. Perhaps they would be stood down. He wondered what would happen, then chided himself. What would be, would be. Right now, he decided, it was better to live in the present.

*

They were finally scrambled at four o'clock that afternoon and ordered to fly to Rochford once again. From there, having refuelled, they were ordered into the air at 7.30 p.m., once more to patrol Dunkirk. The skies were clear apart from the smoke cloud over the port and, after half an hour flying up and down the patrol line, they spotted a flight of enemy bombers. Before they could take them on, however, there were a dozen Me 110s to deal with. Rather than dive for the bombers, Pip chose to confront the fighters. Archie fired at several, saw strikes on two, but could claim nothing. He escaped the dogfight unscathed, as did Ted. The squadron claimed three shot down – Archie certainly saw two diving out of the fray trailing smoke – but they lost two more of their own. Hank McNair, the American, was seen bailing out over the sea, while Paul Hunt, a B Flight pilot, was seen going down in flames.

That night, when they finally reached Northolt once more, they all went to the Mess at Pip's insistence. Lined up along the bar were eight upturned pint glasses.

'To our friends and comrades in the best squadron in the RAF,' said Pip, raising his tankard. 'May they live on and never be forgotten. And,' he said. 'And.' He touched the corner of his eye. 'Let's hope this past week has been the squadron's darkest hour. From now on let's pray things start to get a little bit better.'

Yes, thought Archie. *Let's hope so*. Because if they continued losing pilots at their current rate, within a couple of weeks there wouldn't be one man left standing.

12

VICTORY ROLL

Tuesday 4 June, around 6 a.m. A beautiful morning already, just a light haze over the Channel but it was dispersing fast. Away to the east, Archie could still see the smoke cloud over Dunkirk, that ever-present marker rising high, high into the air, but beyond, in the east, the sun was already well clear of the horizon, and the sky above was clear blue, with nothing more than a few wisps of high cirrus.

It was the squadron's first sortie in three days, but it already felt like a long morning: up at three, before first light, down to dispersal, where their Spitfires were already being run up, the cacophony of Merlins tearing apart the pre-dawn. Then at first light they'd taken off, all twelve aircraft, this time to Eastchurch, known only to Gordon, Tony and Colin who had accidentally flown there five days before. *Five days!* Archie thought as they approached the airfield. It seemed like a lifetime ago.

A quick mug of coffee at Eastchurch, a slice of buttered toast and marmalade, and then a mixed flight of two sections had been sent over to patrol Dunkirk once more, Archie flying as Pip's wingman at Blue Two. They had climbed to eighteen thousand feet, and once again Archie had marvelled at how small the world seemed from that height. As they headed north, then turned south, with France and the sun on their port side, he glanced across at southern England, and there it was, stretching away, the finger of Kent, the Medway and Thames estuaries, the curve of East Anglia, just as it was on the maps. *How did they make maps?* he wondered. *How did they do it before there were aeroplanes? Concentrate,* he chided himself.

He looked around – behind to his left, to his right, up and then down. Below, steaming across the sea, were two ships, the vivid lines of their wakes white against the deep blue sea. As usual, the ships were taking a circuitous route – to avoid minefields, apparently – and so were well north of Dover and still far out at sea.

He looked around him again, then at his dials, then at Pip up ahead, the Spitfire bowing up and down slightly; it was hard to fly perfectly straight and level. Another glance around, and this time he saw a formation of aircraft, about two miles away, he guessed – he could only just make them out. They were heading north-west, in the direction of the ships.

'Nimbus Leader, this is Blue Two,' said Archie over the R/T, remembering his radio procedure for once. 'Twelve bandits, angels twelve, crossing the coast now at ten o'clock.'

'Good spot, Archie.' Pip's voice crackled in his ears. 'We'll turn back north, dropping height, then attack out of the sun. All of you keep a close watch out for the snappers. Over.'

Archie, on the port side of the formation, followed Pip as they banked and turned north. Where were those snappers, those Messerschmitts that always seemed to turn up and spoil the party? He swivelled his head, glad to feel the soft silk of Tess's scarf against his neck. They flew on, the sun bright to the east. Archie felt his heart quicken once more. If the enemy fighters turned up, it would almost certainly be from straight out of the sun.

On they flew, heading north-east, then, keeping themselves between the sun and the advancing enemy aircraft, banked again. As they manoeuvred, Archie lost sight of the enemy bombers – they were still some way off and the sky was a big, big place. It was often hard to spot tiny aircraft until one was almost right on top of them, but then he saw a glint of sunlight on metal or perhaps the perspex of the canopy, and immediately spotted the wake of the two ships. The enemy were almost over the vessels.

'All right, chaps, here we go,' said Pip. Archie glanced around once more – still nothing. The Stukas were now just a mile or so away and a couple of thousand feet below. Another glance behind – *my God, that sun is bright* – and then they were gently diving down towards them and Archie saw to his delight that the enemy formation were Stukas. *Good,* he thought, *now's the chance to test the theory.*

The Stukas were only a mile ahead and about fifteen hundred feet below them, and, it seemed, still oblivious to the threat above and behind them.

'This is Nimbus Leader,' said Pip over the R/T, 'get ready.'

Archie squeezed his legs against the control column, then with both hands lowered his goggles over his eyes and switched the gun button to fire. Suddenly the first of the Stukas began its dive, then the second and third. They had split into flights, one group attacking one ship, the second the other. In front of him, Pip flipped over and dived and he now followed him down. As the first Stuka emerged from its dive, he saw Pip open fire, and saw smoke burst from the dive-bomber's engine. 'Ha!' he said out loud, as he homed in on the second of the Stukas. There went its bomb, way wide of the lead ship, and then the Stuka pulled up and tried to bank away out of trouble. Archie followed, watching it fill his reflector sight. *Hold on, hold on,* he told himself, and then, at less than two hundred yards, with the waddling Stuka big in his target circle, he pressed his thumb down on the tit.

The Spitfire juddered, and wispy tracer fizzed across the sky and appeared to strike the cowling. A moment later, he hurtled over it, thundering past the stricken machine. Archie craned his neck, saw a puff of smoke from the Stuka's engine, then put on full boost and climbed vertically, feeling himself slammed into the back of his seat, until he was upside down. Then he rolled the Spitfire, the sky and sea swivelling the right way up, and dived back down. His Stuka had banked and turned in towards the ship, diving down to the deck, its only chance of escape.

'You're not getting away from me,' muttered Archie to himself. The dive-bomber was just a few hundred feet above the water, barely clearing the lead destroyer, but, swooping down, Archie carefully lined up his target once more. With the Stuka at just a hundred and fifty yards, limping large in his sights, he pressed down again on the gun button and watched bullets and tracer spew towards it. A second later, he was hurtling over the Stuka again. Craning his head, he saw a burst of flame and smoke. Archie banked again for a better view. It was as if the Stuka wobbled in the air, then it plunged into the sea. 'That's for Will,' he said.

He continued his turn and, just a hundred feet off the water, he flashed past the lead ship. As he did so, something caught his eye.

'No,' he said out loud. 'It can't be!'

Archie flew on, climbed and rolled once more, then dived back down towards the destroyer. Although he knew he should climb back into the fray, curiosity got the better of him. Pulling back on the throttle, he slowed the aircraft, lifted his goggles on to his head and glanced out over his port wing. There, at the bow of the ship, he saw one of the soldiers waving an orange scarf. The orange scarf he had given them as he'd left them in Cassel.

'Brilliant!' he said out loud. *They got away.* He laughed and pulled back his canopy and waved, then, opening the throttle, sped on, climbing into the sky and rolling so that he was facing the ship once more. Where were the others? He saw another Stuka plunging into the sea a little distance away, looked up and spotted several wheeling, turning aircraft, then thought, *Oh, well, what the heck.* Archie laughed again, opened the throttle wide, and hurtled towards the starboard side of the ship. A hundred feet off the deck. Three hundred and forty miles per hour. As he went past, he eased back on the stick, felt the Spitfire start to climb, then pushed to the left and saw the horizon spin three hundred and sixty degrees. He whooped with joy, waggled his wings, then turned for home.

Later, in the early afternoon, they flew back to Northolt. The squadron had claimed four Stukas destroyed and two possibles. Archie now had four confirmed kills, Ted three.

'You know what this means,' Pip had said as they'd gathered at dispersal at Eastchurch, 'one more and you'll be an ace.'

'I'll tell you what it means,' said Mike.

'What?' said Archie.

'You're buying the first round of drinks in the bar tonight.'

When they arrived back at Northolt, they were immediately stood down. 'I've just been talking with the adj,' Pip told them. 'The evacuation's over, chaps.'

'So now what?' asked Ted.

Pip shrugged. 'We wait for Jerry, I suppose. And in the meantime, we're all going to have a party in the bar tonight.'

'The PM's speaking on the radio later,' said Reynolds, the adjutant. 'Addressing the nation. We should listen to that, don't you think?'

'Good idea,' said Mike. 'Perhaps he can tell us what on earth is going on.'

They dined early and were in the bar for the prime minister's broadcast. Archie had dutifully bought the first round for the pilots, as well as Calder and Reynolds, and now, with their pints in their hands, they huddled around the radio, listening.

Churchill recounted the events of the past three weeks in his low, rumbling voice, and they listened in silence until he said, 'Meanwhile, the Royal Air Force . . .' whereupon everyone cheered. Their fighters, he said, 'struck at the German bombers, and at the fighters which in large numbers protected them. This struggle was protracted and fierce. Suddenly, the scene has cleared, the crash and thunder has for the moment – but only for the moment – died away. A miracle of deliverance, achieved by valour, by perseverance, by perfect discipline . . .'

'He obviously hasn't heard us on the R/T,' said Pip.

'. . . by resource, by skill, by unconquerable fidelity, is manifest to us all.' He talked of the 'great trial of strength' that had taken place between the German and British air forces, and made it clear that the Germans had paid dear. The Luftwaffe might have four times as many aircraft, but Britain's pilots had not stinted. He likened the young pilots of the RAF to knights of the Round Table, to crusaders. 'May it not also be,' he growled, 'that the cause of civilization itself will be defended by the skill and devotion of a few thousand airmen?'

My word, thought Archie, *he means us.* He swallowed hard.

Churchill rumbled on. No one said a word now. The room was silent but for the tinny growl of the prime minister's voice. 'We shall fight with growing confidence and growing strength in the air,' he promised, 'we shall defend our island, whatever the cost may be, we shall fight on the beaches, we shall fight on the landing grounds, we shall fight in the fields and in the streets, we shall fight in the hills; we shall never surrender.'

When it was over, Reynolds leaned over and switched the radio off, but still no one spoke for a moment. *It was strange,* Archie thought – they all knew they had been taking part in something important over Dunkirk, and yet they had been operating on their own for much of the time – one squadron, a handful of planes and pilots. Churchill's speech underlined the enormity of what had been achieved and what now faced them. Ten days' fighting had been hard enough, but what lay around the corner? He breathed out heavily. *Don't think about it,* he told himself.

On cue, Pip said, 'Well, one thing's pretty certain: the Huns aren't coming tonight. Look, chaps, who knows where we'll be in a week's time, but let's not worry about that now. Tonight we're all here, we're all alive. And I, for one, intend to enjoy myself.'

Yes, thought Archie, *amen to that.*

13

RING THE CHANGES

For more than two weeks, they waited. The squadron was expected to be at various stages of readiness from dawn until dusk – either immediate, which meant being airborne within three minutes, or at fifteen minutes availability, or at thirty. This meant no release day and no leave. New pilots arrived, including the squadron's first sergeant pilots. The old auxiliary squadron was slowly but surely shedding its skin.

Initial relief at having survived the baptism of fire quickly gave way to sullenness among the originals and even a degree of listlessness.

'You know what the trouble is, don't you?' Reynolds said to Archie and Ted one day. 'We've not got enough to do. Too much time to brood.'

They were at half-an-hour readiness, and the two men were ambling around the perimeter, looking at the aircraft for no other reason than for something to do.

'We've all been together a long time,' Reynolds went on. 'Many of these fellows have been friends since childhood. It's a big blow and with all this sitting around at dispersal all day, every day, it's damn tricky to put it out of one's mind.'

Archie liked Reynolds. He was the oldest member of the

squadron, in his early forties, with a kindly face, a trim moustache and hair that was greying at the sides. As ground staff, his age was not the hindrance it had been to Fitz. Everyone called him 'Uncle'.

'You were in the last war, weren't you, Uncle?'

'Yes. Flying too.'

'A few losses, then, I suppose.'

Reynolds smiled. 'Too many. It was always the new chaps, though. We used to reckon that if a new fellow could survive three weeks, he had a pretty good chance of keeping going for a bit. Most were knocked down on their first few trips. It was like lambs to the slaughter, frankly.'

'Weren't they given enough training, then?' asked Ted.

'No, but it wasn't just that. It's the same with you fellows. You might know how to fly a plane, but not how to fly it in combat, and to learn that – and quickly – you need to be able to fly without thinking. I bet when you get in your Spit now and you want to make a one hundred and eighty degree turn, you don't think, *Pull back on the stick a bit, then use the ailerons*. You just do it, like riding a bicycle or driving a car.'

'You're right, Uncle. I don't,' said Archie. 'When I get in, I feel as though I'm strapping myself to the Spit. It's almost as though we become one, if that makes sense.'

'Perfectly. But these chaps would turn up, straight from flying school – much the same sort of age as you two fellows – and they were still thinking about the dials and controls and how to do this and that. When you're in combat, you need to be thinking about shooting down the enemy and making sure you don't get shot down yourself. You need to concentrate on that one hundred per cent. That's why you two have been lucky.

You'd flown before the war started – Ted a fair amount, I know – then had a month or so getting some hours under your belt on Spits, and now you've had proper combat experience. It's chaps like you that the new fellows will be looking to. You're the veterans now.'

'We're only nineteen, Uncle,' Ted laughed.

'But a lot older in combat terms. Share your experience, won't you? It's terribly important.'

Archie nodded thoughtfully, then said, 'Uncle, how did you deal with the deaths in the last war?'

'Well, I'm afraid I got terribly upset to begin with, but it's like most things: one gets used to it. Hardened, I suppose. I used to pretend they hadn't died at all. I used to tell myself they'd simply gone away. A bit like when one moved school and suddenly all those chaps one had been great friends with and had seen every day weren't around any more. You were sorry you didn't see them, but I don't remember feeling particularly sad about it. One made new pals and got on with it.' He paused and felt for his cigarettes. 'That's the trouble at the moment. You're all struggling to get on with things because very little is happening.'

'I know. The mood has changed,' said Ted. '629 Squadron used to be such a jolly bunch of lads. The atmosphere has changed completely. Even Mike's stopped cracking jokes.'

'On the other hand,' said Reynolds, 'this respite is a godsend. Hitler's obviously decided to finish off France first. It's given us a great chance to replenish the stocks. We've got three more pilots due this afternoon.'

'I suppose so,' said Ted. 'But I want to get flying again. I'm fed up with this endless hanging around. I'm fed up with this fighter station.'

Reynolds chuckled. 'Enjoy it while you can. It won't go on like this.'

Later, after they were stood down for the night, Archie and Ted took the Norton and rode to the Tyler house in Pimlico. Ted had managed to ring earlier and for once the family were all there, even the group captain. Tess too, much to Archie's relief. She seemed genuinely pleased to see him, kissing him on the cheek and leading him by the hand straight into the dining room. That flush of excitement he had felt when he had first danced with her at the Bag o' Nails now swept over him once more. He had, of course, played down his feelings for her with Ted, but there had been, as he had hoped, more letters since the scarf. He had treasured each one, and, in truth, during the long days of inactivity over the past fortnight, thinking about Tess, reading her letters and writing his own in return, had helped take his mind off the boredom they had endured at Northolt.

Ted, he knew, had also been writing to Polly and had even seen her once during an evening in town after they had been stood down for the day, but his friend did not talk about her much, just as Archie rarely mentioned Tess. It was funny, Archie had reflected, how they were such close friends, had shared so much together, and yet there was an implicit understanding between them that girls would not be discussed – not much, at any rate.

'Did you hear Churchill's speech?' Ted's mother asked as they sat down to dinner.

'No, 'fraid not,' said Ted. 'We were at dispersal and the wireless has broken. Heard the last one, though, a couple of weeks ago.'

'Was it good, Mrs Tyler?' asked Archie as the maid brought in the soup.

'Oh, it was marvellous,' she said. 'I must say, I used not to think a great deal of Mr Churchill. He took sides with King Edward over that awful abdication business and he always looks, I don't know, a bit unreliable, somehow, but I will admit he's a wonderful orator and does seem to be rallying the nation, rather.'

'Rallying the Empire, darling,' said her husband. 'These speeches are being broadcast all around the free world. They're rallying cries to our imperial allies as much as to us here in the British Isles. And I'll admit it: he certainly knows how to inspire.'

'He said the Battle of France is over and that the Battle of Britain is about to begin,' said Tess. 'That means you boys.' She looked down at her soup, her expression one of sadness.

'Well, it certainly hasn't begun yet,' said Ted. 'I wish it would. Archie and I are sitting by that damned dispersal hut all day bored rigid.'

'Ted! Language!' said his mother.

'Sorry, Mama. But, really, it's such a waste of time. We're expected to be at readiness all the time, when we'd be far better off flying and practising.'

'Your impatience,' said his father. 'Really, Ted. I worry when I hear you talk like that.'

He glanced up at the wall, and Archie followed his gaze to the portrait hanging there. It was of Group Captain Tyler as a young captain in the last war, fresh-faced, flying helmet on his head and wearing a long, leather flying coat.

'I'm not being impatient in the air, Pops, I just don't want to be sitting about doing nothing.'

'Aren't you getting any practice?'

'Some, but not very much. It's difficult when the entire squadron is expected to be at readiness all the time.'

'It's because our numbers are still down, sir,' said Archie. 'Normally, we could have one flight on, one flight off, but there aren't enough of us yet. New pilots are arriving, but until we're back to full strength . . .'

'I see.'

'And we still don't have a new CO,' said Ted. 'Pip's been a good caretaker, but –'

'You need someone to steer the ship.'

'Well, yes.'

Group Captain Tyler dabbed his mouth with his napkin. 'I don't think I'm betraying any state secrets in telling you this,' he said, 'but your new CO is on his way to you.'

'About time,' said Ted. 'Who is he?'

His father smiled. 'A New Zealander.'

'What? Commanding an auxiliary squadron?'

'You're not auxiliaries any more. Those times are long gone, Ted. You're a permanent squadron in Fighter Command. He's called MacIntyre. And he's good. He'll soon whip you all back into shape.' He chuckled.

'And what about Jerry?' asked Ted. 'Where's the Luftwaffe?'

'Finishing off France and frantically building airfields in the Pas de Calais,' he replied, then added, 'and don't ask me any more than that because I can't tell you.'

'Then why aren't we going over there now and shooting them up?' asked Ted.

'We have Bomber Command for that. Your task is to defend this island, not go and get into mischief across the Channel.'

Archie glanced at Ted, who was rubbing his chin thoughtfully. And then he felt something touch his leg and could not help smiling. Sitting opposite him was Tess. Underneath the tablecloth, she was gently knocking his leg with hers.

Squadron Leader Stephen MacIntyre arrived at Northolt the following day, drawing up in a small maroon Austin Ruby and being ushered into the main building. The pilots all watched anxiously, but he did not reappear until later that afternoon, when he walked over to dispersal in his flying gear. Stocky, with dark brown eyes, a wide nose and wearing an expression of ill-disguised impatience, he pointed at one of the new boys and said, 'You. We're going up on a half-hour flight. You first, then you,' he added, turning to another of the arrivals from the day before. 'Be ready to take off as soon as I get back with this one.'

The first, Peter Benson, a young man straight from Operational Training Unit, went into the dispersal hut to collect his flying helmet and parachute. By the time he re-emerged, the new CO was already halfway to one of the waiting Spitfires.

'What d'you make of that?' said Mike as they watched the CO start up and begin taxiing.

'Bit of a stickler by the look of it,' said Tony Simmonds.

Half an hour later, Benson landed again and trudged towards the dispersal hut as the new CO took off again with the next new boy, Joss Flinders.

'Well?' said Pip as Benson reached them.

Benson shook his head. 'I think he shot me down at least three times.'

'What d'you mean?'

'We climbed to eight thousand feet and he told me to follow him,' said Benson. 'He kept diving and turning and in no time I'd lost him completely. Then out of the blue I heard, "Rat-a-tat-a-tat-a-tat," in my ear and looked round and he was right on my tail. He did it three times and each time he said, "You're dead, Red Two."'

Pip and the others sniggered. Benson looked distraught.

Half an hour later, Flinders also came trudging back, just as despondent, while above, the new CO beat up the airfield, flying low over dispersal – so low that everyone ducked.

'Christ,' said Ted to Archie. 'This bloke means business.'

'You're telling me,' agreed Archie.

The CO now landed and told A Flight to get ready to fly in ten minutes.

'But aren't we supposed to be here at readiness, sir?' asked Pip.

'We can't be more ready than being in the air, can we?' snapped MacIntyre.

As they hurried to their Spitfires, Ted said to Archie in a conspiratorial tone, 'He's trying to catch us out. Over my dead body. We mustn't let him.'

'All right. So what do we do?'

'Play him at his own game. He's not going to make asses out of us, Arch.'

They took off, Archie flying at Yellow Two behind Pip, and climbed up to ten thousand feet, London and the Chilterns stretching away beneath them. It was a bright afternoon, but with plenty of towering cumulus. As they climbed, the squadron kept near perfect formation, staying in their tight vics of three, with the CO and Red Section leading, Yellow Section off their port side, and, trailing off the starboard side, Blue and then Green Sections.

'This is Red One,' said the CO, 'I want you all to stick on my tail, all right?'

Archie glanced across at Ted, who waved and then pointed skywards.

'No, Ted,' said Archie to himself, and shook his head. Ted was nodding and signalling upwards once more.

They levelled off and flew towards a giant bank of cumulus. 'What's the CO up to?' mumbled Archie.

Moments later, they flew straight into the thick, white cloud, and Archie felt his Spitfire buck with the turbulence. He could still see Ted, but ahead, Red Section were already disappearing. Then suddenly he saw them dive away to port, but at the same time Ted pulled back on the stick and climbed. Archie knew he had a fraction of a second to decide what to do: follow the new CO, or stick with Ted – which would undoubtedly result in a roasting for both of them.

'Damn you, Ted!' he said out loud, then pulled back on the stick and felt the Spitfire lurch higher into the sky. He glanced across again at his friend, saw him wave and then a moment later they burst through the cloud and into the clear. Climbing still, they circled, looking down below, with the sun behind them.

'There he is!' said Archie out loud. Two thousand feet below, he could see the CO, ahead of the rest of the squadron now, rolling off the top of a climb and plunging back into the cloud. When he reappeared, he was a thousand feet higher and had lost the others, who, a moment later, emerged through the cloud still at around ten thousand feet.

Archie grinned and looked across at Ted, who was now frantically signalling to him, repeatedly holding up his hand.

What does that mean? thought Archie. *Wait?* He craned his neck and saw the CO just below, turning, ready to dive on the others with the sun behind him. Evidently, he had not seen the two rogue Spitfires circling in the glare above him.

Another glance at Ted, who was now pointing furiously downwards, the signal plain enough this time. As MacIntyre began his dive, Ted flipped over and followed, a puff of smoke coming from his engine as the carburettor momentarily flooded. Pushing forward the stick, Archie dived too.

Two thousand feet below them, the rest of the squadron were flying in a wide circle, still roughly in formation, although Pip, at Yellow One, was out on something of a limb. Archie wondered when the CO would say something, but it was not until MacIntyre was about two hundred yards from the rear of the formation that he said, 'Rat-a-tat-a-tat-a-tat,' over the R/T.

Not us, thought Archie, grinning to himself, then looked across at Ted. They were both no more than two hundred yards behind the CO's plane.

He prayed Ted would keep quiet. The temptation to call out, to say, 'You're dead, Red One,' was overwhelming – but would be disastrous. They simply could not humiliate the new CO like that, not in front of the others. In any case, in climbing away on their own, they had blatantly disobeyed orders. 'No!' he mouthed and shook his head. 'Don't say it, Ted!'

MacIntyre flew over the formation and took his position back as Red One. 'All right,' he said, 'let's head home.'

Nothing from Ted, and Archie breathed a sigh of relief and

slipped behind Pip's port wing. He wondered whether Pip had noticed their absence.

After they had all landed, Pip said to Archie and Ted, 'Where did you two get to?'

'Nowhere.' Ted grinned. 'We stuck to you like glue, Pip. Didn't we, Archie?'

'Absolutely. Like glue. May have fallen back a little bit at one point in the cloud, but not for long.'

'Hmm,' said Pip. 'Well, I hope the CO didn't spot you.'

'That's just it,' said Ted. 'I don't think he did.'

Then, on cue, both of them said, 'Rat-a-tat-a-tat-a-tat,' and began laughing.

'Don't you start,' muttered Mike.

At dispersal, MacIntyre eyed them both suspiciously, then strode back towards the main building.

'Do you think he knows?' whispered Ted.

Archie shrugged. 'He didn't say anything, did he?'

Ted grinned. 'Maybe we got away with it, then. Honour satisfied all round, I'd say.'

In the Mess later that evening, the CO showed up briefly, had a quick drink, then disappeared.

'I hope he's going to say something other than rat-a-tat,' said Pip.

'He's making a very clear point, though, isn't he?' said Colin Bishop.

No one answered him. Pip blew four perfect smoke rings.

'What I want to know,' said Mike, 'is where the devil he's come from?'

'Ask Uncle,' said Pip. 'He'll know.'

'Ah. Well,' said Reynolds as the others gathered around him. 'Learned to fly on his parents' farm, apparently. Applied to Cranwell and was accepted. Passed out in '34, then almost immediately went out to Aden. Couple of years there, then back here, where he became an instructor.' By all accounts, the adj told them, he'd been an excellent instructor, but that wasn't all. He'd been in France too, knocking down a number of planes, and had already been given a DFC. 'So he knows his stuff all right.'

Archie looked across at Ted and saw him wink.

Soon after, they headed back to their room. 'I'm still smiling about that trick on the CO,' said Ted.

'I was convinced you were going to say, "rat-a-tat,"' said Archie, laughing, 'and I was so hoping you wouldn't.'

'I'm not that much of a fool. If I'd done that, he'd have probably given me the chop there and then. Still, we proved a point, didn't we?'

'I'd like to think so, yes.'

They were still chatting as they walked down the long corridor that led to their room. When they reached it, they saw a folded note under the door.

'What's this?' said Ted, bending down and pulling it clear.

He unfolded it and immediately his expression changed. 'Oh, blast,' he said.

'What?' said Archie. 'What does it say?'

'Here,' said Ted, passing it to him.

There was just one line: *See me in my office at 4.30 a.m. sharp. S/Ldr S. MacIntyre.*

'We're for it, then, Ted.'

Ted patted him lightly on the shoulder. 'Yes, Archie,' he said. 'I think we probably are.'

14

THE NEW CO

Since the squadron was expected to be at readiness by 5 a.m., it was a daily occurrence for the pilots to be woken at four. It was midsummer and already starting to get light, and so long as there was light, the squadron was expected to fly.

Archie was greeted with a mug of sweet tea, but no sooner was he awake than he remembered with a dull ache in the pit of his stomach that in half an hour he and Ted were expected to report to the new CO. It reminded him of the time he had been caught breaking out of his dormitory at night. He and his friend Dougal had run down the fire escape, across the school yard and to the cricket pitches, where they had peed on the square; it was a school tradition, a rite of passage. But they had been caught by one of the matrons as they tried to sneak back in, and then the headmaster had been summoned.

'See me outside my study in the morning,' they'd been told, leaving them with a night in which to ponder their punishment. That time they had both been given two strokes of the cane. My God, how that had hurt. Two crimson weals had appeared, one on each cheek of their buttocks, and when Archie had tried to sit down, waves of pain had coursed through his entire body. A few days later, the weals turned purple, then greenish yellow. It had taken nearly two weeks for the marks to disappear altogether.

But that had been when he was twelve. He wondered now what had possessed him and Ted to try to take on the new CO on his very first day. Causing trouble did not come naturally; instinctively, he preferred to toe the line.

'It'll be all right,' said Ted, a weak smile on his face. 'Bit of a dressing down, that's all.'

'Let's hope so,' said Archie.

At 4.30 a.m. they were standing outside the door of the CO's office. Ted looked at Archie, then knocked.

'Come!' came the voice.

Gingerly, they opened the door, walked up to the desk and saluted.

MacIntyre waved his hand. 'All right, all right,' he said, then leaned back in his chair, his hands behind his head. 'How old are you two? Nineteen?'

They nodded.

'And you joined the squadron in April.'

'No, sir,' said Ted. 'Back in the autumn of 1938, sir. During our first term at Durham University.'

'Oh, yes, the weekend fliers – a few trips in a Tiger Moth, then dinner and drinks afterwards – yes, I know the kind of thing. You, Tyler, had your civilian licence, which, let's face it, they give to anyone who can take off and land, and you, Jackson, had about twenty hours before they packed you off to training. So, apart from a bit of larking about in the auxiliary squadron, which, frankly, barely counts, you joined the permanent wartime squadron in April. Right?'

'Yes, sir,' they said in unison.

'So you've still got a lot to learn, wouldn't you say?'

'Yes, sir.'

MacIntyre leaned forward. 'Right. This is both a pat on the back and a warning. The point of yesterday's evening sortie was to see how well the squadron flew together once there was a bit of cloud and sun. It's all very well flying in beautiful neat formations, but it doesn't work the moment you're in a cloud bank. So what do you do?'

'Avoid clouds?' said Ted.

'If possible, yes.'

'And don't fly quite so close together, sir,' said Archie.

'Yes, again. Actually, what you two did was the best course of action. Fly up-sun, watch, then dive down with the advantage of height and sun. So from that point of view, well done.'

Archie felt himself relax, but it was short-lived.

'However,' MacIntyre continued, 'in doing so, you disobeyed my orders. I told you all to follow me, didn't I? I wanted to make the point about how disorientating cloud is, and –'

'But we know that, sir,' interrupted Ted, 'that's why we avoid –'

'Be quiet!' MacIntyre glared at him. 'I wanted to make the point about the shortcomings of the vic formation, to get this bunch thinking outside the conventions of normal RAF fighter doctrine. But you two decided not to play ball. You felt you had to try to score points, to show me that you're two pretty damn confident pilots, who know a thing or two about flying. I know you've both got confirmed kills to your names, and you can both obviously handle your aircraft nicely. One, or perhaps both, of you has excellent eyesight, a tremendous asset. But we're not a bunch of individuals here, we're a team. It's not about amassing personal scores, it's about defeating the enemy. Helping one another. I've no place for individuals here, or pilots who are overconfident and think they know it all. In my experience, overconfidence gets people killed.' He paused and eyed them both; his dark eyes seemed to bore into them. Archie guessed he was only in his mid-twenties, but somehow he appeared an age older.

'So,' he said, 'you play by my rules, not yours, all right? This squadron is in a mess. Morale is poor and no one knows what they're doing. God knows how much time we've got, but it isn't going to be much and there is a lot to do. I want you to help not hinder me, all right? Play ball, and we'll all get along just fine. Cross me, and I'll have you run out of this squadron before you can say bandit. And that's no idle threat. Clear?'

'Yes, sir.'

'Good. Now get going. Scram.'

Back out in the corridor, neither spoke until they were well clear of MacIntyre's office, then eventually Ted said, 'Well, that could have been worse.'

'I suppose so,' agreed Archie, 'although I can't say I enjoyed being threatened with the chop.'

Ted waved a hand impatiently. 'Just hot air. He's not going to sack us. He needs us. He said as much.'

'I get the impression he means what he says.'

'You worry too much, Archie. Come on, that's the end of it. We got a rap on the knuckles, but we kept our honour. I'd say that's a pretty fair exchange.' He slapped him lightly on the back. 'Let's forget about it.'

'All right,' said Archie. 'I'll try.'

*

Squadron Leader MacIntyre took out more pilots that morning, but not Ted or Archie. Then at midday, he called the entire squadron together in the Mess – both pilots and ground crew.

'I thought we were supposed to be at readiness,' Ted whispered to Archie.

Archie shrugged. 'I get the feeling the CO can fix things like that.'

The CO sat on the bar, twirling a snooker cue between his fingers while he waited for everyone to arrive. He had laid his cap down beside him, but as soon as everyone appeared to be there, he stood up and took off his jacket, very deliberately rolling up each of his shirtsleeves in turn. The massed gathering – some sixteen pilots and over thirty ground crew – watched this procedure in curious silence.

Then, still twirling the cue, MacIntyre began. 'I don't think I've ever come across a group of men so inadequately placed to be a front-line fighter squadron,' he told them. 'You're a miserable, ignorant bunch. I wanted all of you in here because bad morale seeps down from the very top to the very bottom, and, let's face it, you lot have hit rock bottom. Ten of you here are, according to what I've been told, experienced pilots, but you could have fooled me. You lost nearly half your number over Dunkirk, but you don't seem to have learned anything. Instead, you're moping about, feeling sorry for your mates who got the chop and waiting to be killed yourselves. As for the new pilots, I don't know what you've been taught, but you are quite simply not ready to fly in combat. If I sent you up against the Jerries today, I'd put a lot of money on not one of you coming back.'

There was a slight murmur from the back and one of the pilots coughed.

'Sorry, what was that?' said MacIntyre. 'Did someone say something?' Silence. 'If you've got anything to say,' he said, 'say it now, and we can go outside and fight it out. This is your last chance.' He looked around the room, staring at each of the pilots in turn. 'No? No one want to challenge me?' His eyes glared brightly, and his forearms flexed as he gripped the cue tightly with both hands. The room remained deathly quiet.

'Good,' he said. 'Right, first of all, let's talk about what's gone wrong, and if you want to say something, put up your hand. This is – was – an auxiliary squadron. Most of you know each other, you come from the same part of the world, and your mummies and daddies left you with enough money so you could indulge in a little bit of weekend flying. All jolly good fun, and you felt a bit superior and a bit elite and a bit above everyone else. Then the war comes along, so of course you want to do your bit and you sign on the dotted line and become full-time pilots. Everything carries on much as normal until Jerry decides it's time to liven things up a bit and you are suddenly a part of the action. But although you've all learned your six methods of attack, the reality is very different from the training. For starters, there's rarely one target, but lots, so which do you go for? Secondly, the target does not fly straight and level, but darts all over the place, so your perfect formation flying is suddenly completely useless. So you panic a bit and end up shooting at the nearest thing you see, following it as it dives out of your way and forgetting there might be any number of enemy planes behind you. How many of you who flew over Dunkirk followed a plane down?' A pause, the pilots looking at each other guiltily, then a reluctant show of hands.

'And why did you do that?' No one answered. 'I heard that

the last CO got himself shot down doing just that. Now I'm sure he was a fine fellow, but he left you lot in the lurch a bit, didn't he?' Again, no one answered. 'Follow your enemy down, and you immediately lose the crucial advantage of height and speed and are no longer any use in that particular sortie. Did it ever occur to any of you to sit down and talk about what happened over Dunkirk?' No answer. 'No,' said MacIntyre, 'I didn't think so.' He paced up and down the length of the bar, his cue still in his hands. 'Clearly, most of you know how to handle an aeroplane, but being a reasonable pilot does not make you a reasonable *fighter* pilot.'

He laid down his cue, then gave them a list of golden rules, much the same, Archie noted, as those Group Captain Tyler had given him and Ted a month earlier. They were, Archie now knew, good rules – crucial rules, in fact.

'And never, and I mean never,' repeated MacIntyre, 'follow a plane down. A quick burst of your guns, then get out of there. Another target will come along, believe me.

'So far, the Germans don't seem to want to come out and play, which is very fortunate for you. God knows how long we've got, but we need to work bloody hard right now. I don't care what anyone in the Air Ministry says, the standard command attacks are useless and a complete waste of time.' There was a murmur and turning of heads at this.

'Yes, yes, yes – I know the theory: the more of you that attack in one go, the bigger the punch – but it doesn't work like that. Surprise is everything in air fighting, so I want you all to forget you ever knew them. Second, you're all going to get your guns resynchronized. What have you got them set on at the moment? Four hundred and fifty yards, as prescribed by the Air Ministry?'

A few nods.

'No, sir,' said Ted. 'I've got mine at a hundred and fifty yards.'

MacIntyre nodded. 'That's more like it. No more than two hundred yards at any rate. Let me tell you this: your chances of shooting anything down at more than four hundred yards is slight. The .303 Browning is a pea-shooter. Our machines need cannons like Jerry has, but since we don't have them, we've got to make the best of what we've got. If you get in close, your bullets will be more effective and your target will be bigger and therefore twice as easy to shoot down. If they're more effective, you won't need to fire so many to do the job. And if you don't fire so many at one chap, you won't stay so long exposing yourself to being attacked in turn, and you'll have more bullets to shoot at another target. So from now on, synchronize your guns at between one hundred and fifty and two hundred yards. All right?' He looked around at them all. 'It's common sense, really.

'And another thing. We're going to get rid of tight vics. The Germans don't use them and they don't for a reason. You spend too much time concentrating on keeping a nice, tight formation and not enough on looking around the sky. So we're going to loosen up a bit, and fly at slightly different heights. Trust me, you'll much prefer this way.

'Right,' he said, clapping his hands together. 'We're going to train all day, every day, in flights and individually, and you're all going to learn very quickly, or else, I'm afraid, you're going to get yourselves killed. I'm sorry about your friends, but you must put their deaths to one side now. Feeling miserable about it won't help them and it certainly won't help you. And you, Winters, I don't want to see you wearing your Irvin again, all right? You can't possibly see behind you properly with that bloody great collar of fur. It's better to freeze your bollocks off than get a cannon shell up your arse.' Pip, picking a strand of tobacco from his mouth, glared back at the CO.

'Right,' said MacIntyre, whacking the cue on top of the bar, 'I want to see you lot liven up a bit. Where's your damn fighting spirit? Let's start thinking about avenging those dead colleagues, and making sure we can take on anything the Germans throw at us. Clear?' No one replied, so he said again, 'Clear?'

'Yes,' came the mumbled reply.

'What about being at readiness all the time, sir?' asked Mike Drummond.

'Forget about that,' said MacIntyre. 'I've sorted it. We're moving out of here soon, in any case. There's no point being at readiness if you lot aren't ready to take on the enemy. While there's nothing doing with the Luftwaffe, we're going to train. A much better use of our time than sitting on our arses at dispersal.'

Archie had felt buoyed up by MacIntyre's talk, just as he had had his confidence lifted by Group Captain Tyler's advice after that first sortie over Dunkirk. As the CO said, it was all common sense, really. For the next couple of days, they trained hard, just as MacIntyre had promised. Taking off, they would fly to between ten and fifteen thousand feet, then in turns make attacks, head on, from the side, from beneath, from above, from out of the sun – all against the CO, who manfully coped with the erratic performance of the rest of his pilots.

'Your neck should ache like hell,' MacIntyre told them. 'If it doesn't, you haven't been watching hard enough.'

Nor was it just the pilots who needed working on. Over in France, the CO had learned lessons the Air Ministry had not, and so ordered the ground crew to re-equip all their Spitfires with armour plating behind each of the pilots' seats and to somehow find a number of rear-view car mirrors which were to be bolted on to the outside of the canopy.

'You should have heard him,' Reynolds told Archie, Ted and some of the other pilots in the Mess. 'He said, "The ones we've been given are too small. No good to anyone." Well, Chiefy Butterworth scratched his head and said, "Where are we supposed to get them from, sir?" and the skipper says, "Use your imagination. A scrapyard for the armour plating and steal the mirrors." I mean, priceless, isn't it?'

'And Chiefy's got them, you know,' said Mike. 'They've started fixing them already.'

Reynolds chuckled. 'You can say what you like about him,' he said, 'but Mac's certainly changing things around here.'

'But why aren't we doing anything?' said Ted. 'Why are we waiting for the Luftwaffe? We should be going over there and shooting up these new airfields of theirs while there's a chance.'

'You can if you like, Ted,' said Colin Bishop, 'but I'm quite happy waiting. The longer Jerry leaves it, the better, as far as I'm concerned.'

'Hear, hear,' said Pip.

'I admire your zeal, Ted,' said Reynolds, 'but concentrate on training, eh? The Huns will be here soon enough, you know.'

But later, just as Archie was about to drop off to sleep, Ted said, 'I've got a plan.'

'What?' asked Archie.

'We fly over to the Pas de Calais and strafe a couple of Jerry airfields.'

'No, Ted,' said Archie.

'We could be over there at first light. Those Jerry fighter boys wouldn't know what's hit them.'

'No, Ted,' said Archie again.

'Well, I'm going. I'm going to do it.'

'Don't be ridiculous. We can't do that. If Mac finds out about it, he'll give us the chop.'

'He doesn't need to know about it. We'll get permission to go on an early morning practice flight. We'll only be gone an hour.'

Archie sat up. 'Please, Ted,' he said.

'Come on, Archie. It'd be easy. I know where they are. I saw a map of them in Pops' study. There's about six of them around Calais. We'll fly in low, strafe them to hell and fly back. We could knock out lots of Hun fighter planes, which means there'd be fewer to attack us with.'

'I'm not doing it,' said Archie. 'It's madness.'

'Fine,' said Ted. 'You stay. But I'm going.'

Archie let his head fall back on the pillow. *No,* he thought, *please, no*. Ted was his best friend, but he could be maddening. But, because he was his friend, Archie also knew he could not let him do this on his own. He would need someone to watch his back.

A sinking feeling swept over him. *Sleep,* he thought. *We need to get to sleep.* Perhaps by the morning, Ted would have changed his mind. But he was kidding himself. Once Ted got an idea into his head, he never changed his mind. Not ever . . .

15

CHANNEL DASH

Monday 24 June, around 8 p.m. The Chief of the Air Staff was out that night and so Group Captain Guy Tyler was having a drink with Wing Commander Fred Winterbotham, who headed up an air intelligence section within MI6. They were sitting in Tyler's office in King Charles II Street, both smoking, both clutching a tumbler of Scotch. Tyler had known Winterbotham for some years. He was tall, good-looking, charming and exceedingly clever. And a very useful friend.

'I'm afraid that I simply don't know,' said Winterbotham. 'Before the war I was given a number of tours around airfields and met a number of their squadrons, but I was never told details about an individual squadron's make-up.' Winterbotham had spent much time in Germany before the war, posing as a Nazi sympathizer. In reality, he'd been nothing more than a spy. 'One thing I do know, though,' he continued, 'is that Ernst Udet is no Beaverbrook. A lovely fellow, actually – for a Nazi – but he's a flier. He lives for planes and making jokes and having fun. He's all at sea in the cut-throat world of Nazi politics. Worst appointment Göring ever made. You want a businessman running the aircraft industry, not an airman.' He drew on his cigarette. 'And it's even more astonishing when one considers that Göring is in fact a far better businessman than an airman, even though he was a fighter ace in the last war.'

Tyler smiled. 'But if he's such a good businessman, why did Göring, as commander-in-chief of the Luftwaffe, appoint an old flying chum to head up such a critically important job as the procurement and production of new aircraft? Makes no sense.'

'Because he wants to be surrounded by yes-men. People he can trust. People who will do what he says. General Milch is actually rather competent and rather efficient and, as Göring's deputy, would have been a much better choice, but that would have made him too powerful. Göring doesn't want any threat to his authority.'

'Extraordinary.'

'That's what you get with a military dictatorship like the Nazis. Anyway, the long and short of it is that Udet's making an absolute balls-up of the Luftwaffe's production. Too many private firms and not enough big factories. That, at least, is in our favour.'

Tyler slid across his desk the latest production figures from Lord Beaverbrook's Ministry of Aircraft Production. 'Have a look at these.'

Winterbotham whistled. 'Over four hundred new and repaired aircraft last week. I'm impressed.'

'Sixty-one new Spitfires this last week alone.'

'Well, I can tell you this. Production of Me 109s is much, much lower. Less than half that.'

'Trouble is, they've got so many more aircraft than us at present.'

'But presumably with every day that passes, the gap is closing.'

'Gap? More like a giant chasm. But yes, I suppose so.' Tyler took a sip of his Scotch. 'This delay is incredible, though.'

'Hitler's sightseeing, you know,' said Winterbotham. 'Been to look at the Eiffel Tower.'

'I suppose now that France is out of the war, he wants to savour his victory. He'd be far better off turning on us without delay, though.'

Winterbotham smiled. 'I met him a few times, you know.'

'And was he mad?'

'Deranged is probably a better word.' Winterbotham held up his glass, as though examining the whisky. 'He's a continental man, though. He's read his history. Has a picture of that great warrior Frederick the Great of Prussia in his study. But it's land war that he's interested in, and his air force has been built to support the army, not to act independently. I think he's stalling because he doesn't really quite know what to do now. I suspect all his planning was for this great offensive he's just won. He probably never really considered having physically to conquer Britain.'

'Really? How else was he going to defeat us?'

'By routing our Army. If you're a continental man like Hitler, the army is everything. The navy and air force are merely extensions of that army. He would have thought that, with France out, we would sue for peace. But Winston has other ideas. "We shall never surrender!"' Winterbotham said, in what Tyler thought was a rather good impression of the prime minister. 'Hitler probably still hopes we're going to come to the peace table. And, of course, he's got to get his much-vaunted Luftwaffe ready.'

'They're certainly gradually moving up to the Channel coast,' said Tyler.

'This much I know is true, Guy,' said Winterbotham. 'If we can stop his Luftwaffe gaining air superiority over southern England, Hitler will never, ever be able to invade Britain. And if he doesn't, he'll lose the war.'

'Is that a wager?' asked Tyler.

'If you like. Put it this way, I'm prepared to bet any amount you care to name.'

Tyler smiled and raised his glass. 'So, win the forthcoming air battle and we win the war.'

Winterbotham laughed. 'That's the sum of it, Guy, yes.'

As Tyler was sitting chatting in his office, above London his son was flying a Spitfire, climbing high into the sky alongside Archie. For two days, they had trained as hard as anyone, and Ted, especially, had gone out of his way to be as obliging and conscientious as possible. Nor had there been any further mention of them making a raid on German airfields in the Pas de Calais. Archie had been pleasantly surprised.

They had taken to the air some ten minutes earlier to practise some dogfighting. The rest of the squadron had been stood down, but when Ted had suggested the practice flight, Mac had agreed. 'Keep it local, though, all right?' he'd told them.

As they continued to climb in an easterly direction, Archie looked out. There was London, the River Thames a silvery snake in the evening light. He could see Kent stretching away from them, and all the way down to Sussex and beyond to the sea.

'What about some dogfighting, then, Ted,' said Archie as they finally levelled out.

'A bit further,' Ted's voice crackled in his headset.

They flew on, over London and above north Kent.

'Um, this isn't very local, Ted,' said Archie.

'Perhaps a little further than usual,' said Ted. 'But it's useful to properly familiarize ourselves with this part of England, don't you think?'

Archie thought for a minute and then the penny dropped. *Of course,* he thought. How could he have ever thought Ted would forget about it?

'Ted,' he said now, 'are you thinking what I think you're thinking?'

There was silence for a moment, then Ted's voice crackled, 'Come on, Archie. We can really make a difference. A quick dash for it, under the radar, and give those Huns a bit of a dust-down.'

'Are you mad? If Mac finds out, we'll get the chop for this – and that's if we haven't already been shot down ourselves.'

'Rubbish. He was just trying to put the wind up us. Shoot up a load of Jerry kites and he'll be handing out DFCs.'

'This is madness. Absolute madness. No, Ted – I'm turning round.'

'Look, we're almost at Manston now. Fifteen minutes and we'll be there.'

'No,' said Archie, conscious that he was still flying on Ted's wing.

'Well, I'm going on. Turn round if you like. I'll go alone.'

'Ted, please. As your best friend. Let's turn round.'

'Go if you like, Archie – honestly, I don't mind.'

Archie cursed. He liked the CO. He liked what he was doing for the squadron and he absolutely did not want to be in trouble again. But on the other hand, he couldn't let Ted go on his own. How would he feel if he turned round now and then Ted got in trouble, or, worse, was killed? No, Ted needed someone to watch his back. With his right fist clenched, and gnashing his teeth in frustration, Archie flew on, agonizing over what to do. And they were losing height too. Without even properly realizing it, they had slipped five thousand feet. Archie looked out. Beneath him was Beachy Head and there was Dover away to his left. Now they were at just seven thousand feet and out over the sea.

'Blast you, Ted,' muttered Archie. 'If anything happens to us . . .'

Ted laughed. 'You'll thank me for it one day. Come on, Arch, it'll be great sport. We'll be heroes for pulling this one off.'

Archie kept silent. The sea twinkled beneath them like a burnished carpet. They were losing height rapidly now, so that as the French coast loomed, they were no more than a hundred feet off the water – dizzyingly close to the sea. A strong pocket of turbulence, a sneeze and a knock of the stick, and whoosh – it would all be over. Archie glanced at his dials. *Good – still plenty of fuel.* Everything else normal. His heart had begun to hammer in his chest and he felt a trickle of sweat run down the side of his face.

'OK, Archie, follow me. We go in just south of Calais. The sun's right behind us now. We'll switch our R/T off after this. Just follow me and when we spot a Jerry airfield, we shoot up anything we can see, all right? There might be some ack-ack, but we'll be too fast for them. Then we turn north out to sea and cut back again, following the Thames. OK?'

'Let's just get it over and done with,' said Archie.

'Roger, over and out.'

The coast was now less than a mile away. Archie took a deep breath. *Christ, what am I doing? Why am I tempting fate like this?* The coast hurtled towards them and then they roared over land, just fifty feet above the ground. Archie glanced over at Ted and saw him wave. He took another deep breath, his oxygen mask now hanging free from his face. Below, brown cows began stampeding in a field; a man on a bicycle stopped and looked up as they thundered overhead. *Dear God,* thought Archie, glancing at his dials. Three hundred and twenty miles an hour and they were virtually hedge-hopping. At this speed, it was hard to see much – they were over any landmarks almost before they could be recognized. Up ahead, a village – a church with a spire – but then they were past it. *We're over France,* he thought, and suddenly his fear had gone. Below were the enemy, but the speed they were flying at made him feel strangely invincible. He looked out either side – countryside hurtling by, the sharp, elliptical wings scything through the air. Just ahead of him, Ted climbed a little, then turned slightly to the left and Archie saw him pointing forward. With his thumb, he flicked the gun safety button off and kept his thumb hovering over the tit. Suddenly they were upon an airfield – nothing more than a hastily cleared field, by the look of it, but along one side were a line of 109s, all facing outwards.

Breathing in and out rapidly, he muttered out loud, 'OK, here goes.'

He opened fire, the airframe shuddering as the eight machine guns drummed out bullets. Tracer pumped flashes of orange light as they tore over the line of machines, bullets still pouring from his wings. Men below ran, an explosion to his right – *was that a bowser or a plane?* A glance in the mirror as a Messerschmitt collapsed, broken. Just ahead of him, Ted banked round the edge of the field towards another row of aircraft on the far side. And there was a bowser, Archie now saw – quite definitely a fuel truck. Again he opened fire, saw bullets spit along the ground in line with the truck and then, with a whoosh of angry, billowing flame, it exploded. Archie ducked his head, banked to the right and sped on, away over open fields. A quick glance back. There was another explosion and then another. Ack-ack was hurtling above him now, but it was high and harmless. Ted was on his port side, and Archie quickly looked across and then back as thick smoke began rising over the airfield. He blinked. *Christ, did we really just do that?* A few seconds – that was all – and then they were away, leaving wrecked aircraft, fire and mayhem. Perhaps Ted's idea hadn't been quite so hare-brained after all. *But we're not clear yet.*

Archie followed Ted as they turned for the coast, but then there ahead of them was a second airfield. *Another? So close?* Archie took another deep breath and hovered his thumb over the firing button. This time, most of the German fighters appeared to be better sheltered, parked against a wood that ran along one side of the field, but there were two aircraft which looked as though they were about to take off, taxiing around to the end of the field. Archie and Ted flew straight at them. The panicked German pilots hurriedly began to take off, but it was too late: in a couple of seconds, the Spitfires were upon them, opening fire, lines of tracer hitting the ground first and helping Archie and Ted get a bead on the enemy machines. Archie saw smoke and flame burst from both planes as their full fuel tanks were hit and ignited by the tracer. Then the Spitfires were past and there ahead was the sea. Enemy anti-aircraft fire opened up, but again the flak was too high and too late. Archie looked behind and saw slow tracer pumping into the air. A glance at the dials: fuel OK, oil pressure OK – everything OK. *Thank God*. Beneath them, the coast. A bit of boost – three hundred and forty miles per hour – the ground below a blur, and suddenly they were out over the sea, which twinkled benignly as the sun, like a huge orange, cast its evening glow across the water.

Archie followed Ted as they sped on over the English Channel, still at just a hundred feet above the waves, and only when they were several miles out to sea did Ted begin to climb once more.

'Everything OK?' asked Ted, finally breaking R/T silence. 'Didn't get hit at all, did you?'

'No, I'm fine,' Archie replied.

'And that's at least ten less 109s to worry about. Not bad going!' He whooped with excitement and joy. 'You can't tell me that wasn't exhilarating.'

'Let's just get back, Ted,' said Archie. His heart was still thumping in his chest, his mouth was as dry as sand, and he felt more alert and alive than he had ever been in his life, and yet he dreaded what faced them back at Northolt. Ted had not thought that part through at all, he knew. What were they going to do? Pretend they'd chased after an enemy intruder? Somehow hide the fact that the red patches covering their gun ports were shredded and that gun smoke had streaked back and stained their wings?

As they crossed over Kent, Archie hurriedly switched on his IFF – identification friend or foe – a transmitter that gave a distinct 'blip' and told those manning the radar and sector stations that his was a friendly not a hostile aircraft. He breathed out a heavy sigh of relief, glad that he had remembered in time, then they flew on, at around eight thousand feet, back over English soil once more. But as Kent slipped by and they neared London, so Archie's heart grew heavier and heavier. *What have we done?* he thought. He felt sick with dread.

16

FALL OUT

In the Mess that night, neither Archie nor Ted said a word about what they had done. Of course, it was obvious that they'd fired their guns, but Ted had told the others that they'd just been practising against patches of cloud, doing beam attacks and sharpening their deflection shooting. Archie said little. He hated lying, always had done, and he left early, muttering about having a headache and wanting an early night. But he knew the CO knew: he'd caught his eye at one point, and had looked away guiltily, but not before seeing the flexing cheek muscles of a man barely able to contain his anger. *Darn it, darn it,* he thought.

He struggled to sleep. He couldn't believe he had actually flown over to France and shot up those enemy aircraft. Had that really been him in that Spitfire, hurtling over the French coast at a hundred feet and more than three hundred miles an hour? *I must have been mad,* he said to himself again, for about the hundredth time. And then there was Mac. My God, but they were for it, no doubt about it. He clutched his hands to his head. *No, no, no!* He realized he was more terrified of facing the CO than he was of being confronted by a horde of enemy fighters.

Ted stumbled in an hour later.

'You see, I told you it would be fine. Mac didn't say a thing!'

'It's not fine, Ted. He knows.'

'Rubbish. He'd have hauled us in already if he did.'

'Ted, he knows. I saw his face and he was absolutely livid.'

'You're imagining it. Relax! We'll be fine. You'll see.'

Archie rolled over. What was the point of arguing? But he knew. He knew that Mac knew. And he also knew that, come the morning, they would be for it. Mac had threatened them with the chop and Archie was certain he would stick to his word.

A little while later, as he lay there, eyes wide open, staring at the dark wall and listening to Ted's light snoring, Archie could not remember ever having felt so miserable.

The following morning, things at first did not seem quite so bad, and, as they joined the others in the Mess for some breakfast, Archie wondered briefly whether perhaps they had got away with it after all. Perhaps – *perhaps* – Ted's boundless optimism had been justified.

Such fleeting hopes were soon dashed, however. As they were about to head down to dispersal, Reynolds came over, his face ashen, and said, 'The CO wants to see you in his office now, boys.'

They followed the adjutant in silence as they walked over to the main building, into the hallway, along the corridor and then stood in front of the CO's office. Reynolds looked at them, sighed, then said, 'Deep breath, chaps.'

'Thanks, Uncle,' said Ted.

Archie felt so nauseous he could not speak.

Then they were standing before Mac's desk as he sat there looking over a couple of sheets of paper. The morning sun poured through the window, illuminating the dust motes that swirled idly on the air. There was a smell of stale cigarette smoke and floor polish. Archie closed his eyes.

'I don't know which report to begin with,' said MacIntyre. 'Tell you what, let's start with this one. This is from the Hornchurch Sector reporting two lone Spitfires seen heading out over the Channel at 20.13 last night. Then here's another at 20.46 reporting the same two Spitfires flying back over the coast. They've identified them as being from this squadron by the radio chatter that was picked up.'

Beside him, Archie was conscious of Ted shifting his feet.

'Then there's a report from Air Intelligence in which German radio signals report six 109s destroyed and seven more damaged, plus a fuel truck destroyed and various buildings and other bits of equipment damaged at Coquelles and Calais Guines. On top of that, there are reconnaissance photographs from Medmenham taken first thing this morning that confirm that not inconsiderable damage was caused at both enemy airfields. Finally, there's a note to me from Air Vice-Marshal Park, AOC 11 Group. "Good work across the Channel – well done. But no more trips over the water. Reserve all strength for fight over our own soil."' The CO put the paper down, sighed, then rubbed his forehead, before turning to look at them once more.

'What you did was very brave and, fortunately for you, very successful, but also completely idiotic. If anything had gone wrong – *anything* – you would have had no chance of recovery. Not flying that low. We need every pilot we can get at the moment, and especially two like you who are damned good and know how to handle themselves. You pulled it off, but you might easily not have done. You might easily be dead, the pair of you. Last time I hauled you in here, I warned you that if you crossed me again I'd run you out of the squadron. I also warned you that I was not making an idle threat, and nor was I.' He paused and sighed again. 'You're the two best pilots in this squadron and I had hoped that you'd be the beating heart of 629 in the weeks and months to come. But I need to trust my pilots and I don't trust you. I can't – not any more. Not after what you did last night. You're still very young – kids, really – but you need to grow up, and grow up fast, or else you'll continue to be a danger to yourselves and a danger to those around you.'

'Sir, I'd like to say that it was all my idea,' stammered Ted. 'Pilot Officer Jackson was against the idea from the start and only came with me because he felt honour-bound to watch my tail.'

'Somehow, I can believe that,' said MacIntyre, 'but I'm afraid you're both being posted.'

'Please, sir,' said Ted.

'Sorry,' said MacIntyre. 'I did warn you. You've brought this on yourselves. I don't care how good you are as pilots, it's what's up here that counts.' He tapped the side of his head with his finger. 'Perhaps this will be the making of you both.' He passed over two envelopes. 'Here. Your postings. You're going to join 337 Squadron at Biggin Hill. Squadron Leader Berenson is an old friend of mine from Cranwell days. He's a good bloke.' He stood up and walked around his desk.

'You're not being put on a charge or anything like that. Your records are clean – this is a transfer to a front-line squadron – a squadron that also suffered over Dunkirk and which could use a couple of decent pilots like yourselves.'

'But, sir,' said Ted, 'aren't we needed here? If the squadron loses another two pilots –'

MacIntyre eyed him. 'We're moving to Middle Wallop in 10 Group. Today, as it happens. Much more action in 11 Group, Tyler, which will suit you down to the ground.' He gave them a lopsided smile and held out his hand. 'I wish you luck, fellers, and perhaps one day our paths will cross again.'

Once they had left MacIntyre's office, Archie brushed past Ted and walked on, partly because he did not want to see or speak to him, and partly because he could feel tears pricking at the corner of his eyes.

'Archie, Archie!' called Ted.

'Just keep away from me, Ted,' Archie replied.

Ted hurried up behind him and grabbed Archie's shoulder, but again he brushed him off. 'I'm so sorry,' said Ted, 'really I am. I never thought for a moment that Mac would give us the chop.'

'Why didn't you, Ted? Why the hell not? He said he would. You only have to look at him to know he means what he says. Why the hell d'you think I was so against it? Because I knew this was what would happen.' He strode on, out of the main building and towards the Mess, conscious that Ted was still following. He wished he could be on his own for a bit, that he could get away from Ted, but they both had to pack their things; there was no avoiding it.

Archie could hardly bear to look at him. He had never felt so angry with another person before. The humiliation. The shame! Apart from that one time he'd been caned, he had never really been in trouble. It wasn't in his nature, and now this . . . Given the chop from the squadron he considered to be something of a second home.

'Archie, please,' said Ted, sitting dejectedly on the bed. 'I honestly never thought this would happen, really I didn't.'

'Then you're more stupid than I thought,' snapped Archie.

'Look on the bright side, at least we won't have Mac breathing down our neck any more. And at least we'll still be flying Spitfires. I know 337 aren't on Hurricanes.'

'I like Mac,' said Archie. 'He's a good CO who knows his stuff. And I like 629 Squadron. I was proud to be part of it. To be in the City of Durham Squadron.'

'But 337 Squadron is a permanent squadron in the RAF, Archie – it's got real fliers in it, Cranwell boys, probably. 629 Squadron has been good for us, I agree, but Mac was right, it's full of weekend fliers. In a way, going to 337 Squadron will be a step up.'

Archie turned on Ted. 'No, it isn't, Ted! We've just been given the chop! I was happy about moving to Middle Wallop – but Biggin Hill! We'll be in the front line there all right.'

'Good – then we can bag a few more.' Ted opened the posting letter Mac had given him. 'We're not expected until tomorrow. What shall we do? Go and see my people?'

'I don't know, Ted,' said Archie, closing his case. 'You go. I think I want to be on my own for a bit. I might book into the RAF Club.'

'Oh, come on, Archie, don't be like that. All right, I admit it, I'm sorry to be saying goodbye to 629, but it's not the same squadron any more anyway. Fitz has gone, Dix, Will, Dennis and the others. Mac might know his stuff, but he's hardly the spirit of 629 Squadron, is he?' He looked at Archie. 'Anyway, I think we should be given a pat on the back for taking out all those Jerry machines, not given the damned chop. If that's Mac's attitude, then personally, I'm glad we're being posted.'

'I'm going to say goodbye to the others, Ted,' said Archie. 'I'll see you at Biggin tomorrow.'

'What? Don't I even get a lift into town? Come on, Archie, what's got into you?'

Archie sighed and picked up his case. 'I'll see you tomorrow,' he said.

'Well, fine, then. Be like that,' said Ted. 'I thought we were friends.'

'It's because we're friends that I followed you to France, Ted,' said Archie, opening the door. 'I've been given the chop because of being friends with you.'

'I told you to go back. I never made you come.'

'Don't be ridiculous. You know perfectly well I wasn't going to let you go on your own.'

'I would have been fine. You came because you wanted to. And anyway, where would you be now if it wasn't for me? You might not even be a fighter pilot. Don't forget it was because of me that you joined 629 Squadron in the first place.'

Archie glared at Ted, then shut the door and walked away down the corridor. He had never felt more miserable in his life.

The others wished him well, said they were sorry he and Ted were leaving, and promised they would all meet up again one day soon. For the second time that day, Archie thought he might cry, which would have made the situation worse, so he tried to speak as little as possible, just shaking their hands and mumbling 'Good luck' to them all.

Soon after, he was speeding down the Western Road towards the centre of London, his flying helmet and goggles on his head, wearing his Irvin and flying boots, with his case strapped to the back of the Norton. He cursed Ted. It was not true – he had gone because he knew he couldn't let Ted go on his own. If anything had happened to him, he would never have forgiven himself. And, yes, it was true that Ted had helped get him into 629 Squadron, but that didn't mean he was indebted to him for ever more – and certainly not now. Not after Ted had got him the chop! The chop! Sent away from the squadron! He still couldn't quite believe it had happened. After Dunkirk, he and Ted had been the top scorers in the squadron, the golden boys. Now they had been thrown out in disgrace – and it was disgrace, no matter how Mac liked to paint it.

There was a spare room at the club, even though it was a little more than Archie would have liked to spend for a night's board and lodging. And having reached his room and put down his case, he suddenly felt at a loss as to what to do. Perhaps a sleep, he told himself – God only knew, he hadn't slept much the night before. Taking off his flying boots and jacket, he lay down on the bed, arms behind his head, and closed his eyes. Sleep, however, eluded him, and it suddenly occurred to him that perhaps he didn't want to be on his own after all. Perhaps he'd been too hard on Ted. Perhaps his friend had had a point. He had definitely not wanted to make that Channel dash, and had certainly only done so because of his loyalty to Ted, and yet, if he were being truthful, he had found it an exhilarating experience. All those machines knocked out! It had been quite something. He could see why Mac had felt he had no choice, but perhaps he could have given them another chance. Now that he thought about it, he didn't see why he had been sacked too – not after what Ted had said – and yet the squadron would most certainly not have been the same without him. He rolled on to his side and wondered whether perhaps he'd spoken too hastily earlier. He had thought he wanted to get away from his friend, not to see him for a while, but now that his anger had started to cool, he wished he had gone to the Tyler home in Pimlico. *What am I going to do until tomorrow?* he wondered.

Perhaps he would go down to Biggin straight away, but, then again, he had his room at the club now. He wondered whether maybe he should ring Ted and possibly try to patch things up. But maybe it was a bit *too* soon for that; he would see him tomorrow. They could resolve their differences then.

Suddenly he had an idea. Sitting up again, he unpacked his black shoes then headed downstairs to the phone booth. Lifting the receiver, he was put through to an operator.

'Yes, hello,' he said, 'please could I have Whitehall 921.'

'It'll be a few minutes,' said the operator. 'Are you willing to wait?'

'Yes.'

Archie stood there in the wooden booth, drumming his fingers. Several minutes passed, but then a voice said, 'Putting you through now.'

He heard a click, then a ringing tone and eventually a voice said, 'Hello?'

'Is that you, Tess?'

'Yes, who is – oh, Archie, it's you!'

'Yes, and I'm in town. I was wondering, would you let me

take you out to dinner tonight? Are you free?' He had his fingers crossed, praying.

'Archie, yes, I am, and I'd love to. Where shall I meet you?'

Yes! he thought, then said, 'I can come and find you.'

'No, I'll come to you. Are you with Ted?'

'Er, no – no, I'm not. I'll explain later. How about the RAF Club, then?'

'Perfect. I'll be there about seven-thirty.'

Archie said goodbye and rang off. Already, he could feel his spirits rising.

After all, it turned out to be quite a good afternoon. He wandered up Piccadilly, then went to see a film – *His Girl Friday,* starring Cary Grant and Rosalind Russell – which made him laugh and did much to take his mind off things. Then he went to Foyles and bought a couple of paperbacks – an Agatha Christie and a Jeffery Farnol, both of which he hoped would be a good distraction, then ambled back to the club. There he had a cup of tea in the library and started his Poirot novel. Then a good soak in the bath and a quick walk in Green Park across the way, and then it was almost seven-thirty. Life did not seem quite so bad, after all.

And it improved dramatically when he saw Tess bound up the steps and come through the revolving door into the hallway. Her face lit up when she saw him, and she hurried over and kissed him lightly on the cheek.

'Hello.' She smiled. 'What a treat!'

'Gosh!' said Archie. 'You look – you look lovely, Tess.' He could feel himself blushing. She was wearing her WAAF uniform, and it showed off her trim figure, while her face looked more beautiful than ever. She clutched his arm.

'So where are we going?'

'The Criterion.'

She laughed. 'Very spoiling! That sounds wonderful, Archie.'

She held on to his arm as they ambled slowly back up Piccadilly. Archie had undone the top button of his tunic – the unofficial mark of a fighter pilot – and walked with his back just that little bit straighter. He was conscious that a number of passers-by seemed to notice them – a young, handsome couple, he with his wings and cap at a jaunty angle, she a bright and really rather beautiful young WAAF. His anguish and humiliation of earlier seemed to be melting away.

'So have you been given some leave at long last?' she asked.

'In a manner of speaking.'

'And Ted?'

'Yes, Ted too.'

'Then why are you paying for a room at the club? You know you're always welcome in Winchester Street.'

Archie looked down. 'It's a little complicated,' he said.

She looked up at him. 'Try me.'

'I'll tell you in a while,' he said. 'First I want to know who you've seen at the Air Ministry. Has the PM been in again?'

'No, but I did see Anthony Eden the other day. He's terribly tall and good-looking.' She talked on and then they had reached Eros at Piccadilly Circus, although they could not see the statue at all as it was boarded up, with sandbags around the base.

At the door of the Criterion Archie paused to let Tess go first, then took a deep breath and followed. He had never been to a restaurant as smart as this. Mac had told him and Ted they needed to grow up; well, he felt more grown-up already, taking a girl to dinner somewhere as smart as this. He glanced up at the ceiling, a dazzling mosaic of shimmering golds and blues, and then they were being ushered to their table.

A waiter gently eased Tess's chair in as she sat down. Starched white cotton napkins were draped across their laps and he was handed a wine list. Archie looked down the list. He liked wine, but had rarely drunk it; certainly, he knew nothing about it. *Which to go for?* He suddenly remembered the film he had seen earlier. Cary Grant had ordered two glasses of champagne and then asked, casually, what the waiter recommended.

'Hm,' he said, in what he hoped was a nonchalant manner. 'Two glasses of champagne, please, and which red would you recommend?'

'It all depends on what you are going to eat, sir.'

Archie was stumped by this. 'I tell you what,' he said, 'we'll come back to the wine when we've had a look at the menu.'

The waiter bowed graciously and glided off.

'Champagne! What a treat,' said Tess. 'I wonder how much longer we'll be able to drink it.'

'I just thought we should. It's not every day I have the chance to take you out to dinner.'

'I know,' said Tess, leaning towards him conspiratorially, 'but the Criterion is terribly grand. I've only been here once before, and that was for Pops' last promotion. I do hope this won't clean you out.'

Archie smiled. 'I have to admit the Air Ministry don't exactly pay well, but I've not had much cause to spend it, really. My Mess bill didn't amount to much, all things considered. Anyway, I've never been here before and I'd rather spend what money I have when I can. And on someone I want to spend it on.' He felt himself redden again and looked down, worried he had been overly forward, but Tess smiled at him and took his hand and gave it a squeeze.

'Well, thank you, Archie. It's lovely to see you. Lovely to have you to myself for once.'

They were silent a moment. Archie could feel his heart thumping. Was this dating? Was Tess now his girl? The waiter arrived with the champagne and two menus.

Tess raised her glass and gently chinked it against his. 'So, tell me,' she said. 'What has happened? Is Ted in trouble?'

'Why, is he usually?'

Tess rolled her eyes. 'Always! Haven't you discovered that yet? He was expelled from two schools, you know.'

'Two? He kept that pretty quiet.'

'Mama and Pops despaired of him, but then Pops offered to get him flying lessons if he promised not to get in any more trouble, and so he knuckled down for a bit and even got a place at university. He's older now, so he gets away with things. I'm amazed he didn't get thrown out of flying training, but then he does really love flying.'

'We got the chop,' Archie said suddenly.

'What do you mean?' Tess looked aghast.

'We've been posted to a new squadron – at Biggin Hill.'

'That's a sector station south of London – in Kent,' said Tess.

'I know. 629 Squadron have been posted to Middle Wallop.'

Tess put a hand to her mouth. 'What on earth happened?'

Archie told her – about the arrival of Mac, of the trick he and Ted had played on his first day, and then the trip to France and the shooting up of the German airfields.

'I should have talked him out of it,' he said. 'I did try, but – well . . .'

'He wouldn't listen,' said Tess. 'That's Ted all over. He doesn't listen. Or rather, he only listens to one person – himself.'

'I thought I couldn't let him go over there on his own,' said Archie. 'Actually, I think he would have been fine. After all, one Spitfire is a smaller target than two. He says I went because deep down I wanted to.'

'And did you?'

'No, I didn't, but I will admit it was quite a thrill.'

'But reckless and stupid.'

'Yes.'

'If Pops ever finds out, he'll be absolutely livid,' said Tess.

'I suspect he will find out,' said Archie. 'The intelligence bods picked up a German signal about it. They lost quite a lot of aircraft. Anyway, I was just so furious with him this morning and we had a huge row. I said I didn't want to see him until we're due to report at Biggin tomorrow and that he could make his own way into town.'

Tess laughed. 'Oh, dear. Well, it sounds to me as though he deserved everything you said. I do love my brother very much, but I know he can be awfully pig-headed at times.'

'I don't know why he was so eager to beat up those Jerry airfields, though. He's got three confirmed kills already and everyone in the squadron knows he's the best pilot. He doesn't need to prove anything.'

Tess looked thoughtful. 'I think partly it's just who he is, but it's also because of Pops.'

'He was a very successful ace in the last war, I know.'

'And we both knew that when we were little and growing up.

Not from Pops – he would talk about flying, but not about fighting in the war. It was from other people – people in the RAF we would meet. They were always saying, "Your daddy is a very brave man, you know," or, "Your daddy's a very important flying ace," or suchlike. I suppose Ted wants to live up to that. And now here we are in another war and you and Ted are the next generation of fighter pilots.'

Archie sat in thoughtful silence for a moment. 'I should make up with him. Tomorrow, when we get to Biggin. He's been a very good friend. The best friend I ever had.'

'But maddening at times too.'

Archie grinned. 'I could have brained him this morning.'

She took his hand again. 'And he's been very sweet about us. Not at all jealous and possessive.'

Us, thought Archie. *She said us.* Emboldened, he took his other hand and placed it on top of hers, and she made no motion at all to move it.

Later, after dinner, they walked hand in hand back down Piccadilly and across Green Park. There was a large moon and the sky was so clear that, despite the blackout, they could see quite clearly.

'Before the war, you could never see the stars in London,' Tess said.

'Why not?' said Archie.

'I suppose there were too many lights on. But now, look. I think I prefer it this way.' She squeezed his hand. 'What a time to be alive. Will you write to me still? From Biggin?'

'Of course.' He stopped as they reached the Mall. Buckingham Palace, huge and still, stood dark against the sky. Tess turned to look at him. Archie's heart began thumping again, his mind wracked by teenage uncertainty and nerves that had been stifled by his responsibilities in the war. All of a sudden being behind the controls of a Spitfire seemed like a less daunting place to be.

But Tess gave him a shy smile that was so lovely it felt silly to be nervous. And so, bold as brass, he leaned down and kissed her. Standing there, on the edge of the park, with the palace behind him and the stars overhead, and not a soul but the two of them anywhere to be seen, Archie understood what a wonderful, magical thing life could be.

17

337 SQUADRON

Wednesday 26 June. Although Archie had walked Tess home the night before, he had purposely not gone in, and so it was not until the following day, at RAF Biggin Hill, that he saw Ted once more. It was an overcast day with the threat of rain, and Archie was relieved to reach Biggin before the inevitable downpour came.

He was met at the main gates, then directed to the Mess, a handsome brick building tucked away from the main airfield behind a row of horse chestnuts. There he was met by the squadron adjutant, Flight Lieutenant Wheeler, a small, trim man in his thirties, noticeably younger than Reynolds, but still too old to be flying operationally. However, he told Archie that he had joined the RAF as a pilot and, during his time, had flown in Iraq and India. 'But biplanes – dope and wood and canvas and not much more.' He smiled wistfully. 'Oh, to have been given the chance to fly the kites you chaps have now.'

Archie was given a room to himself in a wing of the Mess, then taken down to the bar.

'We'll just wait for Pilot Officer Tyler to arrive,' Wheeler said, 'then I'll take you to see the skipper.' He raised his glass.

'Cheers. Good to have you on board. Actually, we were rather expecting you to come down together.'

'Oh,' said Archie. 'I'm afraid we went our separate ways yesterday after leaving Northolt.'

'Fair enough. But he's coming by bus, and they can be a little unreliable.'

Archie cursed to himself. *I should have called him this morning*, he thought. The anger he had felt towards Ted had melted away overnight. It still hurt to think they were no longer a part of 629, but his friendship with Ted, he realized, was worth much more to him than belonging to the squadron. After that first sortie over Dunkirk, he had vowed to live for the present. What was the point of bearing grudges? It was not in his nature, in any case. Ted was his best friend; what had happened had happened. At least they were still together. At least they were still on Spitfires. And, actually, perhaps Ted had had a point about Mac – perhaps he had overreacted. No one had been hurt, no aircraft even damaged. That raid had been pretty damn successful. Having thought about it, Archie realized that if he felt any resentment at all, it was towards Mac and not Ted.

Wheeler drained his glass, then looked at his watch. 'Look here,' he said, 'are you all right sitting tight for a little bit? I've got a couple of things to sort out. When Tyler gets here, I'll come and fetch you and take you to see the skip.'

It was nearly forty minutes later, at around 1.20 p.m., that Wheeler reappeared with Ted in tow looking damp from the rain that was now falling.

'Ah, good!' said Wheeler. 'Still here, then. Look who I found, albeit a little on the wet side.'

Archie smiled at Ted but received a scowl in return. 'Hello, Ted,' he said, 'how are you?'

'I'd be a lot better if I hadn't spent half the day getting here.'

Archie held out his hand, but Ted turned away. *Oh, no,* thought Archie. It hadn't occurred to him that Ted might be smarting at *him*. And had Wheeler noticed? He hoped not.

'Follow me,' said Wheeler.

They went out of the Mess and clambered into Wheeler's car, the adjutant chatting affably, Archie and Ted sitting in silence. They drove down a tree-lined track and past a cluster of low brick buildings. Beyond was a large hangar.

'South Camp Belfast Hangar,' said Wheeler. 'We had great excitement here yesterday. The king made a visit. He was awarding gongs to a number of the chaps. There are three squadrons here – 32 and 79, which are Hurricanes, and us in Spits. Our skipper got a DFC and so did Charlie Bannerman. He's B Flight Commander.'

'So that's why we were told not to arrive until today,' said Archie.

'Exactly. There was nothing doing while HM was here.'

'And what did you make of him? The king, I mean?'

'He was charming. Everyone bangs on about his stammer, but he spoke jolly well, I thought. All the chaps were frightfully bucked at his coming here, at any rate.'

They drove past another large hangar, then around the north perimeter. 'Our chaps are down here,' he said. Archie saw a number of Spitfires lined up, and others parked in protective pens – grass mounds built up around them – then Wheeler stopped beside a long, wooden hut. 'Here we are,' he said. 'And, right on cue, it's stopped raining.'

They clambered out, and stepped into the hut. There were windows all along the front, while the walls were lined with an odd assortment of tables and chairs, models of aircraft, radios and a mass of clutter. There was a stove, a number of old armchairs and on the walls were recognition charts and other posters. The pilots were all there – some sleeping, others reading, several playing cards, others writing letters. It was much like the dispersal hut at Northolt.

A tall, blond-haired man with a square chin and slightly bent nose jumped up and came over to them.

'Ah, the strafers!' he said, extending his hand. 'Welcome to 337 Squadron. I'm Jock Berenson, the CO. We're jolly glad to have you.'

Archie and Ted introduced themselves, then Berenson looked around, waving an outstretched hand. 'There are the chaps. A pretty useless bunch, to be honest.'

'Steady on, Skip,' said one, a wide-faced lad with a thick head of ginger hair. He pushed himself up out of his armchair. 'Hello,' he said. 'I'm Donald Clancy, but everyone calls me Ginger. You'd never guess, would you?' He grinned amiably.

Others were getting to their feet now.

'Charlie DFC!' called out Berenson. A good-looking man, almost as tall as the CO, with long, dark hair slicked back off his brow, got to his feet, a smile rising from one corner of his mouth. 'How d'you do? Charlie Bannerman.'

'Charlie's going to be your flight commander in B Flight, Archie. And where's Ivo?'

'Here, Skip,' said a tousle-haired young man. 'Sorry,' he said, rubbing his eyes and yawning. 'You caught me catnapping. Hello – I'm Ivo Rainsby.'

'Ted, you're with Ivo in A Flight. All right?' He introduced them to the others – young men much like any other bunch of young men in any fighter squadron, Archie supposed. One was called Dougal Macfarlane, a pale-faced lad with fair hair and a mild Scottish accent.

'Where are you from?' asked Archie.

'He's a Highlander, aren't you, Dougal?' said Bannerman. 'Another B Flight man.'

'Braemar,' said Dougal. 'And you?'

'Near Pitlochry.'

'You don't say!'

Already Archie felt himself begin to relax. This lot seemed friendly enough, he thought, although he wished he could have a chance to speak to Ted. They had barely spoken yet.

'So,' said Berenson. 'What's all this about shooting up two Jerry airfields the other day?'

Ted shrugged. 'It just seemed like the right thing to do at the time,' he said. 'We were sitting around doing very little and Jerry's bringing all his fighters up to the Pas de Calais, so rather than wait for them to buzz over here, I thought it might be a good idea to go and knock out a few before they had the chance to do the same to us. Unfortunately, our CO didn't quite see it that way.'

'His loss is our gain.' Ginger grinned.

'So what height did you go in at?' asked Berenson.

'About a hundred feet, maybe a bit under.'

'And any ack-ack?'

'A bit,' said Ted. 'But it took them by surprise and their aim was too high. We got back without a scratch.'

Berenson laughed. 'I've known old Mac a good long time.

He's always been a stickler. I mean, I like to think we keep a pretty tight ship here, and maybe if you'd done that on my watch, I might have been a bit binding too, but – well, it was a brave thing to do, at any rate.' He glanced out of the window. 'It's brightening a bit. Let's have a chat outside, and I can introduce you to Chief White, who's in charge of ground crew and all our kites. He's first class. All the erks are, actually.'

Archie and Ted followed him out.

'Look,' he said. 'Personally, I think Mac was mad to give you two the chop, but, having said that, I don't want you tearing off on your own either, is that clear?'

They both nodded.

'I'm not a stickler,' Berenson added. 'I run a pretty easy-going show, but I have to trust my chaps. I'm going to trust you too. Don't let me down, will you?'

'No, sir,' said Ted and Archie together.

'And you can forget the "sir". It's Jock, all right? Although most people call me Skipper.' He patted them both on their backs. 'Good. Glad that's all clear. I'll get you up in the air as soon as possible. It's mainly convoy patrols and X raids at the moment – dashing off after false alarms – but I think everyone senses it won't last for much longer. And I'm afraid, when the balloon really goes up, we're going to be in the thick of it.'

Archie was allocated OK-Z and, with it, a fitter and rigger.

'She's a nice one, sir,' said Corporal Bufton, his fitter. 'Three-blade variable-speed propeller – we've just been fitting them all this past week – and armour plating behind the seat.'

'Good,' said Archie, thinking of the battered two-speed Spitfire he'd taken on after Dunkirk. 'She looks gleaming.'

'Straight off the production line, this one, sir,' said Leading Aircraftsman Lewis. 'Was only flown in a couple of days ago.'

Archie grinned. 'Wonderful!'

''Scuse me for asking, sir,' said Bufton, 'but is it true you got the chop from your last squadron for beating up a couple of Jerry airfields?'

'Er, yes, it is.'

'Well, I think that's bonkers, sir. Should have given you a gong, if you ask me. An' you've seen a bit of action over Dunkirk?'

'A little bit. I've not had that much experience.'

'Got any kills, sir?' asked Lewis. 'Apart from the ones you strafed, I mean?'

'I, er, I've got four confirmed.'

Bufton grinned. 'We'll mark 'em up, then, sir.'

'You'll what?' asked Archie, perplexed.

'We like to paint little swastikas by the cockpit, sir. Just a bit of fun. We do it for all the pilots, sir.'

'Well, as long as it's normal practice,' said Archie. 'I wouldn't want anyone thinking I was shooting a line.'

Archie left them, his spirits rising further, then saw Ted walking towards him.

'At last,' said Archie. 'I've been wanting to talk to you ever since we arrived.'

'And I've been wanting to talk to you,' snapped Ted. 'You've got a nerve!'

'What?' said Archie. 'What do you mean?'

'Saying you wanted to be on your own, then spending the evening with Tess! And then – and then! – binding to her about me. I can't believe you'd be so disloyal!'

'Disloyal? What are you talking about? How have I been disloyal? And I didn't bind about you to Tess.'

'I stuck up for you yesterday, didn't I? Told MacIntyre that it was my fault? I said I was sorry until I was blue in the face, and then I find you've been talking to my sister about me behind my back. I've had a hell of a journey down here as well, nearly got soaked to the skin, and then you bounce up all cheery, as though everything is fine and dandy. Well, it's not.'

'I wanted to say sorry,' said Archie. 'I was upset yesterday. I'm not really any more.'

Ted grunted and walked on.

'Come on, Ted. We're supposed to be friends. I don't want us to fall out. I'm sorry I overreacted, really I am.'

'"Supposed" is the word. And what's going on with you and Tess?'

'What do you mean? You knew we were keen on each other.'

'I didn't mind you writing the odd letter and I didn't mind having her tag along when we were in town, but you were supposed to be *my* friend.'

'And I still am. Ted, this is ridiculous.'

'Am I? Am I, Archie?' he said, turning on him. 'Because the way I look at it, I'm not sure I am. Not any more.'

18

ATTACK ON DOVER

Friday 19 July, around 8 a.m. B Flight was flying at around eighteen thousand feet over the English Channel – two vics of three, Archie leading Green Section, widely spaced apart. Down below he could see an east-coast convoy turning into the beginning of the Thames estuary – eight colliers, tramp steamers, black smoke chugging from their funnels, a small white wake following them. Merriman, the IO, had told them that coal was the lifeblood of the nation. 'If we don't have coal,' he had explained a few days earlier, 'we can't fire the power stations, and if we can't fire the power stations, we won't have any electricity, and if we don't have any electricity, we won't have any factories.'

'Yes, all right, Happy,' Charlie had said, 'we get the picture: no factories, no Spitfires, no Hurricanes, no nothing.'

Large-scale convoys – those bringing food and fuel and other supplies across the Atlantic – had stopped using the east-coast route already, but for the colliers there was no choice – they had to reach London – and it was partly Fighter Command's job to protect them by flying endless patrols overhead. My God, though, it was boring – and Archie was not alone in thinking so: they all did. Grousing about convoy patrols was becoming one of the main activities at dispersal. Every day it was the same: up at first light, fly a patrol, land at Manston, stay there all day, fly a second patrol later and then head back to Biggin at dusk. Once, B Flight had been on patrol and had been vectored towards a lone Dornier 17, but they had lost it in cloud. Otherwise, Archie had not seen a single enemy aircraft since joining 337 Squadron. Not one! Meanwhile, he had heard from Pip Winters that 629 Squadron had had repeated tussles with the enemy high above Southampton and Portland.

'Clover, this is Bison,' he heard Charlie say over the R/T to the ground controller at Manston. 'There's nothing to report. We're heading back to base.'

Archie looked around, craning his neck, but there was nothing, and so, following Charlie's lead, he led Green Section back down in a gradual dive over the north Kent coast. Fifteen minutes later, they landed.

As Archie reached dispersal, Ted looked up. He was sitting outside in the sun, flicking a pack of cards into an upturned Tommy helmet.

'How was it?' he asked.

'Nothing doing,' Archie replied.

Ted nodded and went back to throwing his cards.

It had been like this for the past three weeks: the two of them barely talking to one another – the odd word here and there, a shared conversation in the Mess, but, on the whole, they avoided one another. Archie had felt saddened by this sudden estrangement from his friend, then angered, then saddened again and finally, a kind of resignation had settled over him. He had become pals with Dougal and Charlie and a Canadian in B Flight called Mick Donnelly, and he had reached the point where he wondered whether he and Ted could ever be good friends again, even if they had wanted to be.

'He'll come round,' Tess told him. 'He can be a moody so-and-so. He once didn't talk to me for almost the entire summer holidays.'

'Why?' Archie had asked. 'What did you do?'

'I think I told on him about something to Mama and Pops. I must have been twelve at the time. There's a brooding side to Ted, you know. Always has been.'

Archie had never realized that. He missed their friendship – Ted had always made him laugh – but there was a coolness between them now, an iciness that would not thaw.

The same day, 12.20 p.m. Suddenly some action. In the dispersal hut, the telephone rang, the orderly answered and then there was shouting, 'Squadron, scramble!' and ringing of a handbell. Cards were thrown on the ground, books dropped, cigarettes flicked away as both flights hurriedly got to their feet and ran towards their Spitfires.

Engines were already starting up, and, as Archie reached his, he saw Bufton clamber out of the cockpit. 'She's all ready for you, sir,' he said as Archie grabbed his parachute pack from the wing. Fumbling fingers brought the straps over his shoulders and between his legs and clicked them together, then he was clambering on to the wing, the paintwork not quite so pristine now, rather chipped and flaked. In less than a minute Archie had strapped himself in, plugged in his leads and given the thumbs up to Lewis, who hastily pulled away the chocks. Release the brakes, push the throttle forward a little and then he was moving, taxiing towards the edge of North Field.

A Flight took off first, then Blue Section and then Green. With Mick on his port side and Geoff Williams, one of the sergeant pilots, on his starboard, Archie opened the throttle and followed Blue Section, and, moments later, they were airborne, their shadows below growing smaller and smaller as they rose higher into the air.

Jock's voice over the R/T: 'Clover, this is Bison. Squadron airborne.'

'Roger, Bison,' came the reassuringly calm voice of the ground controller. 'Proceed zero one five, angels fifteen. Bandits, thirty plus. Big jobs attacking Dover, keep a look out for snappers, over.'

'Roger, Clover.' Silence, a crackle of static, then, 'OK, chaps, eyes peeled.'

They were out to sea already, Blue Section two hundred yards ahead. Below, the tip of Kent was disappearing. A glance at his altimeter – climbing steadily. Archie glanced south, towards Dover, and saw smoke rising from around the port. *Damn it,* he thought to himself, *they're there already.*

Geoff was now on the R/T. There was something wrong with his oxygen; he was turning back. Archie watched him peel off and head home, then looked to his left and saw Mick, who waved. *Don't worry – I'm still right here.*

Archie felt his heart quicken. It had been a while since he had been in action, but now the blood was pumping once more. The sky was particularly bright, the sun high above them as they continued their climb, glaring off the perspex of the canopy and off the cowling in front of him. *Where the hell are those Mes?* he wondered. They could be bounced by them at any moment. He craned his neck and tried to scan the blue expanse above him, but it was almost impossible, even with his goggles. *Please don't attack out of that,* he thought. Then, up ahead, a small layer of cloud. He watched Blue Section fly into it, and he and Mick soon followed, bursting through the other side and then levelling out.

They were now around five miles to the east of Dover. Tiny dark puffs of smoke littered the sky above the harbour, where flak was bursting. Archie scanned the skies again and then spotted them, a group of some fifteen Me 110s, and a couple of thousand feet above them about twenty Me 109s, all protecting a group of Stukas diving on Dover. He could see them quite clearly – yes, there were the dive-bombers hurtling down towards several ships in the harbour. Huge columns of spray were erupting into the air.

The squadron was now circling, making sure it was up-sun, and then he heard Jock say, 'All right, tally ho! Go for the fighters.'

A deep breath, an involuntary shiver, and Archie dropped a wing and dived after the others. Below, a squadron of Hurricanes, some three thousand feet beneath them, were tearing into the Me 110s. Immediately, the twin-engine German fighters split up as a large number of individual battles began. Now the 109s were diving in among them too.

My God, thought Archie, grimacing as his Spitfire hurtled down towards the melee. Aircraft swirled all over the sky. One plane – he couldn't tell what – plunged towards the sea, trailing smoke. Another exploded mid-air.

Archie felt his airframe shake. Three hundred and fifty, three seventy-five, four hundred. *Four hundred and ten miles per hour.* To the left of the mass of aircraft he spotted a lone 109, turning – *Back to France, or preparing to make another attack?*

– he couldn't tell. *Stay there, stay there.* The Messerschmitt banked lazily, back towards the fray. It still hadn't seen the Spitfires diving out of the sun. 'Come on, come on,' muttered Archie, flicking his gun button to fire. Thumb hovering over it, then a kind of strange vacuum. His mind had become closed to noise. Four hundred yards, three hundred yards, and then suddenly the Messerschmitt banked hard to the left as a Hurricane emerged from the melee, firing wildly.

Archie cursed, his chance gone. He was going too fast, and he now grimaced as he pulled out of the dive, the huge advantage of height and sun gone. Where were the others? *Hard to tell,* but as he levelled out and banked he saw the 109 – or was it a different one? – turning back towards a Hurricane that was firing madly at an Me 110. A quick glance behind – *clear* – and now the 109 was lining up to fire at the Hurricane.

'Look behind you!' Archie said, as he tried to line up the Messerschmitt in turn. Three hundred yards – *too far* – but tracer was now arcing from the German fighter. Archie applied boost, felt the Spitfire surge forward, but not before the Hurricane suddenly fell away, trailing smoke. The 109 dived after it, but Archie followed.

Come on, come on . . . Another glance in the mirror and behind – there was a parachute opening just below – and then the 109 was filling his sights. He pressed down on the gun button and felt the Spitfire judder and the eight machine guns clatter. Bullets and tracer hurtled through the air but a little too high.

The 109 banked sharply, but Archie followed, the horizon sliding again, and then pulled the stick towards him so that his body was pressed into the seat. He grimaced and pressed down on the gun button for a second burst. Bullets spewed again, but this time just ahead of the Messerschmitt. Archie eased back fractionally on the stick and a moment later it flew straight into his cone of fire. Smoke and flame flickered from the 109's cowling, then a second later the aircraft exploded, jolting Archie in his seat. Debris hurtled through the air, Archie flinched, something smacked the canopy, and the stick was knocked from his hand. Archie gasped, grabbed the control column again as the sky and sea swapped places, felt his stomach heave, then managed to right himself, and looked up to see blood trickling back across his windscreen and over his canopy hood.

Archie gasped again, and glanced around, then realized his mirror had gone – sheared clean off. His heart hammered and he was short of breath. He tried to breathe in a deep lungful of oxygen, but it was no good. He could hear his laboured gasps into the rubber mask as dark red blood continued to streak across the windscreen. *Christ! Christ! Oh, my God!* He tried to look around, but it was hard to see, so he pushed the stick forward and dived – dived out of the fray, the blood slowly clearing as he did so.

He was still gasping as he levelled out at two thousand feet. He could see more clearly now, although blood still streaked the canopy. Above him, the sky seemed strangely empty. For a minute, maybe more, he flew on, his mind still reeling from what had happened. It wasn't supposed to be this way. Air fighting was a detached form of warfare – machine against machine – but now the blood of a man he had killed was spattered across his canopy. It was still there, dried brownish rivulets across the perspex. Archie closed his eyes as a wave of nausea churned his stomach.

More regular breathing returned. *Where am I?* he thought.

Looking at his compass, he realized he was heading almost due north. He banked and saw the coast, some miles away to the south-west. Opening the throttle, he lost more height, then pulled back the canopy, looked all around him and headed back to Manston.

'Blimey, sir,' said Bufton, as Archie switched off the engine and hurriedly clambered out. He leapt from the wing, looked back briefly, then felt another surge of nausea and, running to the hedge, vomited. Still leaning over, he dabbed his mouth, the bile sharp on his tongue, then felt a hand on his back.

'Are you all right, Archie?'

He looked up and saw Ted standing over him.

'Ted,' he gasped. 'I-I think so.' He stood up. 'He just exploded – just like that. Right in front of me.' He leaned forward again, his hands on his knees. 'Christ, it was horrible. There was blood – blood all over the canopy. I couldn't see . . .'

'Just get it off, will you?' he heard Ted say.

'Of course, sir, right away,' said Bufton, and when Archie looked back, he saw his fitter busily cleaning the stained canopy.

'Who was it? One of ours?' asked Ted.

Archie shook his head. 'A 109. He just blew up right in front of me.'

'Come on,' said Ted. 'Let's get to dispersal. You need to tell Happy.'

Excited pilots were recounting their experiences to Merriman with exaggerated arm movements, but the IO, like Calder at 629 Squadron, was hard to convince. Ivo Rainsby was convinced that it was he who had shot down a particular 109, but it seemed two others were also claiming it. Merriman awarded them a third of a kill each. Ted claimed an Me 110, which was confirmed, and then there was Archie's 109. Others had seen it; there could be no doubt.

Mick had had half his rudder shot away and Joe Mazarin, the squadron's lone American, had landed with a burst tyre and had nearly tipped over his Spitfire, but otherwise everyone had made it back – everyone except Ginger Clancy. There were various reports of a Spitfire going into the sea and Charlie swore blind that he'd seen someone bail out and a parachute drifting towards the coast – but whether this had been Ginger, no one could say for certain.

It was not until they were back at Biggin and having supper in the Mess that a car pulled up outside and Ginger stepped out. Through the windows, Archie watched him lean down to say something to the driver, wave cheerily, and then he sauntered in. Everyone clapped as he stepped into the dining room, and he grinned. 'Thank you, thank you!' he said as the CO and Charlie got up and hurried over to him. 'Have you missed me?'

'What are you wearing?' said Charlie, laughing.

Ginger was wearing a pair of grey flannel trousers that were too big for him and an army battle blouse. In his hand was a small case. 'What are you suggesting? You don't like my new design for a uniform?'

'Maybe if it fitted,' said Jock.

'I had a swim,' said Ginger and, holding up his bag, added, 'I'm afraid my kit got a little sodden with seawater.' He looked around. 'On the other hand, there's some good news – I can confirm that both parachute and Mae West work splendidly.'

Everyone laughed, spirits suddenly lifted by his late appearance.

‘What happened?’ asked Charlie. ‘I saw a Spit go down and saw someone bail out. I thought it was you, but wasn’t sure.’

‘Yes, sorry about that. Got one in the glycol tank. It was a fluke shot, though – a one in a thousand chance.’

‘Of course it was,’ said Jock.

‘Anyway, in no time my engine was heating up like a pressure boiler and I thought to myself, *Oi, oi, this old girl’s going to blow any moment. Better get out of here toot sweet, old chum.* So I cut the engine, pulled back the canopy, undid all my clips, flipped her over and pretty much fell out. I pulled the cord, thankfully the parachute opened – they are marvellous those girls that pack ’em – and next thing I know I’m drifting down into the drink. Trouble was, I could see the white cliffs all right, but was that going to be close enough? Anyway, to cut a long story short, I needn’t have worried because I hadn’t been bobbing around for very long when a minesweeping trawler came along and hoisted me out. It was a fishing boat, but now, instead of catching hauls of mackerel or cod, they catch enemy mines instead. Amazing – I had no idea. They were a rough old bunch, absolutely insisted on plying me with rum, then took me into Folkestone. There I was taken to a hotel, given these clothes by some Home Guard wallah, given something else to drink and taken back to Manston, but by then you’d all scarpered, so I had to get another lift, and here I am.’

‘And very glad we are to see you too, Ginge,’ said Jock, then announced that the entire squadron was going to head to the pub – attendance compulsory. They could all do with getting off base, he told them, and in any case, they had cause to celebrate: their first major engagement since Dunkirk and all had made it back.

After supper, they clambered into a truck – the tumbrel, as they called it, which normally took them from the Mess to dispersal – and headed out of the gate to the Old Jail, a mile or so down the road. Tumbling out, shouting and laughing excitedly, they burst into the pub, crowding around the low-beamed bar. The first round, the landlord told them, was 'on the house'. More cheers.

'Quiet! Quiet!' said Jock, holding up a hand to silence them.

'Shhhh!' said Ginger loudly.

'I'm introducing a new rule,' Jock told them. 'We now have our first official member of the Goldfish Club.' More cheers, and Ginger raised his arm in mock acknowledgement. 'From now on, anyone who gets shot down and lives to tell the tale has to sing a song in front of everyone. And it's got to be a song by Cole Porter.'

'Why Cole Porter?' asked Ivo.

'Because I like Cole Porter and because I'm the skipper and I say so.'

'Fair enough, Skip,' said Ivo.

'But I can't sing,' said Ginger.

'No getting out of it, Ginge,' said Jock.

The others began chanting and stamping their feet on the wooden floorboards. Archie laughed as Ginger swayed and put his pint down on the bar.

'All right, all right,' said Ginger, 'but you might want to put your hands over your ears.' He put one hand on his chest, his other outstretched, then began singing 'Ev'ry Time We Say Goodbye', but quickly forgot the words, finishing with, 'I can't remember the words, hum dum-di-dum . . .'

Everyone started laughing. 'That,' said Jock, 'was the worst rendition of a song I've ever heard in my life.'

'I did warn you,' said Ginger.

Jock held up his hands again. 'I've got another new rule to announce.'

'As long as it doesn't involve Ginger singing anything,' said Charlie.

'No, not Ginger, but we've got another reason to celebrate tonight.'

'Have we?' said Ivo. 'What?'

'The squadron's first ace,' said Jock. 'Archie Jackson. Five confirmed kills.' Cheers and wolf whistles. Archie looked down, embarrassed and happy at the same time.

'And Strafer Ted's just behind,' said Jock. 'One to go, Ted!'

'So what's he got to do?' asked Charlie.

'Exactly the same, but afterwards he's got to buy everyone a round. We don't want him getting big-headed.'

Archie laughed and was pushed forward towards the bar.

'And now the song!' called out Jock.

'Song! Song! Song!' chanted the others.

Archie wracked his brains for Cole Porter songs, then suddenly knew which one to choose – it was a recent number, but he and Ted had played it a lot since they had first heard it. He cleared his throat in an exaggerated fashion, then began to sing 'Let's Be Buddies'.

As he finished, everyone cheered and began joining in chanting lines from the chorus over and over. Archie glanced at Ted and caught his eye as the others yelled, stamping their feet at the same time so that the floorboards were vibrating.

He saw Ted push through the others and move towards him.

'Not bad,' he said.

'I told you I used to be in the choir when I was small,' Archie replied.

Ted smiled. 'I haven't heard that song for a few weeks.'

'Me neither.'

Archie looked down and saw Ted was holding out his hand. He took it, gripping it firmly, relief coursing through him. *Thank God.*

'I've been a fool,' said Ted. 'I'm sorry.'

Archie grinned and clasped Ted's hand.

'So, what do you say?' said Ted. 'Let's be pals?'

Archie laughed. 'Yes,' he said. 'Yes, let's.'

19

CANNON SHELL

Saturday 20 July, around eight o'clock in the morning. A bright day, but with plenty of cloud. Down below, Archie could see the convoy as it inched its way along the south coast of England – half a dozen ships sailing so slowly it would be impossible to tell they were moving, were it not for the smoke from the funnels and the stark white of their wakes.

'Hello, Clover, this is Bison.' Jock's voice over the R/T. 'We're at angels eighteen.'

'Roger, Bison. Bandits, forty plus, crossing the Channel now.'

'OK, we'll keep our eyes peeled.' A crackle of static and then Jock said, 'All right, chaps. You heard him. Jerries on their way.'

Archie swallowed and checked his dials. The squadron was spread out in an open formation – four loose vics of three Spitfires. The day before, they had been scrambled to intercept an attack and had arrived too late, but this morning they had flown down at first light to Hawkinge, near Folkestone, and an hour later had been ordered up on a patrol. By chance, the Luftwaffe had played ball. This time the squadron would be waiting.

Archie had discovered that no matter how scared he felt before going into combat, once he was in among the enemy, his fear seemed to melt away. He was too busy concentrating on what he had to do, too charged with adrenalin. There were heart-stopping moments when his heart seemed to lurch and his body jerked with a pulse of terror, but for the most part it was the thought of going into battle that he found the hardest. He could feel his heart racing again now, could feel the dead weight of dread pressing down on him; and there was that knot of nausea in his stomach too.

Forty plus! And there were just twelve of them. He breathed in a lungful of oxygen. The squadron was circling, hovering high over the convoy way below. A bit of turbulence, his Spitfire wobbled, then he was through it. Where were they? He stared as hard as he could towards France, sprawled towards the horizon, patchy green between the cloud.

Then all of a sudden, there they were, like a swarm of insects, tiny black dots, stepped up in layers.

'Bandits, three o'clock!' he said from Green Section's position at the starboard edge of the formation.

'All right, I've got them,' came Jock's reply.

Archie looked across at them as Jock led the squadron into another climb and began turning them west so that by the time the enemy arrived they would be attacking with the sun behind them. It was still quite low in the sky, but any advantage, however slight, had to be taken. The bombers were at the bottom, then the Me 110s and, above them, the Me 109s. The 110s, Archie noticed, appeared to be swaying from side to side, as they tried to keep pace with the much slower bombers – *Stukas?* He couldn't tell yet. But above the 110s, the German single-engine fighters were, he now realized, flying at a more normal speed, ahead of the others.

'Spread out a bit, chaps,' said Jock.

Good idea, thought Archie. The further apart they were, the harder they would be to spot.

The 109s were almost beneath them now, heading west between light banks of white cloud, but at least two thousand feet below them. That was something, thought Archie to himself. He could feel himself tense. *Any moment now.*

'OK, tally ho!' said Jock, and Archie watched Red Section peel off and begin its dive, then he was pushing his stick over and forward and diving too. Twenty thousand feet to fifteen in a matter of moments, the speed on his air-speed indicator flickering at nearly four hundred miles per hour. Suddenly he was into cloud, the Spitfire was buffeting and screaming but the sense of speed was momentarily gone as the light changed from bright morning sunlight to that strange, milky glow. Then the cloud thinned, the intense speed evident once more as the wings sliced through wisps of white, and there were the 109s, a dozen of them at least, spaced wide apart in groups of four. Out of the corner of his eye, Archie saw tracer spitting across the sky and to his left an aircraft was peeling off – *A 109? Yes!* – and diving, smoke trailing. A second later, another 109, with its dark green mottled paintwork, filled his sights and he was firing himself, the Spitfire juddering, his body vibrating, glued into the bucket seat, as bullets and tracer flashed across the sky.

Had he hit his target? He thought so, but it had flipped on to its side and, with a puff of grey smoke, had dived away. *Don't follow it,* he told himself, as he glanced up into his newly fixed mirror and then either side of him. A Spitfire flashed past in front of him as he banked into a tight turn and felt his vision blur with the force of negative gravity. As he pulled himself round back into the fray, he looked down at the tumble of aircraft and saw another Spitfire hammering at a 109.

The Messerschmitt was weaving and turning, the Spitfire glued to his tail, but another 109 was now homing in and about to get behind the Spitfire. Archie pushed his stick forward, applied boost, and pitched himself down towards the attacking German fighter. At a hundred yards, he fired a two-second burst, then realized he would not be able to pull up in time and that the two would surely collide.

'No!' he yelled out loud, pulling the stick towards him. There was the 109, just in front, so big he could see the pilot in his cockpit and the smoke-streaked wings and the stark black and white crosses. The Spitfire was screaming, Archie was pressed into his seat, and then the plane disappeared from view under him. He closed his eyes, waiting for the explosion, the collision of two machines travelling at over three hundred and fifty miles per hour. A fraction of a second to realize his life was over.

A moment later, he opened his eyes, startled to discover he was still alive and that the Spitfire was now climbing once more. He pushed the stick over and the sky swivelled. A quick look – there was the 109, plunging towards the sea, a long trail of smoke following it down – *At least he didn't explode* – and now Archie pulled the Spitfire into a turn. He tried to look around, but his head was like lead from the force of negative gravity. Level out – the horizon swivelling again – and a glance around. Below him, a mass of tangling aircraft: Stukas diving, a ship on fire, Hurricanes tearing into the 110s, a Spitfire still tussling with 109s. He tried to pick out a 109, but then he felt and heard a clatter of bullets across his port wing.

Christ, Christ! I've been hit! He'd taken his eye off the ball for a moment and he'd been hit.

Instinctively, he pushed the stick over and back towards him, throwing the Spitfire into a tight left-hand turn, then frantically looked around him. He felt pressed into his seat, as though by a giant hand, but despite his panic, he remembered to look over his right shoulder, easier to manage than over his left when in a turn. The 109 was behind him, an ill-defined but menacing form at the periphery of his vision. A glance in the mirror – the Messerschmitt clearer now, like a grotesque giant insect. Flashes from its gun ports in the wings and cowling and now more tracer fizzed and whipped under his wings.

Archie brought the stick in closer to his stomach, grimacing with the strain, the Spitfire on its side, almost beyond the vertical, turning, turning ever more tightly. His vision began to blur as the blood drained from his head. He strained to lean forward to ease the gravity loading. *No more tracer.* A glance in the mirror again, and he realized he was stretching away from his pursuer, that he was, incredibly, out-turning his enemy.

Keep turning, he told himself, but for how much longer? *Think, think!* he told himself. His port-side aileron was sluggish, but otherwise his Spitfire seemed to be all right – dials OK, oil temperature a bit high, but not critically so. Suddenly he saw the Messerschmitt pull out of the turn and climb, ready to make another steep turn and dive down on him again, but now more tracer was hurtling past him. Another one – *Where did that come from?* He tried to think calmly, but his mind was racing – panic, terror, shock screaming in his brain, preventing him from thinking rationally at all. *Calm down, calm down.* Tracer fizzed beneath him, and suddenly his brain cleared. Pushing the stick forward and flipping the aircraft over on its starboard wing, he began a dive, the throttle still open, the engine screaming in protest. Archie clutched the stick, and cried out as a stabbing pain shot through his ears from the sudden change in pressure. His air-speed indicator showed more than four hundred and sixty miles per hour, his altimeter needle was spinning, and he could see the wings visibly straining – *bending* – as he hurtled down past twirling Hurricanes and 110s, and on towards the rapidly closing sea. The noise was deafening. Sixteen thousand to six thousand feet in a matter of moments, and now he had to somehow pull out of the dive, but the full weight and momentum of the machine was hurtling towards the water. Could he stop it?

Grimacing, his arms aching, his ears hurting like hell, he pulled back on the stick, but the gravitational force was making everything so heavy, so sluggish – so painful. The control column felt like lead as he heaved it into his stomach, the Spitfire desperate to continue its downward plunge into the water. *Come on, come on!* The blue-green sea getting ever closer. He cried out. His whole body felt crushed. Sweat ran down his face, his arms ached so badly he desperately wanted to let go but he knew he could not. Let go and he would die.

Then a glimmer of hope, as the Spitfire finally began to level. *Please, please, come on, come on*. The Merlin whined pitifully, and now, at last, the horizon rose before him and, instead of the deep dark sea, he saw the white cliffs of Beachy Head appear before him, felt the force that was thrusting him into his seat release its grip, and the unbearable ache in his arms relax with sudden relief.

'Thank you, thank you,' he mumbled, and pulled back the

canopy. Smoke rushed out and he looked around. High above, away to his right, a number of glinting flashes and white contrails streaking the sky, but around him the air was his own.

Despite the damage to his port aileron, his flaps still worked and he was able to land back at Hawkinge without mishap. There were the Hawkinge ground crew, welcoming him back, directing him to his parking spot. Brakes on, engine off and sudden, delicious silence. Would it always be like this, now that the air battle appeared to be underway? Archie wondered how long he could keep it up, how long he could keep chancing death. As he pulled off his helmet, his hair was damp with sweat. Shakily, he got to his feet and eased himself out and down on to the wing and then on to the ground. His legs felt light and unsteady and he gripped the edge of the wing for support.

'You all right, sir?' asked one of the erks.

Archie nodded. 'I'll be fine. Just give me a moment.'

Another of the erks was on the wing now, looking into the cockpit. 'Bloomin' heck,' he said, 'someone's looking after you all right, sir. I reckon that's a cannon shell what's gone up through that.'

Archie looked up. 'I did feel something hit me, actually,' he said, and, taking off his gloves, felt the back of his head. It was damp. Sweat? No, he realized, holding up his hand. Blood.

'I'm not bleedin' surprised, sir,' said the erk. 'That was a cannon shell what hit your armour plating. If we hadn't had that put in – well, I don't reckon you'd have much of a head left, sir.' He jumped down and opened the small hatch behind the cockpit, reached inside and a few moments later re-emerged, grinning, with a piece of metal between his forefinger and thumb.

'Luck of the devil,' he said. 'Here, sir,' he added, handing it to Archie.

Archie looked at it. A flattened 20-mm armour-piercing shell. He breathed out heavily. It was unbelievable. *I should be dead,* he thought.

'You should keep that, sir,' said the other erk. 'Might keep you lucky.'

Archie nodded, then stumbled towards the dispersal hut. A number of others had already landed and more were doing so. *Where's Ted?* he wondered. He felt numb, his legs still light, and his head throbbed. And then there was Mick, walking towards him, asking if he was all right.

'Jeez,' he said, 'I thought you'd gone. I saw that 109 clobber you. Your Spit seemed to jolt in the air. I thought that was you gone, done and dusted.' He stood back and looked Archie up and down. 'But here you are, flesh and bones. It's good to see you, buddy.'

'And you, Mick.' He touched his head again.

'Here, let me see that,' said Mick. He stood behind Archie and peered at his head. 'Can't see much. A nasty graze, I'd say. Reckon you'll live.'

Archie collapsed into a deckchair outside the dispersal hut, and felt the energy drain from his body. His eyes stung; it was a warm day, and he closed his eyes. Another Spitfire landed, but nearer to hand a bee was buzzing among the clover. A moment later, he was asleep.

He was in the air again, firing at the plane in front and then it exploded, but it wasn't a 109, it was a Spitfire and it was Ted hurtling towards him and smacking against his windscreen, his body mashed to a bloody pulp. 'No!' he shouted, then jolted awake. A dream. It was just a dream.

'Easy, Archie,' said Ginger. Archie looked up and saw him standing in front of him.

'Sorry,' he said. 'I must have nodded off.'

'You've been out cold for about three hours.' Ginger laughed.

'Oh,' said Archie. 'Where's Ted?'

'He's gone over to his Spit. He got two today, you know. I wonder what he's going to sing for us tonight. Happy's here and he's noted your one too. Mick and Geoff both saw it go down.'

Archie pushed himself out of his chair, stood up and winced. His head was sore. He rubbed his eyes and said, 'I'm going to find Ted,' then stumbled towards the line of Spitfires, conscious that although the two of them had shaken hands the previous night, there was still much left unsaid. There hadn't really been a chance until now: they had been in the pub with the others and had left all together around eleven. Back at the Mess, everyone had gone straight to bed, Archie and Ted included. Archie had felt so exhausted he had fallen asleep on his bed fully dressed. Four hours later, at 3.30 a.m., he had been woken by his batman and they had taken the tumbrel down to dispersal. No one had felt like talking much, least of all Archie. He had had a headache and his mouth had felt as dry as chalk.

Then they had reached Hawkinge, had been given some coffee and breakfast, and soon after they were scrambled to patrol over the convoy that was clearing the Strait of Dover on its way to Portsmouth. Since he got back, he'd been fast asleep.

He rubbed his eyes again, then spotted Ted, very much alive, standing beside OK-T, supervising the painting of two more swastikas on to the side of his plane.

'Archie!' he called out. 'You're awake at last.'

'Congratulations,' said Archie. 'You got two more.'

Ted grinned and pointed to the six little swastikas in a line beneath the cockpit. 'They look rather good, don't they? Still, a long way to go until I catch up with Pops. It's a shame the ones we strafed don't count.'

'It might be a long war,' said Archie. 'I'm sure you'll have the chance.'

'Maybe.' He scratched his head. 'Look, Archie, I've been meaning to say, about – well, about us falling out – I've behaved like an ass.'

'No, it was my fault. If anyone's been an ass, it was me.'

Ted held up a hand. 'No, I was pig-headed and proud and I've been a prize fool.'

'If anyone's been pig-headed,' said Archie, 'it's me.'

Ted laughed. 'You know, we can't start arguing again over who's most at fault.'

Archie laughed too. 'No, all right. How about we agree that we've both been foolish, and leave it at that?'

'It's a deal.' Ted eyed him, as though he were about to say something, but then stopped. He sighed heavily and said, 'Oh, it all seems so silly now. I've been more cross with myself for letting my pride get in the way than I ever was with you. I've really missed not having you to talk to these past weeks. The chaps in the squadron are all good types, but it's not been the same.'

'Honestly, Ted, I agree with you. I think I knew it before, but for the past few weeks we've been doing nothing but stooging about the place, following convoys and chasing after non-existent Dorniers, and I started to forget that it's a pretty serious business we've got ourselves into.'

'It is now all right.'

'Exactly. I've realized that these past couple of days. God knows how I'm still here, but I can't help thinking my luck will run out any minute. I don't want bad blood with anyone, least of all you.' He looked away a moment, then felt inside his trouser pocket. 'Look,' he said, passing Ted the remains of the cannon shell. 'That hit my armour plating behind my head.'

Ted whistled.

'I had two 109s on me, and had to dive out of the way in a hurry. I thought I was never going to be able to pull out in time. I thought I'd had it.'

Ted nodded grimly. 'Come on,' he said. 'Let's go for a wander.'

'Ted?'

'Yes?'

'About Tess . . .'

'What about her? That my best friend has gone and fallen head over heels with my sister?'

Archie looked down. He could feel the blood rising to his cheeks.

'I admit, I did feel a bit jealous,' said Ted. 'I mean, you were supposed to be *my* friend. Suddenly it seemed you'd rather be with her and she with you. I've always got on well with my little sis. I felt a bit left out, I suppose.'

'But how I feel about Tess is completely different. I still think of you as my best friend and I'm sure I always will.'

'I know. And I'm used to it now. To start with, I wasn't bothered because I didn't think a night of dancing added up to much, but then it was suddenly a bit more serious. But I'm happy for you both now. Honestly I am. I know she's crazy about you, Archie.'

'I'm a bit crazy about her too.'

'And I also know she's been desperate for us to make up.' Above them, a skylark twittered furiously. 'He's full of the joys of life, isn't he?' said Ted as he paused to light a cigarette. 'Maybe he's singing for all of us.'

Archie did not reply, but perhaps Ted had a point. The skylark's song was especially joyful, but he couldn't help feeling rather sad. *I've still got so much to live for,* he thought to himself. *I don't want to die. I don't want Ted to die.*

'What's the matter?' asked Ted.

Archie shrugged. 'I don't know. Nothing, really.'

Ted looked at him again. *Go on.* But when Archie remained silent, he said, 'Is it what happened yesterday? The blood on the canopy? You've got to try to put it out of your mind, you know.'

'I wish I could, but I can't stop thinking about it. The pilot was probably just like us. Alive one moment, in a thousand pieces the next. It's all so – so unfathomable. I keep thinking that might happen to me. Or to you, Ted.'

Ted patted him on the back. 'No, we'll be all right. We know how to handle ourselves now. Remember what Pops said, and what Mac told us. Experience is everything in this game, and we've got that now.'

'It makes a difference, I know, but a lot of it is luck – chance, fate, whatever you want to call it.'

'And as we've already shown, we're lucky.' He grinned. 'Come on, Arch, this isn't like you. And anyway, now that we're pals again, we can't let anything happen to us. We'll be all right, you'll see.'

Archie smiled weakly. 'Maybe you're right.'

In two days of combat he had been a hair's breadth from colliding with a Messerschmitt, had been hit by a cannon shell, his plane peppered with bullets, and he had nearly plunged head first into the sea. And this was almost certainly just the beginning. The beginning of the battle, the beginning of the war. He knew he somehow had to push such thoughts out of his mind, but it seemed to him that the odds of their surviving were stacked against them.

20

FORTY-EIGHT-HOUR LEAVE

At the end of the month, on 26 and 27 July, Archie and Ted were given leave for forty-eight hours. Two whole days! Regular leave was something Air Chief Marshal Dowding had recently introduced: every pilot was to have twenty-four hours off a week and at least forty-eight hours off every three weeks. As far as Archie was concerned, it could not have come at a better moment.

'I think we can survive without our aces for a couple of days,' Jock had told them. 'In any case, Happy tells me the weather forecast is looking poor for the weekend, so I don't suppose Jerry will be coming over much anyway.'

So it had proved, not that Archie minded. He had gone to stay with the Tylers – at Ted's insistence – and for much of that first day had slept. A large bed, crisp, clean sheets, a mattress at least a foot deep, and a room filled with paintings and furniture and a carriage clock that whirred and ticked comfortingly. Biggin seemed a long way away.

When he awoke, early in the evening, it was to see Tess sitting on the edge of his bed.

'Am I in heaven?' he said, opening his eyes.

She laughed and kissed him. 'How are you feeling?'

'Much better. Much, much better.'

'Good, because Ted wants us all to go out.' She stroked his cheek. 'I'm so glad you've patched things up.'

'So am I.'

They headed out soon after: drinks at the Café de Paris, then dinner at Oddenino's before heading back to Pimlico. Eating out was expensive, but Archie saw no point in saving his pay. What's more, it was fun, and made him feel just that little bit older and more grown-up – to be drinking cocktails and dancing at famous clubs like the Café de Paris, and to have Tess at his side in sophisticated Regent Street restaurants, was rather thrilling. He was conscious he walked taller and straighter when Tess was with him.

'Thank you, boys!' she said as they arrived back at Winchester Street later that night. 'It's been lovely – and such a *funny* time too. I've laughed and laughed.'

'It's been very jolly,' agreed Ted. 'If only we could be on leave all the time.'

Group Captain Tyler was home before them this time, sitting in the drawing room with a tumbler of Scotch.

'Ah, boys!' he said, standing up and shaking hands vigorously. 'How good to see you both!'

'I'm an ace, Pops!' said Ted. 'And so is Archie. We've both got six.'

His father smiled. 'Well done. Well done. And how is the squadron?'

'In good form,' said Ted. 'We've not lost a man yet. A few bail-outs but no one's got the chop, thank goodness.'

'It's incredible, really,' said his father. 'The Luftwaffe are still attacking ports and ships and that's all. It's given us the most wonderful breather.'

'But we've been flying non-stop!' said Ted.

'Ah, yes, but how often have you actually engaged the enemy?'

'Not often, but we have had a few big dust-ups the past week or so. Aircraft swirling about all over the place. It's been mayhem.'

'So do you think things are looking a bit more hopeful, sir?' asked Archie.

'Things are better than they were. Put it this way, more and more new aircraft are being built. Production is outdoing wastage. More pilots are being trained. But Göring has got to make an all-out strike soon.'

'Why, Pops?' asked Tess.

'Because if Germany is to have any chance of defeating us, Herr Hitler has to invade, and he cannot successfully invade unless he has control of the skies.'

'Why not? They'll be coming by sea, won't they?'

'Because, my little sis,' said Ted, 'we'd shoot up and bomb all the boats and barges carrying their troops like rats in a barrel if they didn't.'

'But time is a very important factor, darling,' said the group captain. 'Hitler doesn't have a large navy and, in any case, would have to carry most of his troops in barges and small ships.'

'Because,' interjected Ted, 'you can't rapidly unload lots of fighting troops on to beaches from warships – they can't get close enough to the shore. So you need landing boats or flat-bottom barges.'

'Which cannot cross the Channel unless the weather's reasonably fine,' continued their father.

'Which it is in summer?' said Tess.

'Which is most likely in summer,' agreed her father. 'Come the autumn, the sea will be too rough, the days too short and Hitler will have to wait until the spring, by which time we'll be strong enough to defend our skies again.'

'So it really is a race against time,' said Tess.

'Yes,' agreed her father. 'And with every day that passes, our chances of survival improve just that little bit more.'

'Do you have any idea when they might launch their main attack, sir?' asked Archie.

Tyler shook his head. 'I wish we did. I suspect when there's a spell of good, clear weather, but the outlook remains unsettled, thank goodness. Normally, we all moan when it rains, but I'm praying this is the wettest summer on record.'

They all went to bed soon after, heading upstairs together, so Archie could not snatch a brief moment with Tess alone. For a while, he lay in his bed in the guestroom on the first floor, unable to get to sleep, thinking, not of colliding aircraft or pulverized pilots, but of Tess. He felt quite bewitched by her. Was this love? Perhaps he would marry her. Could they? One day? What a great evening it had been, and there was still all of tomorrow. It reminded him of Christmas Eve: the feeling of contentment mixed with expectation that was all too rare these days. He rolled over and was soon asleep, dreaming as usual of dogfights and all the horrors of war that now invaded his dreams.

The following morning a telegram arrived addressed to both Ted and Archie. They were having breakfast and Tess hurried to the door when the knock came.

'I don't know who to give it to,' she said, looking anxious. 'Oh, I do hope it's nothing awful.'

'Probably recalling us from leave,' said Ted. 'Go on, Archie, you open it.'

Archie held the envelope for a moment. No one spoke. The only sound was the rhythmic tick of the wall clock.

He tore open the envelope and pulled out the thin piece of paper with its glued-on words. *I don't believe it!* he thought.

'Well?' said Ted. 'Well?'

'*Congratulations. Stop. Award of DFC confirmed to both Pilot Officers A Jackson and E Tyler. Stop. No bragging allowed. Stop. Skipper. Stop.*' He looked up, a wide grin on his face. 'We've been given the Distinguished Flying Cross!'

Ted's mother and Tess hugged and kissed them both in turn. Archie could not stop smiling.

'We must tell Pops!' said Tess. They called his office and after a brief delay Ted managed to get through.

'He sends his congratulations,' said Ted after he had put down the receiver, 'and says they sell the right ribbon at the Army and Navy store in Victoria Street.' He clasped Archie on the shoulder. 'We should go there now. Mama, you'll sew it on for us, won't you?'

'Of course,' she replied. 'If you boys go now, I'll have it done before lunch. Then you can wear it before you go out tonight.' She looked at them both. 'You are going out tonight, I take it?'

'Of course!' Ted laughed. 'We need to celebrate!'

'Shall I invite a friend?' asked Tess. 'Make up a foursome?'

'Three's a crowd, is it, sis?'

'I just thought you might want to meet my friend Jenny. She's very pretty and isn't stepping out with anyone. You'd like her. She's fun.'

'What about that Polly girl?' asked their mother. 'You seemed frightfully taken with her a little while ago.' Archie was very fond of Mary Tyler. She was a gentle lady – calm and assured but not a stick-in-the-mud at all. She seemed to accept, Archie thought, that times were changing. He adored his own mother, but he could not imagine her being willing to allow him to go out both nights of a precious two-day leave.

'Don't mention Polly,' groaned Ted. 'She's back in the arms of some ghastly army captain now. Apparently, she always was and was only draping herself over me to make him jealous.'

'Then what about Jenny?' asked Tess.

'When you say she's pretty, just how pretty? The last thing I want is to be lumbered with some awful bore all night while you two giggle together in the corner.'

Archie laughed.

'She's blonde, has blue eyes, a pretty nose and is rather clever, but not in a showing-off way. I'm not a boy, but if I were, I'd say she was pretty much perfect.'

Ted grinned. 'All right, ask her. But I'm trusting you, sis. Don't let me down.'

Ted need not have worried. As Archie could tell the moment Jenny walked into the Brevet Club in Shepherd's Market, Ted was instantly smitten. After drinks, they went for dinner at a French restaurant near Berkeley Square and Ted could not keep his eyes off her. When the girls later disappeared together to the ladies' room, Ted turned to Archie and said, 'This time I definitely *am* in love. Isn't she amazing?'

'You've only just met her, Ted.'

'So? I can tell. Jenny's the one for me. And she laughs at all my jokes.'

'I saw.'

'Coup de foudre, Archie, coup de foudre. Love at first sight!' He sat back and sighed. 'I never want this night to end.'

After dinner, they went dancing at the Bag o' Nails, Ted and Jenny glued to each other and Archie happy to be able to hold Tess close to him.

'It's going to get worse, isn't it?' she said. 'The fighting, I mean.'

Archie nodded. 'I think so.'

She leaned her head on his shoulder as they drifted slowly round the dance floor. The band was playing 'Blue Skies', at a gentle, unhurried tempo, the female singer crooning huskily.

'I couldn't bear it if anything happened to you or Ted.'

'We'll be all right,' he said. He wished he meant it.

'Do you get frightened?'

Archie nodded. 'Before our leave I had a couple of bad days. A few close calls. It's very tiring. The Spit's a beauty, but it's still very hard work moving it this way and that at three hundred miles an hour. Your arms ache, your legs ache, then there're centrifugal forces to contend with too. I very nearly didn't pull out of a dive the other day. The trouble is, gravity is pulling it one way and you're trying to make it go another – it's a massive strain on the aircraft and on our bodies. Fortunately, I did manage to pull up in time on that occasion, but I felt a bit windy after that. But it taught me a lesson. I shan't make that mistake again.'

She held him tight, and then the singer breathed into the microphone, 'Since we have a few airmen out there tonight, this one's for you.'

It was 'A Pair of Silver Wings'.

Ted brushed past with Jenny, grinning from ear to ear. 'How about that, hey, you two?'

'Can we sit down?' Archie said. 'I don't really like this one.'

'Good idea. I don't either. It's depressing.' She smiled. 'Ted's happy.'

'He's in love.'

'Already?'

'So he says.'

Tess took his hand in hers. 'I wish we could go away somewhere.'

'Why don't we? This won't go on for ever. At some point, I'll be given leave. I could show you Scotland. I could take you to Loch Rannoch. Or we could go to the West Coast. I haven't been there since I was a boy scout, but it's wonderful. Mountains and glens, and the sea. It'll probably rain, but who cares?'

Her face lit up. 'I would love that.'

Archie suddenly became quite animated. 'I could get a bike with a sidecar. We could go by motorbike. Wouldn't that be fun?'

'Do you think we could? Honestly?'

'Of course we could. If your parents didn't mind.'

'I wouldn't tell them – I'd say I was going with a girlfriend.'

'That's so wicked.'

'Not very. Not really. You'd have to get me a leather flying helmet and goggles specially.'

'And an Irvin. I could raid the stores and nab one.'

She laughed.

'Oh, Tess, let's do it,' said Archie. 'It's a wonderful country. So beautiful. We could go on a tour.'

She put her arms around him and kissed him. 'That would

be heavenly! And something we can both dream about. I can't think of anything I'd rather do.'

The band had stopped playing 'A Pair of Silver Wings' and was beginning a rendition of 'I Get a Kick Out of You'. Tess held Archie's hand and stood up. 'I want to dance again now. That's made me so happy just thinking about it.'

Archie grinned, and pulled her back on to the dance floor.

'You've got to promise to look after yourself,' she said. 'No more gadding about, flying over to France. I need you in one piece for our Grand Tour of Scotland.' Her eyes twinkled. 'Promise me?'

'I promise.' He laughed. And at that moment, he wondered whether he had ever been happier in his entire life.

21

NEVER FOLLOW AN ENEMY DOWN

Tess had given Archie a journal before he and Ted had left the following morning. It was bound in black leather with lined paper, and in it she had written,

> Everyone should keep a diary at this time. Who knows what things you will write in these pages, but I know in years to come we will look back at these days and marvel at what took place.
>
> Your loving Tess
>
> 27 July 1940

'I thought about getting you a diary,' she had told him, 'but then I decided a journal was better. You can write what you want, when you want.'

'Thank you,' he had said. 'I will write in it. I'll enjoy it. It'll give me something to do while we're waiting at dispersal.'

When they arrived back at Biggin on Archie's Norton, it seemed as though they had never been away. Just as Jock had predicted, there had been little flying; that Sunday, the squadron had remained at Biggin. Archie and Ted found the pilots at dispersal. Outside it was raining.

But the rain did not last. They were up again at dawn the next day, flying down to Hawkinge, patrolling the south coast in the morning, before being scrambled and sent off after a reported enemy raid. They saw nothing.

Archie scribbled in his journal as they sat outside dispersal at Hawkinge later that afternoon:

Monday 29 July

Another X raid. We flew to sixteen thousand feet and were then vectored to an enemy raid reported as being 'twenty plus' but there was a bit of cloud about and we couldn't see an enemy plane anywhere. One thinks one should be able to see a plot of twenty enemy bombers and fighters, but when you can see an aeroplane no more than a few miles away, it's actually difficult to spot them sometimes. The sky is a big place.

I've just bought a camera from Mick. His people sent him a new one for his birthday, which was three weeks ago – it arrived a tad late – so I've taken on his old one. I'm going to take snaps of everyone and stick them in my journal.

Archie reckoned he had got a bargain: an Argus 35 mm, only about three years old, Mick told him, and all for sixteen shillings – about a day and a half's pay. Mick had also included a Kodak film, so Archie spent an evening going around taking photographs of the pilots.

'Here,' said Mick just before they flew back to Biggin. 'Let me take a shot of you and Ted. You should have one of the pair of you.'

They sat on the step of the dispersal hut and grinned at

Mick: hair unkempt, scarves instead of ties, sheepskin-lined flying boots battered and scuffed.

'Perfect,' he said. 'One for posterity.'

Twenty-four hours later, Mick was dead. It was the second scramble of the day. One minute they had all been lying out in the sun at Hawkinge, the next the telephone rang and B Flight were ordered off. Books and cards were flung down, Archie dropped his journal and then they were running for their Spitfires. Engines roaring into life. Snatch the parachute from the wing, fumble frantically with the straps and catches, then clamber into the cockpit, chocks away and off, quickly taxiing around the perimeter and, moments later, throttles wide, nine Spitfires thundering across the grass and into the air. Three minutes – that was all it had taken.

They were vectored towards a formation of twenty plus, reportedly heading for Folkestone. By the time they were at angels sixteen, there was no sign of any enemy bombers but suddenly they were being bounced by twenty 109s.

The Messerschmitts were upon them in a flash.

'Bandits, eleven o'clock,' Archie heard Charlie shout, and then turned to see them passing on their right, no more than a hundred yards away. So close were they, he could see the pilots quite clearly in their cockpits, leaning forward, and then they were turning towards them and opening fire, luminous tracer spitting across the sky.

In a moment, all cohesion was lost. Archie flung his Spitfire into a roll and passed under a 109 that rushed over him, then saw two on Ginger's tail, so pulled up and, banking, followed them. Ginger was rolling and banking and weaving but could not shake them. Archie cursed to himself – he had to do something to get those 109s off Ginger's tail, so although he was out of range, he pressed his thumb down on the gun button and let off a couple of two-second bursts. It did the trick: both Messerschmitts hastily broke away. Suddenly he spotted an opportunity. Climbing steeply, he half rolled so that before the 109s could complete the half-circle of their turn, he was able to dive down and latch on to the tail of the second. In his reflector sight, the Messerschmitt was just flickering to the right. A bit of rudder, and – *Yes!* – a clear target, just a slight deflection.

A quick look in the mirror and around him – thank God for his silk scarf – and then a gentle squeeze on the gun button. Bullets spewed from his guns and Archie saw the tracer rounds flashing along the German's fuselage. Flames licked from ruptured fuel tanks, then the cockpit was engulfed in thick dark smoke, the flames flickering through the swirling clouds. The pilot threw his machine into a turn, then flipped it on to its back and a moment later a figure tumbled free, the trail of the parachute following behind. Archie circled and watched it billow open and the pilot waft down towards the sea.

Moments later, tracer was fizzing over Archie once more. A half-roll, then a tight turn, the centrifugal force pinning him to his seat and making the muscles in his arms burn. Fading vision, then someone was screaming in his ear, 'I've been hit! I've been goddam hit!' Frantically, Archie levelled and quarter rolled. *Mick!*

'Christ! Oh, Christ!' screamed Mick, and now Charlie was shouting, 'Just get out of there, Mick, get out of there!'

Archie saw it now – a Spitfire burning away to his left.

'Oh, God! Help me!' Mick screamed again. Archie winced,

the cry of pain and terror violently loud in his ear. He flipped his Spitfire on to its back and dived. There was another 109 and he opened fire, but he was past him before his bullets could strike home and all he could hear in his ears were Mick's screams and then a broken note of high-pitched static. Spiralling down towards the sea, still burning and trailing thick smoke, was Mick's Spitfire. Moments later, there was a splash of white spray and then the Spitfire, with Mick still inside, disappeared.

Later that evening after they finally landed back down at Biggin, he wrote in his journal:

> Mick's gone. I know I'm going to hear his screams for the rest of my life.

*

Monday 12 August, around 4.30 p.m. Another long day, but although both flights had been scrambled that morning, they had seen nothing. At dispersal at Hawkinge, the pilots had been playing cricket with a tennis ball since their sandwich lunch. It was certainly perfect cricketing weather, even though a few cumulus and high cirrus clouds had lazily appeared in the clear blue sky. The game had now broken up, and pilots had drifted back towards the collection of deckchairs and armchairs outside the dispersal hut. A fair few were now asleep, snatching the chance to snooze while they could. Ted and Archie were both busily writing at a table brought out from the hut. Absolute quiet had descended over the airfield, and, as Archie paused to think, he could hear the scratch of Ted's nib on paper.

'What do you find to write about?' asked Ivo, breaking the silence, standing behind them in the doorway of the hut. 'You only wrote to her yesterday.'

'When you're in love, Ivo,' said Ted, 'there are always things to say. You need to get yourself a girl, then you'd understand.'

'I wouldn't want the responsibility of having to write every day,' he said.

'Well, I like writing every day. It makes me think of a lovely, sweet, beautiful girl rather than you lot, and gives me something to do while we hang about here, waiting for Jerry to show himself. It's better than loitering in doorways.'

Ivo smirked. 'And what on earth do you put in that journal of yours, Archie?'

Archie shrugged. 'What we've been doing, mainly.'

Jock, who had been reading a magazine in an armchair next to them, now put it down. 'Got up at dawn, took tumbrel to Spits, flew to Hawkinge, stooged about a bit, occasionally saw the odd Hun, flew back to Biggin, dinner in Mess, then pub, then bed.'

They all laughed.

'It has been a bit like that,' said Archie, glancing back through his entries. 'Here: *8 August. Plenty of cloud, scrambled and saw Dornier disappear into cloud. Lost it.*'

'My sister thought he'd write something interesting in it,' said Ted. 'She thinks we're living in historic times and that he should be writing things down for posterity. When Archie here is old and grey, he can look back at it and think, *Oh, yes, the summer of 1940. Sat on my backside at dispersal waiting for Jerry.*'

'Don't get me wrong,' said Jock. 'Long may it continue, but you could hardly write a book about it, could you?'

Ivo said, 'You don't think maybe we're tempting fate with this kind of chat?'

The telephone suddenly rang. Archie felt himself tense. Those asleep were instantly awake, looking towards the hut expectantly.

'I told you,' said Ivo.

'You spoke too soon, Skipper,' said Ted.

'Yes,' said the orderly from inside the hut. 'Yes, right. Right, sir.' A pause as he replaced the receiver, then he yelled, 'Squadron scramble!' He began furiously ringing the handbell.

Archie glanced at Ted as they put down their pens and pushed back their chairs. 'Good luck,' he said.

Ted patted him on the shoulder, winked – *calm as you like* – then they were running along with the others towards their waiting Spitfires.

4.50 p.m. Climbing into the sky, twelve Spitfires. They passed through cloud, then back out into the clear, the sun still high and bright above them. Archie, at Blue Two behind Charlie Bannerman, looked across at the squadron, spread out in four vics, Yellow Section just ahead to their left, Green Section on their right and slightly behind. His curving, elliptical wings looked sharp and vivid, but seemed suspended in the air, the sense of speed lost to him the higher they climbed. Five minutes passed, the drone of the Merlin becoming a kind of neutral background, like a rather heavy silence. The enclosed space in the cockpit: the smell of rubber and metal and oil. Archie smacked his leg, stinging himself out of his reverie.

'Hello, Bison, this is Clover,' he heard in his headset. 'Patrol Dungeness at angels ten.'

'Hello, Clover, Bison answering.' *Jock*. 'Repeat: angels ten?'

'Hello, Bison, yes, angels ten. No Hurris to take on big jobs.

Bandits, eighty plus. Go for big jobs. Steer 012 degrees, zero, one, two. Over.'

'Roger, Clover. Out.' A crackle and then Jock said, 'All right, chaps, you heard what he said. Eyes peeled.'

Eighty, thought Archie. *Christ. There's just twelve of us.*

He was certainly wide awake now, his body tensing, heart hammering and his throat heavy and dry. Then he saw them, just as Billy Barrow at Green Three called out, 'Bandits, four o'clock!'

There were, he guessed, thirty or forty twin-engine bombers – *Junkers 88s or Dorniers?* He craned his neck, squinted into the sun and then saw a swarm of around twenty 109s a couple of thousand feet above them. He could taste the gall in his throat.

'Hello, Red One, this is Blue Two,' he said. 'Twenty little jobs at two o'clock, angels twelve.'

'All right, Blue Two, I see them. Get ready to attack, but for God's sake keep a watch on your backs. Tally ho.'

He peeled off but Archie could see the 109s were already beginning their dives too, little dark crosses glinting in the sun, white contrails following. Archie took a deep breath – *Here goes* – then turned on to his back to prevent the engine from cutting out and looped down in a curving dive. The enemy bombers had yet to see them, droning on towards, he guessed, Dover. Archie felt the airframe shake and clatter as the bombers rapidly loomed towards him. Four hundred on the clock, and now he could see they were Dorniers. Spitfires were converging on them – the first clatter of machine guns and tracer spitting across the sky – and now the bombers had seen them and were scattering. Return fire – stabs of luminous red tracer criss-crossing the sky – was that a Dornier falling already? All cohesion had gone as Archie picked out one, opened fire – the chatter of guns, the smell of cordite, the shake of the aircraft – bits falling off the Dornier – and then he was past it, a blurred impression of the black and white cross on the wing a matter of yards away. Pull back on the stick – arms aching, the centrifugal force pinning him to his seat – and banking in a wide arc and there was another one, out on a limb, desperately trying to get away. A slight deflection shot, but he could see it filling his gun reflector sight – another squeeze of the gun button and he saw his tracer sparking along the starboard side of the fuselage. The Dornier hung there for a moment, then suddenly dropped forward as one of the fuel tanks caught; flames flickered, then rippled along the wing. A glance behind – *Christ, 109s!* – bank the Spit, open the throttle wide – *Thank God, got him off my tail* – a weave back and forth, and a glance around – a mass of incoherent images: a parachute opening, bits of an aircraft fluttering through the air like leaves – swirling fighter planes – criss-crosses of tracer – chatter, German and English – 'I've got one!' – *Charlie?* – and then, 'Can't get these damn 109s off my tail!' *Ginger.*

'Ginger,' said Archie out loud, and now saw, a little below him, two 109s chasing a lone Spitfire. Ginger was weaving back and forth, tracer following him, but as Archie pushed the stick forward and dived towards them, he saw Ginger put his Spit into a tight left-hand turn and one of the 109s detach itself, climb and roll inverted, before swooping down for another attack. Archie latched on to Ginger's other pursuer, but it was too late.

'Break, Ginger, break!' he shouted, but already the Spitfire had been hit. A puff of smoke and Ginger's voice shouting, 'I'm bailing out, I'm bailing out!' A moment later, a dark figure fell, followed by the blossoming of a white parachute. *Thank God*, thought Archie, but then saw one of the 109s circling and preparing to dive down towards the falling 'chute. Archie frantically looked around – were there other targets? – then saw the Messerschmitt thunder over Ginger as he gently drifted down towards the sea. As it did so, the parachute folded in on itself and suddenly Ginger wasn't floating downwards, but plummeting.

'No!' shouted Archie. Banking his Spitfire, he dived after the 109, who was now circling lazily five hundred feet below.

Anger welled inside him as he swooped down, but as he neared, the German pulled out of his turn and headed straight towards him. 'Come on, come on!' muttered Archie. Stabs of tracer were arcing towards him, lazily at first, then whizzing past, and the 109 was rapidly filling his sights, its yellow spinner bright against the dark airframe. Archie rolled, firing, felt bullets clattering and saw a blur as the Messerschmitt shot past. Archie pulled the stick towards him, the horizon tilted and then on the top he half-rolled, levelled out and prepared to dive again. Where was his 109? *There!* Below him, diving gently out of the fray, smoke trailing.

Never follow a plane down, he remembered Mac saying. *To hell with that*, thought Archie. Mac hadn't just seen his friend plunge to his death because of what that Jerry pilot had done. Another surge of anger as he made a curving dive after the ailing Messerschmitt. He was soon gaining on him. The German saw him and began to weave furiously from side to side, but the smoke from his engine was getting worse and his speed faltering. Four hundred yards, the 109 flickering across his gun sight. Archie eased the stick forward, saw the Messerschmitt rise and then, adding a bit of rudder to yaw the plane, he pulled back on the control column and at two hundred yards opened fire. Bullets streamed from his guns then stopped – *Damn, out of ammo!* – but he had done enough. The 109 had dropped into a spiralling vertical dive. Had he killed the pilot? There was no sign of any parachute. Archie looked around him, craning his neck – nothing – empty skies, then banked gently and watched as the 109 plunged into the sea, just as Ginger had done just a few minutes earlier.

Archie sighed, his anger spent. There was little satisfaction, he realized, in taking his revenge. *Poor Ginger*, he thought.

A clatter of bullets and a loud bang and Archie was jolted in his seat. *Jesus! Jesus!* A thunderous roar and a dark shape swooped directly overhead. Archie craned his neck back to see a 109 waggle its wings and fly on back towards France.

'Damn it! Damn it!' Frantically, he looked at his dials – oil pressure rising, manifold pressure diving. He could see the coast – it was only a few miles away – but his engine was dying. Smoke was gushing from the cowling and the Merlin was groaning. Archie cursed again. He'd committed two cardinal sins: not only following the 109 down, but also failing to spot his attacker.

At least he had height – six thousand feet on the clock, and, although it was steadily falling, he still had plenty of height in which to bail out. But bailing out hardly appealed. He swallowed hard, his mind suddenly addled. One hand loosely on the stick, the engine spluttering and coughing and belching thick smoke. A deep breath, nausea in his stomach, but the Spitfire was still flying. Getting closer to the coast.

Four thousand feet. Two miles to go? The coast looming – he could see Folkestone and the white cliffs and then the long, curving beach at Dymchurch and the low spit of Dungeness reaching out to sea. And what was that? Smoke rising – billowing – from beyond Folkestone. *Hawkinge?* Had they bombed Hawkinge?

Another bang, Archie started, a renewed belch of smoke, and the Merlin died. He was drifting, falling in a gentle dive. *Please*, he prayed, *let me reach the coast*. Steadily, his altimeter fell. Three thousand, two thousand. *Nearly there.* Sixteen hundred. Fifteen hundred feet.

Archie closed his eyes a moment. He had to get out – leave it too late, and he'd die. Just up ahead, he could see Dymchurch – could almost touch it.

'Come on, Archie,' he told himself. 'Do it.'

He could feel the sweat running down his face and back and yet he was shivering, his heart banging like a hammer in his chest. With his shaking hands, he unplugged his leads, unclipped the Sutton harness and pulled back the canopy. A waft of oily smoke made him cough and splutter, then he banked the Spitfire so that it pointed east, out to sea, pushed the stick hard to the left and felt the horizon swivel, and then he was falling, falling, tumbling towards the sea, the air gushing past him and wondering whether these were his last moments alive.

22

MASSING OF THE EAGLES

Tumbling ever closer towards the sea – or was it land, after all? – he tried to pull the cord, but it was difficult, plunging through the air, to think clearly. Then he yanked it, felt a jolt of panic, but a moment later, with a shoulder-wrenching jerk, the parachute ballooned and he was no longer plunging to his death but drifting to his survival. And he was over land! *Hooray!* he thought, but then realized with the breeze he was drifting back out to sea. Despair engulfed him, only to be replaced with relief once more as he dropped gently into the sea not thirty yards from the shore.

Bitingly cold water closed around him and then the parachute seemed to be tugging him, pulling him under. He flailed desperately, his boots and uniform weighing him down as he fumbled with the release. Panic nearly got the better of him, but then he was free and rising to the surface. He inflated his Mae West and began swimming towards the beach, his arms and legs splashing like a child's.

It wasn't far, but it seemed to take for ever: fully clothed, heavy, fur-lined boots on his feet, helmet still on his head – it wasn't the best swimming kit. At last he felt his feet touch the ground and staggered clear of the water.

A shout, followed by another, and Archie looked around to see several soldiers on the tufty headland above the beach waving their arms at him. Did they think he was German? He couldn't understand and so pulled off his flying helmet and took another couple of paces, his hand cupped to his ear.

'Stop!' yelled one of the men. 'Don't move!'

Archie stood still, looking around at the coils of wire that now ran along the beach.

'Mines!' shouted the man. 'The beach is mined!'

Archie froze. Mines! It hadn't even occurred to him, but it should have been obvious – he was on a beach the Germans would land on if they ever attempted an invasion.

Seawater ran down his face, his clothes clung to him, cold and sodden, and his teeth began to chatter. He could see one of the soldiers inching carefully on to the beach, passing through a gap in the wire.

'Hold on!' he yelled. 'Won't be long!'

Archie watched as he stepped left and right, then hopped and gradually drew closer.

'Jolly lucky we were there when you came down,' he said as he finally reached Archie. He held out his hand. 'How d'you do? Lieutenant James Masterton.'

'Archie Jackson. Thank you for coming.'

'Don't mention it. Just got to get you off again.' He eyed Archie carefully. 'Just do exactly as I do, all right? And I mean exactly.'

Archie nodded, then took his first step.

They were soon clear, even though Archie nearly lost his balance at one point. Managing to recover, his heart in his mouth, he had never felt more relieved to be walking on grass again.

'Well done,' said the lieutenant. 'Safe and sound. If you're not being shot at by the Luftwaffe, it's our own mines, eh?' He chuckled, then said, 'Look here, let's get you back to our HQ, then we can get you some dry clothes and a drink of something and get you back to your squadron. Where are you?'

'Thank you,' said Archie. 'I'm at Biggin Hill, but my forward base is Hawkinge.'

'Hawkinge? Got a pasting this afternoon.'

'I saw the smoke. I hoped I was wrong.'

''Fraid not. Not sure what the damage is yet. Anyway, we can get you back there – that'll be no trouble.' He turned to his men. 'Stay here, chaps, and I'll sort out Pilot Officer Jackson.' He set off, then suddenly stopped and turned to Archie. 'You're not injured or anything, are you?'

'No. No, I'm fine. Not a scratch.'

'Lucky you. Saw a chap get his parachute blown in earlier. Straight in I'm afraid.'

'That was Ginger,' said Archie. 'He was a friend of mine.'

'I'm so sorry. I'm afraid I didn't see what happened to the blighter that did it.'

'I shot him down and killed him, actually.'

Masterton looked at him and frowned. 'Oh,' he said. 'Oh, well. One less to worry about, I suppose.'

'I suppose so,' said Archie.

He was back at Hawkinge by half-past six and was shocked by what he saw: one hangar completely wrecked, machine-gun bullet marks across a number of the buildings. The main stores had been partially burned to the ground – the fire had been put out but it looked like a blackened wreck, the air was thick with the stench of burning and smoke. Craters pitted the airfield.

He found the pilots at dispersal.

'Archie – you're back!' Ted sprang up and vigorously shook his hand. 'We heard you were all right. Some army wallah rang through. What happened to you?'

A number of them clustered around him now.

'I went after that Nazi that blew in Ginger's parachute,' he said. 'I know we're not supposed to follow anyone down, but I'm afraid I saw red. He killed Ginger with his prop wash – I saw it all.'

'And you got him?' asked Charlie.

Archie nodded. 'But not before he got me in the engine. I managed to get back to the coast and bailed out, but the wind took me back out to sea. Then I nearly walked on a mine on the beach. Fortunately, some army chaps saw me and got me safely off.'

Jock patted him on the back. 'You've the luck of the devil, Archie. I think you should be called "Lucky" from now on.'

Archie looked around at the scene of devastation. Hawkinge had seemed so quiet, so peaceful earlier on. Now it appeared utterly wrecked. Following his gaze, Jock said, 'Can you believe what we were saying before we were scrambled?'

'Nazis,' muttered Archie. 'They're murderers.'

'Five killed here this afternoon, six more injured,' said Merriman. 'A couple of Spits damaged. And no less than twenty-eight craters.'

'Made landing a bit hairy,' said Ted. 'Couldn't see much because of the smoke, and then we all had to dodge the potholes.'

'Any prangs?' asked Archie.

Jock shook his head. 'Jimmy and Dougal bailed out too, but they rather sensibly managed to do so over land.'

Archie looked at Dougal, who grinned at him. 'Piece of cake,' he said.

'Anyway,' said Jock, 'we'll be staying at Biggin tomorrow while they patch this place up. We're being stood down, so we're about to fly back. You can get a ride with Dougal and Jimmy in Happy's car. See you in the pub – you know the rules, Archie. You've a song to sing. And anyway, we need to raise a glass to Ginger.'

Archie smiled weakly and thought about Ginger and his appalling singing the last time. It made him sad. He didn't feel like going to the pub at all; he felt exhausted. He thought: *I want to get back to Biggin and go to sleep.*

'You'll all have new kites tomorrow,' said Merriman as they set off for Biggin. 'The ATA are bringing in three more.'

'My sister's joined the ATA,' said Archie. 'I got a letter from her yesterday – on headed paper from her EFTS. She's learning to fly.'

'Good for her.'

'Yes, that's what I think. My parents weren't terribly keen to start with, but I gather they've come round. It really is amazing, you know, how these new kites keep appearing. One day four get lost, and the next morning there are four new ones. Lord Beaverbrook must be performing miracles.'

'A lot of people working round the clock,' said Happy. 'Those damaged Spits looked a right mess, but they've already been taken by the CRU, and will be made to fly again. So perhaps Jerry won't beat us after all.'

'Ted's father says it's pilots that we're a bit short of, rather than planes.'

'Which, if the Luftwaffe ever ventures inland, will give us a huge advantage,' said Happy. 'Look at today. None of the pilots and crews of the seven aircraft you all shot down will ever fly against us again, but we lost just the one pilot.'

'Poor Ginger,' said Archie. 'He was a good fellow. He made me laugh.'

'We don't know the German did it deliberately, though,' said Dougal.

'I saw it,' said Archie. 'He flew straight over him. Of course it was deliberate. Anyway, I got him back.'

'And lost your Spit in the process,' said Happy.

'I'm here, aren't I?' He knew he sounded petulant. He sighed and leaned against the window. 'Sorry,' he said. 'Just a bit tired, that's all. And I don't want to have to sing a song in the pub.'

Happy smiled. 'It's just a bit of fun. It's far better to get off the station and all go out together and have a few drinks than to mope about at the Mess. Jock's a terrific CO.'

'I know. We're lucky to have him.'

'Go out tonight and try having a bit of fun, Archie. It's good for you to let your hair down a bit after a hard day like this.'

Much later, just before midnight, Archie stumbled back out of the Old Jail pub with the rest of the pilots. He'd sung 'I Get a Kick Out of You', pointing to all of them as he'd done so, and had been drowned out with cheers for his pains. *It was good to take one's mind off things*, he thought to himself as they rumbled home in the tumbrel. And what better way to do so than to sing and be merry? The IO, as usual, had been quite right.

*

About the same time as the boys of 337 Squadron were heading back to base in the truck, singing Archie's song at the top of their voices, Group Captain Guy Tyler put the key in the door of his house in Pimlico and stepped into the darkened hall. He put his cap on the small semicircular cherrywood table, then went into the kitchen to fix himself a drink. A generous measure of Scotch, a squirt of soda from the siphon, and then he wandered into the drawing room, switched on a lamp, and sat himself down in his favourite wing-backed armchair.

Tyler rubbed his eyes and yawned. He was exhausted, but knew he could not sleep – not yet. It was, he reflected, so much easier when he'd been flying. In the last show he'd known so very little of what was going on, and only towards the end, when he'd been given his own squadron, had he had any responsibility to anyone other than himself.

Now he felt consumed by a sense of helplessness. His task was to accumulate information; information about the enemy, an enemy that seemed so much stronger than their own RAF. For the past few weeks, they'd been holding on, desperately trying not to get drawn into an air battle over the Channel in which precious pilots shot down over the water would most likely never return. But that phase of the battle was over. The all-out attack that Hitler had been boasting about, that had been so inevitable since Dunkirk, was about to start.

Reconnaissance aircraft, flying over France, had now identified a large number of enemy airfields in northern France. No wonder it had taken the Luftwaffe a while to get themselves organized; since the fall of France, the Germans had built some ten new airfields, complete with anti-aircraft defences, blast shelters, vast repair tents, fuel supplies and camouflage netting.

Fighter aircraft were now massed in the Pas de Calais and in Normandy, while the Luftwaffe's bomber force had taken over a large number of airfields a little further inland, all the way from Brittany to Holland, with a further air fleet operating from Norway.

It was true that the RAF's Bomber Command were flying over these airfields and trying to bomb them daily, but these were nuisance raids and little more. The Luftwaffe had now massed a large proportion of their air force along the continental coast, all ready for their assault on Britain. Air Intelligence not only had aerial photographs of all these airfields, the Y Service – the radio listening service – had also pinpointed which unit was where. Tyler knew, for example, that the bomber group KG4 was now based at Schiphol, near Amsterdam, in Holland, and that the fighter group JG2 had squadrons at Cherbourg and Beaumont-le-Roger in Normandy. He knew that JG3, JG26, JG51, JG52 and JG54, with four squadrons each, were formed up and ready in the Pas de Calais. To have this information, yet be unable to act upon it, was a heavy burden to carry.

And now the main assault was beginning. *Adlerangriff*, Göring was calling it, apparently. 'Attack of the Eagles' – the phrase had been picked up by the Y Service. His son had been fighting with some of the German fighters and bombers earlier that afternoon. Ted had rung home earlier – he'd shot down a Dornier and a 109, he had told his mother. Archie had been shot down, but word had reached the squadron that he was all right just before Ted had made his call.

Mary had then rung Guy at the Air Ministry. 'Ted says they were attacking Dover again,' she'd said. 'Our poor boy. I can't bear the thought of him caught up in this. And if anything happens to Archie, I don't know how Tess will survive. Or Ted, for that matter.'

'They're very good pilots,' he had told her. 'And experienced now. They'll be just fine.'

Except that he worried daily – hourly – that they might not be. Experience counted for a lot, that was true, but death in wartime could be quite arbitrary. A chance bullet, a momentary lack of concentration, mechanical failure – any one of these things could cut down the very best. What's more, it wasn't Dover the Huns had been going for – it had been the RDF stations at Dover. And not just Dover – other RDF stations had been targeted, as had Manston and Hawkinge.

So that meant the Germans knew about their radar. It was true that the chain of metal lattice pylons strung out along the southern and eastern coasts of Britain were only one link in the chain of the air-defence network, but it was a critical link all the same. Without radar, they would be dependent solely on the Observer Corps to warn them of incoming raids, which would not happen until the enemy formations had almost reached the coast. And that would be too late. The only chance they had of stopping the Luftwaffe was to be in the air, ready and waiting to attack when the enemy reached England – and for that they needed radar, and both networks: Chain Home, with its hundred-mile range, and Chain Home Low, with its ability to pick up enemy aircraft flying at low level.

By the grace of God – and perhaps because of the work done by 337 Squadron, among others, that day – the RDF stations in Kent were still working; damage had been slight. But they were clearly a prime target, and Tyler reckoned he had a pretty good idea of the pattern the battle would now take: first the radar stations would be knocked out by the Stukas. Without radar, Fighter Command would be virtually blind. The rest of the Luftwaffe would then be able to concentrate on the airfields, hoping to destroy Fighter Command both on the ground and in the air. It would be just like France all over again: Fighter Command constantly responding to enemy attacks rather than anticipating them. Their fighters would always be too late, or surprised entirely. And then they would lose.

He took a sip of his whisky and rubbed his brow, then looked around the room. It was a lovely room, he'd always thought so, and over the years they'd collected some equally lovely things to adorn their house. Paintings, trinkets, some mementoes from their postings abroad, some wonderful pieces of furniture – the walnut bureau, for example, or the baby grand piano in the corner. This room, more than any other in the house, represented them – his family, their life. It was his castle, his piece of England, and the thought of some Nazi storming in and taking it from him made him quiver with rage.

'Over my dead body,' he muttered, his fingers gripping his tumbler.

He looked up suddenly as the door opened gently.

'Pops? Are you all right?'

Tess. 'Hello, darling. What are you doing up?'

'I heard you come in.' She came and sat next to him, on the arm of his chair. 'You look tired, Pops. You should go to bed.'

'I know. I just thought I'd have a quick nightcap before I turn in.'

'Is it looking very bad?'

'No – no, we'll be all right. I'm sure of it.' He forced a smile.

'Darling Pops, I know you're only saying that.'

He breathed in heavily. 'The next two weeks,' he said. 'We'll know where we stand in a fortnight. If the Luftwaffe haven't broken us by then, I'd say they're never going to.'

'And Ted and Archie will be in the thick of it,' said Tess.

'Yes,' said her father, 'they will. And we must pray they get through it.'

23

ATTACK OF THE EAGLES

Sunday 18 August. Second scramble of the day, the air battle frenetic once more after a day of rain and low cloud, and now here they were, at twenty-eight thousand feet, way higher than they had ever operated before, ready to intercept a large raid that the plotters on the ground reckoned was heading for Biggin and Kenley.

And there it was, a far bigger formation of enemy aircraft than Archie had ever seen before. From their position high over Kent, he could see staggered layers of bombers and fighters crossing the coast near the Swale estuary.

'Good God,' he mouthed to himself. He glanced either side of him: Geoff Williams on his left, Billy Barrow and Robbie Dinsdale, the new boy, on his right; the entire squadron had been scrambled, and that meant all available aircraft – sixteen in all. That also meant sections of four, not three. 'They don't want any shot up on the ground!' Jock had yelled as they'd run to their aircraft. Jock was leading them now: Red and Yellow Sections were up ahead, about half a mile in front. Sixteen Spitfires turning towards the black swarm rolling towards south London.

A day of dazzling hot sun, unthinkable just twenty-four

hours earlier. Jock turned the squadron so that they could attack out of the sun. Perhaps there was an enormous advantage in attacking with height and out of the sun, but right now, looking at the mass of enemy aircraft – a hundred at least – Archie felt as though they were minnows attacking sharks.

They completed their gentle turn, so that they were now facing the stacks of enemy formations – at the bottom there were the Dorniers and Ju 88s, then above them the twin-engine Me 110s, and above them, weaving from side to side, were the 109s, perhaps four thousand feet below them. And beneath them all, the familiar toe of Kent and the south Essex coastline, hazy through a filtered light, the English coast disappearing to a faint green curve on the distant horizon.

A crackle in his headset, then, 'Hello, Bison Leader, this is Turban. Jacko Squadron about to engage. Go for the big jobs too, over.'

Jacko Squadron – the Hurricanes from Biggin.

'Hello, Turban, this is Bison. Roger. We're about to engage. Out.' Another crackle and then Jock's tinny voice said, 'Red and Yellow Sections will dive down and fly through the 110s and go for the bombers. Blue and Green Sections distract the 109s.'

Archie felt the familiar eruption of nausea in his stomach, then checked his dials – *all OK* – and glanced around. They were outnumbered, but if they broke up the formations and managed to shoot down a few, then perhaps they would have done their job. *Even so . . .*

He lifted his goggles, and pushed his helmet back from his brow, then glanced in the mirror, but the sun flashed off the glass, making him squint. *Damn!* That was all he needed.

'All right, chaps,' said Jock. 'Tally ho!'

A Flight dived and now Archie looked around and saw Geoff, Billy and Robbie fall in line astern behind him. A deep breath, then he half-rolled and began his dive, his ears popping with the sudden drop in height, the 109s getting closer, his air-speed indicator rising. *Throttle back slightly.*

Below, the bomber formation was breaking up as the Spitfires and Hurricanes swirled and turned among them. The tier of Me 110s also peeled off and dived towards them. Was that a 110 diving in flames? Parachutes were opening, white circles in the sky, two more aircraft were plunging downwards trailing smoke. *Just seconds away now.* Archie braced himself, tensing his stomach muscles to cope with any centrifugal forces. *Find a target.* Frantically, he scanned the sky as the 109s began diving in turn towards the massed melee. He picked one, followed it, but it banked suddenly and was attacked by a Spitfire – *Billy?* – he couldn't tell. Then he saw a lone Me 110 crossing a few hundred yards ahead. Applying boost, he watched the Messerschmitt fill his sights – *five-degree deflection* – and opened fire, the Spitfire juddering as he did so. Tracer spewed towards it, but his aim was wide and now he had lost it. *Damn!* He pulled his plane into a tight turn, gasping as he was forced back into his seat, his arms aching with the effort, but then saw another Messerschmitt, a 109, only a hundred yards away, turning right in front of him – a sitting duck. He pressed down his thumb again – *one, two, three seconds* – saw the tracer sparking across the enemy's cowling. A burst of flame and black smoke and it dropped away. Archie looked back up only to see a 110 hurtle past in front of him, so close that he ducked – not that it would do him any good.

That was close. He gasped heavily into the rubber oxygen mask, his chest heaving.

'Look out! Break! Break!' someone shouted in his ear. *You mean me?* Archie broke left as tracer fizzed past his starboard wing and then found himself parallel with two 109s. He could see their squadron markings and black crosses stark on their fuselages, and he saw one of the pilots wave. Archie waved back, then turned to starboard and dived away.

The melee was breaking up. A quick glance around – the 109s were turning back – *Good* – but up ahead he could see a number of Ju 88s pushing on. *Just fourteen thousand feet now* – and where was he? *Ah, there's London.* He opened the throttle wide and dived after the Junkers. As he neared, orange flashes of tracer arced towards him, but the rear gunner's aim was high. Archie dived below them, then pulled up and pressed his thumb down on the gun button, raking two of the bombers as he sped past them.

He continued his climb so that the sky and earth swivelled and for a moment he flew inverted, looking down on the Junkers below. One was falling away with smoke gushing from one of the engines, while the other two were dropping their bombs and turning for home. Far below, over the fields of Kent, a ripple of explosions – flashes of orange and smoke – and then Archie half-rolled and swept down towards them again. *Another pass*, he thought, but as the nearest filled his sights, he pressed down on his gun button. Only a second's worth of bullets spat from his guns and then there was silence. *Out of ammo! Damn it all!*

Archie banked, opened his throttle and sped away, marvelling again to find himself in a suddenly empty sky once more.

*

Only a few bombers had reached Biggin and they had caused little damage – a handful of craters, that was all. The squadron initially claimed twelve aircraft shot down, although this was reduced to eight after careful interrogation by Happy. Three from 337 had been shot down: Joe Mazarin, the American, had been seen falling in flames, but had bailed out and was apparently safe; Harry Pierce in A Flight had broken a leg bailing out; and Billy Barrow had also been forced to jump for it.

'*All in all,*' Archie wrote in his journal, '*a pretty successful engagement.*'

It was now around four in the afternoon, the sun still high in the sky. A number of the pilots were asleep, but Archie had brought one of the tables out of the dispersal hut and set it in the shade of the hut and the horse chestnut behind. On the grass in front of him the dappled shadows of the leaves flickered slightly in the breeze and, although there was a residual whiff of smoke and cordite hanging over the airfield, Biggin Hill was otherwise a picture of peace and tranquillity once more.

No one said much. Archie could hear the gramophone playing from inside the hut – an American dance band – and the low hubbub of Jock talking to Charlie and Happy. In front of him, half in the sun, Ted was asleep in a deckchair, head lolled on one side, hands folded across his lap. Flying boots on, Mae West over his shirt – ready to fly again.

Archie paused, and read back over his past few entries. My word, but they'd done a lot of flying. Since bailing out six days before, he'd flown twice the following day, once on Wednesday 14 August, three times on the Thursday, and four times on the Friday. On 15 August he had written:

Got up 4 a.m. Mug of tea, then hastily got dressed. We all stamped around outside the Mess, waiting for the tumbrel. Looked like being a peach of a day as first light began streaking across the airfield. It's always rather chilly, though, at that time of day, and made worse by the thought of having been snug in bed just a short while before. The tumbrel drew up and we clambered in. As we neared dispersal, the erks were already firing up our Spits, the noise of sixteen Spits tearing apart the morning calm. 4.45 a.m., take off and fly to Hawkinge. Pockets of mist in the valleys. England looking peaceful and very beautiful. Probably most of the country was still fast asleep, but I don't mind being awake on mornings like this. A couple of deep breaths of oxygen usually wakes me up anyway. It's good to fly at this time: no Jerries to worry about. Just me and my Spit. 5 a.m., touch down at Hawkinge, still looking a bit battered. We clamber out and wander over to our second home from home, the dispersal hut. Some new posters have been put up inside, pictures with captions: 'The Hun is always in the sun.' 'Never go after a Jerry you have hit. Another will get you for certain.' They are next to the aircraft recognition posters: black shapes of Me 110s and Ju 88s and so on. We all know them pretty well by now.

The food wagon comes round with tea and coffee and bacon sandwiches. The bacon's a bit fatty and cold, but the bread's thickly cut and not bad at all. I never used to be able to stomach it, I was so nervous, but now I wolf mine down like an old hand. You need food, and I've not once been sick since that Jerry blew up in my face.

Ted's mooning about Jenny. Swears he's going to marry her. I pointed out that he's still not quite twenty. Sometimes I still feel like the kid I always was, and sometimes I feel a lot older.

Archie paused. He remembered those soldiers who had rescued him in France – one had been just sixteen. Sixteen! Even Jock was only twenty-four, and he was a squadron leader and CO. He thought of home, and the childhood he had had. A happy childhood – a very happy childhood of wonderful freedom. Never once had it crossed his mind that just a few years later he'd be flying for his life – flying for Britain – and trying to shoot down and kill Germans. It was incredible, almost impossible to take in. Was he a different person now? He didn't think so. Not really, and yet he had shown that he was capable of taking another man's life, something he would never have thought possible when he'd been a teenage boy tramping the hills or trying to put a motorcycle engine back together.

His mind turned back to three days earlier: 15 August. That had been some day. First scramble at a little after eleven in the morning and a short, sharp tussle with some 109s in which Gordon Hemmings in A Flight had been killed. When they got back to Hawkinge, it was to discover the airfield shrouded in smoke and another mass of craters. Archie had found it surprisingly easy to dodge the bomb holes as he landed, but a barracks block had been destroyed and another hangar damaged.

The second scramble had been a little after two in the afternoon, to intercept a raid that looked like it was making for the south coast but which then headed towards the Thames estuary. They'd been vectored north, across the north Kent coast and had eventually seen a number of 109s near Harwich, but the Messerschmitts turned back before they could engage.

Finally, they had been scrambled again at 5.20 p.m. and ordered to try to intercept a raid on Selsey Bill, near Portsmouth. They had spotted around thirty Ju 88s and had attacked, only to be attacked in turn by the same number of 109s. Archie had taken bits out of a Junkers but had been forced to break off to deal with two 109s that got on his tail. They had woven and turned about the sky, Archie pushing further and further inland until Charlie and Dougal had chased them off and the 109s had cut and run for home. Ivo Rainsby had bailed out, landing unhurt on the cricket field beneath Arundel Castle. When they landed again, they discovered Hawkinge had been hit for the second time that day – not hard, but there were a few more craters on the airfield.

Later that day, he had scribbled in his journal:

No one who hasn't flown in combat can understand how tiring it is. You might think three combat sorties in a day doesn't sound much – perhaps four hours' flying. But each one means constant concentration, which in itself is tiring. Sometimes I get out of my Spit and my brain can hardly think straight at all. It is also physically exhausting. Flying straight and level is one thing – stooging about the sky is a cinch. Any fool could do it. But every time you bank your Spit and pull a tight turn, the centrifugal forces really weigh you down. The controls become incredibly heavy, the blood drains from your head, your arms and legs ache, your neck doesn't want to move – it's as though it's been clamped in a tight lock. These dogfights don't ever last long – five minutes, maybe ten – but, boy, at the end of them, you're washed out. Your head is damp with sweat, your back drenched. Your whole body aches, and when you finally land again and clamber down, it's all you can do to stand up and not fall over.

It's also very frightening, I don't mind admitting it. My stomach starts to feel knotted and sometimes I find I'm shaking. I can't help myself. Then there are moments of feeling wonderful, of incredible exhilaration. It's strange.

Ivo had bailed out, so we had to go to the pub and hear him sing his song. I didn't feel like going, but then I was glad I did. It takes your mind off things. I think it helps to have a sing-song and a laugh and not think about flying for a couple of hours, even if it does mean not getting to bed until midnight. At least we can sleep between sorties. We're all so dog-tired, most of us can drop off at the click of a finger.

Archie looked at his watch: 4.20 p.m. He prayed they would not be scrambled again that day. He and Ted were due twenty-four hours' leave that night when they were stood down, and planned to go straight to Pimlico to have dinner with Tess and Mary Tyler. Archie couldn't wait – both to see Tess and to be back within the comforting surroundings of the Tyler home. The thought of that bed! Crisp, clean sheets, a mattress deep and wide enough to stretch out in. *Bliss.*

He began to doze, then slumped forward, his head in his arms on the table. Around him the low chatter from the hut, a blackbird singing nearby, a bee buzzing busily, the warmth of the sun lulling him to sleep . . .

Someone was shouting, a bell was clanging loudly, and Archie woke with a start.

'Wake up, Arch!' Ted said beside him, tugging him up from his chair.

'All right, all right.' Chair pushed back, and then he was running, engines starting up and the airfield suddenly alive with activity. On the far side of the airfield, the Hurricanes were also bursting into life, pilots running towards their machines.

Archie grabbed his parachute, hurriedly stepped into it, then leapt up on to the wing and hoisted himself inside. Helmet and goggles snatched from where they had been hanging on the mirror and hastily shoved on to his head. Harness in, leads in, check dials – all OK – then a thumbs up to Bufton and Lewis, and he was rolling forward. A quick rub of the eyes – *I was asleep two minutes ago* – and then switch on R/T, his IFF and Huff-Duff, check gauges and turn for take-off.

Blue Section all in a line, a glance across – *Yes, all four there* – and then throttles open and bumping across the grass. Fifty, sixty, tail up, seventy, eighty, ninety miles per hour, pull back on the stick, throttle open and gently ease the plane into the air, over the valley at the far end of the runway, the shadows of their Spitfires getting smaller and smaller.

'Hello, Bison Leader, this is Turban. A hundred plus bandits heading your way, steer 010, zero one zero, angels eighteen.'

So much for getting to London early, thought Archie, as they climbed once more to meet the enemy.

24

IN A SPIN OVER KENT

Sunday 25 August. Another lovely summer's morning and as Group Captain Tyler had walked to work, he wished he could spend his Sunday with Mary and Tess – a walk in St James's Park, then a roast for lunch, out in the garden, perhaps. The capital seemed calm enough that morning, yet bombs had fallen on the city the night before – for the first time. Three suburbs had been hit: Millwall, Tottenham and Islington; word had reached them at the Air Ministry late the previous night before he had left for home.

No doubt the bombers had dropped them accidentally – at any rate, it had hardly been a concentrated attack. A number of houses had been destroyed, but casualties were few. Still, it was a new experience for Londoners in this war.

Over Whitehall huge, bulbous, silvery-grey barrage balloons hung suspended. Sandbags were stacked up beside every entrance, guards stood watch, no longer in scarlet tunics but in khaki battledress; the visual reminders that London was at war. But in other ways, there was little to suggest Britain was fighting for her life.

What's more, Tyler was beginning to feel faint stirrings of hope. Two weeks earlier, it had all seemed impossibly bleak.

The next fortnight, he'd told Tess, would be decisive. Yet here they were, Fighter Command still fighting, her numbers of fighter aircraft barely dented thanks to the speed with which new ones were being built and damaged ones repaired. And miracle of miracles, the Luftwaffe had almost immediately called off their attacks on Britain's RDF stations. Why? It was unfathomable. What's more, Fighter Command's airfields were holding up well. Only one – Manston – had been made inoperable so far, and that was just two days ago, when it had been pummelled during a particularly heavy raid. Fighter Command could manage without Manston, however. Nor were the Luftwaffe targeting Fighter Command airfields only. It was now quite clear that Luftwaffe intelligence was faulty in the extreme; they seemed to have no idea that the RAF was split into three commands and that it was Fighter Command they needed to destroy in order to win air superiority. A third of the airfields hit had been Coastal Command and Fleet Air Arm. Tyler felt Fighter Command was doing a lot right, but also that the Luftwaffe were making many mistakes. He had said as much to AVM Sholto Douglas that morning.

'Well, let's hope they keep doing so,' he'd replied with a chuckle.

The intelligence summaries that morning had brought even better news: first, that Göring had expected to destroy the RAF in just four days, and, second, that the Stukas were being withdrawn from the battle.

'It's incredible!' Douglas had exclaimed. 'The much-vaunted Stuka dive-bomber! What can Göring be thinking?'

'Presumably he feels he's lost too many, sir,' Tyler replied.

'And remind me,' said Douglas, as he stood by his window,

glancing over the summaries Tyler had given him, 'how many Stukas did we think they had two weeks ago?'

'Between five and six hundred, sir.'

Douglas whistled. 'And they've been completely withdrawn?'

'Yes, sir. You may recall me mentioning a young pilot who pointed out how vulnerable Stukas were as they came out of their dive?'

'I do.'

'It seems he was quite right. Our boys have shot down more Stukas since Dunkirk than any other kind of German aircraft. They appear to work well in support of ground troops, but not so well independently.'

Douglas chuckled. 'Good. So we live to fight another day, eh?'

'It would seem so, sir.'

Douglas had sat down again behind his desk and, having lit a cigarette, said, 'I've already had the PM's office on the phone this morning about the bombs that fell on London last night.'

'Almost certainly by mistake.'

'Well, that's as maybe. But it seems the War Cabinet want us to retaliate with an attack on Berlin.'

'An attack on Berlin, sir? Is that wise?'

'You don't think so, Tyler?'

'No, sir. Fighter Command is containing the Luftwaffe at the moment, but if we hit Berlin Hitler is bound to retaliate. If they send the full force of their air fleets over London, the devastation might be untold. The loss of life could be appalling.'

Douglas looked thoughtful. 'But if they retaliate on London then they can't be attacking any airfields at all. It might give our boys a breather. I know Dowding is worried about pilot shortage. We're all right for the time being, but in another week . . . well, it might be very different. Not even Dowding is convinced we can keep up this intensity for too much longer.'

'I don't think the Luftwaffe can either. We're doing better than we could have hoped two weeks ago, sir,' said Tyler. 'Luftwaffe losses have been high – both in terms of aircraft and aircrew. Have you seen the transcripts from Trent Park, sir?'

Douglas shook his head.

'We've been taking Luftwaffe officers down there, sir, and not only interrogating them, but bugging their rooms. The conversations they have when they're together have been most illuminating. Morale is taking a nosedive. The fighter pilots hate flying over water and they resent being ordered to stick to the bombers. It means losing their advantage of height and speed. Some squadrons have less than ten aircraft. Don't get me wrong, sir, I still think they are immensely strong, but it's not going their way at the moment, and especially not now that the Stukas have been withdrawn. Fighter Command is holding up. We don't need to lure the Luftwaffe on to London in order to protect our airfields.'

'Hmm,' said Douglas. 'I take your point. All right, let me head over to Number 10 myself. I think, on reflection, you might be right, Tyler.'

*

Monday 26 August, around 12.05 p.m. 'Christ, I can't get this Hun off my tail!' Muffled sounds of machine-gun and cannon fire, then, 'Jesus, that was close!'

'I'm on to him, Ted, hold on!' Archie called back. Opening the throttle wide, he turned his plane on to its side and dived down towards the Spitfire and the 109 locked in a deadly game of cat and mouse. Archie could see it all: Ted's Spit on its side, pulling as tight a left turn as he dared, the 109 following, firing short, sharp bursts of tracer that whipped past Ted's tail but were getting ever closer. In a few more seconds they were going to rip Ted's plane to pieces. It was all wrong: everyone knew a Spitfire could always out-turn a 109, and yet this German was gaining on him.

But he hadn't seen Archie, who now dived down on the German's blind side and at a hundred yards pressed down on the gun button and gave him a two-second burst, until he was almost at point-blank range. As he hurtled over, the Messerschmitt exploded, knocking Archie's Spitfire with its force.

'You got him! You got him!' shouted Ted. 'Thank God, you got him!'

Archie could hear the shortness of Ted's breath – the panic, the relief – *the fear.* He looked down. A tumbling ball of flame and metal was plunging towards the ground, while a lone wing fluttered and twirled on its long descent.

A loud crack, then another, deafening in his ears, and the Spitfire was knocked forward, as if smashed by a giant hammer. Smoke filled the cockpit, thick and swirling and hot, and Archie was blinded. He was spinning – spinning and falling, the centrifugal force pinning him to his seat, pressing down on his head as if two hands were holding it there. *Panic.* His eyes could not see, his mind could not think. *I'm dying,* he thought.

The force on his body was immense. Round and round, the engine screaming, the airframe rattling. *Think, think, think.*

'Get out! Archie, get out! Archie! Archie! For God's sake, get out of there!'

Was that his own voice? Or Ted's? Terror gripped him, paralysed him. *Get out* – he had to get out. The hood – he had to get the canopy open. Despite the weight pressing down on him, he forced his hands to where the canopy hooked on to the windscreen and yanked the handle. A jolt, and the canopy slipped back an inch and smoke gushed out, sucked from the cockpit, and now he could see, the ground spinning towards him. He yanked the canopy again, but it was stuck.

Oh, Jesus, no. He pulled again – nothing. *Calm down and think. THINK*. His mind cleared – he'd been here before. It wasn't so hard. Stick forward, kick on full rudder, open the throttle, and suddenly the spinning stopped and the Spitfire swooped, inverted, out of its spiralling dive. Again Archie yanked the canopy, and this time, with the strength in his arms returning, it slid open. *Quick, quick, get out!* The Spitfire had had it, flames licking back along the cowling, but the ground was horribly close now. Ripping off his oxygen and radio leads, he released the harness catch and felt himself falling, tumbling. Gripping the cord, he pulled, felt the pack release and a moment later the parachute billowed open, yanking his shoulders. He cried out, then saw his Spitfire hit the ground half a mile away and explode.

Seconds later, the ground was rushing up towards him – a cornfield, a wood at one end, the vague impression of a farmhouse a short distance away, and then, *whoomp*, he landed. A bolt of pain shot from his leg right up his back. Gasping, he hit the quick-release catch on his harness and lay back, grimacing. His right leg was sticky with blood. *But I'm alive,* he thought. *I am alive*.

For some minutes he lay there, surrounded by ripe, unharvested wheat. It smelled of earth and dust, and somehow gentle and good and peaceful. An image flashed across his mind: the plunging, spinning Spitfire, the cockpit filled with smoke, the paralysing panic. He'd not seen his attacker. Not seen him at all. He thought of the poster in the dispersal hut, a cartoon with the warning, 'Look out! It's the one you don't see who gets you!' He'd thought he'd developed into quite a good fighter pilot, but who was he trying to fool? He'd been shot down three times. Three times! And yet he'd survived every time – and here he was again, not eviscerated, but alive, even if his leg was agony. No wonder Jock had started to call him Lucky. Above him, the sky from which he had fallen at such speed. Deep and endless blue, but marked with swirls of white contrails. At least he'd saved Ted, he thought. He hoped they'd all got back all right.

Shouts not far away, then rustling, and suddenly a black Labrador was standing over him, snuffling and licking his face.

'Nelson! Nelson!' someone shouted. The dog looked up and barked. A moment later, a boy – maybe eleven or twelve – appeared.

'Dad! He's here!' he yelled. Turning to Archie he said, 'Are you all right?' and at the same time saw his bloodied leg.

'I think so,' said Archie, 'although my leg hurts rather.'

'We saw you coming down.' He made a diving movement with his arm. 'Your plane hit the field over there.' He pointed.

'I know – I saw it hit before I landed.'

A middle-aged man appeared, wearing an open-necked cotton shirt and soft brown hat, and with gaiters round his legs.

'Don't worry,' he said, 'we'll get you sorted. How bad d'you think your leg is? Let me have a look.' He crouched down.

'I'm not really sure. I wasn't aware of it until I landed. I'm sorry about your field.'

The man waved a hand. 'Don't worry. You very considerately crashed it into a pasture. Gave the sheep a bit of scare, but no crops lost.' He smiled. 'I'm David Galloway, by the way,' he said, holding out his hand. 'I'm the farmer here.'

'Archie Jackson. Where am I? Last time I looked we were over north Kent.'

'You've come down on the North Downs. Between Wye and Canterbury. Quite a battle going on up there.' Galloway peered at Archie's leg. 'Looks like you've been hit in a couple of places.' He pulled out a large spotted handkerchief. 'I'm going to tie this around the top of your thigh, then, if you think you can manage, we'll get you up and I can help you to the house. All right?'

Archie nodded, then, as Galloway tied the tourniquet, clenched his teeth as new barbs of pain shot through him.

'Shall we try?' said Galloway.

Archie gasped and nodded again.

'Put your arm around my neck,' said Galloway. 'One, two, three!' He straightened and Archie was pulled up, hopping on one leg. He gasped again, his breathing heavy.

'All right?' said Galloway.

'Yes – yes, thank you.'

Ahead, hurrying from the farm, were several soldiers. 'The Home Guard to the rescue.'

Good, thought Archie, *because this hurts like hell.*

'We'll wait, shall we?' said Galloway.

'Did you get any?' the boy now asked Archie.

'Er, yes, I did as a matter of fact,' Archie replied. 'A 109, just before I was hit.'

The boy looked impressed. 'Have you got many?'

'Eddie!' said his father. 'You shouldn't ask things like that. It's enough that he's getting into the sky every day.'

'It's quite all right,' said Archie. 'Actually, I've got eleven and a half confirmed.'

'Blimey!' said Eddie. 'An ace twice over!'

'You might not be adding to that for a bit, though,' said Galloway.

Archie hadn't thought of that. He felt his spirits rise. Perhaps he would see Tess. *Maybe I'll get some leave.* Then he chided himself; there were the others to think about. More than that – there was the small matter of stopping the Germans invading their country. According to what he'd read in the papers, Britain was facing the greatest threat since Napoleon – and here he was, thinking of leave and Tess!

The four men from the Home Guard reached them. They were all middle-aged except for the officer, who wore a colonel's uniform from the last war, and, Archie guessed, was in his sixties.

'Colonel Hanbury from the Wye Home Guard,' he said. 'Come on, chaps,' he said to his men, 'let's lift this young man.'

Two of them made a cradle with their hands, and the third helped to hoist Archie up. He felt embarrassed, a ridiculous figure being carried through the corn. It reminded him of being lifted from the rugby field with a broken leg as a twelve-year-old. The memory of that sense of shame flooded back now.

'I'm so sorry to be such a nuisance,' he said.

'Not at all, not at all,' said the colonel, who appeared to have assumed command of the situation. 'Have you right as rain in no time.'

At the farmhouse, they laid him on a sofa, Mrs Galloway cutting away his trouser leg and gently dabbing at the wounds with warm water.

'How old are you?' she asked. She had a soft, gentle face.

'Nineteen,' he said.

'Goodness,' she replied. 'So young. You're still a boy.'

Soon after, an army ambulance arrived. Archie was given a shot of morphine and put on to a stretcher. He felt suddenly very tired.

'Good luck,' he heard the Galloways say. The Home Guard seemed to have gone.

'Thank you,' said Archie. 'Thank you for helping me.' He put his hand to his neck. *Good*, the scarf was still there. He really did feel very tired. He was vaguely conscious of being in sunlight again, and then almost immediately it was shut out and he was bumping down a lane. And at that point, consciousness left him.

The same day, around four in the afternoon. Group Captain Guy Tyler was in his office in King Charles II Street when the Air Ministry operator put a call through to him.

'Hello, Pops?'

'Ted, are you all right?'

'Yes, I'm fine, although I nearly wasn't. Look, I'm sorry to ring you at work – I know how busy you are, but –'

'Ted, it's all right – honestly. What's happened?'

'It's Archie.'

Oh, no, thought Tyler. He was very fond of Archie – and he knew what a good friend he was to Ted and how much Tess thought of him.

'He's been wounded. Not too badly, though.'

'Thank God for that.'

'Pops, he was saving my life. I was being hammered – this 109 – I don't know how he did it, because we all thought a 109 couldn't out-turn a Spit – but he was turning inside me and I couldn't dive because a 109 can definitely dive faster than a Spitfire, and I was moments away from being badly clobbered, and then Archie swooped in and shot him down, but was then shot down in turn, and I watched him go into a vertical spin, trailing smoke, and I honestly thought he'd been killed – God only knows how he got out of that spin, but he did and bailed out, but he's been shot up in the legs and he's now in the Kent and Canterbury Hospital.'

'All right, all right, Ted – calm down.'

'Actually, I am all right – I'm not calm, but I am all right, anyway. Skipper says I can go down and see him later, but I wanted you to tell Tess. Will you do that, Pops?'

'Of course I will. And well done – all of you.' He cleared his throat. 'I'm very proud of you, Ted.'

'And tell Mama I'll be back tomorrow. I know I said tonight, but it'll have to be tomorrow now.'

'Of course. And I'll go and find Tess right away.'

Ted rang off and Tyler sat at his desk and thought for a moment. He had seen plenty of vertical spins in the last war, and only one when a pilot had managed to pull out successfully. The problem was that they had had no parachutes then – Trenchard wouldn't allow them. If one ever got into a vertical spin, the chances were that your kite was finished already, even if one did manage to pull out of it. *Terrifying,* he thought. *Absolutely terrifying.* Thank God they had parachutes now.

He also knew that a 109 could out-turn a Spitfire. Tests had been carried out on a captured model and had proved it conclusively. They had decided, however, to keep that one quiet; it was a difficult manoeuvre and there was felt to be no benefit in undermining the confidence they all had in the manoeuvrability of both the Spitfire and the Hurricane. But perhaps, he thought, he would explain it to Ted. After all, forewarned was forearmed. *Hmm.* He would think about it.

Having told his secretary he was stepping out for ten minutes, he walked down the stairs and along a corridor to where Tess was working, then, having spoken to her superior, waited for his daughter to appear.

'What is it, Pops?' she said, worry etched on her face.

'Archie's been wounded.'

She put her hands to her face. 'Oh, no. Badly? He's not burned, is he?'

'No, no, he's all right. He's going to be fine. Wounded in the leg, that's all.' He put his arm around her. 'Come on,' he said. 'Let's go out and get some tea. We'll go to that café in the park. The war can wait for us for twenty minutes.'

She nodded, then said, 'What happened, Pops?'

He repeated what Ted had told him.

'Can I go and see him?'

'I'm sure. Let me have a word. Perhaps you can go down tomorrow.'

'I am owed a day off, actually, because I worked all weekend.'

'There you are, then.'

They found the café, bought two cups of sweet tea and a bun each, and sat down at a small table in the sun overlooking the lake.

'Poor Archie,' she said.

'Or perhaps he's been rather fortunate. He'll be out of the battle for a bit.'

She brightened. 'I suppose so. I hadn't thought of that. I can't bear the thought of them both being at Biggin and so in the front line. You should read Archie's letters. He tries to be cheery and to make light of it all, but they've been flying three sorties a day, and meeting formations of aircraft sometimes sixty and even a hundred strong. They're exhausted.'

'I know.' In fact, he was aware that 337 Squadron were about to be rotated out of the front line. He wasn't quite sure when, but any day now. Dowding and Park had concluded it was time for a different squadron to take the flak at Biggin.

'Pops, two weeks ago, you said we'd know by now which way the battle was going. Do we? Are we winning, do you think?'

Tyler took his daughter's hand and smiled. 'I think we might just be starting to, yes.'

25

CONVALESCENCE

Saturday 31 August, around seven in the evening. King's Cross Station was busy. A mass of uniforms – soldiers, sailors, airmen – as well as civilians clambering down from trains, boarding trains; some hurrying along the platform, others ambling; porters with trolleys piled high with luggage. The hiss of steam, the clack of shutting doors, the shrill blast of the guard's whistle. A low hubbub of British men, women and children, and, Archie noticed, a fair few foreigners besides: some Canadian troops, for example, stood together, smoking, as he and Tess walked past towards his train.

Reaching the sleeper, he stopped and turned, putting down his case.

'Thank you for meeting me today,' he said, 'and for seeing me off.'

She hugged him. 'Have a good time with your family.'

'I will. And thank you for coming to visit me in hospital too.'

'I'll miss you,' she said. 'Scotland seems such an awfully long way.'

'I'll miss you too, but it's only a week. It'll go by in a flash.'

'Let's hope we won't have been invaded by then.'

Archie smiled. 'No chance.'

She squeezed him tightly, then kissed him, and he turned and swung his case on to the train, then carefully hoisted himself up using his crutch. The door shut with a loud clack, but he turned and leaned out of the window and took her hands in his. Steam swirled along the platform from the locomotive, then suddenly a whistle blasted and with a slow, deliberate *chunt, chunt*, the train began to move. Tess kept pace, walking then running along the platform. Then, as the train slowly gathered speed, she let go and Archie watched her waving from the platform, until, in a flurry of steam, she disappeared from view.

He found his cabin and, although it was a twin, was pleased to discover he had it to himself. The bed had yet to be made up and so for a while he sat on the seat, his leg straight up in front of him, staring out of the window.

The fragments of a cannon shell had done for him. His leg had been lacerated in several places, but no bone had been broken, and no artery severed. All the pieces had been taken out – the surgeon had presented them to him in a small tin pot – the wounds stitched and dressed, and five days later he had been discharged, the doctor assuring him that with a bit of rest, he would soon be 'as right as rain'.

'Take a week's rest, young man,' the doctor had told him. 'Where's home?'

'Perthshire, sir.'

'Perfect – best place for you. Get away from it all. Rest the mind as well as the body.' He had signed Archie's release form. 'Good luck. You've been lucky, Jackson. A half-inch to the left with that big piece and it might have been a very different story, but, as it is, I'm expecting your leg to heal very nicely. You have a GP up in Perthshire?'

'My father's a GP, sir.'

The doctor had laughed. 'Well, well – you are lucky. Your father can take out the stitches for you. I'll book you in for a medical on Sunday 8 September. Then, assuming all is well, you should be fit enough to rejoin your squadron.'

Archie opened his bag and took out a paperback and his journal. Ted had brought it down that first evening. He'd still been a bit dazed then, doped up as he was with morphine, but Ted had been profusely grateful to him. 'You'd have done the same,' Archie had told him, 'and, anyway, I didn't see the blighter that got me. That was my fault and because I forgot to look round rather than because I nobbled your Hun.'

The next day Tess had arrived. One minute he'd been asleep, the journal resting on his lap, the next he had opened his eyes and there she was, a vision of loveliness, standing before him. She'd stayed all afternoon, and outside the rain had poured down. There had been little going on in the air that day. She had told him that her father was more optimistic now, that he thought the RAF was slowly but surely winning.

'But he's worried about London,' she said, 'now that we've bombed Berlin.'

'Have we?' Archie had replied. 'I didn't know. I didn't think we could fly that far.'

'Pops was against it,' she told him. 'He told them that the RAF was surviving without too much damage to their airfields and that if we bombed Berlin, the Luftwaffe would turn on London in retaliation. Apparently, Churchill said that if the RAF bombed Berlin, it would show the world we could fight back and hit at the heart of the Reich.'

'And so we really have bombed Berlin?'

'Yes. It's a little frightening to think they might start bombing us.'

'I don't think I like the thought of that at all,' Archie had told her. 'I'd be worried stiff about you.'

'Well, they haven't yet. Maybe they won't after all.'

They had also talked of their plans – their tour of Scotland on the motorcycle and sidecar – of things that one day they would like to do and how they wanted to live their lives. There was so much future to be had: there was the perfect house to live in, or owning an open-topped sports car, in which they would travel around Europe after the war; and there was an unspoken understanding that these things would be done together, even though Archie thought, *But I'm still only nineteen, and you're the only girl I've ever really known.*

Two days on, the weather had once again closed in, and later in the afternoon Ted had turned up again, this time with Jock and Charlie Bannerman. And they brought news: they were moving. 337 Squadron had been posted to Boscombe Down, near Salisbury, in 10 Group.

'So hopefully we can put our feet up a bit.' Jock grinned. 'God knows, we could all do with a breather. We lost a couple more yesterday, I'm afraid.'

'Who?'

'Billy – his parachute didn't open – and one of the new boys. He's alive, but badly burned. He's been packed off to the burns place at East Grinstead.' Jock rubbed his brow; he suddenly looked exhausted. 'So we're a few pilots down, which means more flying for everyone else. We keep being sent new sprogs, but I can't send them up. They'll be more of a hindrance than a help and will get themselves shot down in a trice. At least at Boscombe we might get a chance to train them up a bit.'

'I'm not sure it'll be that easy there, Skip,' Archie had said. 'Our old pals at 629 Squadron have been pretty busy.'

'Not so much now the fighting's moved inland,' said Ted. 'It's down here that the Jerries are really interested in.'

'It should be a bit easier,' said Jock. 'I don't think we'll be called upon so much, but we'll be there if we're really needed. That's what Happy told me.'

'How do you think it's going?' asked Archie. 'The battle, I mean? Do you think Jerry really will invade?'

Jock smiled. 'He's not doing that well so far, is he? We're still here. We're still fighting.'

'There's the Navy too, don't forget,' said Charlie. 'And all those mines in the Channel. I'm telling you, an invasion won't be easy.'

Jock pushed Charlie gently. 'We won't need to call on the Navy. We'll see them off on our own. Look,' he added, 'they've not even knocked out one airfield yet, have they?'

'I thought Manston had been abandoned,' said Charlie.

'All right – but that's only one. It's been hard going, I'll admit, but I can't see Jerry beating us. I can't see it at all.'

'So there's your answer, Archie.' Charlie grinned.

Jock had yawned and stretched. 'You know what? I should get myself a little flesh wound. A few days being looked after by the nurses and a bit of time off to convalesce would suit me to a tee right now.'

'You didn't mention you got shot down yesterday, Skip,' said Charlie.

'Sadly for me, I was unscathed,' he said with a grin.

'Did you sing a song?' asked Archie.

'Did he sing a song? Did he ever!' said Charlie.

'My favourite ever Cole Porter,' said Jock. '"Anything Goes". Went down a storm, though I say it myself.'

'Skipper's got a surprisingly good voice,' agreed Charlie. 'I almost think he got shot down on purpose, just so he could show off.'

Jock held up his hands in mock surrender. 'I've been found out.'

'Just think, Skip,' said Archie, 'you wouldn't have been able to do the song if you'd got yourself wounded.'

'That,' said Jock, 'is a very good point.'

Then Ted had said, 'By the way, apparently a 109 can turn inside a Spitfire.'

'I know. I saw it.'

'They've been testing one at Farnborough,' Ted continued. 'The 109 has got slats to help it land and they can be released at around one hundred and forty miles per hour.'

'And when you're circling you lose speed.'

'Exactly. So the canny Hun can drop his slats and out-turn a Spit. Doesn't seem like a lot of Jerries have worked this out, though, but it's worth bearing in mind.'

'We learn something new every day,' said Jock.

They had left soon after, driving back in the skipper's car for one last night at Biggin. Archie thought of them all now, away in the west: new digs, a new Mess, new dispersal. And a small part of him felt slightly left out.

His father was there to meet him at Waverley. Archie stepped down on to the platform, having had a surprisingly good night's sleep, and looked around at the dark red buildings that towered over Edinburgh's station and then up at the castle, as immovable as ever, and felt time shrink. It all looked so familiar, so unchanged; it was as though he had never been away, and yet it had been three and a half very long months, before 629 Squadron had been posted south from Drem.

As the steam cleared, he saw his father wave and stride towards him.

'Dear boy!' he called out.

'Hello, Dad,' said Archie, grinning bashfully.

His father embraced him, then, still clutching his son's arms, said, 'Let me look at you. How do you feel? You don't look too bad.'

'I'm fine. Leg twinges a bit. Itches more than anything and it's a bit stiff, but otherwise I feel OK. Really.'

'And you slept all right?'

'Like a log.'

'Well, your mother's dying to see you. Has been preparing your favourite dinner especially.'

'Thank you for coming to get me,' said Archie. 'I hope you haven't used up too many petrol coupons.'

His father waved a dismissive hand. 'Oh, don't you worry about that. Doctor's perks.'

The drive took the best part of two hours, and then there they were, turning off the road from Aberfeldy, and running alongside the Tay.

'You've managed to get some fishing in this year, then, Dad?' said Archie.

'A bit. I got a beauty one evening a few weeks ago – a lovely six-pounder. Fought like hell, but I landed him eventually. Tasted pretty good too.'

'And is Strathtay still open? I wouldn't mind a round or two if I can manage it before the week's out.'

'Yes, just about. But I'd take it a little steady, Archie. See how you go.'

'I will,' said Archie, although he was going to try his hardest to get at least one round of golf in.

Nearly there, he thought, as they passed along the winding valley he knew so well, and then they were turning left up the track, bumping and jolting up the hill, past the farm and along the drive to their home. It was a glorious day; the house and the hillside on which it perched were bathed in sunlight. His father beeped the horn, Duff, their dog, began barking and running towards them, then his mother emerged, smiling, from the house. But no Maggie. He wished she could be there too – the whole family.

'Hello, boy!' he said, easing himself out of the car and making a fuss of his Labrador, who whined and turned in circles, his tail thumping against Archie's leg. 'Ow, Duff!' he said, laughing, as his mother reached him. She hugged him tightly and for a moment Archie thought he might cry.

'We've been so worried,' she said, dabbing her eye. 'It's so wonderful to see you alive and looking so well – all things considered. I'm sorry,' she said, wiping her eyes again. 'It's just been such a worry.'

'You'll get me started in a minute,' said Archie, laughing, but feeling a lump rise in his throat. 'Anyway, I'm here, I'm all right.'

She led him inside. It smelled just how it always smelled: of woodsmoke and bread, with a residual odour of damp dog, even in summer.

'You're limping a bit,' said his mother.

'Well, I did have six fragments of a Jerry cannon shell in my leg.' He grinned. 'But it's getting better every day. I'm rather hoping Dad might take my stitches out in a day or two.'

'Can you manage the stairs?'

'Of course,' he said, and began climbing them, one at a time, his mother behind him.

'Don't fuss the boy, Kitty,' said his father from the hallway.

Archie turned and smiled. 'You're not fussing, Mum. It's lovely to be here. To see you both. There are definitely advantages to being wounded.'

His mother retreated all the same, and he was glad of that. He wanted to be alone when he went back to his old room. It had always been his: a room at the back of the house, that looked up to the hill behind, with stone walls and sheep on the lower slopes, and gorse and heather and bracken as it rose to the summit. There had been many times when he had lain in bed as a boy, the world beyond the window still bathed in golden summer evening light, the gentle bleating of sheep lulling him to sleep.

Gently, he pushed open the door and stepped in. Everything was as he had left it: his golf clubs in the corner alongside his fishing rod and cricket bat. On the chest of drawers were team photographs from school, a rugby ball, now soft, and a row of books: Biggles, Jeffery Farnol adventure stories, *A Primer of the Internal Combustion Engine* by Harold Wimperis. He picked it up – a dog-eared, battered copy, still smudged with oil stains. It had been a bible to him. Then he spotted the toy dog, long ago lost and then found again by his mother. On the walls were the same pictures: a framed map of the world, and a poster advertising the Schneider Trophy air races. And on his bed, there was Babbit – the worn and patched toy rabbit he had had since a baby.

It was, he realized, the room of the boy he had once been – the teenager who had lived for machines and golf and tramping the hills. An innocent. A boy uncorrupted by killing and war.

He slept that night with the sheep bleating on the hill, with Babbit beside him on his pillow and with the hope that his youth had not gone for ever. The following day, the weather was once again fine. He dug out some of his old clothes – a pair of bags and a cotton shirt and pullover. He was glad to be able to put the uniform away.

'What are you going to do with yourself while you're here, Archie?' asked his father at breakfast as they ate their kippers.

'Get some rest,' said his mother.

Archie rolled his eyes. 'Of course, but I'd like to see McAllister tomorrow. That is, if you could give me a lift, Dad.'

'I expect so,' said his father amiably, 'although perhaps we should go this afternoon – after lunch. He's usually tinkering with something and I'm sure he'd want to see you. I've given myself a day off today, but I'm afraid I've got my rounds and surgery tomorrow.'

'That would be great,' said Archie. 'Sooner the better.'

His father raised an eyebrow. 'Oh, yes?'

'I want to get a motorcycle with a sidecar and I remember McAllister had one, stuck away at the back of his garage. I was hoping it might still be there.'

'I've a feeling it is. I seem to remember seeing it not long ago

– although what condition it's in, I couldn't say. Another of McAllister's half-finished projects that never seem to see the light of day.' He chuckled to himself. 'He's a good fellow, though.'

'Well, if he's willing to let it go, I thought I might try to do it up.'

'What, in your condition?' said his mother.

'I don't need my leg to take an engine to pieces, Mum.'

'Why can't you add a sidecar to your Norton?'

Archie rolled his eyes. 'I could never do that to my Norton.'

'Probably not powerful enough,' said his father.

'Exactly,' said Archie.

His father said, 'You might find McAllister could do with the money. Have you got some stashed away, then?'

'Not very much. Twelve shillings a day doesn't go that far, and, to be honest, we tend to spend most of it, because you never quite know if –' He stopped, seeing his mother's anxious glance at his father. 'Sorry,' he said. 'I didn't mean it like that. It's just . . .'

'It's all right,' said his father. '*Carpe diem*, eh? Seize the day.'

'Yes,' said Archie. 'Something like that.'

After breakfast, he went with his mother to the farm to get milk and eggs. The McAndrewses were pleased to see him, as was old Mrs Lyall, who had called by. Mrs McAndrews told him how proud she was of him, and that she was certain Britain could stop Hitler. Mrs Lyall berated Hitler. What did he want? Why couldn't he go back to Germany and leave everyone alone? Had he heard Churchill's latest speech, Mr McAndrews asked? He then did a decent impression of the PM. 'Never was so much owed by so many to so few!' he said with a flourish, then he slapped Archie on the back and said, 'That's you, Archie my boy. How does it feel to be one of the Few, eh?'

'There was a bit of a joke about that, actually,' Archie told him. 'We thought he was talking about our Mess bills.'

McAndrews laughed and laughed at that. 'Ha, ha, very good, Archie! I like that!'

'Everyone's so proud of you,' said his mother as they walked back along the track. 'They're thrilled to see you.'

'It was rather embarrassing,' said Archie. 'I mean, I know they meant well, but we don't feel like heroes, you know. In the squadron – well, no one's allowed to get above themselves. And we're pretty self-contained. We get up, go to dispersal, fly – do what we're told – hope we make it back again and then perhaps have a few drinks in the evening. We don't see anyone, really, outside the squadron. The only reason I reckon I know anything about what is going on is because of Ted's father. To be honest, in many ways I'd rather not know either. We try not to dwell on things too much.'

After lunch, Archie and his father drove back down the valley road to Pitlochry. As his father had predicted, the wooden sliding door at the front of the garage was open.

'McAllister!' called out Archie's father. 'I've someone to see you.'

A head appeared from a dark cavity at the back, then McAllister emerged. He was a small, wiry man with dishevelled, greying hair and a face etched with lines, especially at the corners of his eyes. McAllister was never a man to take life too seriously.

'Ah, young Archie!' he said, wiping oily hands on his boiler suit. 'Now there's a sight for sore eyes.' Then, noticing Archie was leaning on one of his father's sticks, he added, 'What sort of tomfoolery have you been doing to yourself?'

'It wasn't me,' said Archie, 'it was some Hun. Riddled my leg with cannon shell splinters.'

McAllister shook his head. 'Well, you're in one piece still, so that's something, and by the look of things it's earned you a wee bit of time off from larking around the sky too.' He winked. 'Anyway, it's good to see you. How long have you got?'

'A week.'

'And you'll be needing something to do, no doubt.' He grinned at Archie's father.

Archie looked sheepish. 'That old Royal Enfield you had with the sidecar – have you still got it?'

McAllister was rolling himself a cigarette. 'Follow me,' he said, leading them to the back of the garage. Archie loved the place. It was lined with workbenches filled with bits of engine, wrenches and other tools, there were old bicycles, and oil cans, and it smelled of oil and rubber and wood and dust. At the rear stood a dusty Model T Ford on blocks, but behind, in a dark corner, was a tarpaulin, which McAllister now pulled off to reveal the Royal Enfield with its sidecar still attached.

'You mean this one?'

'Yes,' said Archie, his face breaking into a smile.

'There's a strange story about this one. A fellow brought it in, way back in – oh, let me see . . .' He thought for a moment. 'Must be 1932. Said it wasn't firing properly. Anyway, I did some work on it and then wrote to him at the address he left and waited for a reply. I'm still waiting. The beggar's still not paid me.'

'So it's not really yours, then, is it?' said Archie's father.

McAllister lit his cigarette. 'Oh, I don't know. It's been eight years. And he never paid me and never showed his face again. I reckon it's mine all right now, don't you? Mind you, Archie, you might not want the sidecar.'

'Really? Why not?'

'It's a Steib. German. Made by the enemy.'

'I don't give a fig about that,' said Archie. 'It's perfect. And a 976 cc V-twin Enfield – it's an absolute beauty. But the thing is, would you be willing to sell?'

McAllister narrowed his eyes. 'Would I be willing to sell? Hmm . . .' He drew on his cigarette. 'I'll admit, I've not touched her in eight years now. And will I in the next eight? Probably not, truth be known. I tell you what, how about this: if you can get her up and running before your leave's over, then you can take her with you. Consider it a kind of permanent loan, but if that mister ever shows his face again and demands his motorcycle back, then we might have to talk terms. But if you don't get her going, then she stays here. That seem fair?'

'Fair? That's incredible! Wonderful! McAllister – thank you!' Archie shook his hand vigorously.

'I'm guessing you've got someone to go in the sidecar, then?' Another wink at Archie's father.

Archie felt himself redden. 'Yes, as a matter of fact, I have. And I'll bring her to see you.'

'If you get the bike working again.' He smiled and said, 'Well, let's wheel her out.'

A number of boxes and old engine parts had to be moved, but eventually the path was clear and, between them, they rolled the bike out on to the forecourt.

'She looks pretty good to me,' said Archie's father. 'A bit dusty, the wheels need some air, and the sidecar could do with a spruce, but otherwise . . .'

'She's a beautiful bike, all right. "Made like a gun, goes like a bullet." That's what they say about these,' said McAllister. 'But you'll need to strip that engine down. It's been sat idle too long, and I reckon I thought one of the piston rings might need replacing. It was burning too much oil. I'll bring her up to yours tomorrow morning.' He looked at his watch. 'On second thoughts, let's do it now, while the Doc's here to help. We'll get her on to the back of the pick-up.'

Archie could not stop grinning. 'I can't thank you enough, McAllister. Really I can't.'

'So you think you'll manage it, then? By Saturday?'

'I know I will,' said Archie. 'I'm not going to let this one slip through my hands.'

McAllister chuckled. 'Good for you, Archie. Good for you.'

26

BLACK SATURDAY

Saturday 7 September. A call at home at eight in the morning. It was Douglas Evill, Dowding's Senior Air Staff Officer, on the line.

'I'm sorry, Guy,' he said. 'But Stuffy needs you here by nine. He's called a meeting with Park and Sholto Douglas and wants you there too. Can you get here?'

Tyler had looked at his watch. *One hour – it'll be tight*. 'Yes, I'll be there.' He quickly shaved, dousing his face with cold water, then hastily dressed and left the house. The journey to Stanmore did not take long – half an hour if the roads were clear, and they usually were these days.

He was now Air Commodore Tyler – a promotion, and with it a new job on Air Chief Marshal Dowding's staff at Fighter Command Headquarters. It had come about very quickly, a week before, with an unexpected summons to Bentley Priory, not by Dowding, but by Air Vice-Marshal Evill.

His new job was to be one of three duty officers overseeing the vast underground Operations and Filter Rooms. Each worked an eight-hour shift, during which complete concentration was of paramount importance.

'This is the hub, Guy,' Evill had explained as they'd sat on a bench underneath a large cedar tree in the Bentley Priory grounds. 'As you well know, all the different pieces of information we get about the enemy's movements are delivered to the Filter Room. Signals from every RDF station, every Observer Corps sector station, and every other piece of intelligence, like the information from the bods we send up to thirty-five thousand feet to stooge about and spot enemy raids forming up over France – it all feeds into the Filter Room. There it's checked and cross-referenced, then the enemy movements are plotted in the Operations Room and passed on to the groups, who in turn pass it on to the sectors and then the squadrons. The system is so refined we can get the information to the squadrons in about three minutes and our boys in the air in a further three. So that's information received to airborne in six minutes. Your task, Guy, is to oversee it all – make sure information is acted upon. Don't get involved in the tactical running of the squadrons – we leave that to the group commanders. Your job is to ensure everything runs smoothly.'

He had then been taken to see Dowding. The C-in-C looked strained and tired, Tyler had thought, more than once removing his spectacles and rubbing his eyes. Neither Dowding nor Evill seemed hopeful; pilot shortage was their concern.

'I brought with me a brief appreciation of the German situation, sir,' Tyler told the chief. 'The Luftwaffe is suffering. Aircraft production is running at about a third of the rate of our own, and some squadrons seem to have no more than half a dozen aircraft. One prisoner revealed that his squadron spent two days last week with only two aircraft available. It's meant that their senior pilots have been flying more than they should.'

'Don't want the new chaps let loose in their precious aircraft, I suppose,' said Dowding, allowing himself a slight smirk.

'Exactly, sir,' agreed Tyler. 'But it also seems we were wrong in our estimation of enemy strength. Prisoner interrogations have shown that their squadrons are not as large as ours. We have twenty-two pilots and eighteen aircraft, with an optimum of twelve airborne, but the Germans only have twelve aircraft per squadron, and rarely have more than six airborne at any one time. We've been overestimating their strength by at least a third, if not more.'

Dowding had sat back in his chair. 'Hallelujah!' he said. 'That's the best news I've heard this past month.'

'If the Luftwaffe keep losing fighter aircraft at the rate they are doing, sir,' Tyler had continued, 'I think Göring will call his battle off in the next two weeks or so.'

A week on, Tyler hoped he had not given false hope. The Luftwaffe had kept coming – he'd been able to see them on the huge plotting table in the Operations Room. From his balcony view, he'd looked down on the huge map, the plotters calmly, efficiently pushing plots across the Channel. Fifteen-plus bombers would be picked up by radar in St Omer and a further thirty in Lille. As they neared the French coast, they would be joined by fifteen-plus, then thirty-plus fighters, until a mass of seventy or even a hundred aircraft was moving across the Channel.

A clearer picture of the size of enemy raids and the direction they were heading would be picked up by the Observer Corps as they reached the English coast. A number of different observer posts would report the same plot, which would then be compared and cross-referenced. In response, their own squadrons would also be plotted. It was all done so quietly, so calmly. So efficiently. Yet Tyler knew what it was like for those boys who were scrambled to intercept – the fear, the confusion, the moments of panic. So far, 337 Squadron had been called into action just once from Boscombe Down, but he dreaded the moment he would have to see his son's squadron moved across the map towards one of the Luftwaffe's largest raids.

His shift during this past week had been from 4 p.m. until midnight, which was why, when Evill had rung, he had still been in bed. There was no question of even a second's sleep while on duty, and Tyler had discovered that by the time he arrived back home, he slept like the dead. Evill had warned him that it was essential he should get enough rest. 'We need your mind fresh and alert each day, Guy. You're no use to us if you're overly tired.' And so far, enough sleep and plenty of coffee had done the trick.

Reaching Bentley Priory with five minutes to spare, he made straight for Dowding's office and was soon ushered in. Evill was already there, then Douglas, the Deputy Chief of the Air Staff, arrived and then finally so did Air Vice-Marshal Park.

'I've asked you to join us, Tyler,' said Dowding, 'because of your intelligence background. Now I heard what you had to say last week and all of us here have read your report. What you wrote about Luftwaffe strength may be quite correct, but I'm rather more concerned about our own situation. If we can keep our squadrons in decent shape, then we don't need to worry about what the Luftwaffe may or may not have.' He paused and looked at them all over his half-moon glasses. 'The fact is, our squadrons are falling under strength. So far, we've been able to rotate the hardest hit and most exhausted squadrons out of the front line and put fresh ones in, but the pace of the battle has increased so much that some of the new squadrons are falling behind after just a few days. I'm determined to keep 11 Group at full strength come what may, but I'm not entirely sure how we're going to be able to do that. Not without severely weakening other parts of the country.'

Sholto Douglas cleared his throat and took his pipe from his mouth. 'I think you're being too pessimistic. I've been looking at the pilot figures this morning and we've got plenty coming through the OTUs who can cover the shortfall.'

'Forgive me, Sholto,' said Dowding, 'but I think you're missing the point here. It is one thing to be a trained pilot, and quite another to be a combat-ready fighter pilot. At current rates, we are losing one hundred and twenty pilots a week, which is outstripping the number of pilots coming out of the OTUs, according to the figures that I have. We've already cut the OTU course by two weeks. Squadron leaders are receiving pilots with just fifteen to twenty hours on Spitfires and Hurricanes – and, quite understandably, most are refusing to send them into battle because they know they usually get shot down in a trice.'

'I agree,' said Park. 'You can't expect COs to send these sprogs straight into the air. They won't do it. It's little short of murder to them.'

'I think we all have to accept, gentlemen,' said Dowding, 'that right now we are going downhill.'

Tyler now interjected. 'Excuse me, sir, but so are the Luftwaffe.'

'Exactly,' said Douglas.

'Yes, but the Luftwaffe still has many more aircraft than us,' said Dowding, 'and while I accept that, as it stands, we now probably have more single-engine fighters than they do, that counts for nothing if we don't have skilled fighter pilots to fly them.' He looked at Tyler. 'You said last week that you thought the Luftwaffe would be forced to call the battle off by the middle of the month. That's still a week away and they won't do so without a maximum effort. We have reached the critical moment in the battle, gentlemen. Never have we needed experienced pilots more than now.'

'I think I may have the answer,' said Park. 'We can send our new pilots straight out of OTU to the north or to the far south-west. They can join operational squadrons but, because they are likely to see little action, they can use the time to build up their flying hours. Should a lone raider appear from Norway, for example, they can be scrambled and go after it. They will get some invaluable operational experience but at limited risk. At the same time, we can send fully trained and experienced pilots south.'

'But we need fresh operational squadrons to exchange with your own battle-exhausted squadrons,' said Dowding.

'The two schemes could run in tandem,' Park replied. 'I'm only suggesting importing individual pilots in 11 Group squadrons, and this might only take place if a squadron's number of fully trained pilots falls below, say, fifteen in total.'

'Go on,' said Dowding.

'We will categorize squadrons,' said Park. 'Class A are those in 11 Group and one or stwo in 10 and 12 Groups that have fifteen or more combat-ready pilots. Class B squadrons could contain up to six non-operational pilots from OTUs, and a final category, Class C, would retain at least three fully operational pilots who will teach the sprogs the ropes.'

Sholto Douglas nodded. 'Good idea, Keith. Seems sound to me.'

'So Category C squadrons would mostly be in 13 Group in the north,' said Dowding.

'Exactly. And we can act on this right away. We've sent a number of squadrons out of 11 Group in the past week.' He reeled off several numbers, using his fingers to count them off. 'There's 32 Squadron at Acklington. They've had ten days out of the firing line. Several of their experienced pilots can be posted back to squadrons in 11 Group.'

Tyler sat there, rigid, waiting for what was coming.

'And there's 337 Squadron at Boscombe. Strictly speaking, they might be considered a borderline Class A, but they've not done much this past week. And there are men coming back from convalescence. Good, experienced pilots. These men could make all the difference.'

'All right,' said Dowding. 'So are we all agreed?'

Reluctantly, Tyler nodded his head.

'Good. Douglas, can you and your staff draw up moving lists and send a note out in my name to every squadron?'

'Of course, sir.'

Dowding took off his spectacles and stroked his trim moustache thoughtfully. 'God willing, this scheme of yours might just work, Keith.'

'Let's hope so, sir. Let's hope so.'

An hour later, having agreed to the transfer of over a hundred new pilots to new Class C squadrons in the north, and posted more than forty combat-ready pilots back to the south, Evill turned to 337 Squadron at Boscombe Down.

'We need to do something about 599 Squadron at Kenley. They've lost their CO and a flight commander and three others this past week. Can we reinforce them from 337?'

A call was put through to the squadron adjutant by Group Captain Saunders, one of Evill's staff. Tyler listened, a sickening feeling creeping over him. They were running through the entire squadron: age, experience, date when joined. Number of kills.

'Really?' he heard Saunders say. 'That's rather good. Yes, I'm sure you'd be sorry to lose them . . . No, look, I'm awfully sorry about this, Wheeler, but that's all there is to it . . . They're desperately needed back in 11 Group. Yes . . . yes . . . All right, Wheeler. Yes, so that's four, and who's this other chap?' A pause. 'And when is he due back? Oh, good. Well, we can get him checked by an MO at Kingsway then send him straight on to Kenley with the others . . . Tomorrow, yes . . . All right, goodbye.' He put down the phone. 'Not a happy fellow,' he said, 'but that's Flight Lieutenant Bannerman, Flying Officers Macfarlane and Mazarin, and Pilot Officer Tyler and, all being well, Pilot Officer Jackson.' He stopped a moment. 'Tyler – is he your boy, sir?'

'Yes,' said Tyler. He felt numb. *They're sending him back.*

'And we need to get a telegram to this chap Jackson. Apparently, he's on convalescence leave but due back tomorrow.'

Tyler rubbed his brow. 'It's all right, I can tell him. He's staying at my house tonight.'

He felt a hand on his shoulder and looked up to see Evill standing beside him. 'I'm sorry, Guy,' he said. 'Now, why don't you go home and get some rest?'

*

Of course Archie had managed to get the bike running. He'd worked hard in the shed at home, but it had brought him many contented hours, in which he had been able to put the war to one side and return to the pleasures that had filled his boyhood. He loved that shed, with its workbench and smell of dust and oil. His father had helped too, and even his mother had scrubbed and cleaned the Steib sidecar.

His leg had also improved with every day, so much so that he had even walked halfway to the top of the hill behind the house. There he sat and marvelled at the view and vowed that if he managed to survive the war, he would come back and live out the rest of his days there. And who with? Tess? *Perhaps.*

His mother wept when he left, early on Saturday morning, and he had again felt like crying himself. With his case in the sidecar and wearing his Irvin and flying helmet and goggles, he had rumbled off down the drive, feeling a lead weight heavy in his throat. It was as though he had been given a brief chance to return to the life he had left at the start of the war, but which he knew he could never return to again. He must go back to the war and to an adult life; in a few months he would be twenty. It was a strange feeling; he yearned to see Tess, and to be with Ted and the boys, but it was as though he were leaving a part of himself behind for ever.

It was a long journey, and, if he were honest, he supposed he'd been foolish to try to ride such a distance in one day, but his leg, although stiff and itching rather, was not causing him any pain. Fresh air and plenty of rest had been as wondrous a medicine as any.

It was around seven o'clock when he crested Hampstead and saw huge clouds of smoke billowing high into the sky from the east of London, the black and grey of the smoke darkly sinister against the deep azure blue of the canopy above. *They've hit London,* he thought. Guy Tyler had been right. He pressed on and saw that the fires were not only in the docks. Smoke was rising from Tottenham too. A fire engine hurried past, its bells clanging. *My God,* he thought.

It was after half past seven when he finally pulled into Winchester Street and drew up outside the Tylers' house. Stiffly, he eased himself off the Enfield, and, grabbing his bag, climbed the steps to the front door.

A rap of the knocker and, a moment later, footsteps within, and then the door opened and there was Tess.

'Archie! You're back!' She flung her arms around him, then Ted emerged too.

'Archie, old chap – welcome back.'

'What's been happening? When was London hit?'

'This afternoon – it's been awful,' said Tess. 'Nothing here, thank goodness.'

'But they've hammered the East End,' said Ted. 'We watched it from the roof.'

'Pops said this would happen,' said Tess, then she saw the bike on the road outside. 'My gosh, Archie, where did you get that?'

Archie grinned. 'A friend. I've been doing it up all week. He's given it to me on a kind of permanent loan.'

'I thought you were supposed to be convalescing,' said Ted.

'I was. The best rest I ever had, doing that up. Isn't she a beauty?' The bike gleamed in the evening light. 'Built like a gun, goes like a bullet,' he said, repeating McAllister's phrase.

'Good,' said Ted, 'you can give me a lift to Kenley tomorrow.'

'Kenley?'

'We've been posted – and promoted. We're both Flying Officers now.'

'Posted? From 337 Squadron? Why? What have we done this time?'

'Nothing. I'll explain later, but we're joining 599 Squadron. Dougal and Jimmy too, and Charlie Bannerman. He's been made CO – Squadron Leader now.'

'What about Jock?'

'He's staying at Boscombe. Apparently, they need more experienced pilots in the front line. They think a week of having it quiet is rest enough.'

Archie was ushered inside to where dinner was almost ready – his timing, Mary told him, was perfect.

'Gosh,' he said, 'I'd rather forgotten about dinner. I assumed that with the bombing –'

'We still need to eat, bombing or not,' said Mary. 'And I imagine you must be ravenous. Scotland to London in a day! My goodness!'

'Well, yes, I am rather,' Archie confessed. 'Thank you.'

'I, for one, intend to carry on absolutely as normal,' said Mary. 'It seems to me that if we all turn into cowering wrecks, Hitler will know he's won half the battle.'

No sooner had she said this than the baleful whine of the air-raid siren started up again.

'Not again,' she said.

'That'll be Pops,' said Ted. 'Part of his new job is to give the signal for the air-raid sirens to be sounded.'

'Well, I can't hear anything yet,' said Mary. 'I suggest we sit down and have our soup before it gets cold.'

They ate the soup, but ten minutes later they heard the distant muffled blasts of anti-aircraft fire and a moment later the dull explosion of bombs.

'Let's go to the attic and watch,' said Ted. 'Would that be all right, Ma?'

'What about your cutlets?'

'D'you think we could ask Mrs Atkins to keep them warm for a bit? This will probably be over in ten minutes or so.'

'All right,' said his mother. 'You three go on. I'll be up in a minute.'

The three of them hurried to the attic. There was a dormer window facing east around which they crowded. Dusk had settled over the city; the long, summer nights were beginning to draw in at last. Anti-aircraft fire peppered the sky, black smudges of smoke where the shell had detonated still visible in the gloaming, but large fires gave a flickering orange glow to the horizon, while the moon had turned blood red. Relays of bombers, mostly in twos and threes, droned overhead.

Searchlights suddenly criss-crossed the sky, anti-aircraft guns continued to burst like fireflies, and then over the boom of guns and the drone of engines came the whistle of bombs, the dull blast of the explosions and another pear-shaped burst of orange light rose above the rooftops. Smoke lay heavy in the air, even where they were in Pimlico, several miles from the focus of the Luftwaffe's attack. As the bombers continued droning overhead, so the smoke thickened and the light faded. The searchlights stood out more sharply, vivid beams of light crossing the sky but unable to penetrate the thick roof of smoke. Fire engines clattered through the streets, their bells near one moment, then gradually fading as they sped towards the burning East End.

Half an hour after the raid had begun, the bombers were gone, the lights were suddenly switched off and darkness fell on the city, but away to the east they could still see the flickering glow of fires.

'It's like the Great Fire all over again,' said Tess. She wrapped her arms around her. Archie shivered too. It had grown cold. 'To think they're actually attacking London,' she added. 'It's incredible. I can hardly believe what we've just seen.'

Mrs Atkins had done her best, but the cutlets were lukewarm by the time they sat down again. Archie no longer felt particularly hungry. He sensed the others felt rather the same. Even Mary's determination not to be cowed seemed to have been dented by this third raid of the day, and so they sat around the table, picking at their food, the conversation subdued.

They slept little, the bombers returning throughout the night. And each time the city again became alive to the sound of sirens and explosions. Air Commodore Tyler arrived back just before one in the morning, a grim expression on his face.

'Why aren't you all in the shelters?' he asked as he confronted his family and Archie, all wearing nightclothes and dressing gowns.

'It's the east they're after, Pops,' said Ted. 'Nothing's fallen near us yet.'

Tyler rubbed his brow and poured himself a drink, then joined them in the drawing room. As he sat down, the all-clear siren wailed over the city.

'A grim night, Pops?' said Ted.

His father nodded and smiled weakly. London was now under attack, just as he had known it would be. The RAF had bombed Berlin four times now, and Hitler's patience had finally snapped. He wondered how long the Luftwaffe's bombers would be turned on the capital. Another night? A week? Longer? He wondered how he was going to protect his family. Later that day, his only son – his beloved son – would be thrown into the jaws of the beast once more, but now he had his wife and daughter to worry about too. How easy it would be for a stray bomb to land on their house, and he would be powerless to stop it; all he could do was watch the battle from the safety of an underground concrete bunker.

And there was worse, something he knew he could not share with any of them. Large numbers of troop-carrying barges had been spotted in Rotterdam, Dunkirk, Calais and Le Havre; the weather, tides and moon over the next three days and nights were all favourable for a crossing; and German troops were known to be massing along the continental coast.

At seven minutes past eight on Saturday evening, as the third raid on London began, the signal 'Cromwell' reached him at Fighter Command Headquarters. *Cromwell:* the code word that warned all troops in Britain to go at once to their battle stations. An invasion was now considered imminent.

27

THE GERMAN PILOT

Sunday 15 September, 10.30 a.m. At their dispersal hut at Kenley, the 599 Squadron pilots continued to wait. It had been cold at first light, so they had lit the stove in the centre of the room, and now the last of the embers were dying out. Lingering smoky air filled the hut, a mixture of beech and tobacco. A number of the pilots had ventured outside, but Archie stayed sitting in the armchair in the corner, beneath the poster that said, 'It's better to come back with a probable than to be shot down with the one you've confirmed.' A mug of coffee was balanced precariously on the arm, while on his lap lay his journal. He'd not written much in it this past week, but as the long morning hours of inactivity continued, he'd decided it was time to add to it once more. Perhaps if he did, something would happen.

> We've now been at readiness since five this morning. It was pretty hazy to begin with – Chalkie, the IO, seems to think it's partly the smoke from the fires in London. At any rate, it's beginning to disperse now and it's turning into a beautiful late summer's Sunday, which means that Jerry's bound to be over before long.

He paused, the first knots of apprehension twisting in his stomach.

> It's been a quieter week than we had all expected. We arrived at Kenley a week ago to discover we were on invasion alert – it was news to us, but as Ted and I were driving up to the airfield we were accosted by a number of Home Guard types who were manning a road block. Ted had lost his identity papers – not for the first time – and to begin with they wouldn't let him through. They said, 'How do we know you're not a spy?' Ted got very cross and asked them whether he looked or sounded like a Hun. Another of them told us we were all on invasion alert. I said, 'We've been on one all summer,' but their commander then said that we were now on a high-level alert, whatever that is. Ted then rather lost his rag and told them in no uncertain terms that he and I were supposed to be shooting down the enemy and stopping the damned invasion, so could they stop wasting our time and let us get on with it. He pointed out that they'd seen my papers and that should be enough. They all looked at each other for a while, wondering what they should do, then eventually waved us on. I sometimes think the Home Guard are just itching for the Germans to invade – after all, it must be pretty boring being on invasion alert if nothing ever happens. But nothing has happened, and actually we've not even flown that much – a big raid on Monday, but otherwise it's been quite quiet. Two sorties a day for the most part and mostly that's been stooging about on X raids.

He paused again, and looked up. Charlie was talking to Chalkie and Dougal by the orderly's table. Beside him, Ted was asleep, snoring lightly.

Charlie's doing really well. He's a natural leader. A bit like Jock, really, but he's introduced new flying tactics, which I think are better.

The three-man vics had gone; instead, they were flying in fours and pairs, eight per flight, four per section rather than six and three.

'But we're trained to fly in vics,' Pete Milner, the A Flight commander had said.

'Well, now we're going to train in finger fours and pairs,' Charlie had told him. He had held up a hand. 'Like this: the first pair ahead of the second pair, the leader ahead of his wingman on his port side, the wingman of the second pair behind his leader on his starboard side. Like four fingers, Pete.'

'I'm not sure we're allowed to fly like that,' Pete had said.

'Nonsense,' Charlie had said. 'I'm CO. We'll fly how I want us to fly. Anyway, it's what the Jerries do.'

And that had been that. Charlie had put them all into new flights and new sections, laid down a few laws and then, in the evening after they had been stood down, insisted they all go to the pub. The following day, flying in pairs, they'd claimed three Dorniers and two 109s and lost just one aircraft. 'Buster' Harvey had reappeared later that evening, having bailed out near Maidstone. That night they'd gone to the pub again, and Buster had been made to tell them a joke. 'Not a song?' Archie had said.

'I've got to make my own mark,' Charlie had replied, then, turning back to Buster, had said, 'And it better be funny.'

Beside Archie, Ted now stirred, stretched and yawned, and then turned to Archie. 'Fancy a wander?'

'All right,' he agreed.

'Don't go far,' said Charlie as they brushed past him.

'Aye, aye, Skipper,' said Ted.

Skylarks were singing above them once more, but, despite the calm, the airfield looked a wreck. Patches of gravel and stone littered it where bomb craters had been hastily filled and rolled. Many of the buildings had been wrecked or destroyed. The operations room had been moved to the reserve building away from the airfield, while the pilots were in shared digs away from the Mess.

'I wish Jenny's transfer would come through,' said Ted. 'And Tess's for that matter.'

'Me too. I'm sure your father's doing what he can.'

'I just hate the thought of them being stuck in London with Jerry bombing it. I know the raids have been lighter this week, but it only takes one bomb, doesn't it?'

'They'll be all right,' said Archie. 'They've good shelters at the Air Ministry, and don't forget your father's made Tess and your mother promise to use the Anderson shelter if there are night raids.'

'I know.' Ted kicked the ground. 'It's just that I don't want to have to worry about them. We've enough to think about trying to look after ourselves.'

'It's mid-September,' said Archie. 'Jerry can't keep this up for ever. The evenings are really drawing in now. Before we know it, winter will be here.'

'Good,' said Ted. 'Then maybe we can be given some proper leave. I never thought I'd say this, but I'm looking forward to a rest from flying. I feel exhausted, to be honest.' He looked up. 'But one thing's for certain: we'll be flying today. Look at that.'

Archie followed his gaze. Above lay an endless azure blue.

'A perfect day for flying,' said Ted. 'There's something brewing today, Arch. I can feel it in my bones.'

So could his father. Air Commodore Tyler had been on the 8 a.m. to 4 p.m. shift for the past two days, and since his drive up to Bentley Priory, with the morning haze dispersing before his eyes, he had known they could expect heavy raids that day. And now, at eleven o'clock, he was proved right.

The RDF had picked up a number of enemy formations massing on the other side of the Channel. This information had immediately been relayed to 11 Group Headquarters at Uxbridge as well as to 12 and 10 Groups. Air Vice-Marshal Park was now scrambling a number of squadrons. From the viewing balcony, Tyler watched silently as the plotters inched the enemy raids across the Channel, their croupier sticks pushing the little stands. On the ops board on the wall in front of him stood the list of sectors and squadrons. He could see pairs of squadrons being scrambled: 92 and 72 from Biggin, and now 605 and 599 at Kenley, the lights on the board changing from 'Ordered on "I" Patrol' to 'Left Ground'.

Tyler clenched his fist, his cheeks flexing as he stared at the plotting table – at the air battle that was about to begin.

Ted was right. Barely had they stopped to look at the vast blue sky above them than the telephone rang and they were scrambled. Twelve aircraft, three sections, Charlie leading, with Ted and Archie as Red Three and Red Four. The familiar dash to their aircraft, and, minutes later, thundering down the airfield and into the air.

A gradual climb in a left-hand circuit, London away to their right, the Thames winding and silvery, although the city itself was still veiled in thin mist. Archie looked across, wondering whether Tess was at home still or at work. Barrage balloons hung listlessly over the capital, the sun glinting on their grey backs.

'Hello, Tonto Leader, this is Carfax calling,' crackled the ground controller in Archie's ear. 'RV with Tennis and Gannic Squadrons, then patrol Canterbury. Over.'

Charlie acknowledged, and they were soon vectored towards 92 and 72 Squadrons from Biggin, who had been scrambled at the same time. Climbing to twenty-six thousand feet, they levelled out and were soon over their patrol base, the finger of Kent stretching beneath them.

The airwaves crackled again. 'Hello, Tonto Leader. This is Carfax. Two hundred plus coming in over Red Queen. Vector 120, angels twenty-two.'

Two hundred, thought Archie. *Good God*. Ahead and to his left, Ted's Spitfire bobbing gently.

'Hello, Carfax,' Charlie replied, his voice as calm as ever. 'Message received. Over.'

Archie's heart began to quicken and his throat felt dry. There beneath his starboard wing he saw two huge Vs of enemy bombers. Puffs of flak burst around them as they crossed the coast. He glanced up, and could just see the 'snappers' – the 109s – glinting in the sun, white contrails following them.

'Right, let's go,' said Charlie. 'Tally ho!'

Archie watched Charlie peel off and begin his dive, then Ted was doing the same and Archie followed. The formation of Dorniers loomed suddenly and Archie was conscious of Ted opening fire. He flicked his own gun button off and watched a Dornier fill his sights. He pressed down on the gun button and bullets and tracer spat from his wings. He saw sparks strike the target and chew up the cowling around the port engine. The bomber hastily began dropping its bombs, then flames licked back across the wing. Archie glanced around and followed Ted as they banked and turned for another attack. Planes were dropping from the sky, parachutes opening, excited chatter shrieking in his ears. A glance up, 109s diving down towards them, but ahead was another Dornier. Archie pressed down again, felt the aircraft judder and saw bits of engine cowling flying off like flakes of old paint. As he thundered over it, he felt his Spitfire buckle in the slipstream. Behind, two 109s were lining up.

'Break, Ted!' he called out as tracer spat towards them. They dived again, firing at a lone Dornier as they descended. Had they hit it? Archie couldn't see, but he was now almost out of ammunition.

'I'm out of ammo.' Ted's voice in his ears. He saw Ted waggle his wings and then turn for home.

As more squadrons were committed to the battle, Air Commodore Tyler kept an eye on 599 Squadron's column on the ops board. A little under an hour after they had been scrambled, he saw the lights brighten beneath 'Landed and refuelling'. Ten minutes later, news arrived that 599 had suffered no losses. *Thank goodness,* he thought. Others that morning had not been so fortunate.

He wondered what the Germans were making of this battle. Two hundred plus meant it was among their bigger raids, and yet here they were, in the middle of September, facing more

British fighters than they had ever seen in the air before. In pairs, and singly, every squadron in 11 Group had been thrown into the battle. From what he could follow, it appeared that the large bomber formations had broken up well before they reached London. Pressing on towards the capital were smaller enemy formations, those that had managed to keep going. It was hard to tell from the plots exactly how many had managed to hit London, but he reckoned it could not be more than about twenty. From 12 Group, the Duxford Wing of three squadrons operating together had now joined the battle from the north, while from 10 Group, 609 and 629 Squadrons were also entering the fray, harrying the bombers as they turned back. He had to take his hat off to Park: the battle had been brilliantly co-ordinated; he'd never seen so many squadrons brought together for one action. From the moment the German formations had crossed the coast to the moment they flew back over it, they had been harried continually. And if the reports coming in from the pilots and ground controllers were anything to go by, the RAF had been successful too: German aircraft dropping out of the sky like ninepins, as far as he could make out.

Is this the crux of it? he wondered. *The culmination of the summer's air battle?* He glanced at the clock. Half past twelve. There was still a long afternoon and evening to go. *Only time will tell*, he thought.

2.05 p.m. The squadron was scrambled again, although this time they were to rendezvous with one of the Kenley Hurricane squadrons and climb to angels eighteen. Another massed raid was reported, this time four hundred and fifty plus.

'Go for the big jobs,' the ground controller told them. 'Repeat, attack the big jobs.'

They were over Ashford when they saw them, between eighty and a hundred bombers, Archie guessed, but it was the 'snappers' that worried him: hundreds of them, stacked up in tiers above them, like a swarm of wasps.

'Watch out for those little jobs,' Charlie called out. 'We go in, hit the bombers hard, then make sure we're ready for the snappers. All right?'

They were diving now, hurtling towards the bomber formations. Below, the Hurricanes were already in among them, and Archie spotted another pair of fighter squadrons approaching from the north. Below and ahead, a formation of Heinkels – bulkier, with larger, rounder wings than Dorniers or Ju 88s – but already they were scattering.

Charlie was leading them down to the rear of the formation – diving down lower, below the bomber stream, so they could then climb back up, losing speed as they did so and giving them more of a chance to rake the undefended undersides of the bombers. Tracer from the Heinkel rear gunners fizzed towards them, but they were too far away and now dropped beneath their line of fire. Several Heinkels were dropping their loads, and rising with the sudden loss of weight.

Ahead, Charlie and his wingman opened fire as Archie lined up his own target, a big, fat, grey-green Heinkel. From the corner of his eye, he saw a bomber drop, trailing smoke. Press down on the gun button – bullets spewing towards the target, sparks, a fizz of electrics from the cockpit, a puff of smoke from the port engine and the Heinkel tipped and fell, its pale underside streaking in front of his nose, so that he ducked, his heart hammering in his chest. Where was Ted? *Ah, yes, there.* He followed him as Ted banked, tightly, and grimaced as he pulled the stick towards him, negative-G pressing him into his seat – vision greying – then easing again. A glance up – *Christ!* – 109s everywhere, tearing down towards them.

A Hurricane hurtled in front of him, followed by two 109s, and now Ted was turning towards two more as they closed in on a Spitfire. Archie followed, frantically craning his neck. Aircraft were falling from the sky, someone shouted, 'I've been hit!' Someone else, 'Break! Break!' There were German voices too – and there was a parachute opening. A glance at the dials – *all OK* – and now Ted was opening fire and the two 109s were banking right, turning away from the fray. *What were they thinking?*

As the leader banked, Ted turned inside and opened fire. Bullets streaked across the sky and a split second later, as Archie fired an unsuccessful two-second burst at the wingman, the lead 109 flew straight into Ted's line of fire. Bits of cowling fluttered off, the engine exploded and the Messerschmitt fell away, but as Archie heard Ted cry, 'I've got him! I've got him!' he also saw the German's wingman barrel roll under Ted's flight path.

'No!' said Archie, instant panic enveloping him. *I can't get a shot, I can't get a shot!* 'Break, Ted, break!' he yelled but it was too late. The German had manoeuvred on to Ted's blind side and at just fifty yards' range opened fire.

'No!' shouted Archie. For a brief moment, Ted's Spitfire seemed to hang there, suspended, then a flash of orange, and Archie felt his Spitfire jolt and flip over. *No, no, no, this can't be.* Frantically, he regained control. 'Ted!' he shouted, 'Ted!' but his friend was gone, the Spitfire plunging in a ball of fire and debris.

'No!' yelled Archie. The Messerschmitt crossed his path, four hundred yards ahead, and Archie now opened the throttle wide, applied burst, and surged towards it. Numb – he felt numb. All sound seemed to have gone – the drone of the Merlin, the chatter of machine guns; it was as though he were in some strange vacuum where the only thing that mattered was catching the man who had killed Ted.

The 109 banked lazily, turning back towards the coast, as Archie swooped in behind, latching on to the 109's tail and giving him a quick burst. He saw his bullets strike home, but the 109 flipped over and dived, and Archie followed after. For a brief moment, his engine cut as the carburettor flooded, then caught again, but already the German was getting away from him.

No, you don't, thought Archie.

His Spitfire screamed and his airframe shook as they plunged from sixteen thousand feet to three thousand in a matter of seconds, the lush Kent countryside visible once more. At two thousand feet the German pulled out, and Archie followed, grimacing with the strain, but at last he was level again, the weight on his arms lessening and the controls lightening. As they sped over the long finger of Kent, the gap began to close once more, and Archie now saw a wisp of smoke coming from the 109's engine cowling. They were losing height, the German dropping down towards the deck.

Villages and towns rushed by beneath them as they fell to just a hundred and fifty feet, and then they were passing through valleys, sweeping around church spires, almost brushing the treetops. *Two hundred yards now.* The Messerschmitt filled Archie's reflector sight. A river snaked below as they sped over another village, the Downs to their right. *One hundred and fifty yards.*

Archie held his thumb over the gun button then pressed down, his eight machine guns spitting bullets. Another puff of smoke and the German dropped further still and began weaving frantically from side to side, so that Archie was forced to pull back on the throttle. Another burst of bullets and then nothing.

'No!' shouted Archie again. He could not be out of ammo already – surely not! But smoke was belching from the 109, and the German banked his aircraft, circling. *He's looking for somewhere to land,* Archie thought. He saw a school below, with long swathes of playing fields stretching away from the main buildings.

The German had clearly had the same thought. Archie circled overhead as he watched the enemy pilot glide towards the flat open grassland. Wheels up, the Messerschmitt hit the ground, sliding and yawing a long furrow of churned-up grass, before finally coming to a halt. Was he dead? No – there he was, hurriedly clambering out. *The man who killed Ted.*

Archie looked out at the playing fields. *Long enough,* he thought. Pulling back on the throttle, he circled, then, lowering his flaps and undercarriage, came in to land. Touching down, he bounced, landed again, then throttled back and turned his Spitfire towards the smouldering Messerschmitt. The pilot was hurrying away from the plane towards him as Archie cut the engine, unclipped his leads and jumped down.

Ten yards from the pilot he stopped, his mind suddenly clearing. What was he going to do now? What should he say to this man, this German who had killed his friend?

The German continued walking towards him, slowly, uncertainly, then took off his helmet. The resemblance to Ted was uncanny – long, dark hair, brown eyes – similar height and build too – and for a moment Archie wondered whether he was dreaming, whether this was some terrible nightmare from which he would soon awake.

'Well done,' said the man, his English heavily accented. 'I offer you my congratulations.'

Archie stared at him, his mind racing, then said, 'What do you mean?'

'You brought me down. And Lieutenant Hartmann.'

'You killed my best friend,' said Archie. Some people were shouting behind him. The German glanced towards the school then back at Archie.

'And your friend killed my friend.'

'Your friend?' Archie frowned, puzzled. 'What do you mean?' he said again.

The German stared back at him. 'Lieutenant Hartmann. Mani. We were like brothers.' He took another step towards him. This German man was young too. For so long the enemy had been the 'Hun' or 'Jerry' – a nameless automaton, Nazis one and all, and somehow a quite different breed, barely human. But here before him was a young man just like him and Ted – a young man who had also lost his best friend. Archie did not know what to say, but his anger – his intense rage – was already melting away.

'Mani and I,' said the German. 'We were friends since childhood.' He blinked and looked up. 'This war,' he said. 'So pointless. It's not us who should be shooting at each other, but our leaders. Let them fight it out, not us.'

Archie nodded.

For a moment, the two men continued to stare at each other and then suddenly the young German's face began to crumple, his head dropped and he brought a hand to his face and began to weep. Archie stood there, dumbstruck, then felt something rise from deep inside and flood over him, and he knew he could not control it. Tears ran down his own cheeks and he was sobbing – sobbing like he had never sobbed before, he and the German together, united in their grief and despair.

28

GETTING TO THE PARTY

Saturday 21 June 1941. Midsummer. Sitting outside the dispersal hut at Kenley, Archie Jackson was thinking. He had his journal on his lap, his pen in his hand, poised, about to write. A skylark was twittering away nearby and he immediately thought of Ted. It happened often, and when it did, Archie was always overcome by a wave of sadness that seemed to enclose him like a heavy shroud.

He had become rather fatalistic about the war. He had survived thirteen months of almost continuous front-line action and was still alive. He now felt a curious sense of certainty that he would somehow survive – something that he had rather doubted last year. It was based on little. Just a feeling.

So many hadn't made it, of course. Henry Dix had become a prisoner of war, Will Merton-Moore had been shot down in flames. Dennis Cotton had ended up in the Channel. At Biggin, poor old Ginger had had that dodgy parachute, Mick had been burned to a cinder, and then there was Ted. *Ted . . .*

Those were just his good friends. He couldn't even remember the names of half the others – some had been with the squadron less than an hour. Of course he missed them, and their deaths upset him dreadfully, but after Ted's death, he'd become an expert at not dwelling on it, even if one of his close friends died – like Dougal, for instance, who had been killed in a flying accident back in April. He had not forgotten something Reynolds, the adjutant of 629 Squadron, had told him: that back in the last war, he'd tried not to think of them as dead, but as having simply gone away.

And it worked, to a large extent. Archie would have his nightly bath and think about them very hard, imagining them in the place he thought was most appropriate. He felt sure, for example, that Mick would be back in Canada, living in some log cabin and hunting bear and elk. As soon as an image of his friend's death came into view, or he thought of the screams in his earpiece, he concentrated for a few moments and there was Mick surrounded by furs, and wood fires, and a big hunting rifle. Ginger would have gone to the South Pacific – Tahiti, for example. If he thought of Ginger's parachute plummeting to the ground, he pushed it from his mind and instead pictured his friend lying on a beach, surrounded by nubile Tahitian girls, the shadows of the palm trees flickering gently across his face. It was as though he had gone off on his travels, but had liked the place so much he'd not bothered coming back, or as though Mick had simply decided to head home across the Atlantic to the Canadian Rockies. Or Dougal was stalking some deer in the Highlands.

It was harder with Ted. He thought of Ted with Jenny, imagining them in America, in California – only because Ted had once said that he fancied visiting Hollywood and becoming a film star. But his ploy didn't work so well with Ted, his very best friend. When thoughts of Ted entered his mind, he found himself swallowing hard and wishing he could think of something entirely different.

It wasn't easy to do. The end was still so vivid – Ted's Spitfire engulfed in flame, disintegrating as it fell from the sky. There'd been a funeral, but God knows what they'd put in the coffin. Tess had told him that their father had learned his son was dead while he'd been in the Operations Room at Bentley Priory, that he'd waited until his watch was over, then driven home to tell his wife. Ted's parents had not been the same since. Archie felt their pain every time he saw them. There was guilt too – guilt that Ted had died and not him. It was ridiculous, he knew, but he couldn't help it.

And it had happened so near the end of the Battle of Britain, as it was now called. That Sunday had been the last of the really big air battles; the Germans had continued to come over, men had continued to be shot down, but there had been no invasion. The barges massed in the ports across the Channel had been taken away and gradually the daylight battles petered out until, towards the end of October, Archie and the others at 599 Squadron realized they'd not once been scrambled in four days on the trot.

It was nine months now since Ted had died, and, sad though he felt whenever he thought of his friend, Archie recognized that life went on. Ted would not have wanted him to brood, as Tess often reminded him. *Ah, Tess.* How lucky he was to have her – and working in the Operations Room at Kenley too, where 599 Squadron were still stationed.

'Having an air commodore as a father has its advantages,' she had said when her posting came through. They still didn't see each other as much as they'd like – she was in the Ops Room away from the airfield, and he was either flying or at dispersal, but they could meet up some evenings when she wasn't on duty, and they usually managed to make their leave coincide. One day, he thought to himself, they would get married and, when the war was over, they would live happily ever after. He had written in his journal:

> Really, I have a lot to be thankful for. Far better flying around the sky at three hundred and fifty miles an hour in one of the most beautiful machines ever built, than slogging my guts out on the ground. Think of those poor beggars who rescued me in France. If I have to die – and I don't think I will – far better to do so in style.

And as a fighter pilot, rationing barely affected him, especially since they had started taking the fight to the enemy. Instead of waiting for the Germans to come over when they chose, it was the turn of the RAF to decide when attacks would occur. Since December, he'd had three hot meals a day. He felt a bit guilty that his family in Scotland were going hungry, but then, as his mother had said in a letter to him, he needed to keep his strength up if he were to fight to the best of his ability. And he had Tess. He would put up with quite a lot to keep hold of her.

It was a beautiful midsummer's day. A few wispy white clouds, but otherwise blue all over. Archie and the other pilots had moved some of the old chairs from the dispersal hut outside, and he sat in one of these, his backside low in the seat, legs stretched out, his eyelids flickering gently in the brightness. A bee was busily visiting the daisies in the grass. In the distance an occasional clang of a spanner or wrench on metal could be heard. Otherwise, all was still and peaceful. No one spoke.

He was thinking about Tess – the perfect antidote to more maudlin thoughts of Ted; the ten days of leave they had had in May: the tour of Scotland they had talked of so often. It had been wonderful – a time he would never, ever forget, even if he lived to a hundred. He couldn't imagine ever tiring of her. Mrs Tess Jackson. He liked that – it had a good ring to it.

The telephone rang, shattering the peace of the slumbering pilots. It was rarely a scramble these days, but, after the previous summer, living on a knife-edge waiting for the dreaded call, it still made Archie jump.

'For you, Archie.' Tom Wilson, the current Intelligence Officer, was standing by the open window, holding the receiver.

Archie eased himself out of his armchair with a sigh, wondering who it could be.

'Archie?'

'Hello. Tess!'

'I know I shouldn't be ringing on this line, but I was worried you'd forgotten about tonight.'

Tonight. Tonight? His mind raced. What was happening? Then he suddenly remembered: Diana Thorpe's engagement party at her parents' house near Tonbridge. He cursed to himself. How could he have been so stupid?

'Of course I haven't. How would I ever forget that?'

'Well, I didn't think you had, only I was wondering how we're going to get there.'

'Oh, don't you worry, I've got it sorted,' he said hurriedly. 'Er, tell you what: why don't you meet me outside the Mess at six-thirty. Sound all right?'

'Perfect. And, Archie?'

'Yes?'

'I can't wait to see you. Bye.'

'Bye.'

Archie put the receiver down and thought for a moment. Damn! He hadn't a clue how they were going to get there. They'd left the Enfield at his parents' house, and his Norton was in pieces after Barnie Fuller had crashed it two days before. The train would take too long, so would a bus, and it was unlikely he'd be able to find another motorbike in time. He gently thumped his head against the door frame, then ambled back outside. There *had* to be an alternative.

At six-thirty, Archie was pacing up and down outside the Mess when Tess appeared. She had changed from her WAAF uniform into a sleek, pale blue evening dress, with a small cape to keep her shoulders warm.

'You look wonderful,' said Archie, meaning it.

She smiled at him, and kissed him. 'Thank you. So do you.' Then she looked around and seeing no obvious means of transport said, 'Did you manage to get a car?'

'No – I've done better than that. Follow me.' He took her hand and led her round the back of the Mess towards one of the airfield hangars.

'Archie?' A note of alarm in her voice.

'Trust me,' said Archie, and he beamed, then even gave her a quick wink. Round to the front, away from the main buildings of the airfield, stood a lone Spitfire, its wings and perspex canopy glinting in the early evening sun. Archie stopped and bowed.

'My lady, your carriage awaits.'

'Archie!' exclaimed Tess, her hands clasping her face. 'We can't really be going in that!'

'We can and we will. Come on, it'll be fun. All this time, and you've never been in one. Don't you think it's about time?'

Slowly, her face turned from an expression of shocked horror to one of capricious delight. Inwardly, Archie gave a sigh of relief. Outwardly, he hoped he was maintaining the debonair attitude he'd been trying to convey.

'Archie, I can't believe it,' said Tess, gripping his hand tightly and giving him one of her most radiant smiles.

Archie quickly manipulated the pumps, switched on the magnetos, then gave a signal to his ground crew, already waiting by the plane. They waved back, and then the propeller slowly and silently began to turn until, with a puff of smoke and flame from the exhaust stubs, the engine roared into life.

'Come on,' said Archie, 'let's go, although we've got to be quick.' Glancing around, he led her briskly to the plane.

'Thanks, you two,' he said to Barlow and Lucas, who were now standing by the wing waiting for them.

'Let the lady get in first, sir, then you,' said Barlow.

Archie nodded, then clambered on to the wing and held out a hand for Tess. Holding up her dress, she took his arm and allowed him to pull her up. Balancing gingerly beside him, she looked at him apprehensively, then hopped into the cockpit.

'Good job you're not some huge fat oaf,' she said, laughing, as Archie lowered himself on to her lap.

'Sorry, but there's no other way. Normally, I'm sitting on a parachute, you see.' He was a bit closer to the instrument panel than he was used to but, actually, his all-round vision was improved by sitting so far forward. Now he knew how people had managed before.

'Are you all right? I'll try not to squash you completely.'

'I'm fine. Anyway, I'm far too excited to mind.'

Archie signalled to Barlow and Lucas, then slowly opened the throttle. The Merlin engine roared and the airframe shook, and they began rolling briskly towards the start of the runway.

'Great thing about a Spit,' shouted Archie, 'they don't need much to take off. Let's hope no one spots you.' He released the brakes and opened the throttle further, the engine responding with a deep, guttural bellow. They surged down the grass strip. Either side, the wings began to wobble with the increased power. It felt as though they were racing over a rough, potholed track. Then they were airborne, and the shaking had gone, replaced by a soothing gentle vibration. In moments, the horizon had slid beneath them as the Spitfire sped skywards.

Archie had to remind himself that he was not climbing into battle, but taking Tess on a gentle jaunt. The Spitfire always seemed to want to fly faster and turn tighter, revelling in its own speed and manoeuvrability; but today, he must rein her in. He gently pulled the canopy shut and turned them with the gentlest of sweeps. The horizon slowly tilted as they turned back and circled wide.

'Are you all right?' yelled Archie.

'Couldn't be better!'

Archie grinned. What a good idea this had been. He took them higher – although not too high: six thousand feet should be plenty, as he wanted Tess to be able to see the countryside clearly below.

In the calm evening light, England lay spread out before them. A patchwork of green and gold. Ridges of hills clearly defined by light and shade. Snaking rivers silvery and gleaming. Dense woods. Such a shame, Archie thought, that they could only do this because of the war. And what a shame that his Spitfire, so beautiful, so sleek, such a joy to fly, should be designed not for pleasure, but for shooting other planes out of the sky. For killing people.

'I can see the house!' shouted Tess. They'd been airborne for about twenty minutes.

Archie brought the plane lower and circled, looking for the right field. There was a long grass paddock running alongside the house. It looked flat enough.

'Do a fly-past, won't you?' said Tess in his ear.

'If you want – hold on.'

Pushing the stick forward and opening the throttle, Archie dived towards the house, then pulled back as they whistled past. Tess screamed with delight.

'Hang on tight!' shouted Archie. As they turned and swept past again, he rolled the plane.

'Oh, my gosh!' yelled Tess, then began laughing.

Moments later, they were coming in to land. The field was perfect – quite long enough – and Archie was thinking how glad he was that he'd forgotten about the party earlier and not organized a car.

'Thank you!' gushed Tess as they came to a halt. 'I think that was the most wonderful thing I've ever done. I can't believe I've just been in a Spitfire! Diana will be *so* impressed.'

Archie kissed her cheek. 'Rather fun, wasn't it? England looks pretty good from up there, don't you think?'

'Beautiful. *Thank* you, Archie.' She gave him another kiss and took his hand as they headed inside.

Diana Thorpe's mother and father had some concerns about the sense and safety of two people flying in a single-seater plane with no parachute or harness, but were polite and kind to Archie all the same, and they and their guests had all enjoyed his fly-past. To make it home before it was completely dark, Archie and Tess had to leave just before ten o'clock, but Diana's parents didn't seem in the least bit offended.

'That's all right, young man,' Mr Thorpe told him. 'Jolly good of you to come at all. After all, there is a war on.' They shook hands, Archie and Tess thanked him and his wife profusely, then they turned to walk back to the Spitfire, standing in the field with its nose pointing imperiously towards the sky.

'Do be careful, though, won't you?' Mrs Thorpe called after them.

The rest of the party had come out to watch. Once they were back in the cockpit, Archie prayed the engine would start, but, having primed it, the propeller turned and it fired almost immediately. Soon they were airborne once more. Archie couldn't resist one last sweep past the house, waggling his wings in salute. Tess laughed happily and tightened her arms around his waist.

'I love you, Archie Jackson!' she shouted.

What a perfect evening, thought Archie as they landed back at the airfield safely and taxied over to the hangar. He knew that even if he lived to a hundred, he would remember every part of it. What a strange thing war was.

*

The following morning, it was raining. It was impossible to believe the previous day had been so warm, clear and sunny. To make matters worse, at breakfast the adjutant told Archie the station commander wanted to see him immediately afterwards. 'Brace yourself,' said the adj.

Archie felt a knot tighten in his stomach. He must have been spotted the previous evening.

He was right. Wing Commander Deakin was furious and gave full vent to his anger: What the hell did he think he'd been playing at? Did he have any idea how expensive those planes were? What if something had gone wrong? And to take a young girl out just because he was trying to impress her! Really, it was unforgivable. 'I need people like you,' Deakin yelled, 'experience doesn't grow on trees, you know. It takes time, not to say money. If anything had happened to you just because of some silly prank – well, I'd be furious. I *am* furious.'

Archie could say nothing. The Wingco was right, of course, but he'd long ago stopped worrying about such things. Compared with flying low-level and beating up two German airfields, this was small fry.

'You should be court-martialled for this, you know,' Deakin continued.

Archie nodded meekly.

The station commander sighed, rubbed his forehead vigorously, then pulled out a cigarette and lit it. Through a cloud of smoke, he reached into a drawer and pulled out a letter.

'Here,' he said, handing it to Archie. 'This has just come through.'

Archie took it silently, slowly tore open the envelope and

read the perfunctory note. He'd been promoted from flight lieutenant to squadron leader.

'Congratulations,' said Deakin.

Archie stood there, stupefied, for a moment, then said, 'Thank you, sir.'

'You're going to need to act a bit more responsibly from now on. And by the way, you're grounded.' The Wingco rapped his fingers on the desk. 'If this had been peacetime, you *would* have been court-martialled, you know. Now leave me alone.'

My God, thought Archie. *Squadron leader.* 'Am I being posted, sir?'

'Yes.' Deakin sighed. 'You're getting your own squadron, Archie. I know you're still only twenty, but, for the most part, I think you do act a bit more mature than that. You've a lot of experience. Use it, and use it wisely. Now get out of here. I'll see you in the Mess later, where I'm insisting you buy everyone a round of drinks.'

And sing a song, thought Archie.

'Yes, sir,' he said. He saluted and went out, whistling 'Let's Be Buddies' to himself.

HISTORICAL NOTE

The Battle of Britain occurred much as has been described in the book, and many of the characters, situations and places mentioned are real. Ted and Tess's father, Air Commodore Guy Tyler, is made up, but the two jobs he held during the summer of 1940, and the burdens he carried and dilemmas he faced, are based very closely on those of Tommy Elmhirst, later an Air Marshal, who, in partnership with Air Vice-Marshal Arthur Coningham, helped turn round the fortunes of the Desert Air Force in North Africa in 1942, and later pioneered the first Allied tactical air force. The US Air Force and the RAF still use the principles laid down by Coningham and Elmhirst during the war.

The official dates of the Battle of Britain are 10 July to 31 October 1940, but I've always believed that it really began with the air battle over Dunkirk. This was when Fighter Command was first properly blooded and when, it turned out, Britain faced its greatest peril. After that, the threat facing Britain was not as great as her war leaders feared at the time. British intelligence overestimated German strength, not least because for most of the battle they thought German squadrons – or *Staffeln*, as they were known – had the same numbers of aircraft and pilots as

British squadrons. In fact, they were about half the size and by the beginning of September 1940, when Park and Dowding were so worried about pilot losses, the Luftwaffe – and especially the fighter units – were in dire straits.

Dowding and Park were worried about pilot strength dropping to below fifteen per squadron; at that time German squadrons often had just two or three aircraft available. This meant the experienced pilots tended to fly and fly and fly. British pilots would rarely fly more than three combat sorties a day and often no more than two; by September, it was not uncommon for German fighter pilots to be flying seven times a day. The three hundred and fifty Luftwaffe fighters massed on the afternoon of 15 September represented just about every single aircraft the Germans could lay their hands on – single-seater 109s and twin-engine 110s. In contrast, the RAF had over seven hundred Spitfires and Hurricanes at that stage. In fact, Fighter Command ended the Battle of Britain with more aircraft and pilots than when it started. Still, as the British discovered, it was better to overestimate your enemy's strength than to underestimate it.

Most pilots were very young, aged between nineteen and twenty-five for the most part. The rotation of squadrons and the categorization suggested by Park on 7 September were adopted, and the meeting on the morning of that fateful day took place as described. Traditionally, Hitler's decision to turn his bombers on London is seen as a fatal mistake, because diverting them away from attacking the airfields gave Fighter Command a crucial lifeline. In fact, as Guy Tyler points out in the book (as did the real-life Tommy Elmhirst), the German attacks on the airfields had not proved terribly successful. A lot of damage had been caused at places like Kenley and Biggin Hill, but wide, open grass airfields were easily repaired and the reserve operations rooms, set up for just such a purpose, were quickly activated. The Germans failed to appreciate that they needed a vast amount of bombs to render a grass airfield unserviceable. One Battle of Britain veteran once told me about how he had been flying from North Weald on 3 September 1940 and had seen the airfield come under attack and disappear under a cloud of smoke. He had wondered how they were ever going to be able to land, and yet they all did, without a scratch. 'We just dodged the potholes,' he told me.

I have been lucky enough to sit inside an Me 109, a Hurricane and even to fly in a Spitfire. I've also had the privilege of interviewing a number of veterans from both sides. Most of these conversations were recorded and have been transcribed and are now up on my website: www.griffonmerlin.com. Please do feel free to read them. Those with Geoffrey Wellum, Tom Neil, Roland 'Bee' Beamont, Pete Brothers and Hans-Ekkehard Bob are, I think, particularly fascinating. In fact, the story of getting to the party in the Spitfire at the end of the book was based very much on a conversation with the late Bee Beamont. He was a great pilot: he fought with 74 Squadron in France and throughout the Battle of Britain, then later test-flew the Hawker Typhoon and went on to command 629 Squadron. It was Bee Beamont who later realized it was possible to catch up to a V2 rocket and, by knocking it with the wing of his Typhoon, turn it to fly straight into the ground rather than falling on London, its target. Here's a link to that story: http://www.griffonmerlin.com/ww2_interviews/wing-commander-roland-bee-beamont/

It's pretty near the beginning of the interview.

The squadron numbers I have used were never made operational by the RAF. 629 Squadron is based largely on 609 West Riding Squadron; 337 is based on a combination of 32 Squadron and 92 Squadron, as is 599 Squadron. To get a sense of how often pilots were flying, I used the logbooks of David Crook, who flew with 609 Squadron, and also Pete Brothers, who flew Hurricanes with 32 Squadron for much of the battle. Sadly, David Crook did not make it through the war, while Pete Brothers passed away in 2009. Both were great heroes.

James Holland

ACKNOWLEDGEMENTS

I owe some thanks: to the incomparable Shannon Park and all at Puffin, to Daphne Tagg, and to Nick Wharmby and Rick Hillum for their flying expertise, and to Steve Boultbee Brooks and Matt Jones for taking me up in their Spit. I also owe thanks to Patti and Robin Bell, who own Drumnacarf in Perthshire, on which Archie's home is very firmly based, and to their son, Pete, a great pal, for inviting me there a number of times over the years. And last but definitely not least, thank you to Rachel, Ned and Daisy.